Arata
THE LEGEND

11

WE ARE MAN, BORN OF HEAVEN AND EARTH,
MOON AND SUN AND EVERYTHING UNDER THEM.

EYES, EARS, NOSE, TONGUE, BODY, MIND...

PURITY WILL PIERCE EVIL AND
OPEN UP THE WORLD OF DARKNESS.

ALL LIFE WILL BE REBORN AND INVIGORATED.

APPEAR NOW.

STORY & ART BY
YUU WATASE

Arata: The Legend

Characters

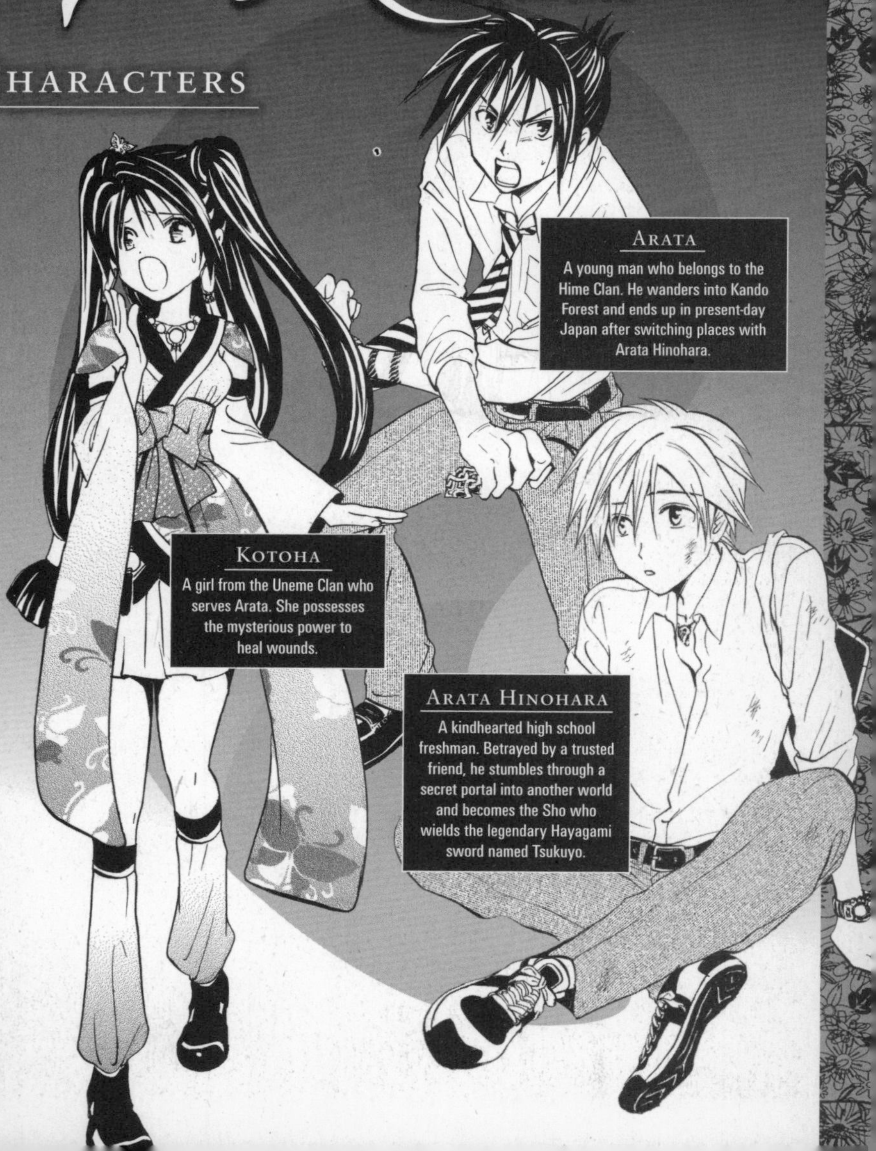
Arata
A young man who belongs to the Hime Clan. He wanders into Kando Forest and ends up in present-day Japan after switching places with Arata Hinohara.
Kotoha
A girl from the Uneme Clan who serves Arata. She possesses the mysterious power to heal wounds.
Arata Hinohara
A kindhearted high school freshman. Betrayed by a trusted friend, he stumbles through a secret portal into another world and becomes the Sho who wields the legendary Hayagami sword named Tsukuyo.

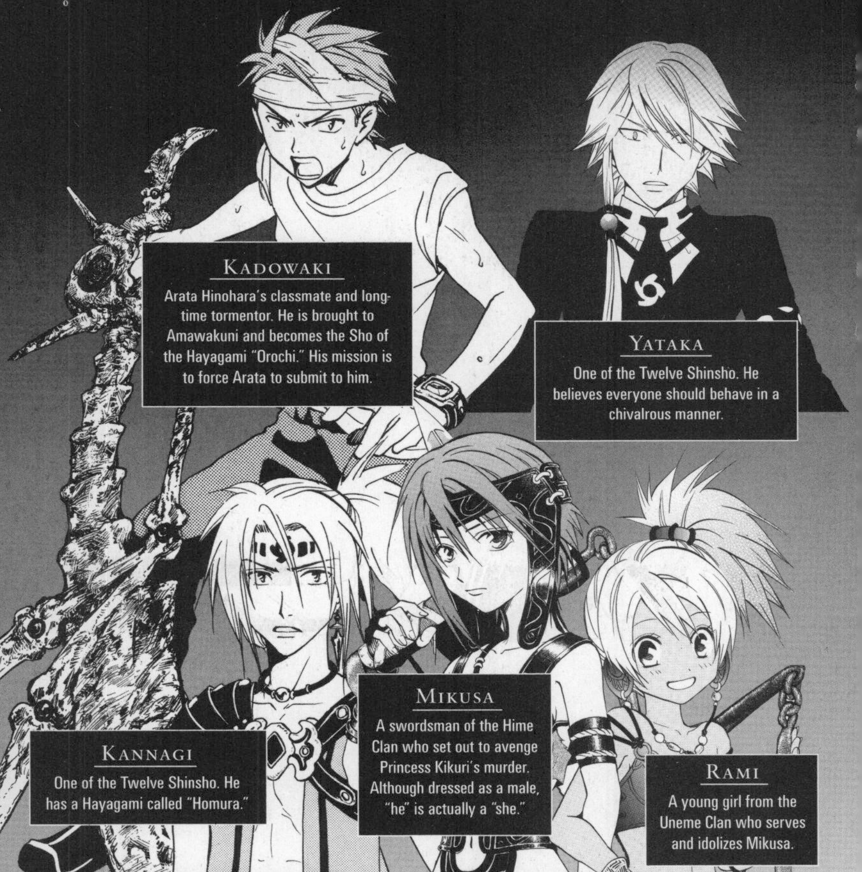

Kadowaki

Arata Hinohara's classmate and long-time tormentor. He is brought to Amawakuni and becomes the Sho of the Hayagami "Orochi." His mission is to force Arata to submit to him.

Yataka

One of the Twelve Shinsho. He believes everyone should behave in a chivalrous manner.

Kannagi

One of the Twelve Shinsho. He has a Hayagami called "Homura."

Mikusa

A swordsman of the Hime Clan who set out to avenge Princess Kikuri's murder. Although dressed as a male, "he" is actually a "she."

Rami

A young girl from the Uneme Clan who serves and idolizes Mikusa.

The Story Thus Far

Betrayed by his best friend, Arata Hinohara—a high school student in present-day Japan—wanders through a portal into another world where he and his companions journey onward to deliver his Hayagami sword "Tsukuyo" to Princess Kikuri.

Arata Hinohara, who is believed to be the King of Hinowa, the ruler of the Hime Clan, is attacked by two Zokusho of the Sho Yataka, who, for unknown reasons, harbors an intense hatred for Princess Kikuri. Due to the power of the Melting Pot of Souls, Arata and a spirit named Teko trade bodies. Then, in the middle of an intense battle, the Melting Pot of Souls appears again, and Arata finds himself in the body of Okima, Yataka's Zokusho. Thus disguised, Arata infiltrates Yataka's domain undetected, only to find himself trapped in a time warp with his enemy!

11

Arata
THE LEGEND

CONTENTS

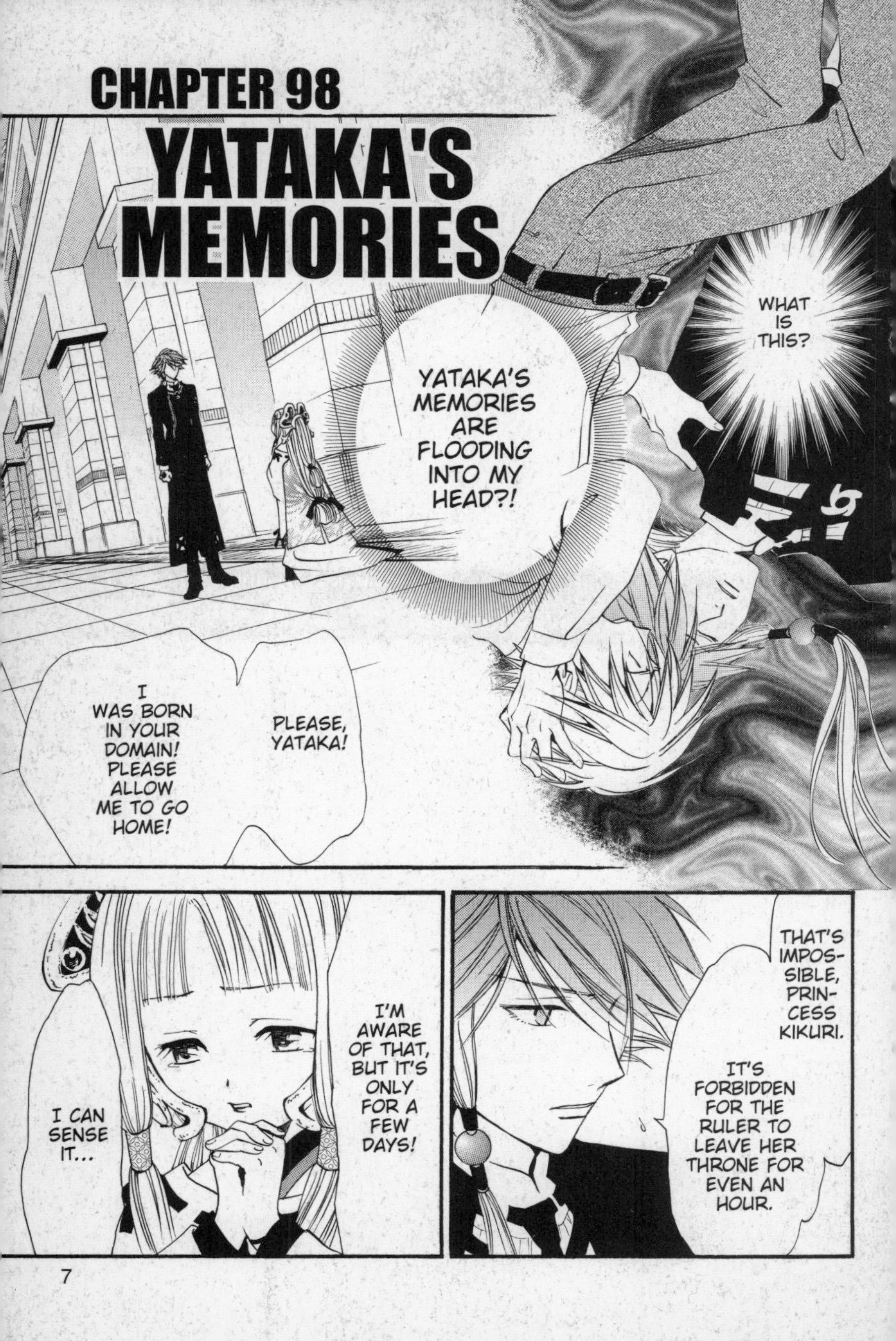
CHAPTER 98
YATAKA'S MEMORIES
WHAT IS THIS?
YATAKA'S MEMORIES ARE FLOODING INTO MY HEAD?!
PLEASE, YATAKA!
I WAS BORN IN YOUR DOMAIN! PLEASE ALLOW ME TO GO HOME!
THAT'S IMPOSSIBLE, PRINCESS KIKURI.
IT'S FORBIDDEN FOR THE RULER TO LEAVE HER THRONE FOR EVEN AN HOUR.
I'M AWARE OF THAT, BUT IT'S ONLY FOR A FEW DAYS!
I CAN SENSE IT...

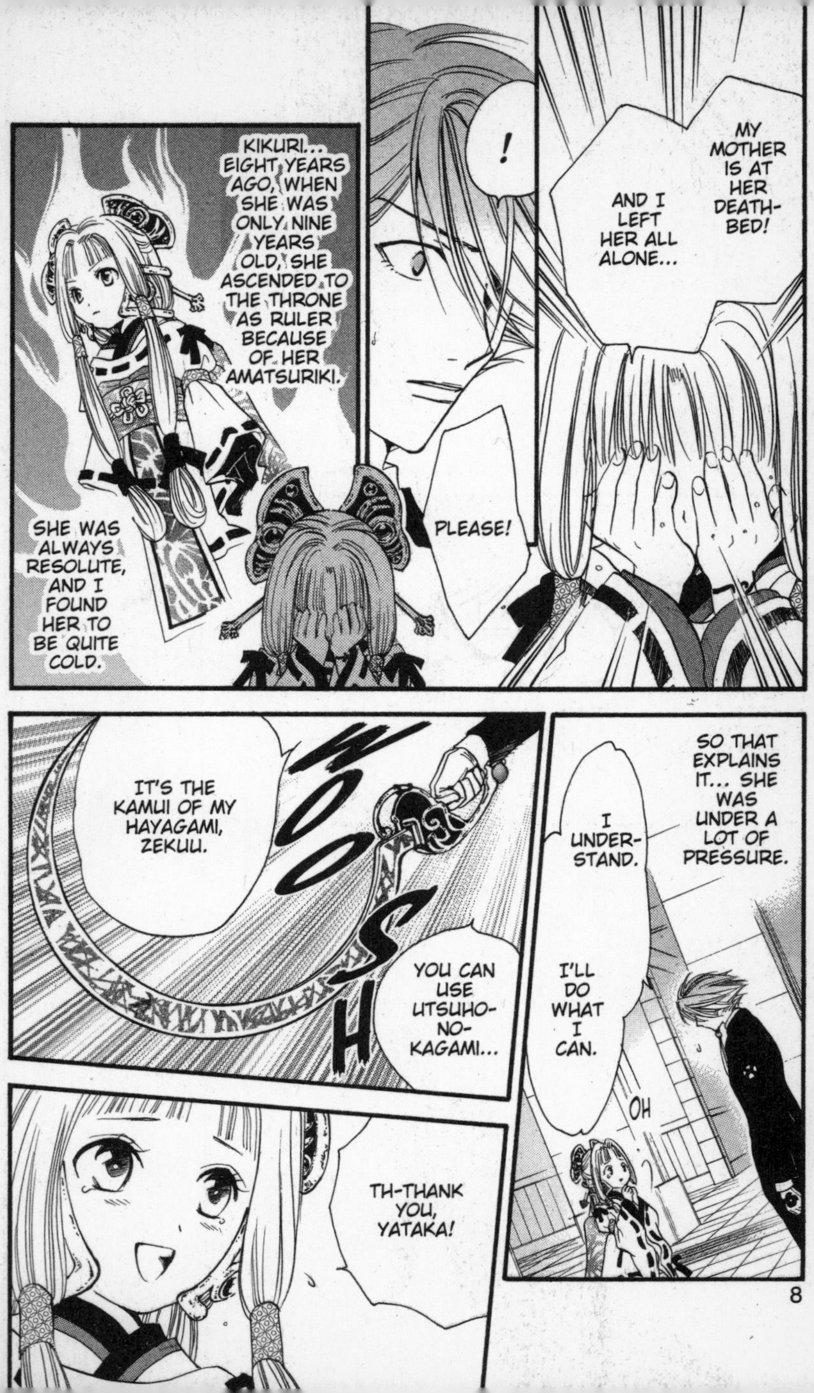
MY MOTHER IS AT HER DEATH-BED!
AND I LEFT HER ALL ALONE...
!
PLEASE!
KIKURI... EIGHT YEARS AGO, WHEN SHE WAS ONLY NINE YEARS OLD, SHE ASCENDED TO THE THRONE AS RULER BECAUSE OF HER AMATSURIKI.
SHE WAS ALWAYS RESOLUTE, AND I FOUND HER TO BE QUITE COLD.
SO THAT EXPLAINS IT... SHE WAS UNDER A LOT OF PRESSURE.
I UNDER-STAND.
I'LL DO WHAT I CAN.
OH
IT'S THE KAMUI OF MY HAYAGAMI, ZEKUU.
WOOOSH
YOU CAN USE UTSUHO-NO-KAGAMI...
TH-THANK YOU, YATAKA!

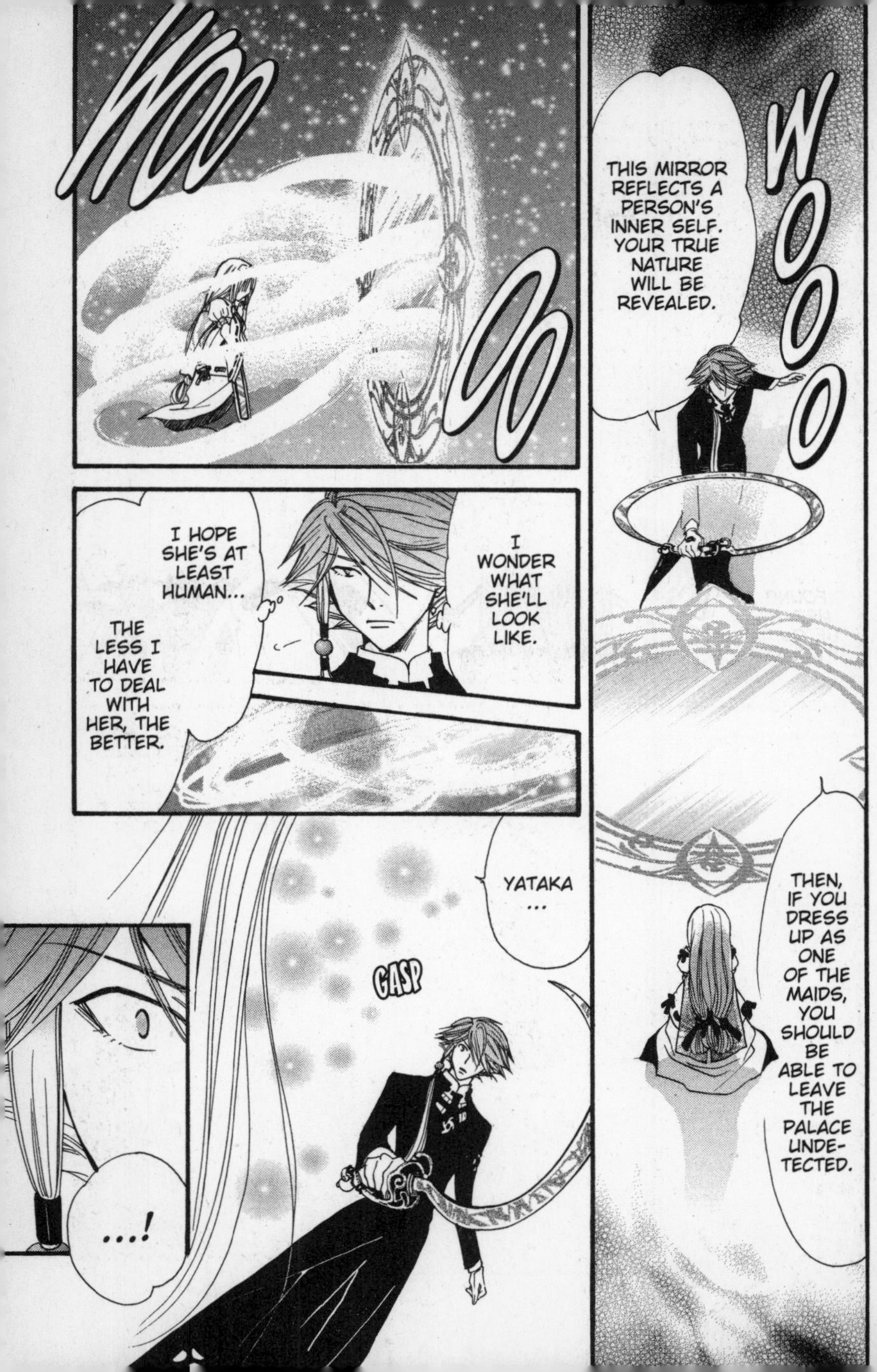
WOOOO
THIS MIRROR REFLECTS A PERSON'S INNER SELF. YOUR TRUE NATURE WILL BE REVEALED.
THEN, IF YOU DRESS UP AS ONE OF THE MAIDS, YOU SHOULD BE ABLE TO LEAVE THE PALACE UNDETECTED.
I WONDER WHAT SHE'LL LOOK LIKE.
I HOPE SHE'S AT LEAST HUMAN...
THE LESS I HAVE TO DEAL WITH HER, THE BETTER.
YATAKA ...
GASP
...!

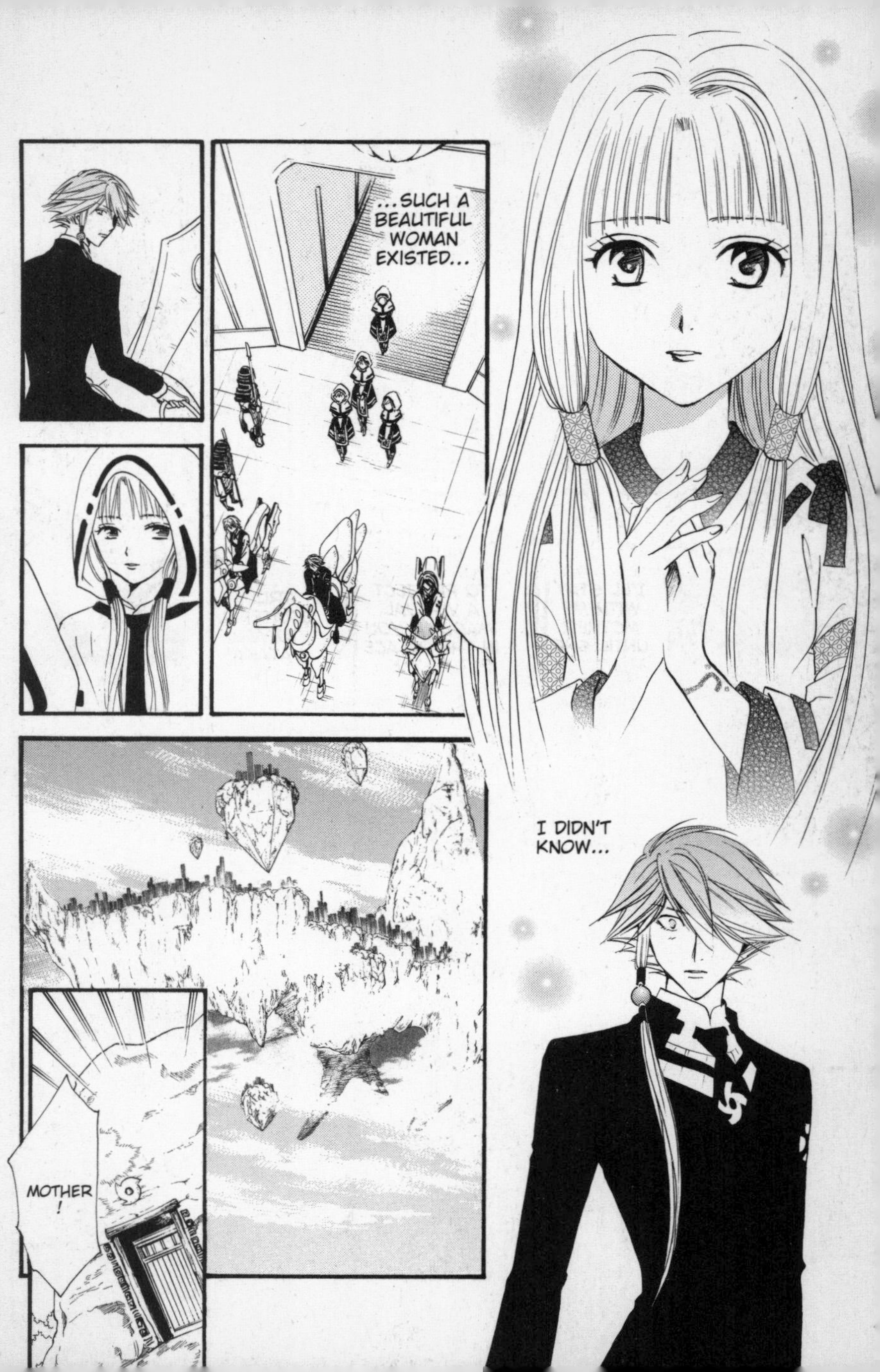
I DIDN'T KNOW...
...SUCH A BEAUTIFUL WOMAN EXISTED...
MOTHER!

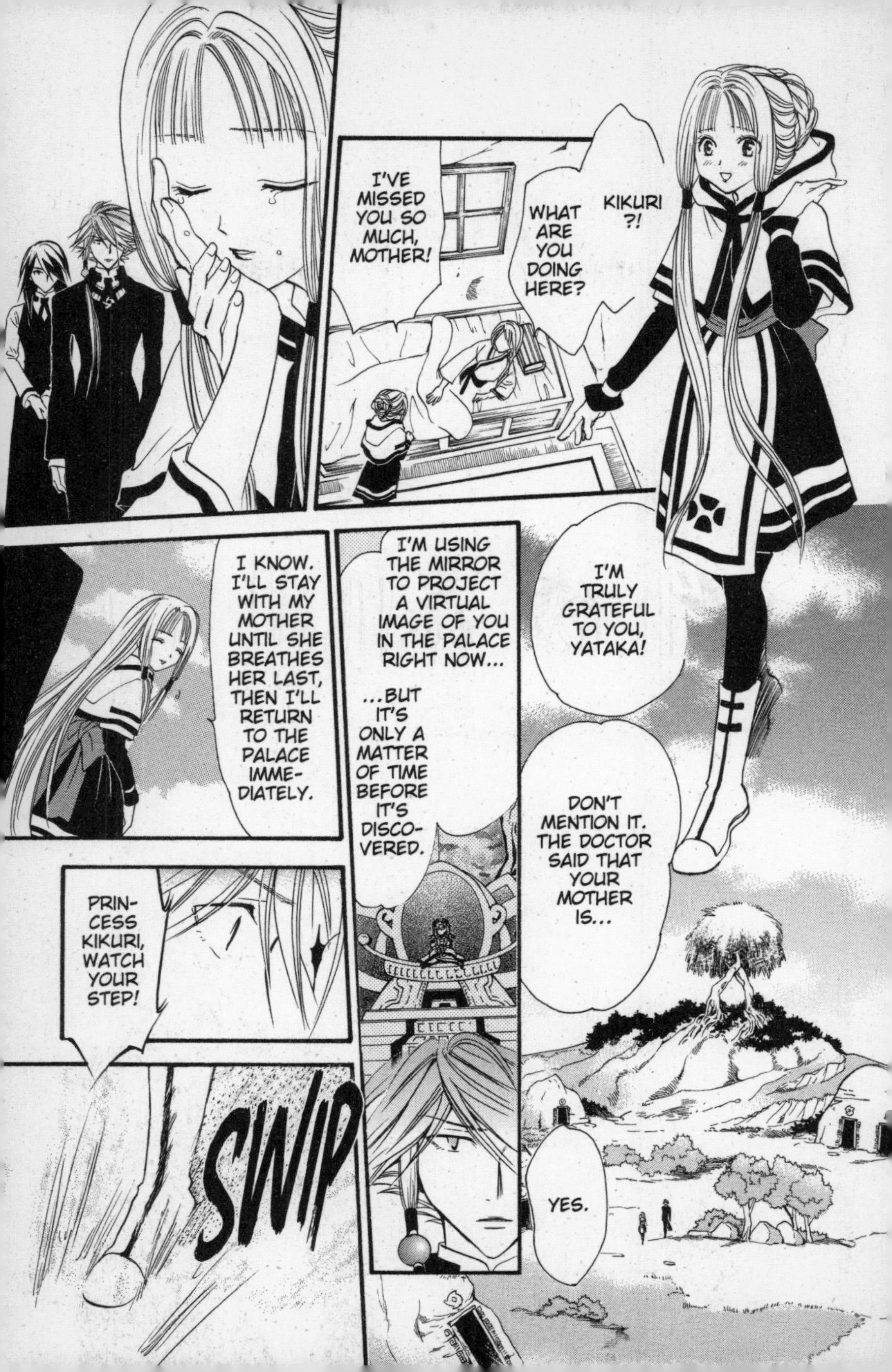
KIKURI ?!
WHAT ARE YOU DOING HERE?
I'VE MISSED YOU SO MUCH, MOTHER!
I'M TRULY GRATEFUL TO YOU, YATAKA!
DON'T MENTION IT. THE DOCTOR SAID THAT YOUR MOTHER IS...
YES.
I'M USING THE MIRROR TO PROJECT A VIRTUAL IMAGE OF YOU IN THE PALACE RIGHT NOW...
...BUT IT'S ONLY A MATTER OF TIME BEFORE IT'S DISCO-VERED.
I KNOW. I'LL STAY WITH MY MOTHER UNTIL SHE BREATHES HER LAST, THEN I'LL RETURN TO THE PALACE IMME-DIATELY.
PRIN-CESS KIKURI, WATCH YOUR STEP!
SWIP

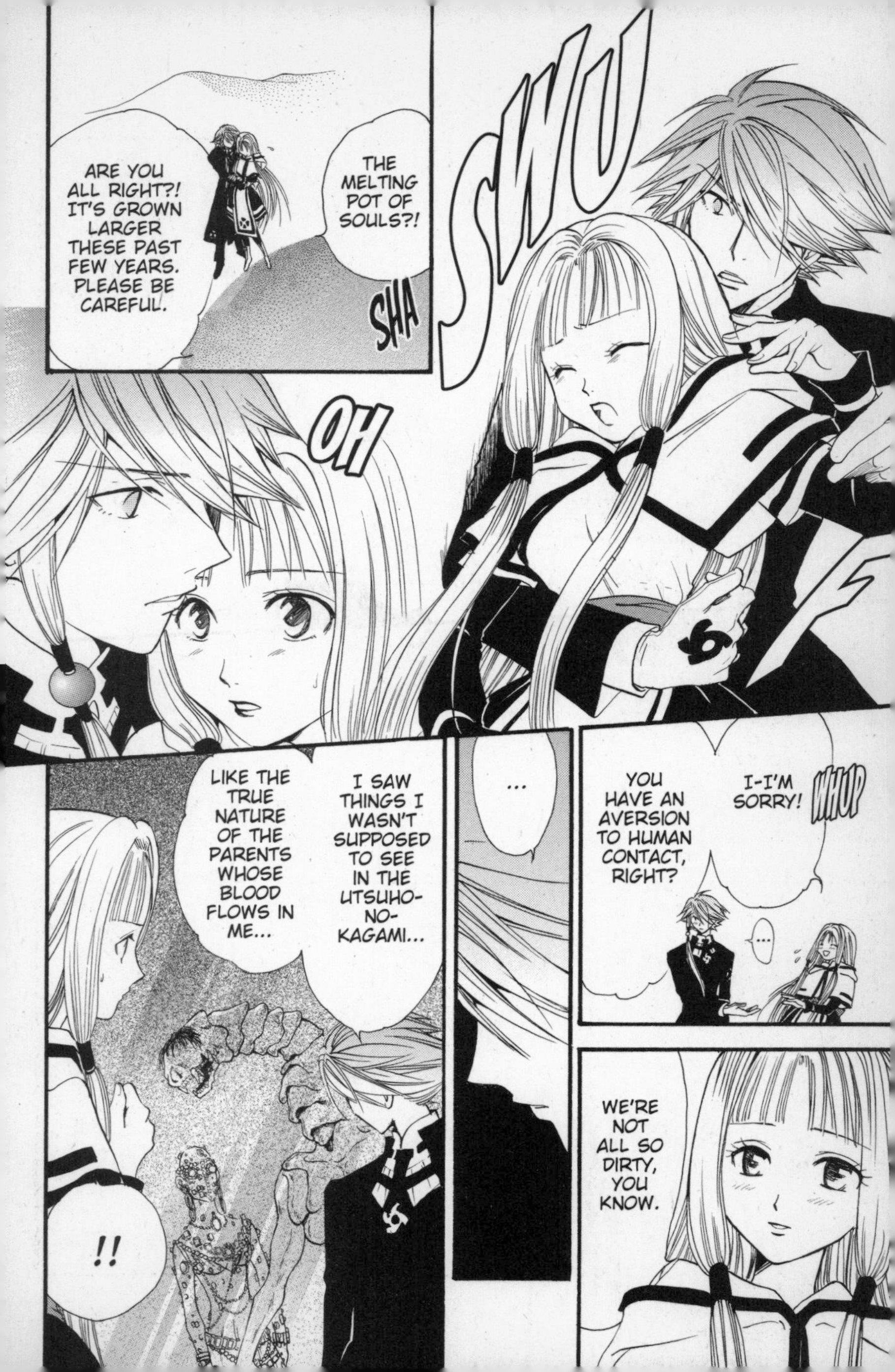
SHWU
THE MELTING POT OF SOULS?!
ARE YOU ALL RIGHT?! IT'S GROWN LARGER THESE PAST FEW YEARS. PLEASE BE CAREFUL.
SHA
OH
I-I'M SORRY!
WHUP
YOU HAVE AN AVERSION TO HUMAN CONTACT, RIGHT?
...
WE'RE NOT ALL SO DIRTY, YOU KNOW.
...
I SAW THINGS I WASN'T SUPPOSED TO SEE IN THE UTSUHO-NO-KAGAMI...
LIKE THE TRUE NATURE OF THE PARENTS WHOSE BLOOD FLOWS IN ME...
!!

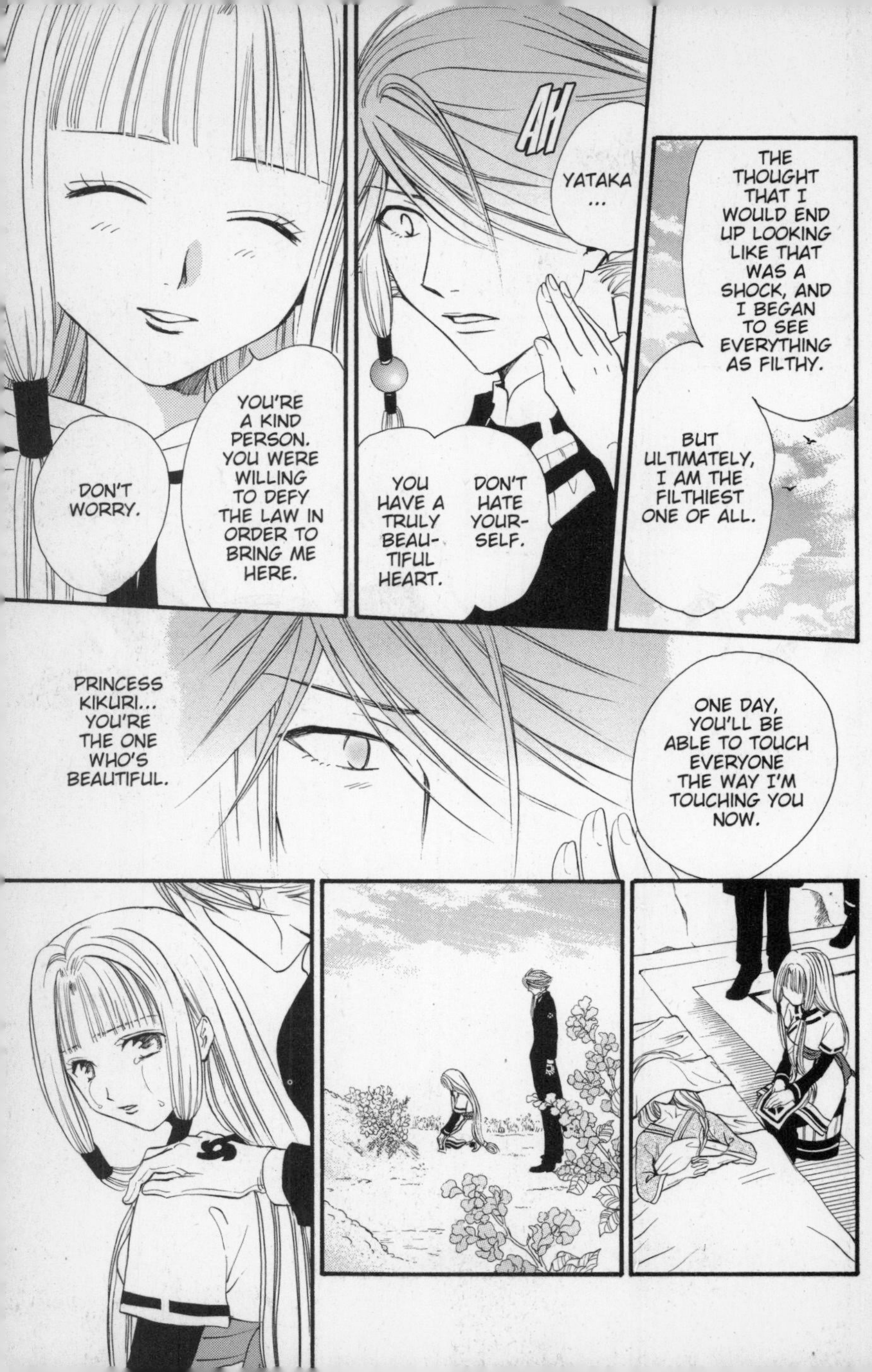
THE THOUGHT THAT I WOULD END UP LOOKING LIKE THAT WAS A SHOCK, AND I BEGAN TO SEE EVERYTHING AS FILTHY.
BUT ULTIMATELY, I AM THE FILTHIEST ONE OF ALL.
AH
YATAKA ...
DON'T HATE YOUR-SELF.
YOU HAVE A TRULY BEAU-TIFUL HEART.
YOU'RE A KIND PERSON. YOU WERE WILLING TO DEFY THE LAW IN ORDER TO BRING ME HERE.
DON'T WORRY.
ONE DAY, YOU'LL BE ABLE TO TOUCH EVERYONE THE WAY I'M TOUCHING YOU NOW.
PRINCESS KIKURI... YOU'RE THE ONE WHO'S BEAUTIFUL.

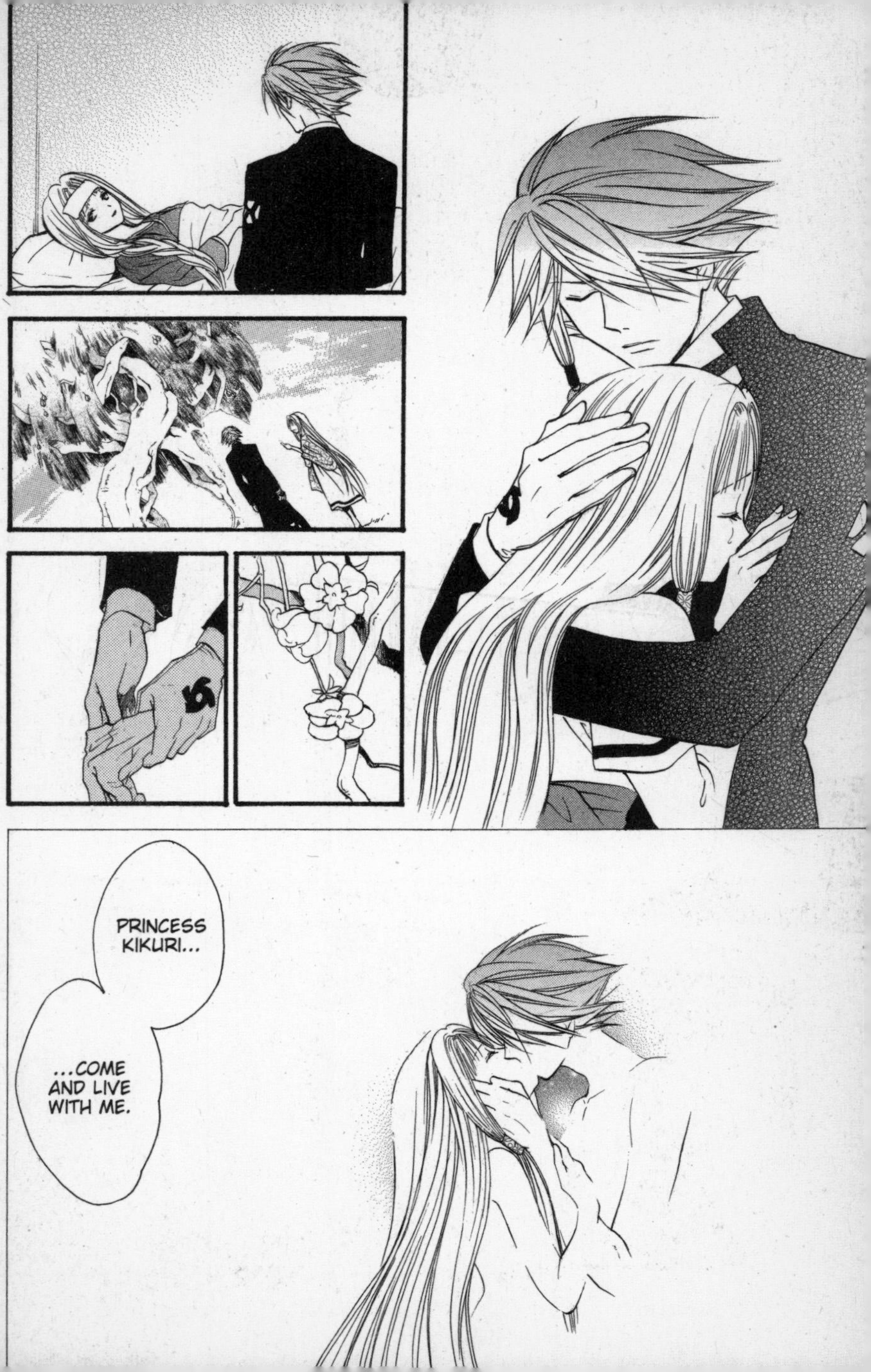
PRINCESS KIKURI...
...COME AND LIVE WITH ME.

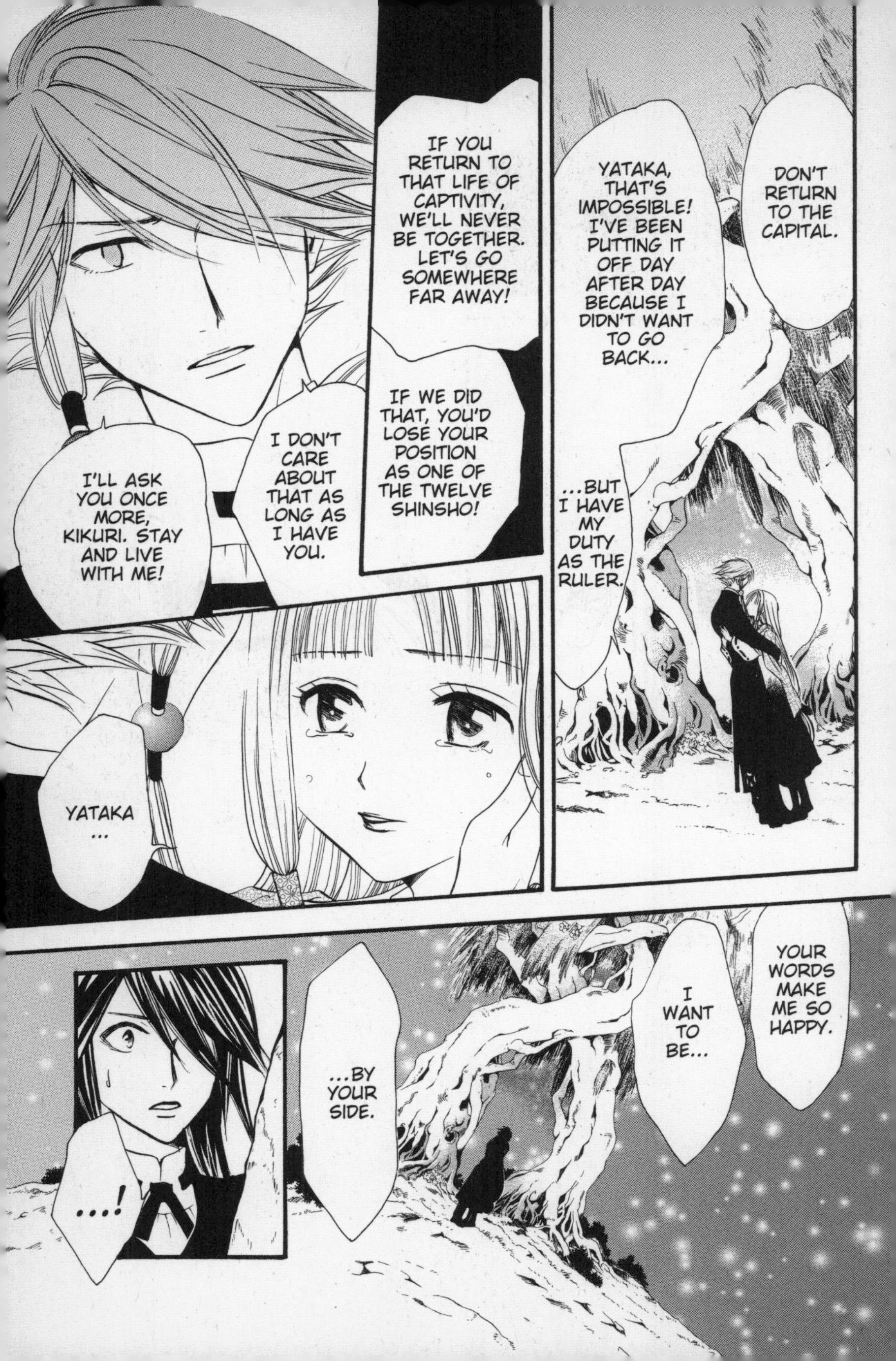
DON'T RETURN TO THE CAPITAL.
YATAKA, THAT'S IMPOSSIBLE! I'VE BEEN PUTTING IT OFF DAY AFTER DAY BECAUSE I DIDN'T WANT TO GO BACK...
...BUT I HAVE MY DUTY AS THE RULER.
IF YOU RETURN TO THAT LIFE OF CAPTIVITY, WE'LL NEVER BE TOGETHER. LET'S GO SOMEWHERE FAR AWAY!
IF WE DID THAT, YOU'D LOSE YOUR POSITION AS ONE OF THE TWELVE SHINSHO!
I DON'T CARE ABOUT THAT AS LONG AS I HAVE YOU.
I'LL ASK YOU ONCE MORE, KIKURI. STAY AND LIVE WITH ME!
YATAKA...
YOUR WORDS MAKE ME SO HAPPY.
I WANT TO BE...
...BY YOUR SIDE.
...!

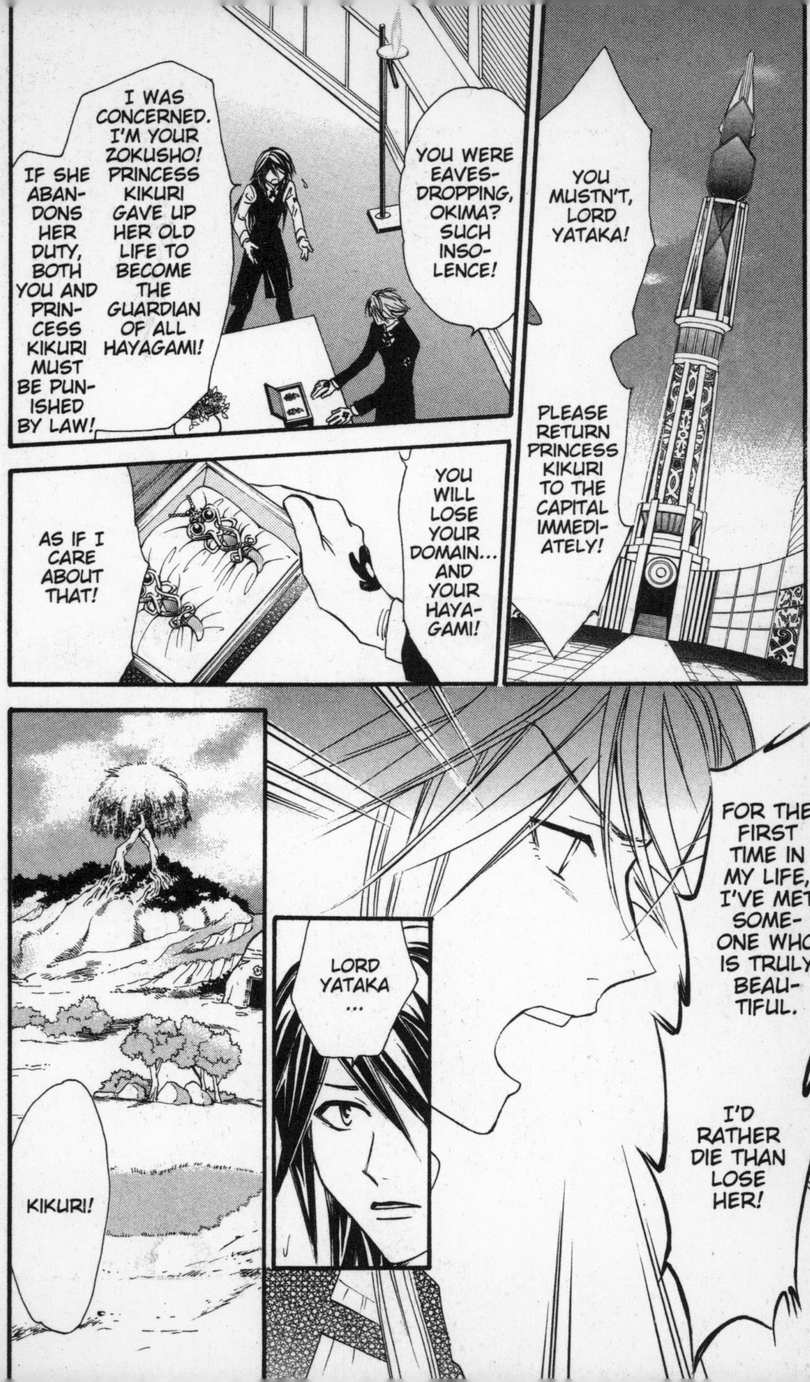
YOU MUSTN'T, LORD YATAKA!
PLEASE RETURN PRINCESS KIKURI TO THE CAPITAL IMMEDIATELY!
YOU WERE EAVES-DROPPING, OKIMA? SUCH INSO-LENCE!
I WAS CONCERNED. I'M YOUR ZOKUSHO! PRINCESS KIKURI GAVE UP HER OLD LIFE TO BECOME THE GUARDIAN OF ALL HAYAGAMI!
IF SHE ABAN-DONS HER DUTY, BOTH YOU AND PRIN-CESS KIKURI MUST BE PUN-ISHED BY LAW!
YOU WILL LOSE YOUR DOMAIN... AND YOUR HAYA-GAMI!
AS IF I CARE ABOUT THAT!
FOR THE FIRST TIME IN MY LIFE, I'VE MET SOME-ONE WHO IS TRULY BEAU-TIFUL.
I'D RATHER DIE THAN LOSE HER!
LORD YATAKA ...
KIKURI!

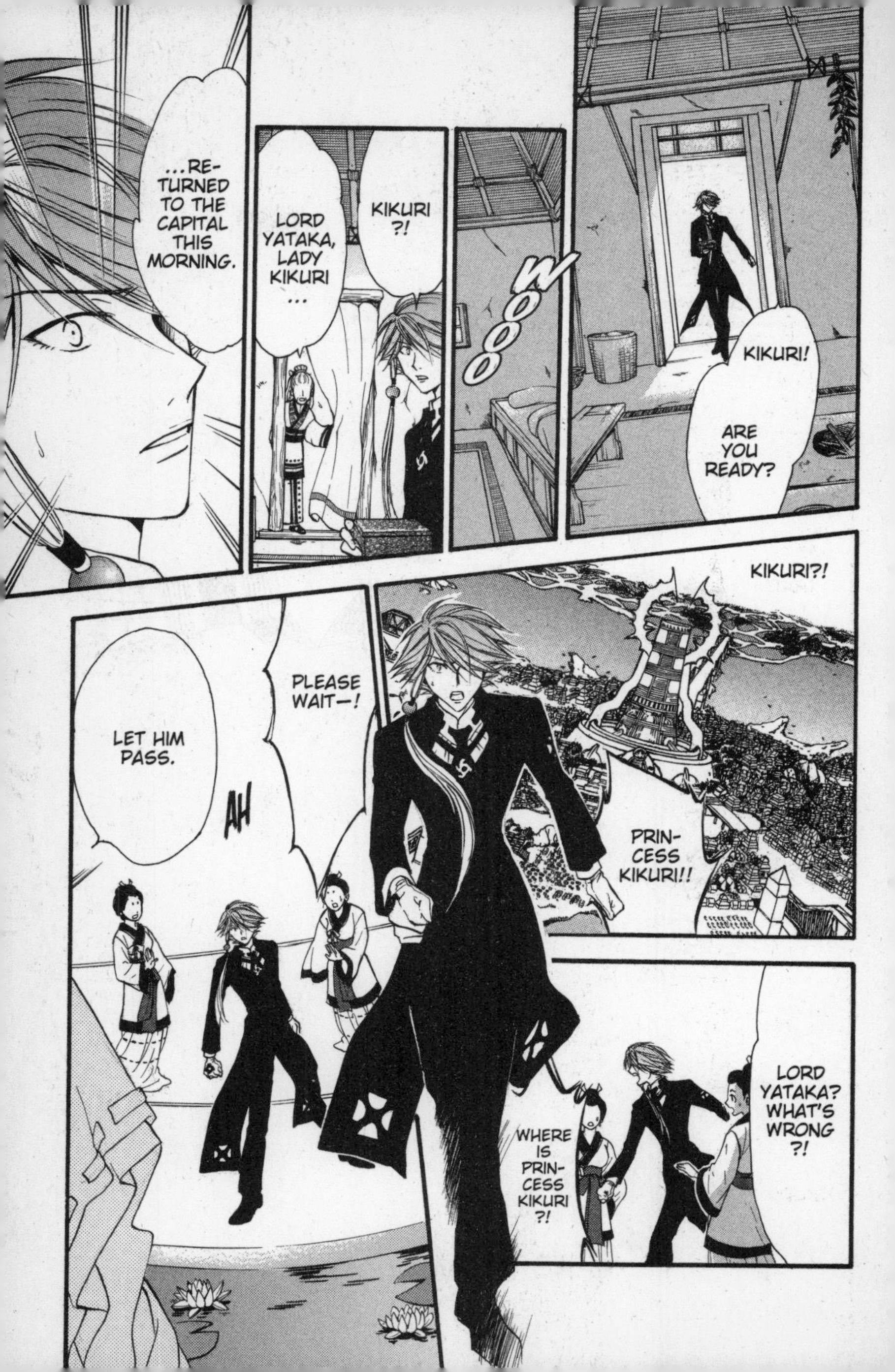
KIKURI!
ARE YOU READY?
WOOOOO
KIKURI ?!
LORD YATAKA, LADY KIKURI ...
...RE-TURNED TO THE CAPITAL THIS MORNING.
KIKURI?!
PRIN-CESS KIKURI!!
LORD YATAKA? WHAT'S WRONG ?!
WHERE IS PRIN-CESS KIKURI ?!
PLEASE WAIT—!
AH
LET HIM PASS.

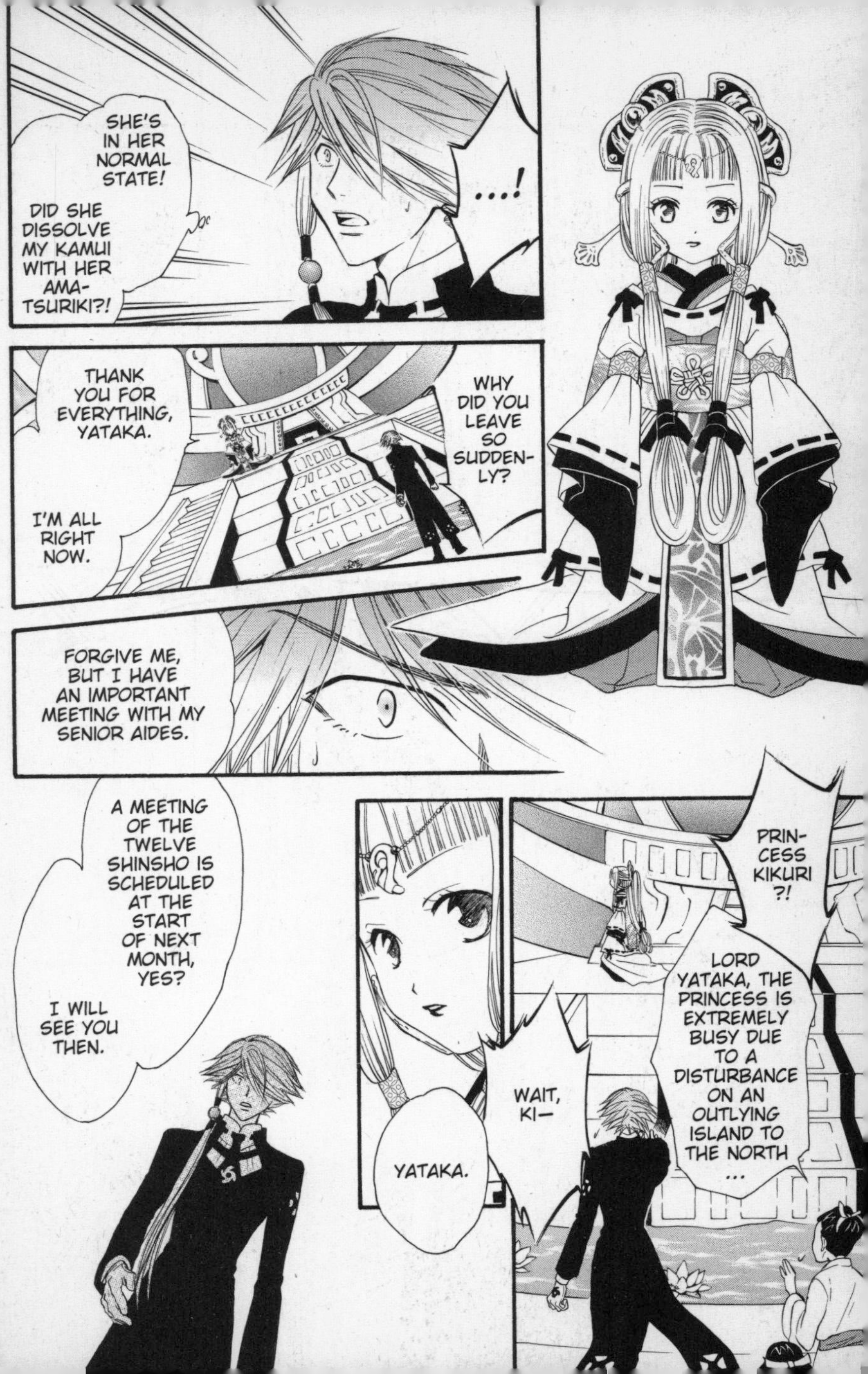
...!
SHE'S IN HER NORMAL STATE!
DID SHE DISSOLVE MY KAMUI WITH HER AMA-TSURIKI?!
WHY DID YOU LEAVE SO SUDDEN-LY?
THANK YOU FOR EVERYTHING, YATAKA.
I'M ALL RIGHT NOW.
FORGIVE ME, BUT I HAVE AN IMPORTANT MEETING WITH MY SENIOR AIDES.
PRIN-CESS KIKURI ?!
LORD YATAKA, THE PRINCESS IS EXTREMELY BUSY DUE TO A DISTURBANCE ON AN OUTLYING ISLAND TO THE NORTH ...
WAIT, KI—
YATAKA.
A MEETING OF THE TWELVE SHINSHO IS SCHEDULED AT THE START OF NEXT MONTH, YES?
I WILL SEE YOU THEN.

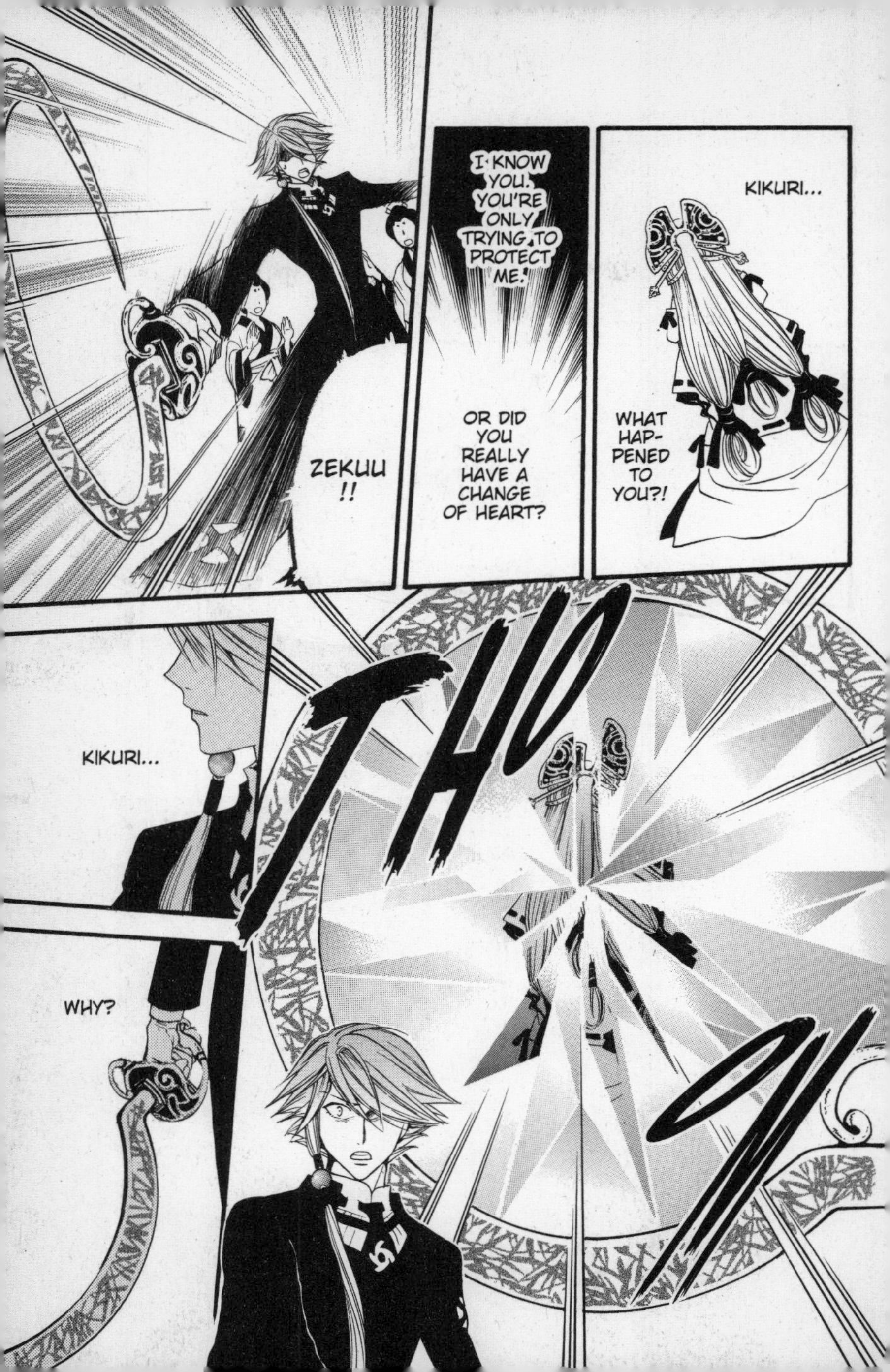
KIKURI...
WHAT HAPPENED TO YOU?!
I KNOW YOU. YOU'RE ONLY TRYING TO PROTECT ME.
OR DID YOU REALLY HAVE A CHANGE OF HEART?
ZEKUU!!
KIKURI...
WHY?

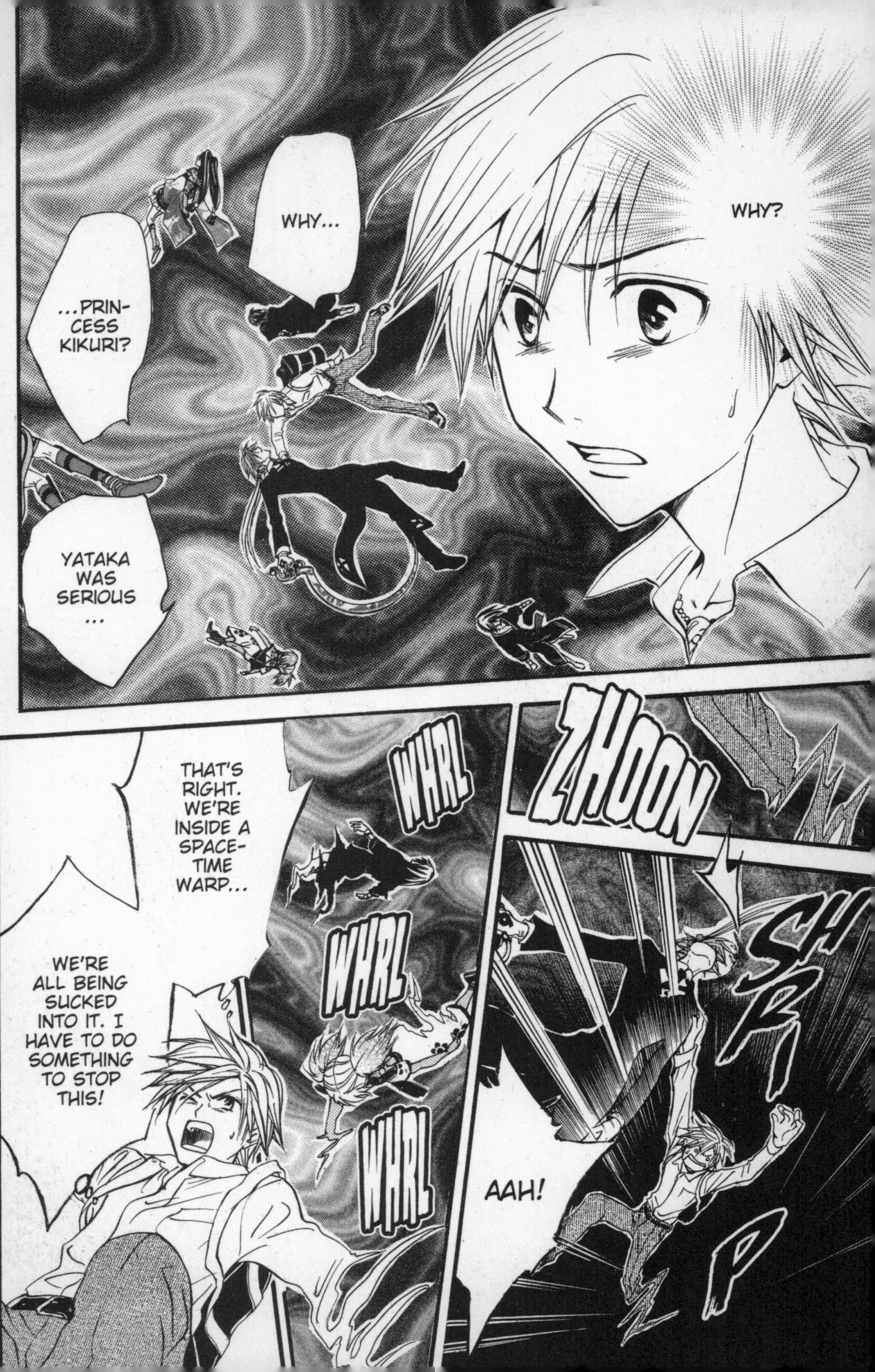
WHY?
WHY...
...PRIN-
CESS
KIKURI?
YATAKA
WAS
SERIOUS
...
ZHOON
SHRIP
AAH!
WHRL
WHRL
WHRL
THAT'S
RIGHT.
WE'RE
INSIDE A
SPACE-
TIME
WARP...
WE'RE
ALL BEING
SUCKED
INTO IT. I
HAVE TO DO
SOMETHING
TO STOP
THIS!

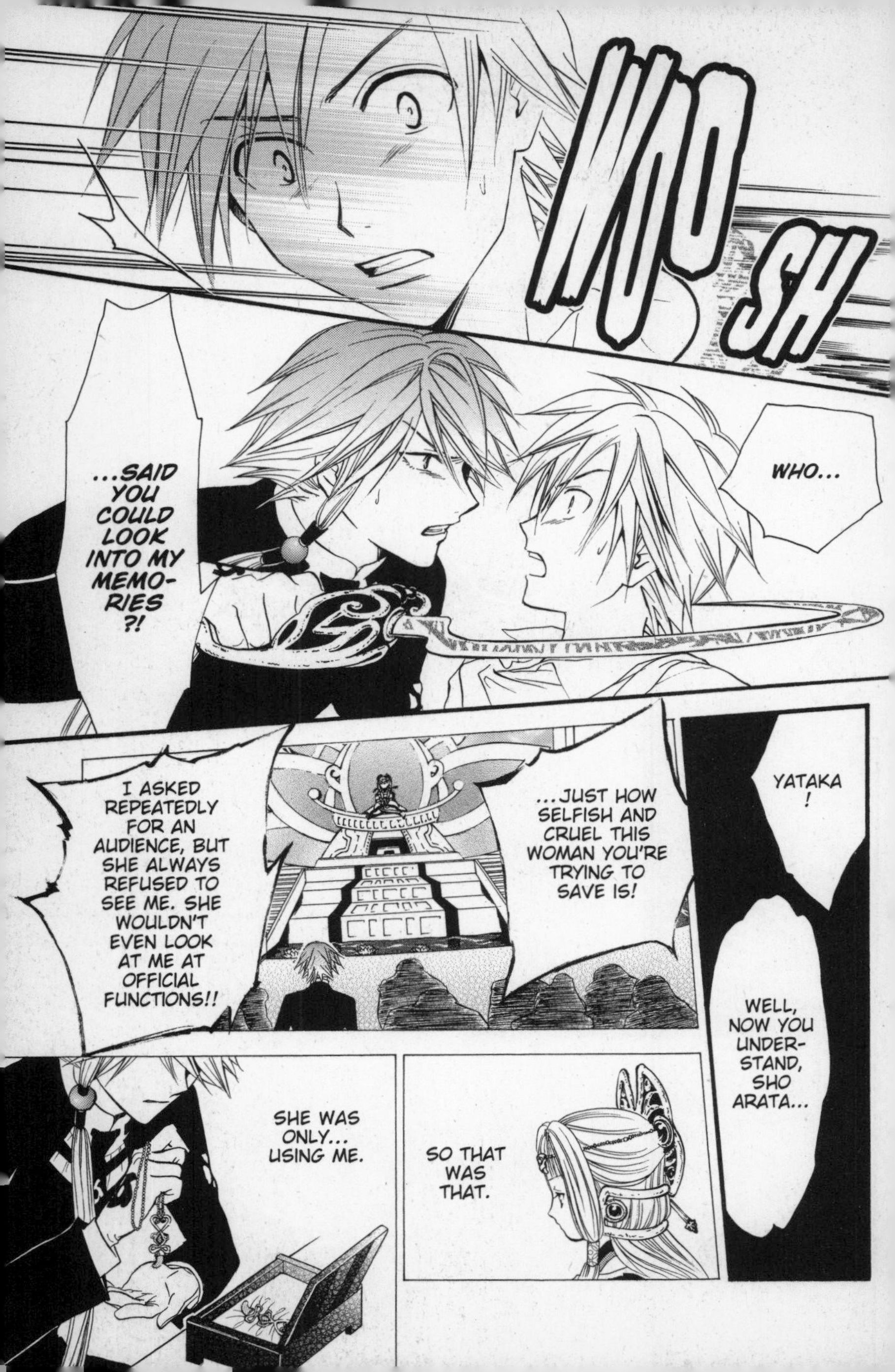
WHOSH
WHO...
...SAID YOU COULD LOOK INTO MY MEMO-RIES?!
YATAKA!
WELL, NOW YOU UNDER-STAND, SHO ARATA...
...JUST HOW SELFISH AND CRUEL THIS WOMAN YOU'RE TRYING TO SAVE IS!
I ASKED REPEATEDLY FOR AN AUDIENCE, BUT SHE ALWAYS REFUSED TO SEE ME. SHE WOULDN'T EVEN LOOK AT ME AT OFFICIAL FUNCTIONS!!
SO THAT WAS THAT.
SHE WAS ONLY... USING ME.

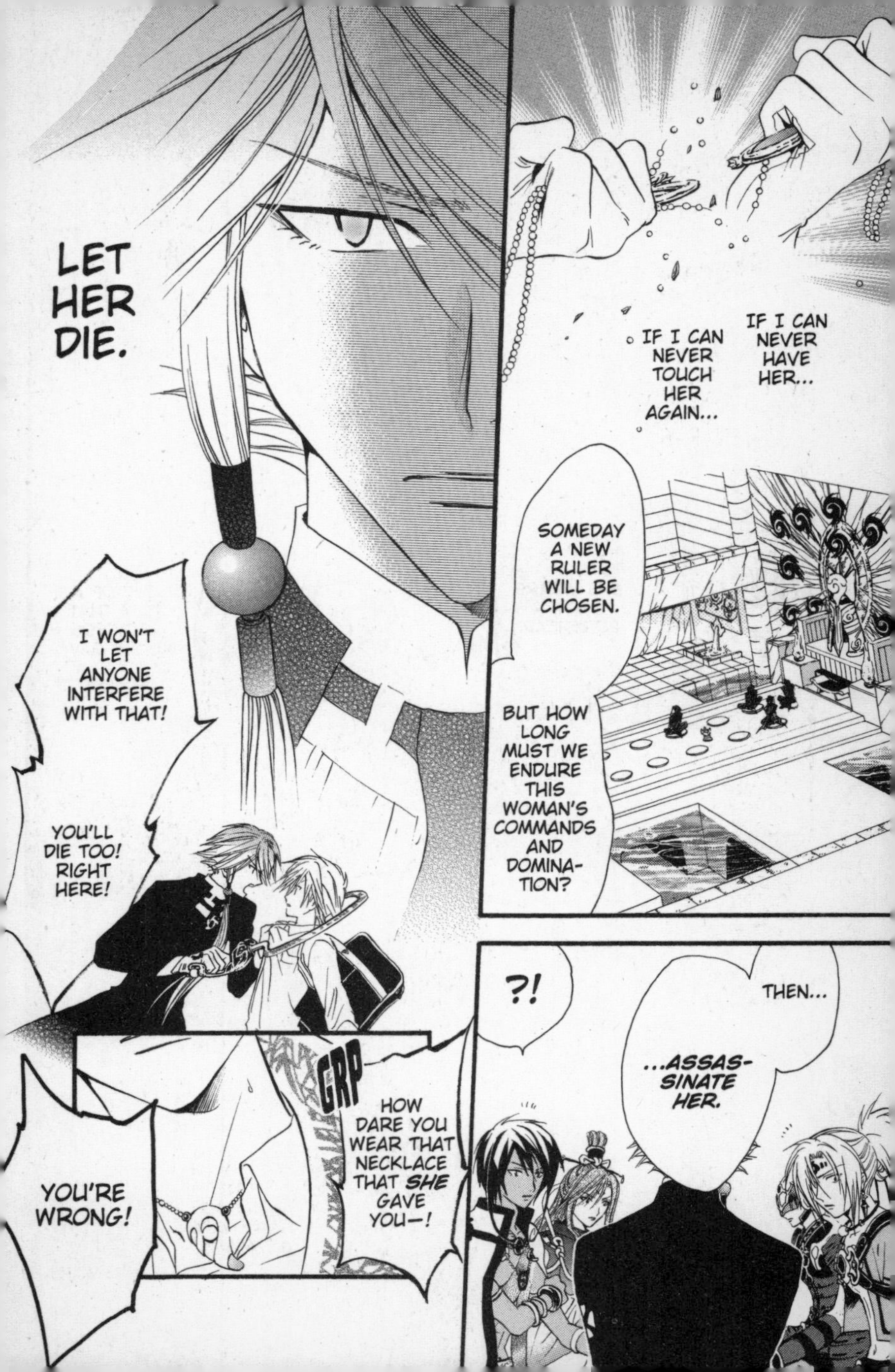
IF I CAN NEVER HAVE HER...
IF I CAN NEVER TOUCH HER AGAIN...
SOMEDAY A NEW RULER WILL BE CHOSEN.
BUT HOW LONG MUST WE ENDURE THIS WOMAN'S COMMANDS AND DOMINA- TION?
THEN...
?!
...ASSAS- SINATE HER.
LET HER DIE.
I WON'T LET ANYONE INTERFERE WITH THAT!
YOU'LL DIE TOO! RIGHT HERE!
GRP
HOW DARE YOU WEAR THAT NECKLACE THAT *SHE* GAVE YOU—!
YOU'RE WRONG!

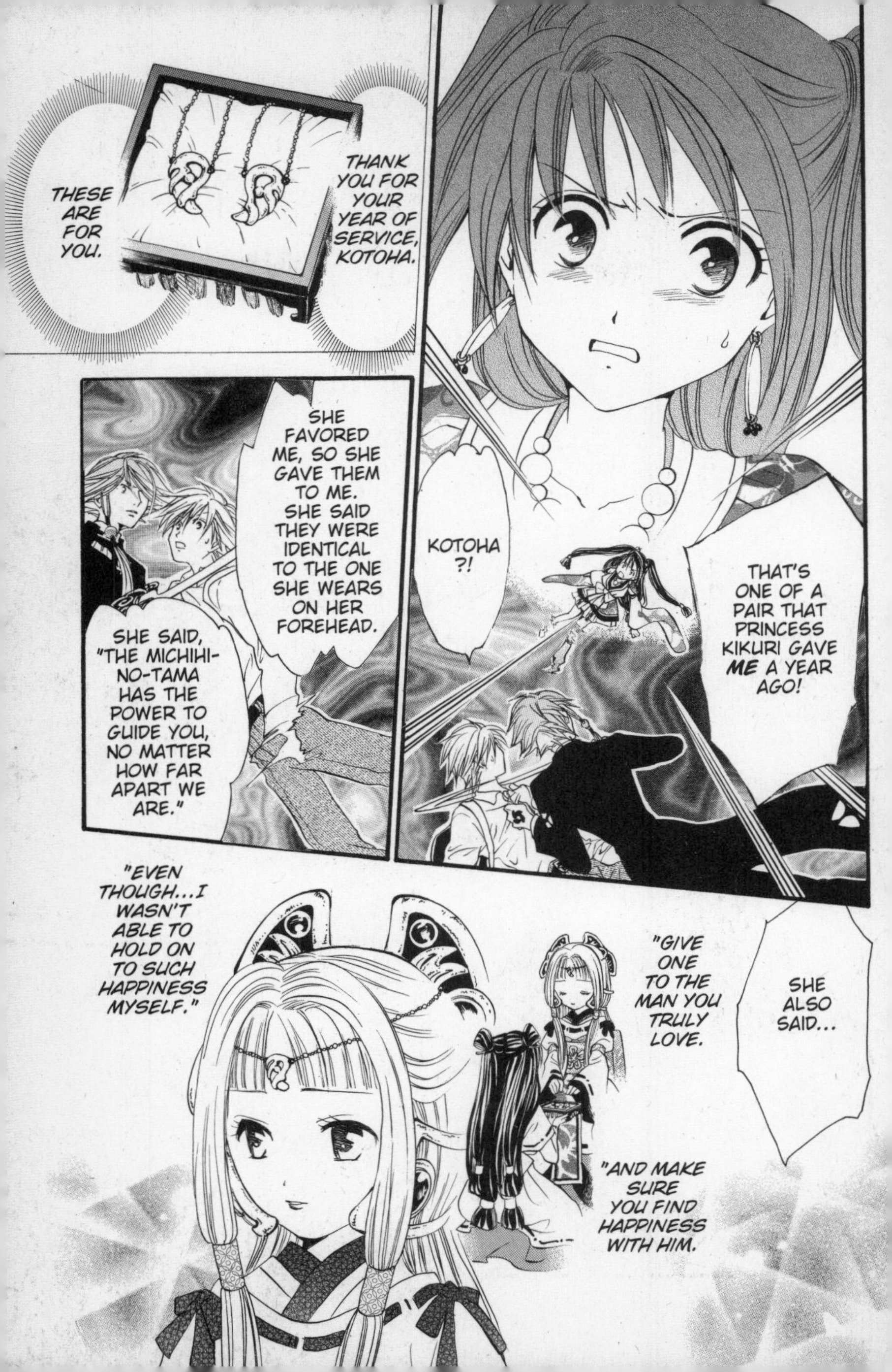
THAT'S ONE OF A PAIR THAT PRINCESS KIKURI GAVE *ME* A YEAR AGO!
KOTOHA ?!
THANK YOU FOR YOUR YEAR OF SERVICE, KOTOHA.
THESE ARE FOR YOU.
SHE FAVORED ME, SO SHE GAVE THEM TO ME. SHE SAID THEY WERE IDENTICAL TO THE ONE SHE WEARS ON HER FOREHEAD.
SHE SAID, "THE MICHIHI-NO-TAMA HAS THE POWER TO GUIDE YOU, NO MATTER HOW FAR APART WE ARE."
SHE ALSO SAID...
"GIVE ONE TO THE MAN YOU TRULY LOVE.
"AND MAKE SURE YOU FIND HAPPINESS WITH HIM.
"EVEN THOUGH...I WASN'T ABLE TO HOLD ON TO SUCH HAPPINESS MYSELF."

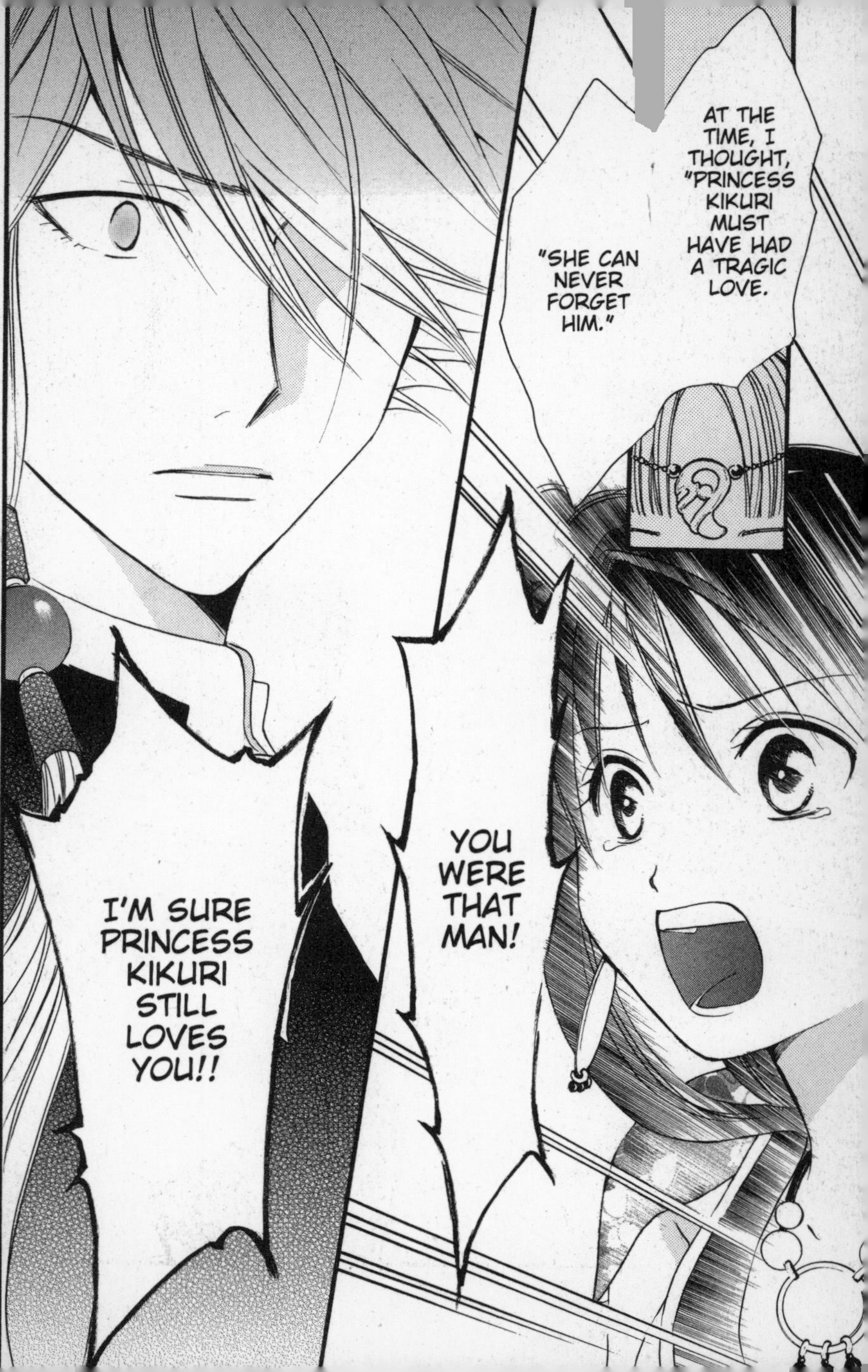
AT THE TIME, I THOUGHT, "PRINCESS KIKURI MUST HAVE HAD A TRAGIC LOVE.
"SHE CAN NEVER FORGET HIM."
YOU WERE THAT MAN!
I'M SURE PRINCESS KIKURI STILL LOVES YOU!!

CHAPTER 99
IT'S NOT OVER

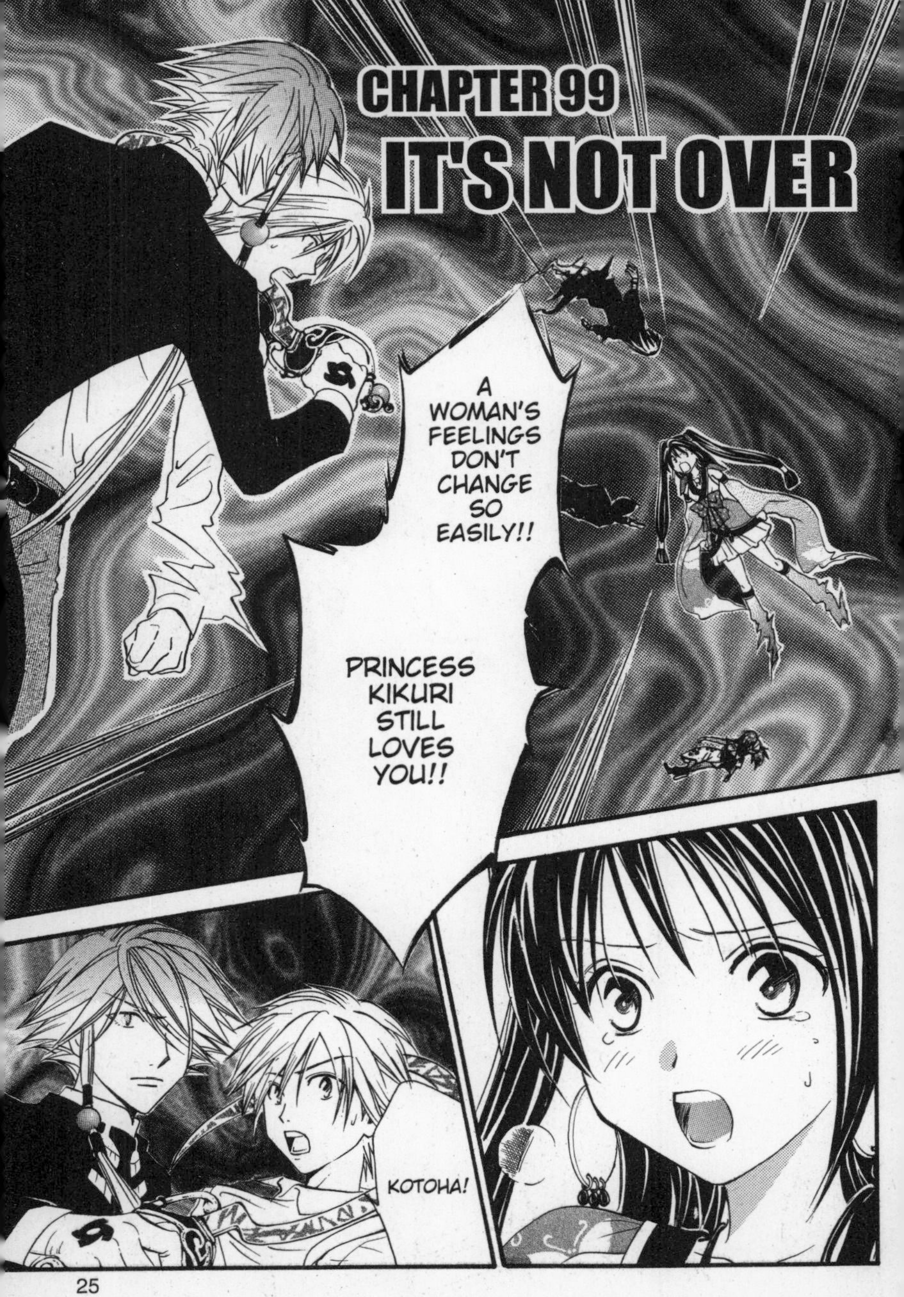

A WOMAN'S FEELINGS DON'T CHANGE SO EASILY!!
PRINCESS KIKURI STILL LOVES YOU!!
KOTOHA!

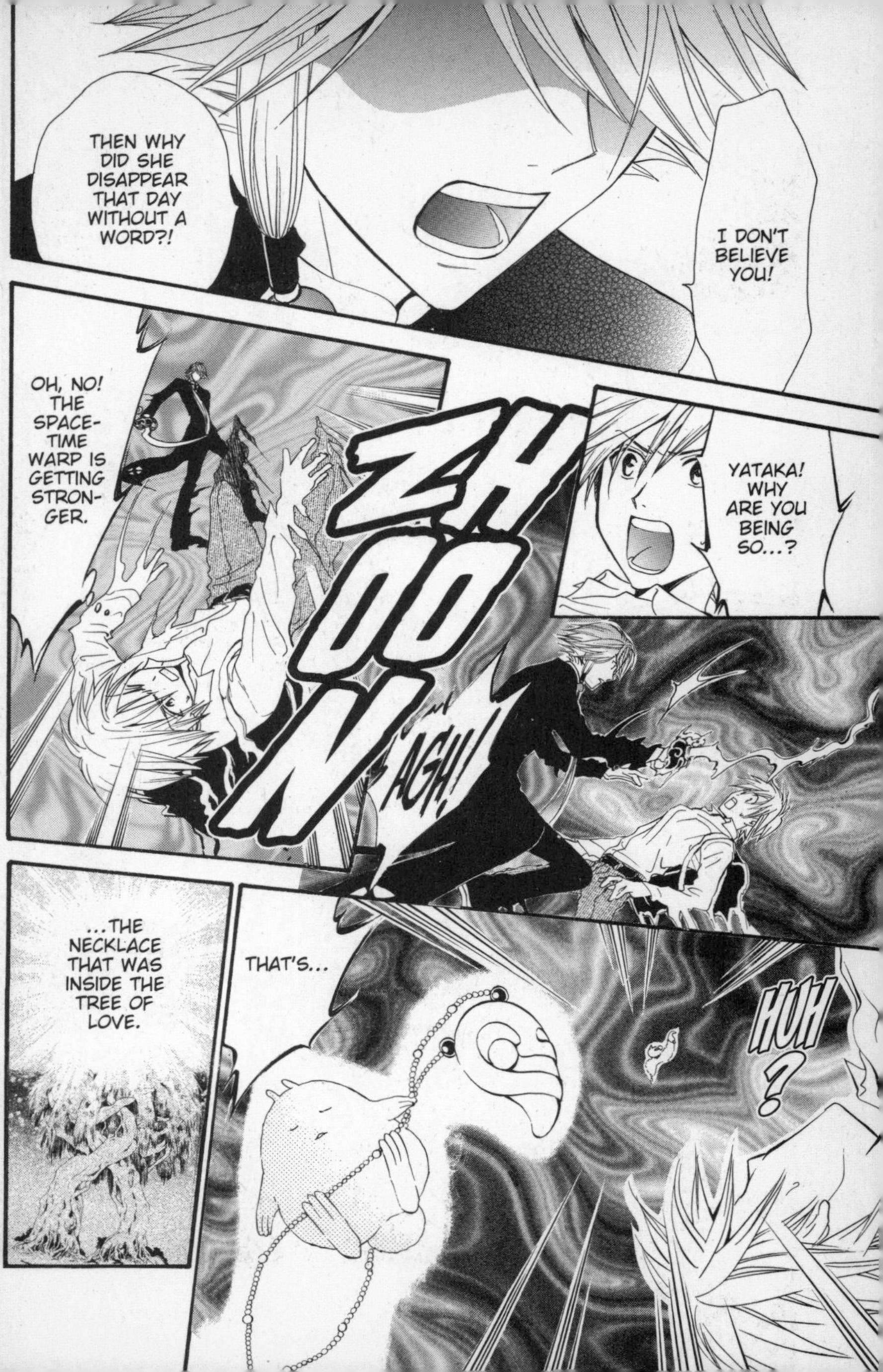
I DON'T BELIEVE YOU!
THEN WHY DID SHE DISAPPEAR THAT DAY WITHOUT A WORD?!
YATAKA! WHY ARE YOU BEING SO...?
OH, NO! THE SPACE-TIME WARP IS GETTING STRONGER.
ZHOON
AGH!
HUH?
THAT'S...
...THE NECKLACE THAT WAS INSIDE THE TREE OF LOVE.

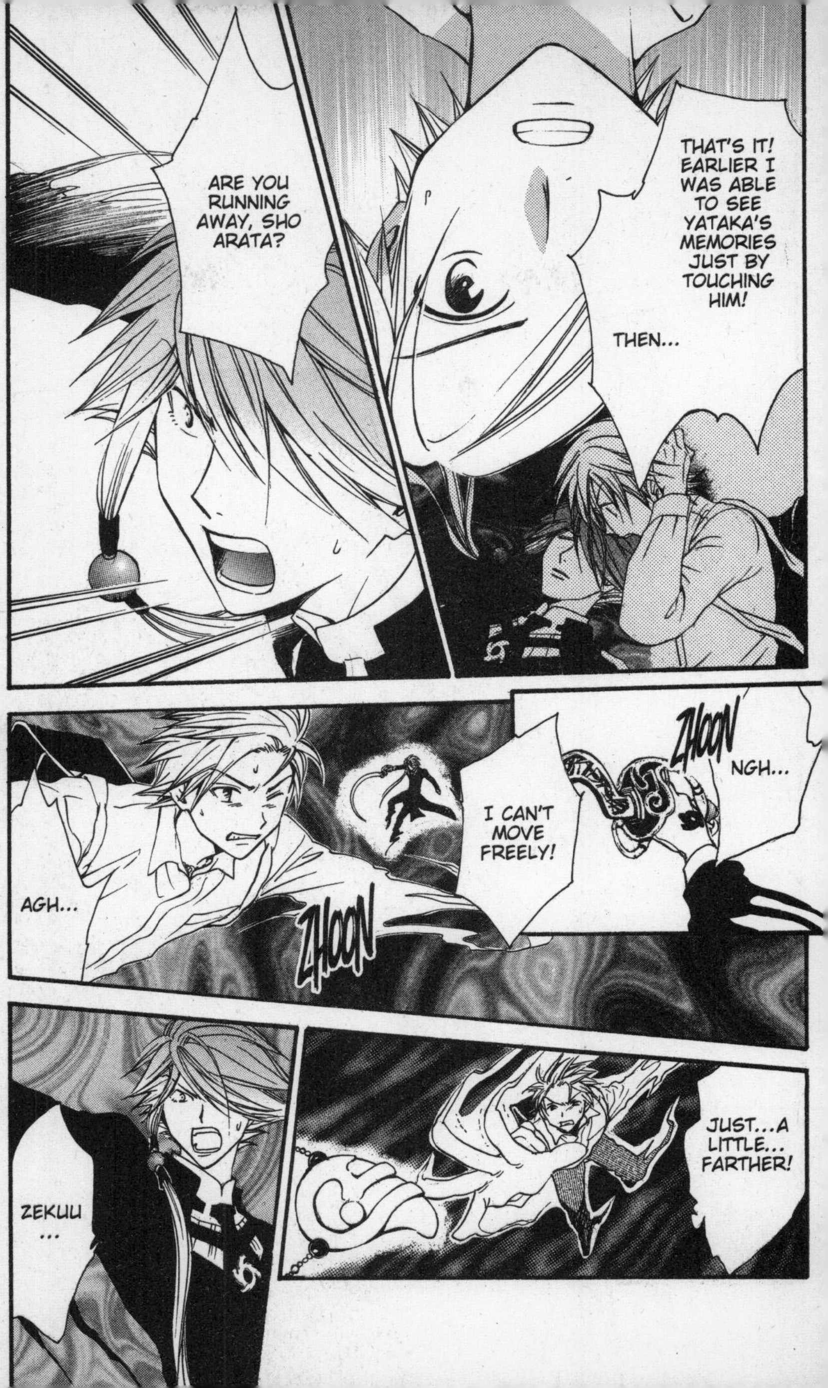
THAT'S IT! EARLIER I WAS ABLE TO SEE YATAKA'S MEMORIES JUST BY TOUCHING HIM!
THEN...
ARE YOU RUNNING AWAY, SHO ARATA?
ZHOON
NGH...
I CAN'T MOVE FREELY!
ZHOON
AGH...
JUST...A LITTLE...FARTHER!
ZEKUU...

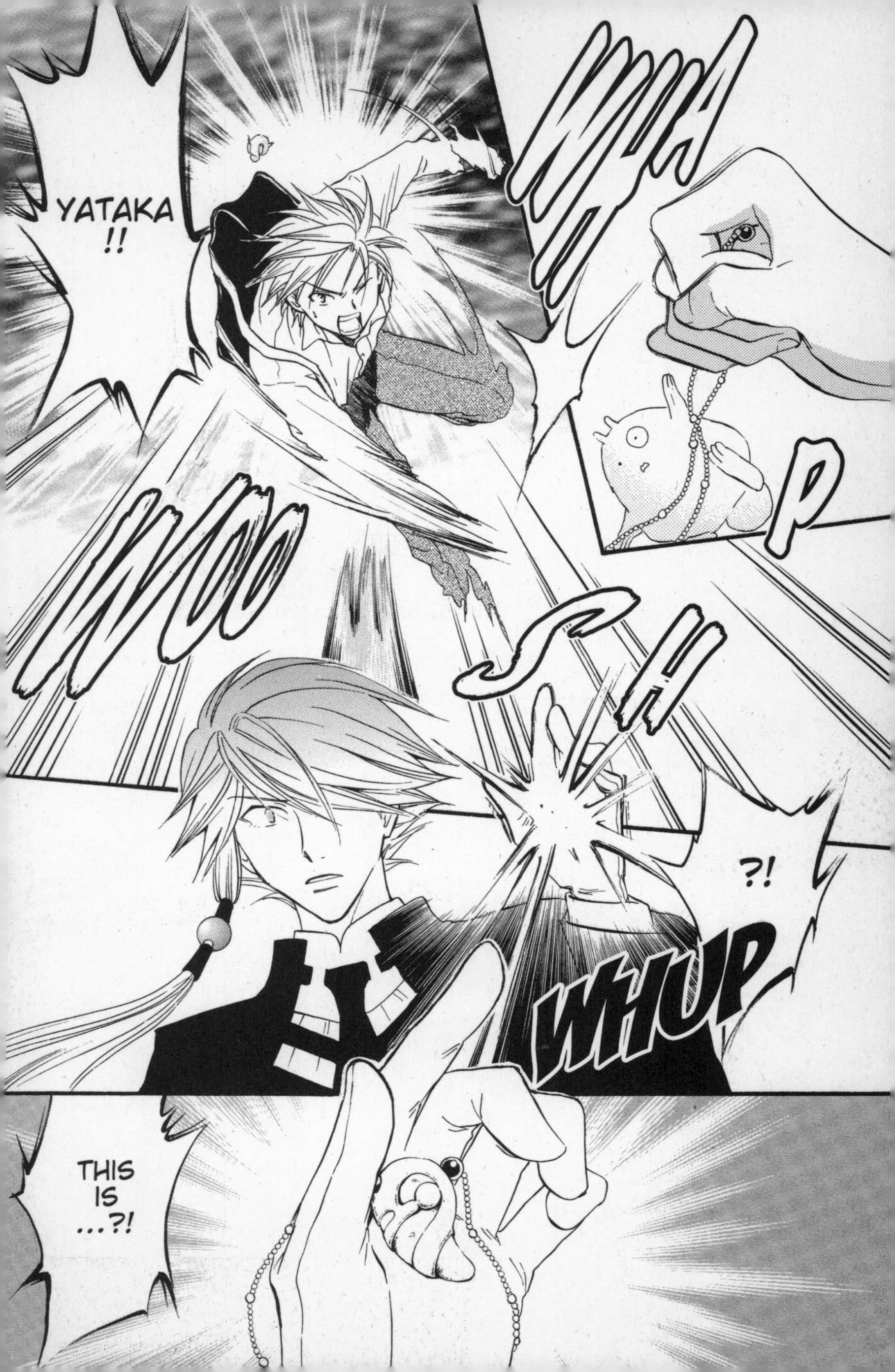
P
YATAKA !!
WOOSH
?!
WHUP
THIS IS ...?!

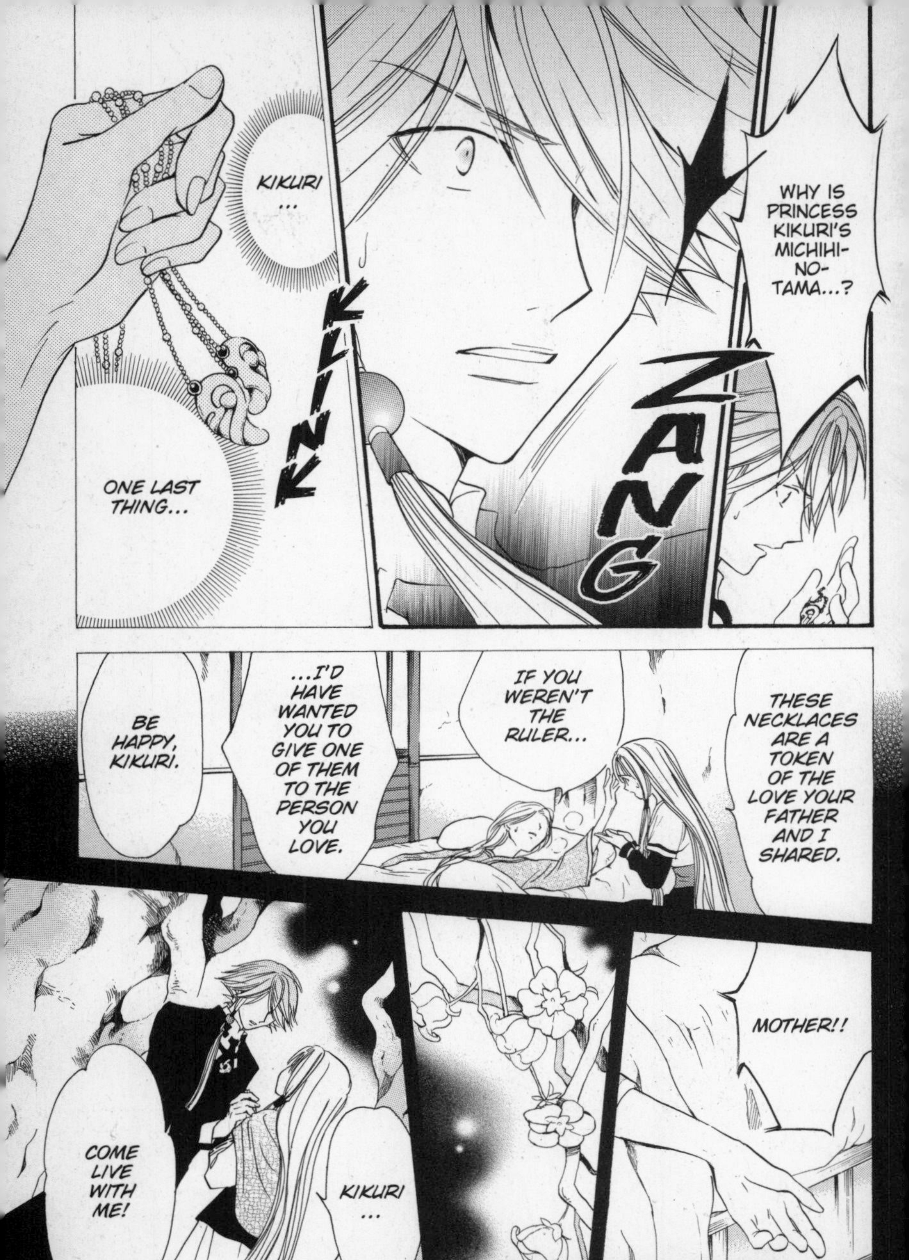
WHY IS PRINCESS KIKURI'S MICHIHI-NO-TAMA...?
ZANG
KLINK
KIKURI ...
ONE LAST THING...
THESE NECKLACES ARE A TOKEN OF THE LOVE YOUR FATHER AND I SHARED.
IF YOU WEREN'T THE RULER...
...I'D HAVE WANTED YOU TO GIVE ONE OF THEM TO THE PERSON YOU LOVE.
BE HAPPY, KIKURI.
MOTHER!!
KIKURI ...
COME LIVE WITH ME!

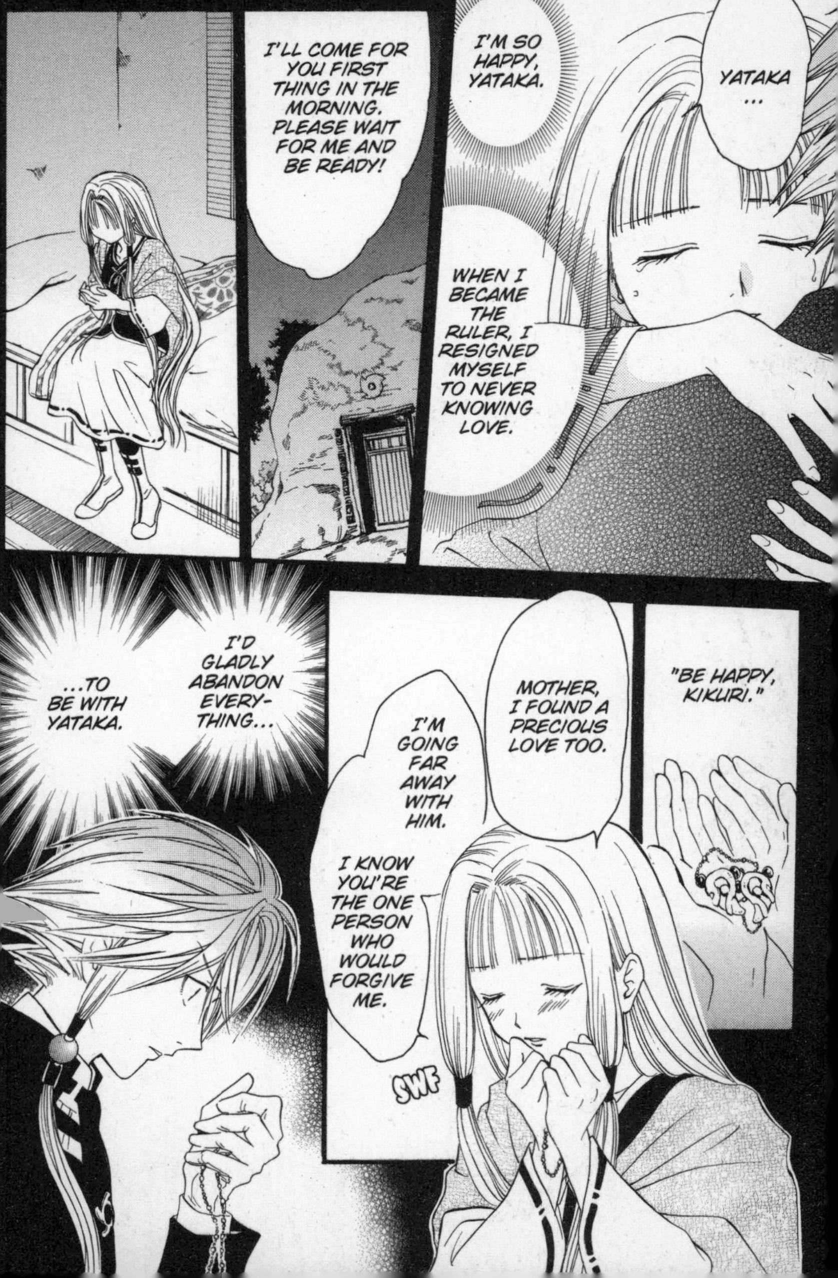
YATAKA ...
I'M SO HAPPY, YATAKA.
WHEN I BECAME THE RULER, I RESIGNED MYSELF TO NEVER KNOWING LOVE.
I'LL COME FOR YOU FIRST THING IN THE MORNING. PLEASE WAIT FOR ME AND BE READY!
"BE HAPPY, KIKURI."
MOTHER, I FOUND A PRECIOUS LOVE TOO.
I'M GOING FAR AWAY WITH HIM.
I KNOW YOU'RE THE ONE PERSON WHO WOULD FORGIVE ME.
SWF
I'D GLADLY ABANDON EVERY-THING...
...TO BE WITH YATAKA.

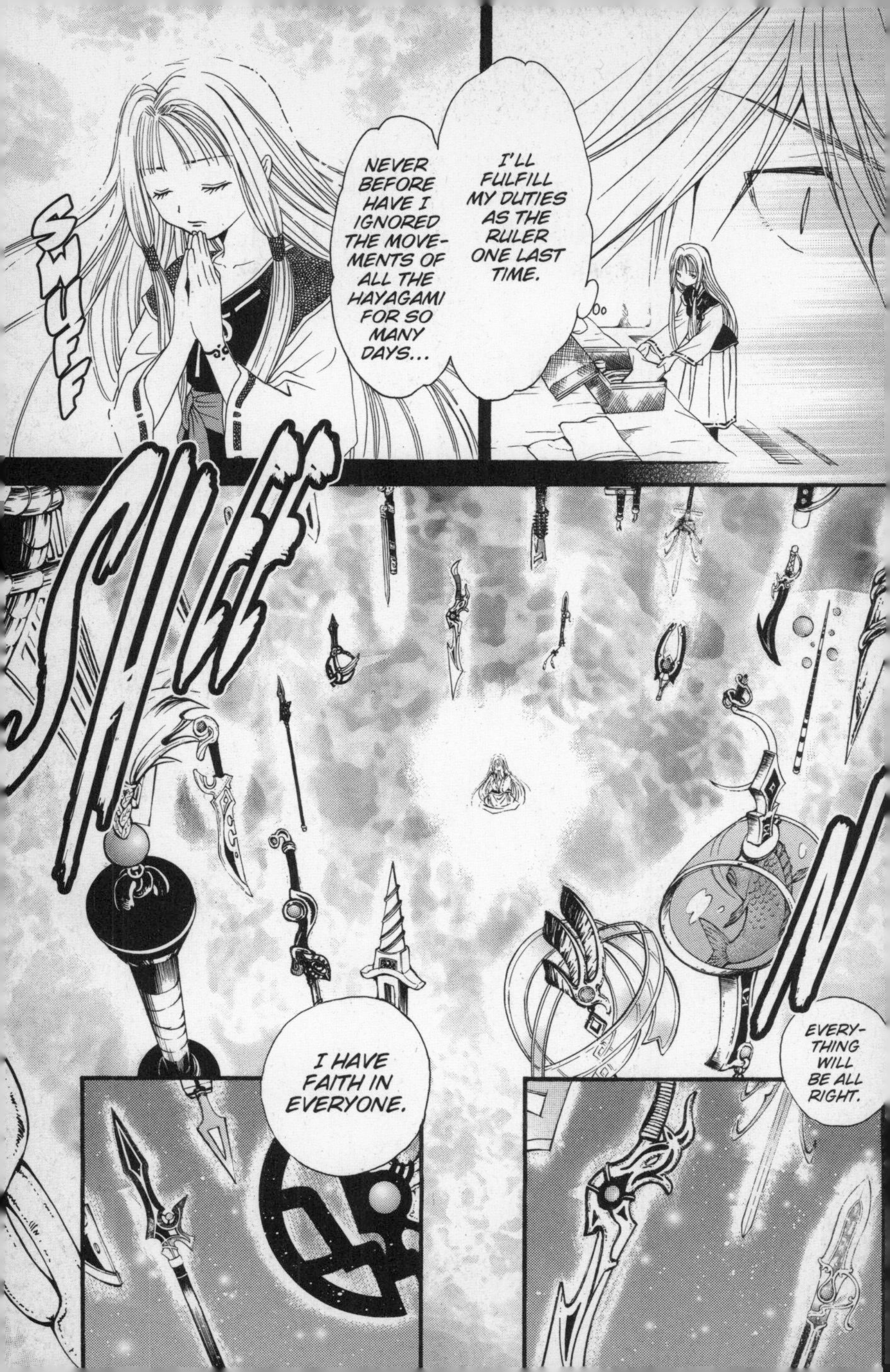
I'LL FULFILL MY DUTIES AS THE RULER ONE LAST TIME.
NEVER BEFORE HAVE I IGNORED THE MOVEMENTS OF ALL THE HAYAGAMI FOR SO MANY DAYS...
SWUFF
EVERYTHING WILL BE ALL RIGHT.
I HAVE FAITH IN EVERYONE.

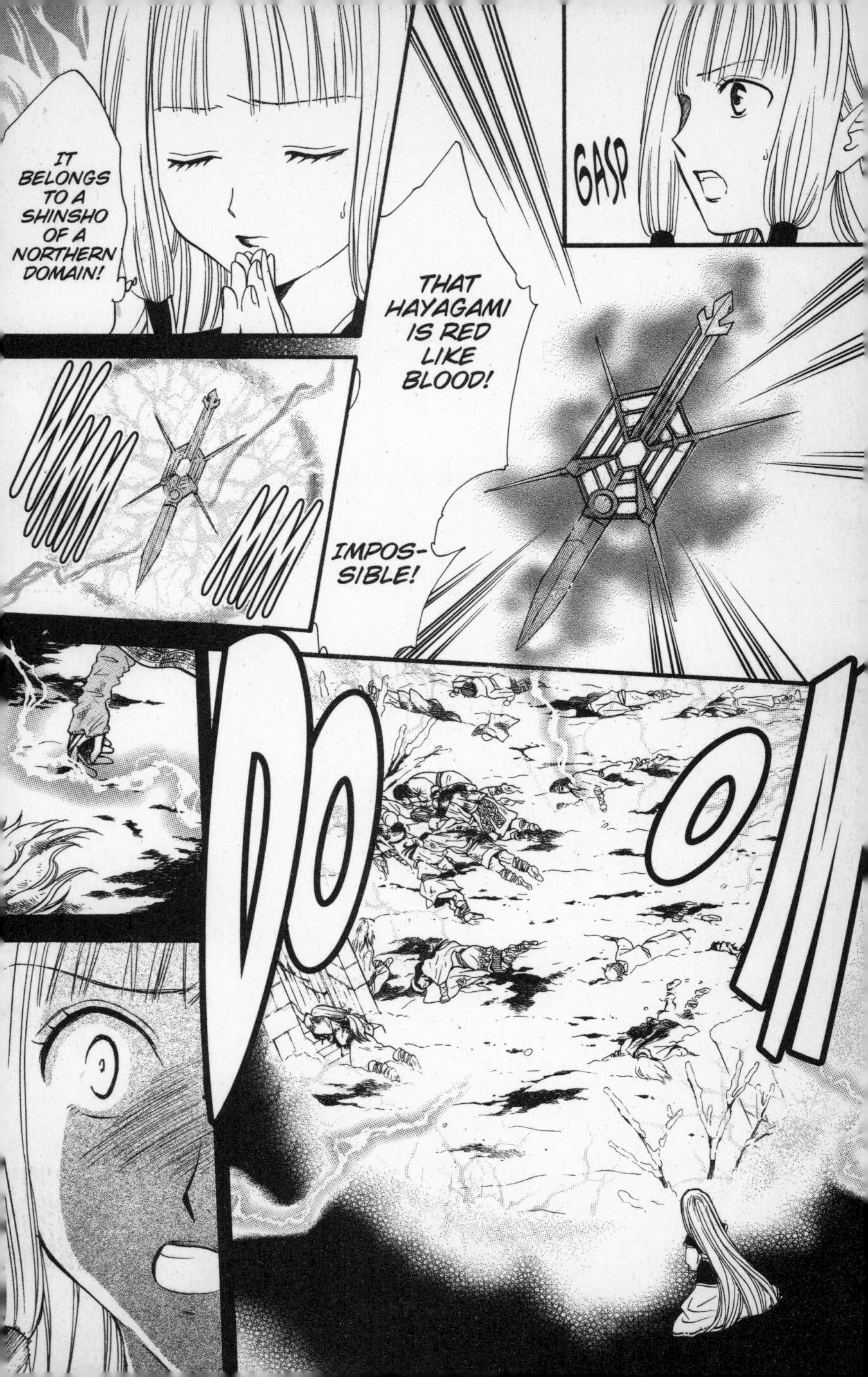
GASP
IT BELONGS TO A SHINSHO OF A NORTHERN DOMAIN!
THAT HAYAGAMI IS RED LIKE BLOOD!
IMPOS-SIBLE!

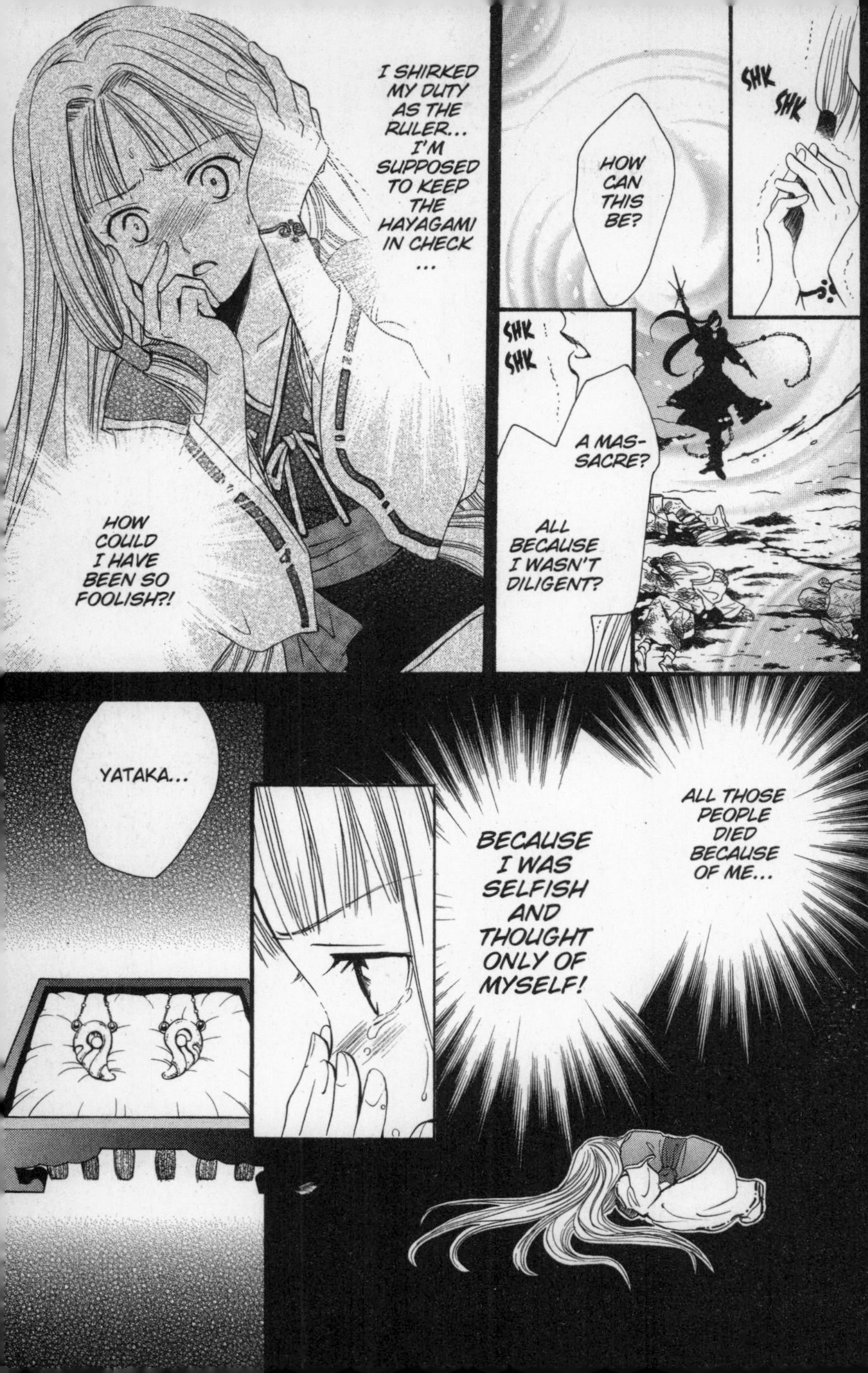
SHK SHK
HOW CAN THIS BE?
SHK SHK
A MAS-SACRE?
ALL BECAUSE I WASN'T DILIGENT?
I SHIRKED MY DUTY AS THE RULER... I'M SUPPOSED TO KEEP THE HAYAGAMI IN CHECK...
HOW COULD I HAVE BEEN SO FOOLISH?!
ALL THOSE PEOPLE DIED BECAUSE OF ME...
BECAUSE I WAS SELFISH AND THOUGHT ONLY OF MYSELF!
YATAKA...

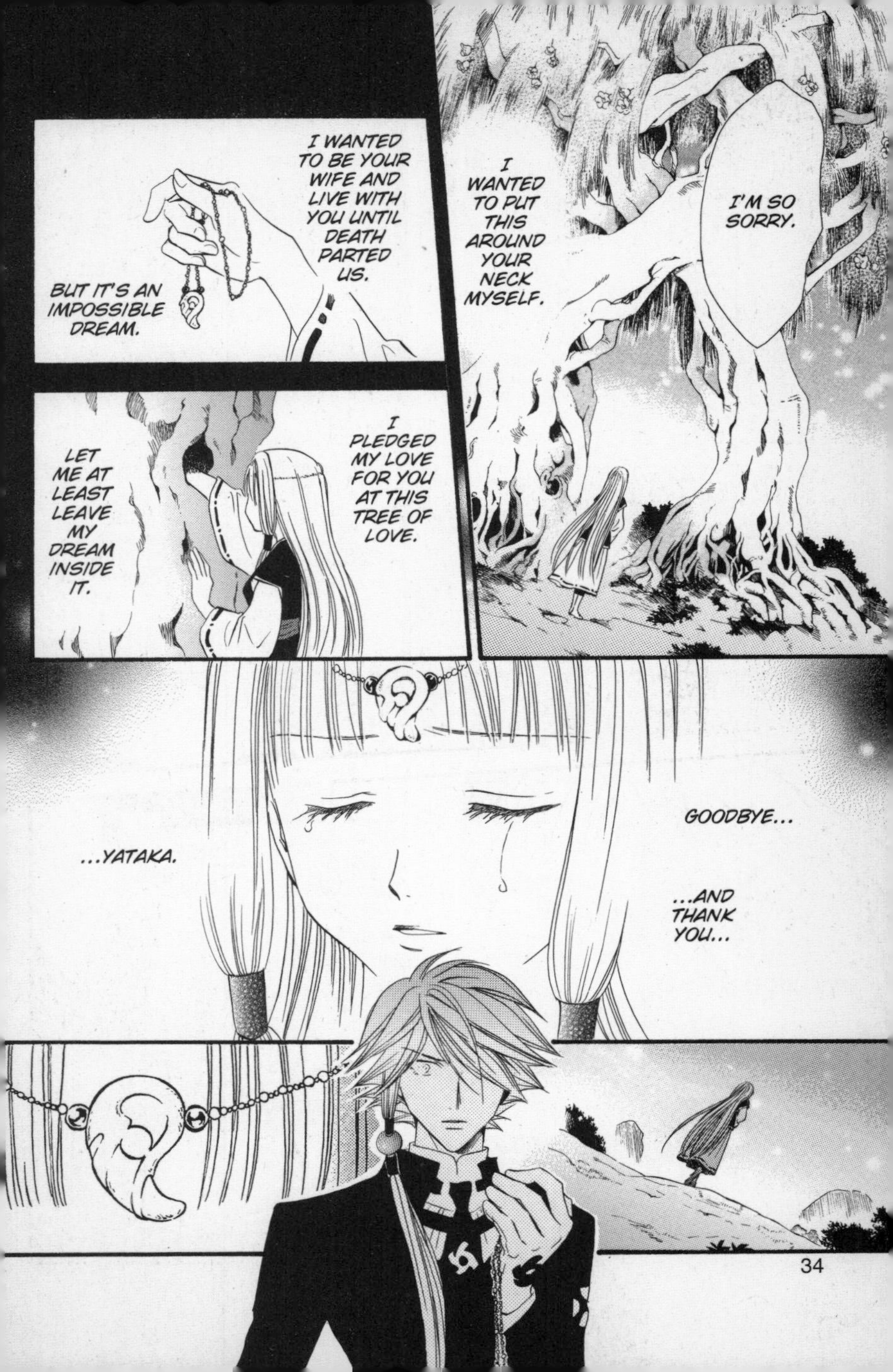
I'M SO SORRY.
I WANTED TO PUT THIS AROUND YOUR NECK MYSELF.
I WANTED TO BE YOUR WIFE AND LIVE WITH YOU UNTIL DEATH PARTED US.
BUT IT'S AN IMPOSSIBLE DREAM.
I PLEDGED MY LOVE FOR YOU AT THIS TREE OF LOVE.
LET ME AT LEAST LEAVE MY DREAM INSIDE IT.
GOODBYE...
...AND THANK YOU...
...YATAKA.

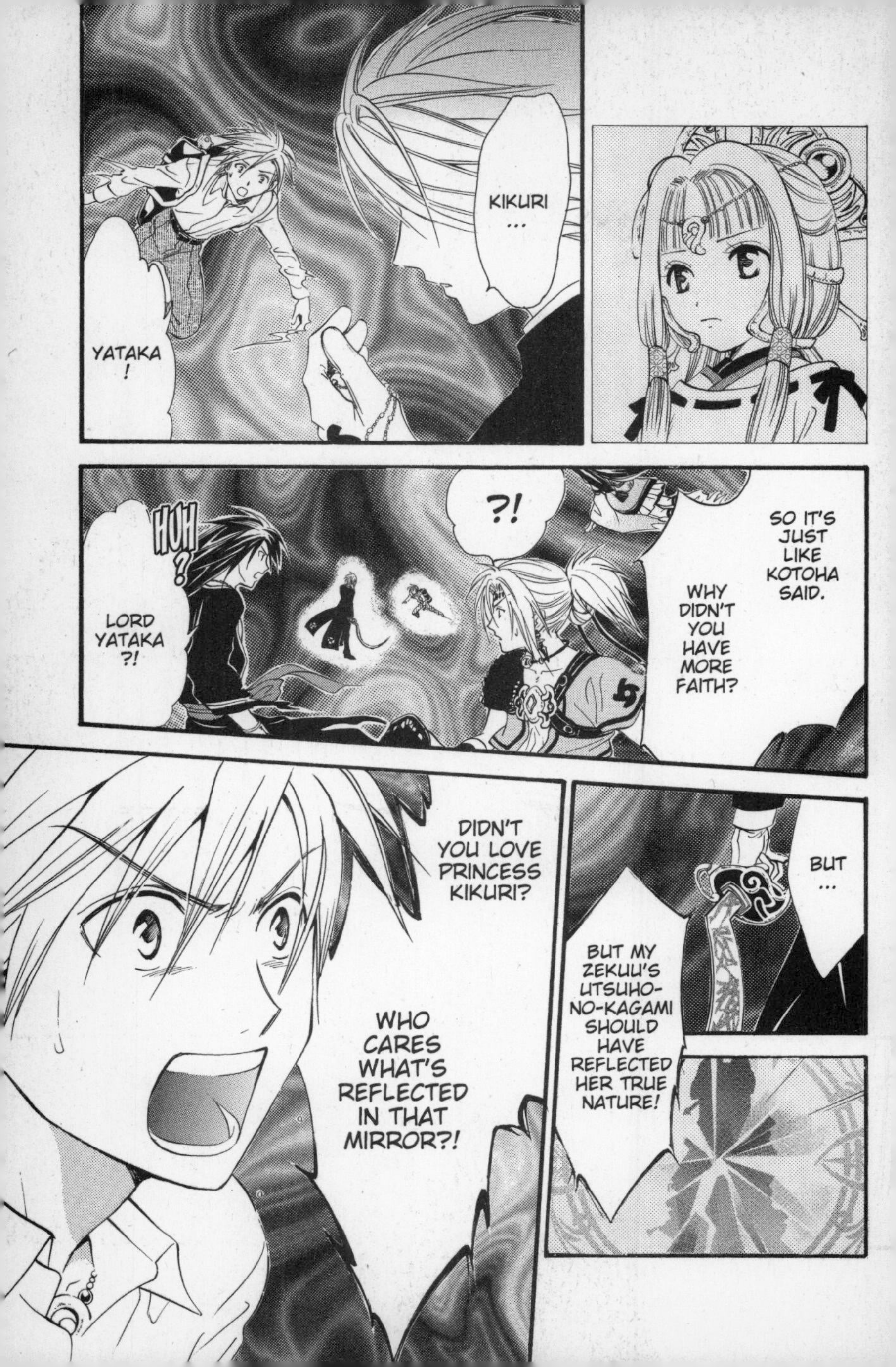
KIKURI ...
YATAKA !
SO IT'S JUST LIKE KOTOHA SAID.
WHY DIDN'T YOU HAVE MORE FAITH?
?!
HUH ?
LORD YATAKA ?!
BUT ...
BUT MY ZEKUU'S UTSUHO-NO-KAGAMI SHOULD HAVE REFLECTED HER TRUE NATURE!
DIDN'T YOU LOVE PRINCESS KIKURI?
WHO CARES WHAT'S REFLECTED IN THAT MIRROR?!

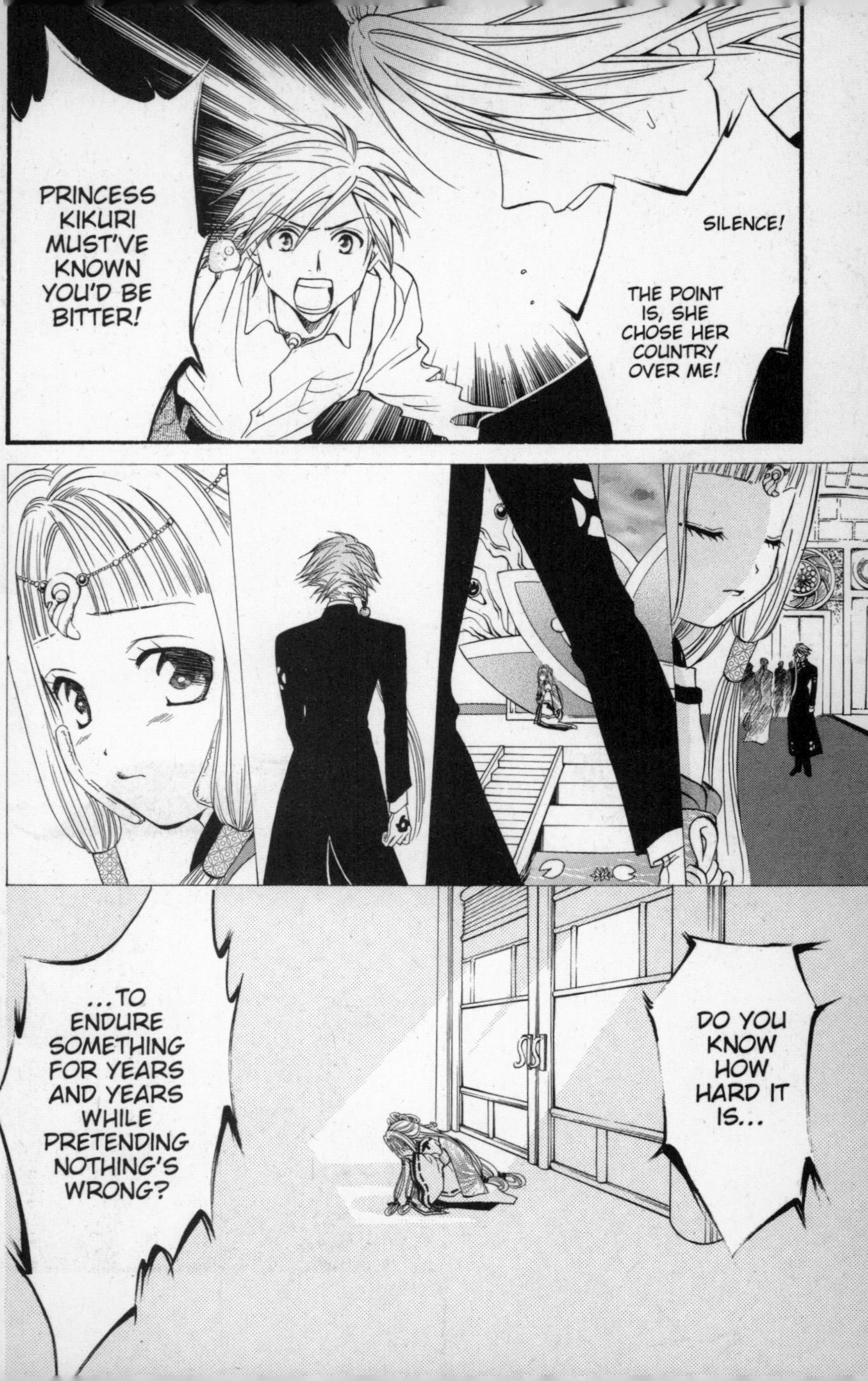
SILENCE!
THE POINT IS, SHE CHOSE HER COUNTRY OVER ME!
PRINCESS KIKURI MUST'VE KNOWN YOU'D BE BITTER!
DO YOU KNOW HOW HARD IT IS...
...TO ENDURE SOMETHING FOR YEARS AND YEARS WHILE PRETENDING NOTHING'S WRONG?

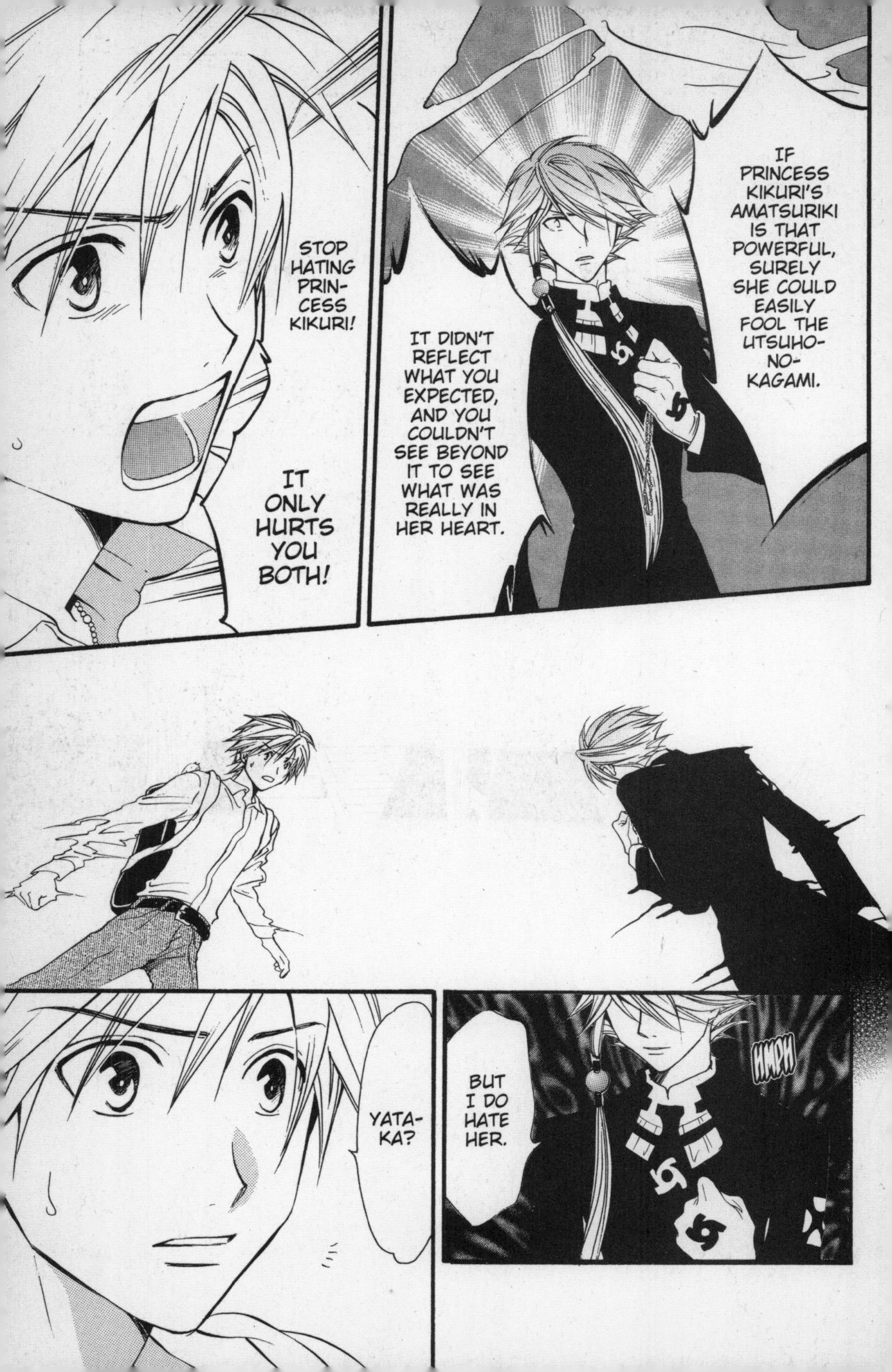
IF PRINCESS KIKURI'S AMATSURIKI IS THAT POWERFUL, SURELY SHE COULD EASILY FOOL THE UTSUHO-NO-KAGAMI.
IT DIDN'T REFLECT WHAT YOU EXPECTED, AND YOU COULDN'T SEE BEYOND IT TO SEE WHAT WAS REALLY IN HER HEART.
STOP HATING PRINCESS KIKURI!
IT ONLY HURTS YOU BOTH!
HMPH
BUT I DO HATE HER.
YATAKA?

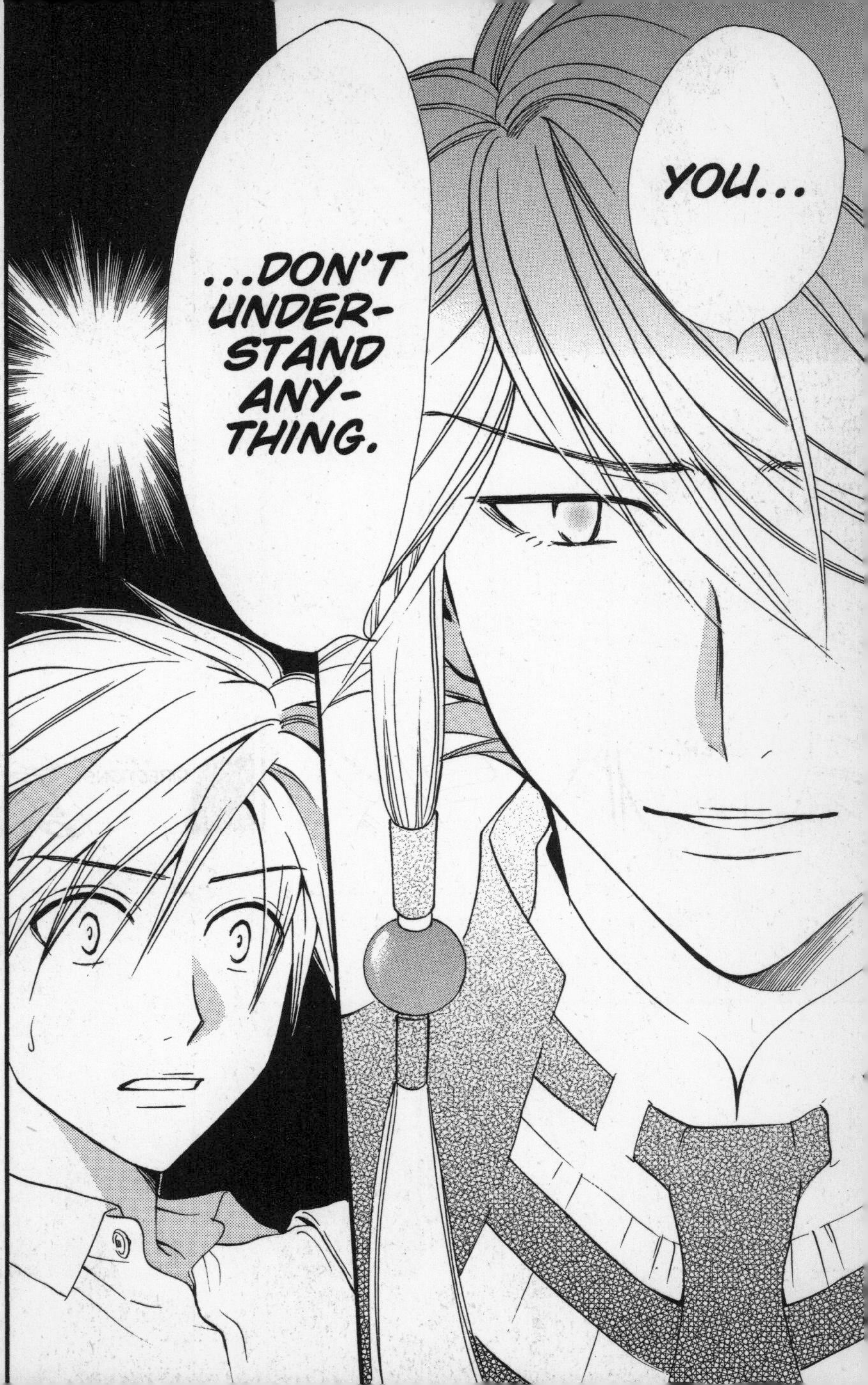
YOU...
...DON'T UNDER-STAND ANY-THING.

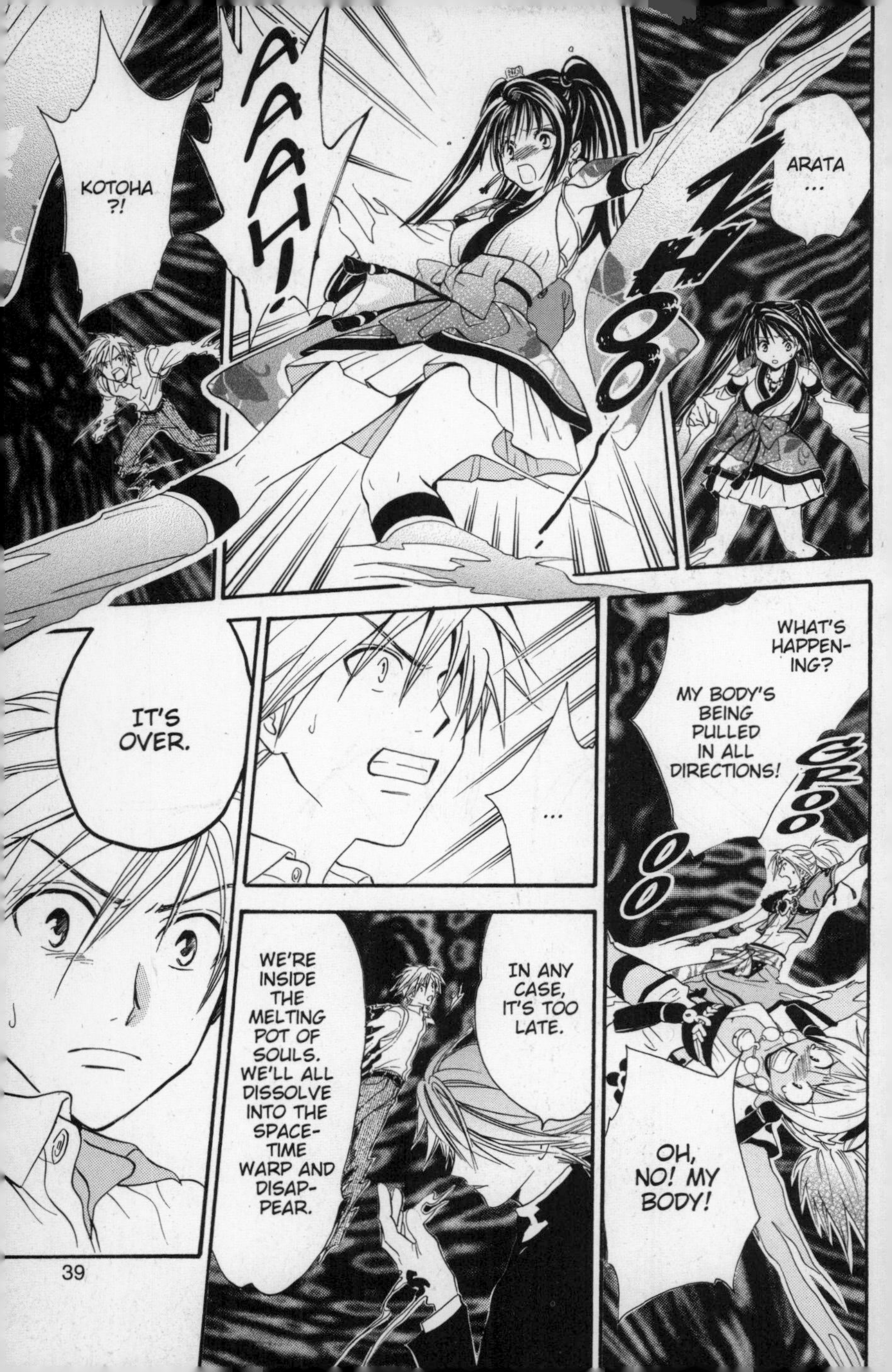
ARATA ...
ZHOO
AAAH!
KOTOHA ?!
WHAT'S HAPPEN-ING?
MY BODY'S BEING PULLED IN ALL DIRECTIONS!
GROOOO
OH, NO! MY BODY!
...
IT'S OVER.
IN ANY CASE, IT'S TOO LATE.
WE'RE INSIDE THE MELTING POT OF SOULS. WE'LL ALL DISSOLVE INTO THE SPACE-TIME WARP AND DISAP-PEAR.

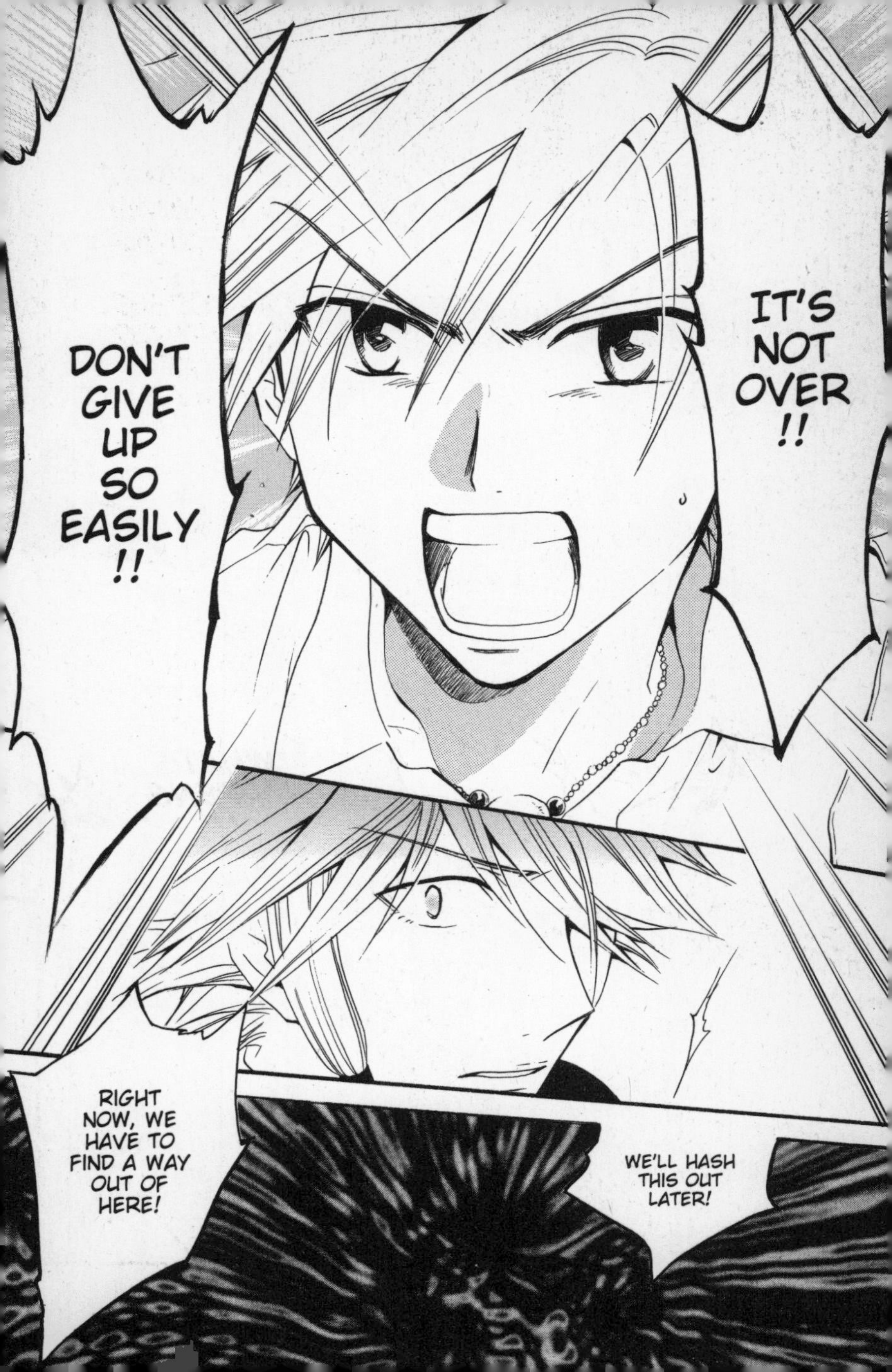
IT'S NOT OVER!!
DON'T GIVE UP SO EASILY!!
WE'LL HASH THIS OUT LATER!
RIGHT NOW, WE HAVE TO FIND A WAY OUT OF HERE!

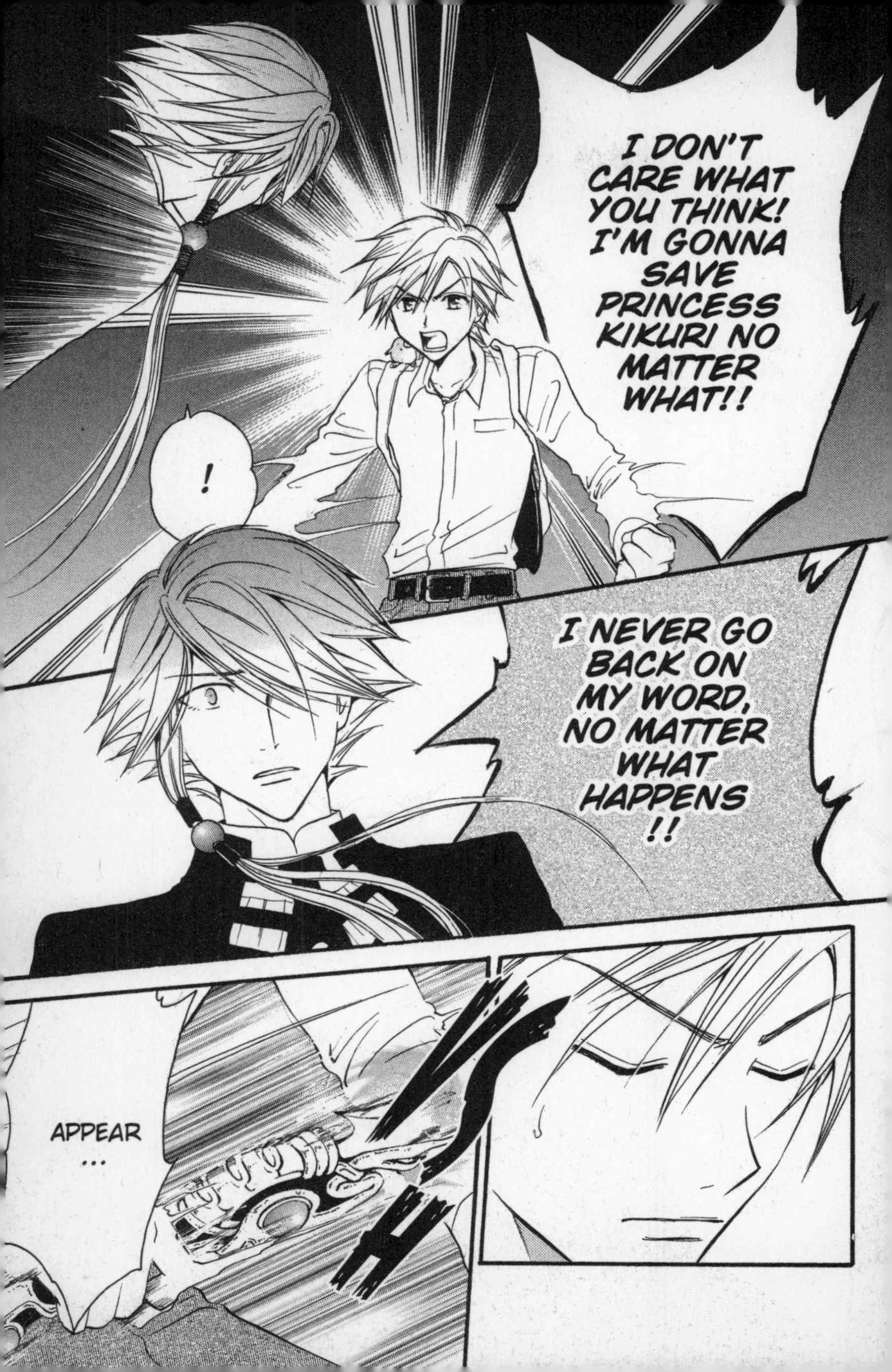
I DON'T CARE WHAT YOU THINK! I'M GONNA SAVE PRINCESS KIKURI NO MATTER WHAT!!
!
I NEVER GO BACK ON MY WORD, NO MATTER WHAT HAPPENS!!
APPEAR...

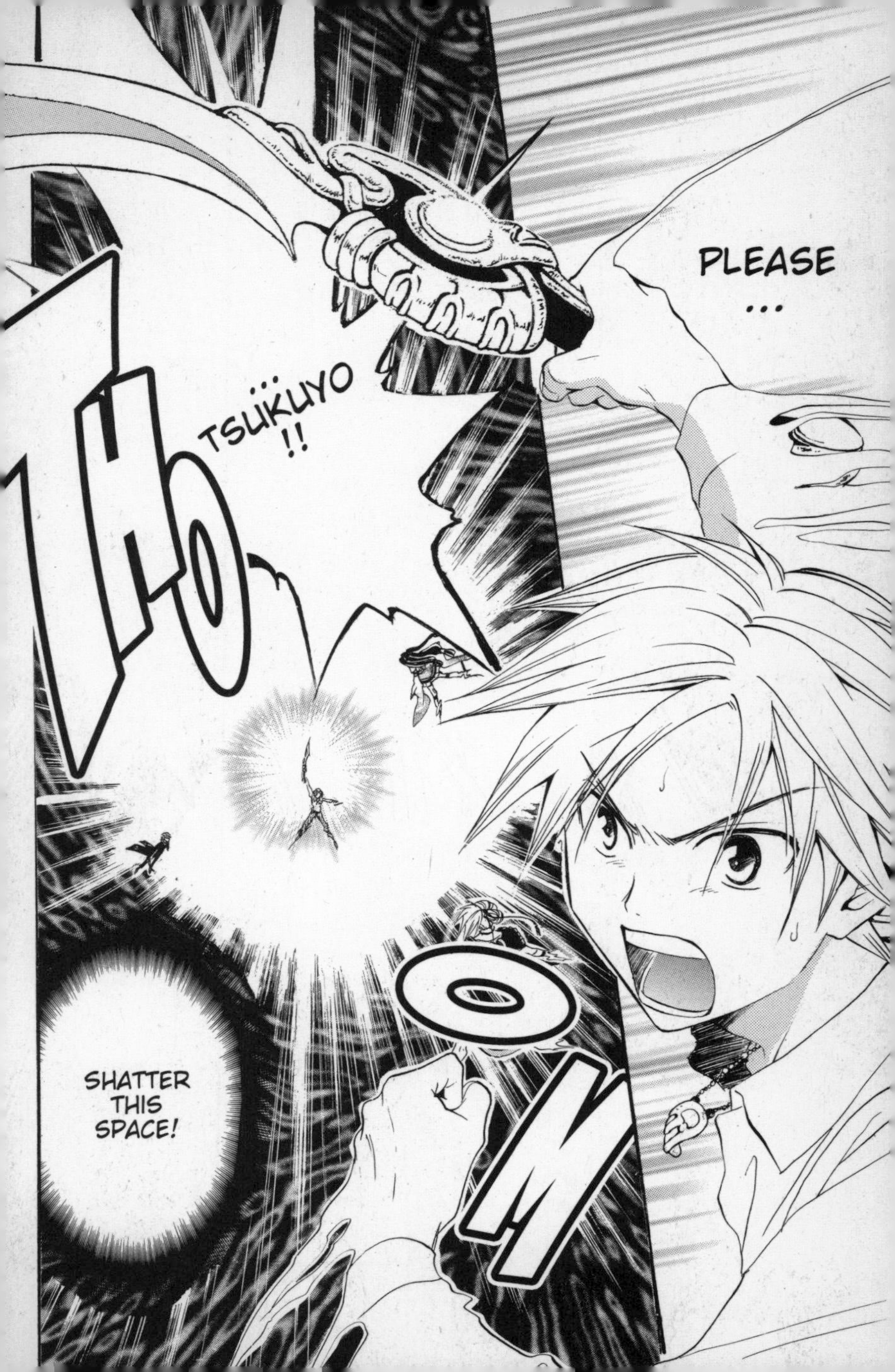
PLEASE ...
... TSUKUYO !!
THOOM
SHATTER THIS SPACE!

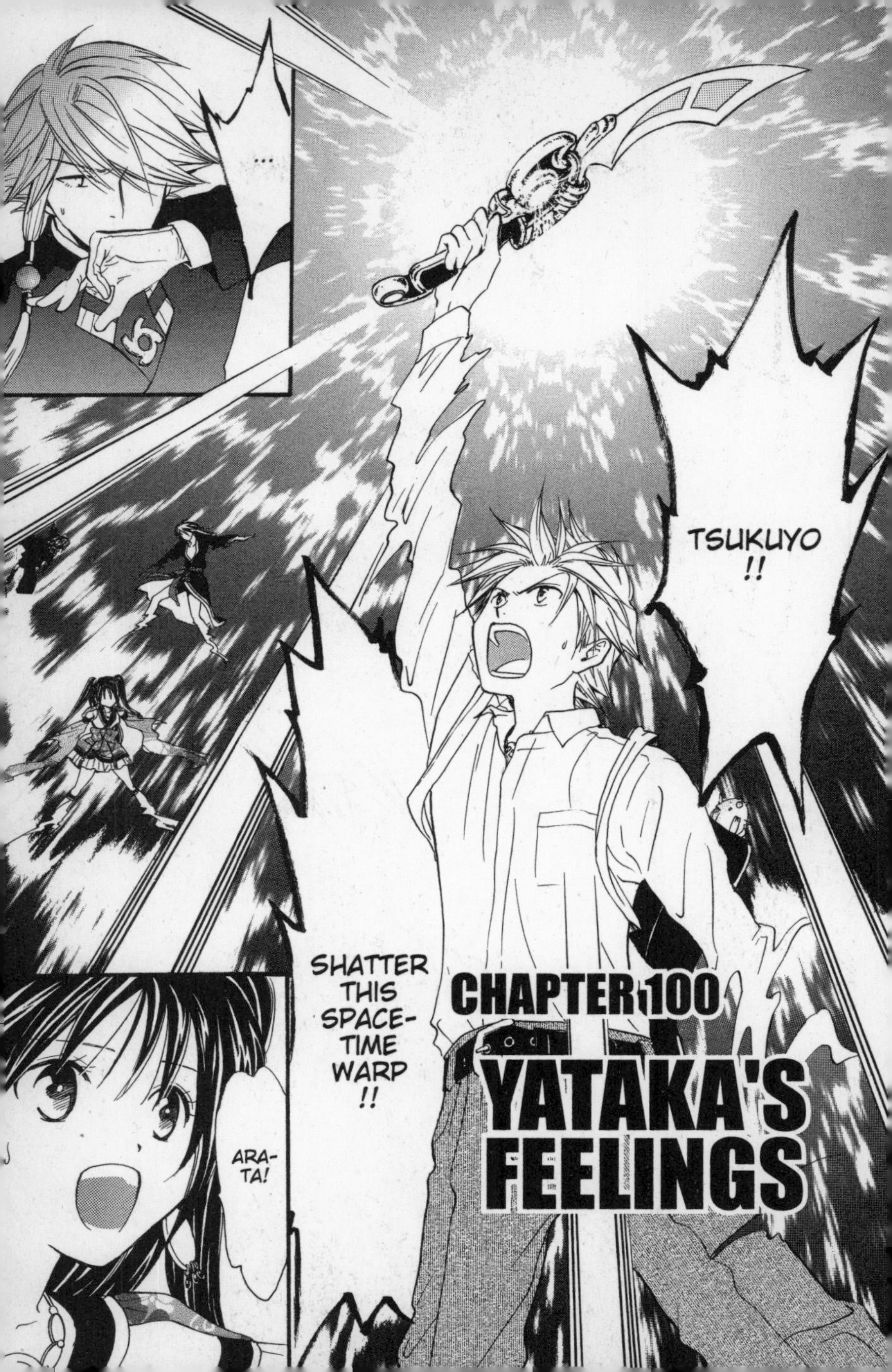
TSUKUYO !!
SHATTER THIS SPACE-TIME WARP !!
CHAPTER 100
YATAKA'S FEELINGS
...
ARA-TA!

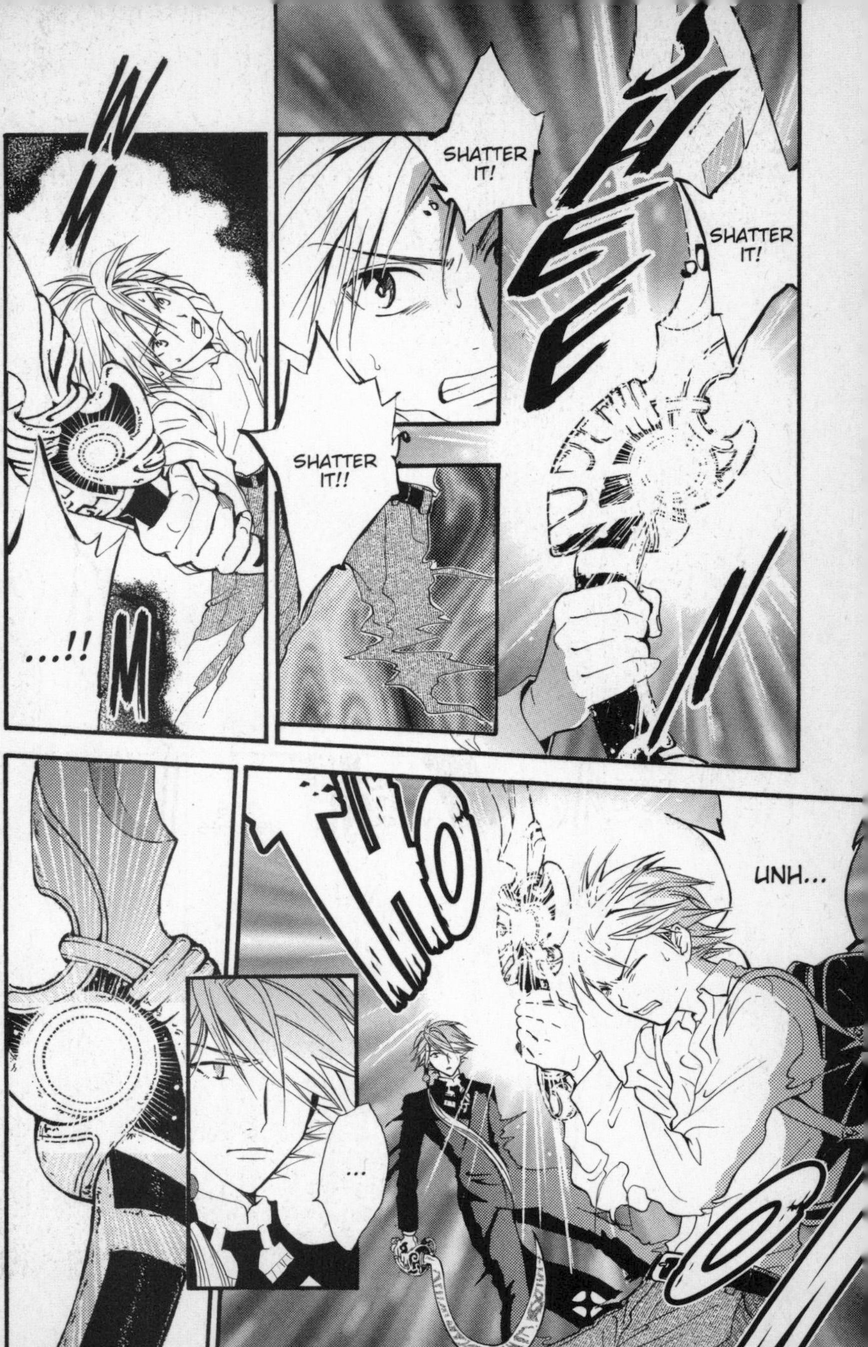
SHEEN
SHATTER IT!
SHATTER IT!
SHATTER IT!!
WMM
...!!
THOO
UNH...
...

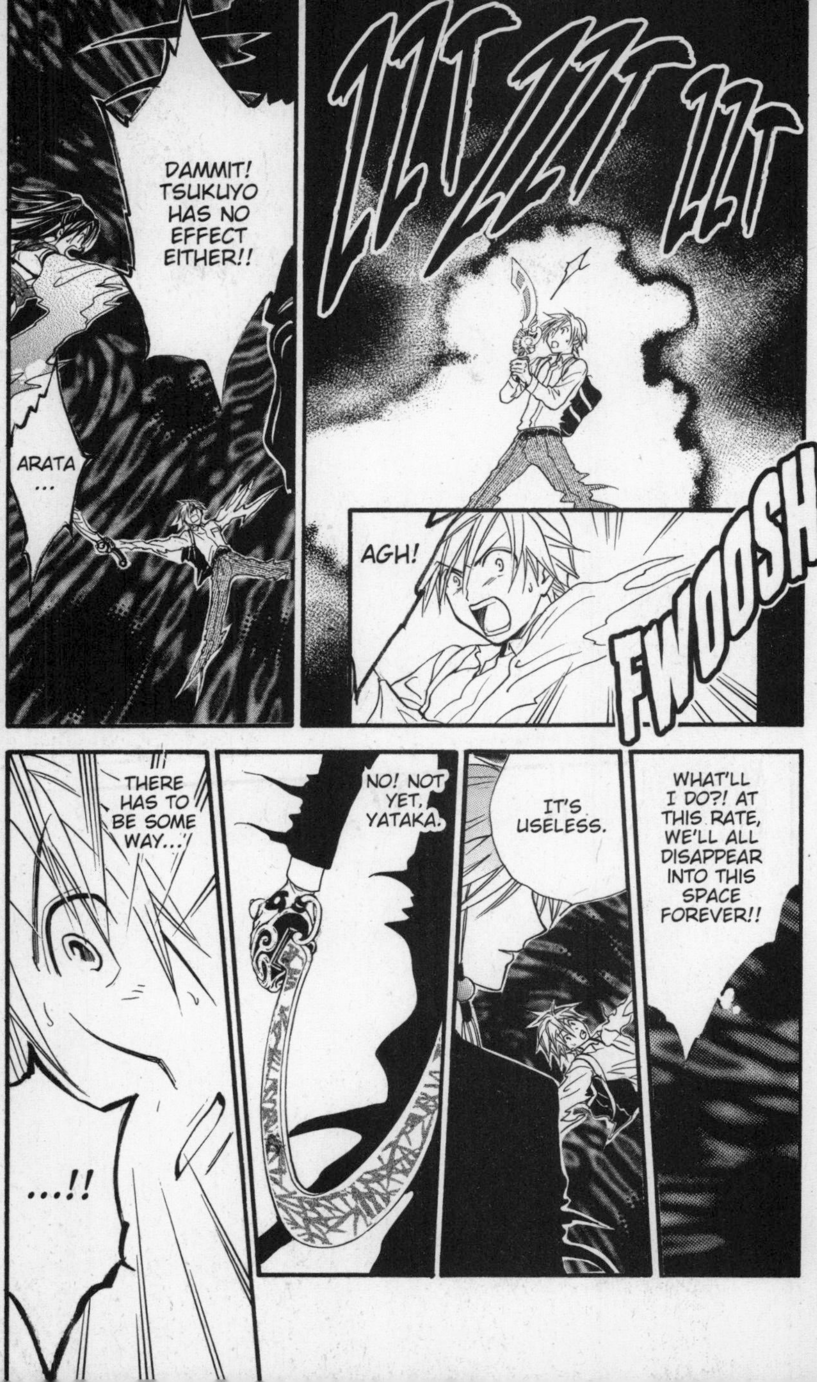
ZZZT ZZZT ZZZT
AGH!
FWOOSH
DAMMIT! TSUKUYO HAS NO EFFECT EITHER!!
ARATA...
WHAT'LL I DO?! AT THIS RATE, WE'LL ALL DISAPPEAR INTO THIS SPACE FOREVER!!
IT'S USELESS.
NO! NOT YET, YATAKA.
THERE HAS TO BE SOME WAY...
...!!

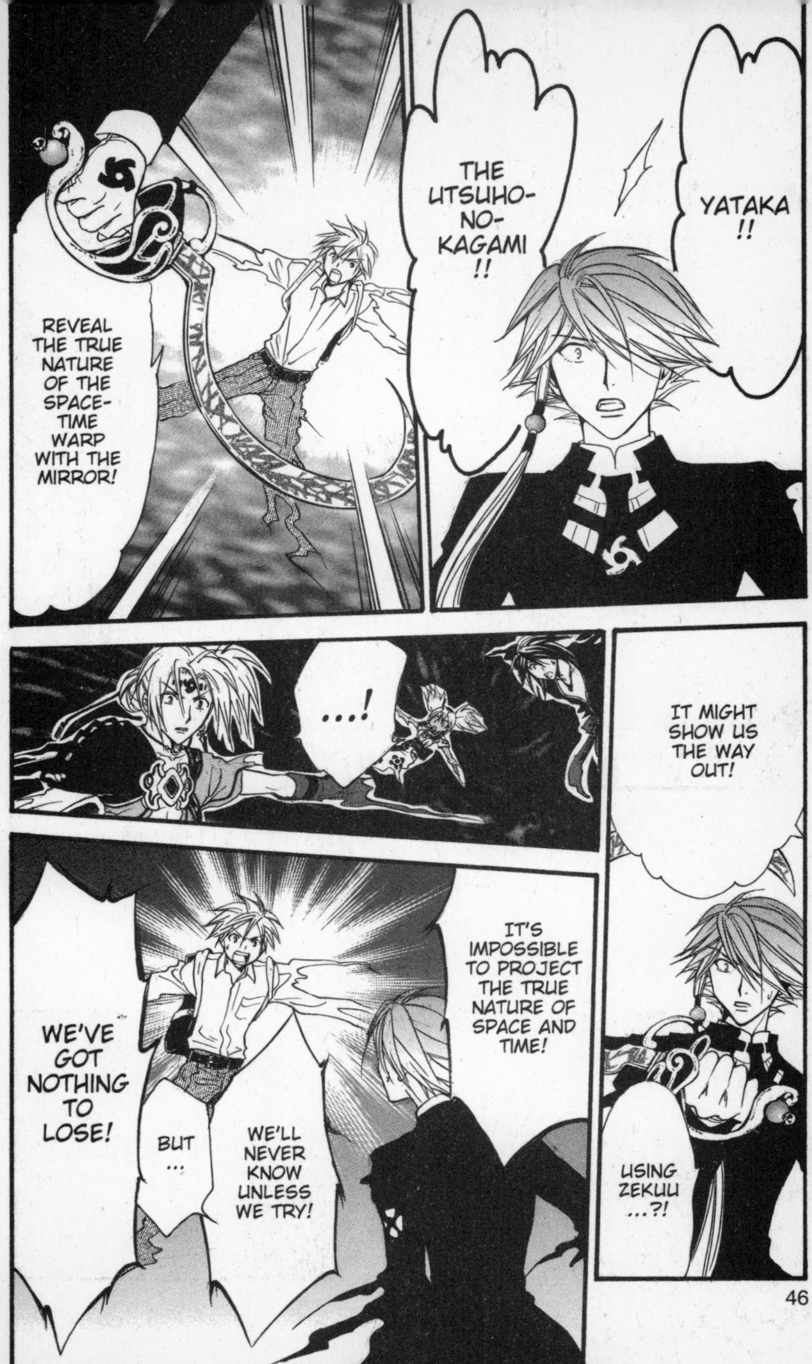
YATAKA !!
THE UTSUHO-NO-KAGAMI !!
REVEAL THE TRUE NATURE OF THE SPACE-TIME WARP WITH THE MIRROR!
IT MIGHT SHOW US THE WAY OUT!
USING ZEKUU ...?!
...!
IT'S IMPOSSIBLE TO PROJECT THE TRUE NATURE OF SPACE AND TIME!
BUT ...
WE'LL NEVER KNOW UNLESS WE TRY!
WE'VE GOT NOTHING TO LOSE!

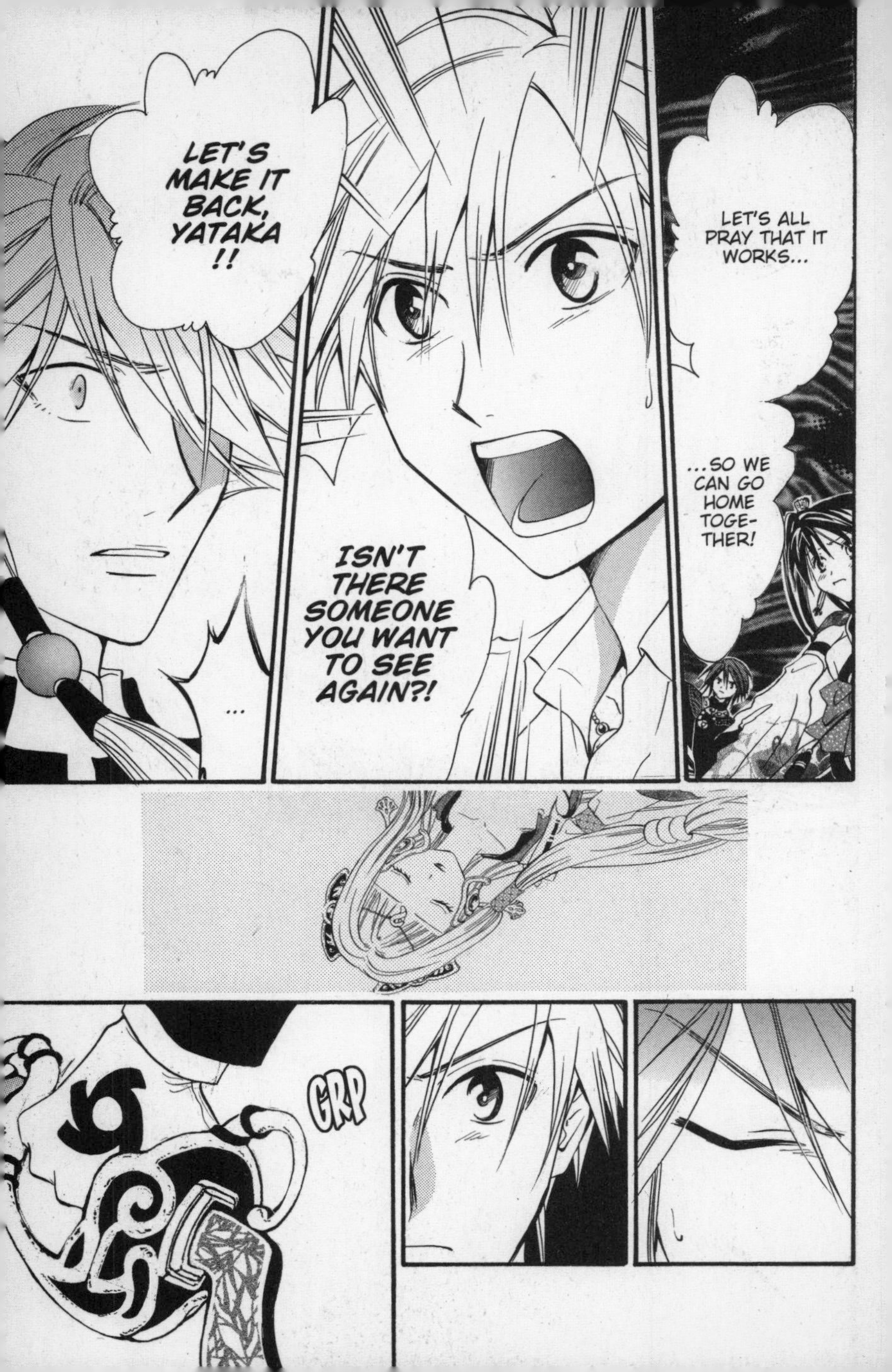
LET'S ALL PRAY THAT IT WORKS...
...SO WE CAN GO HOME TOGE-THER!
ISN'T THERE SOMEONE YOU WANT TO SEE AGAIN?!
LET'S MAKE IT BACK, YATAKA !!
...
GRP

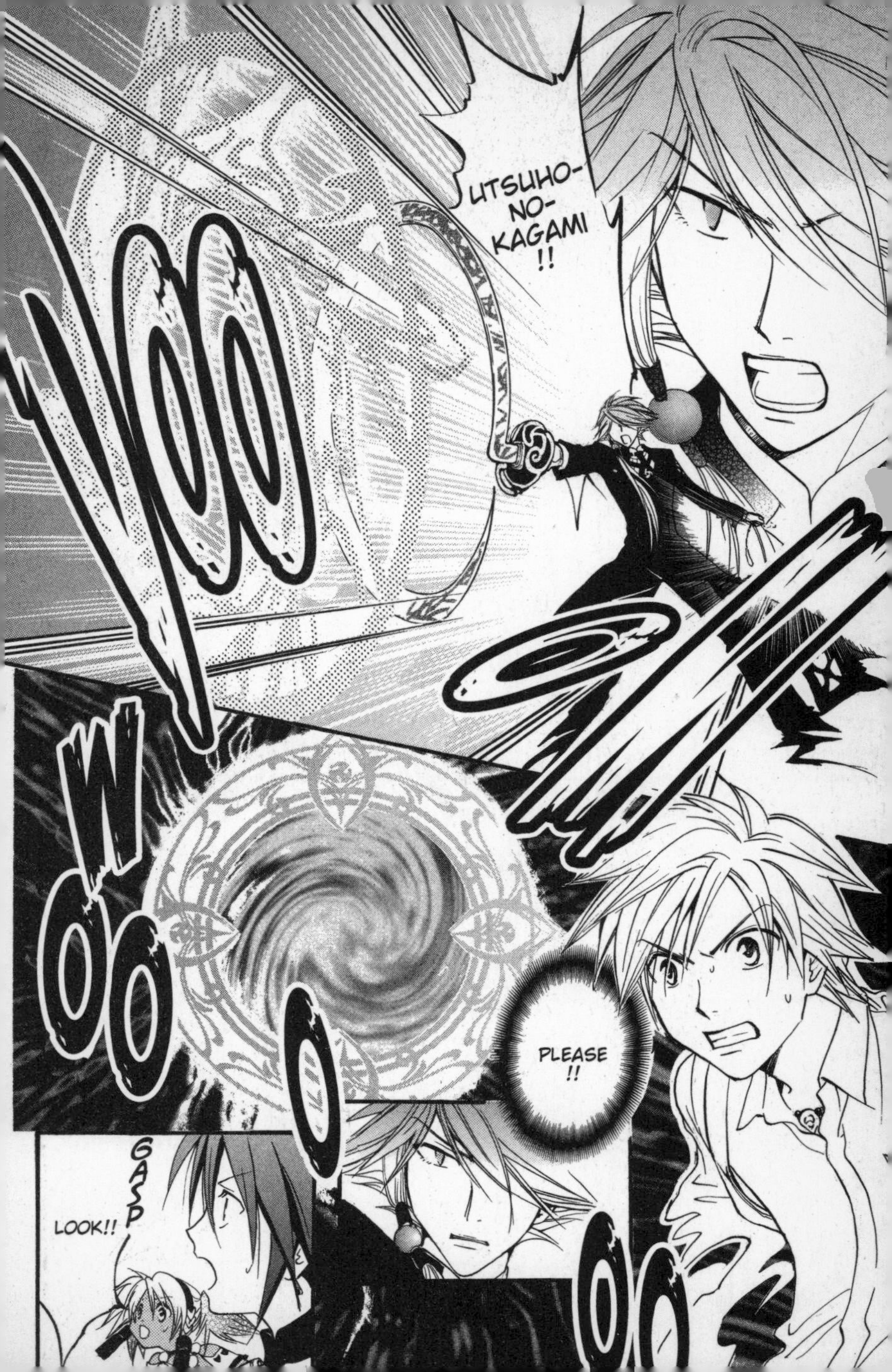
UTSUHO-NO-KAGAMI !!
PLEASE !!
GASP
LOOK!!

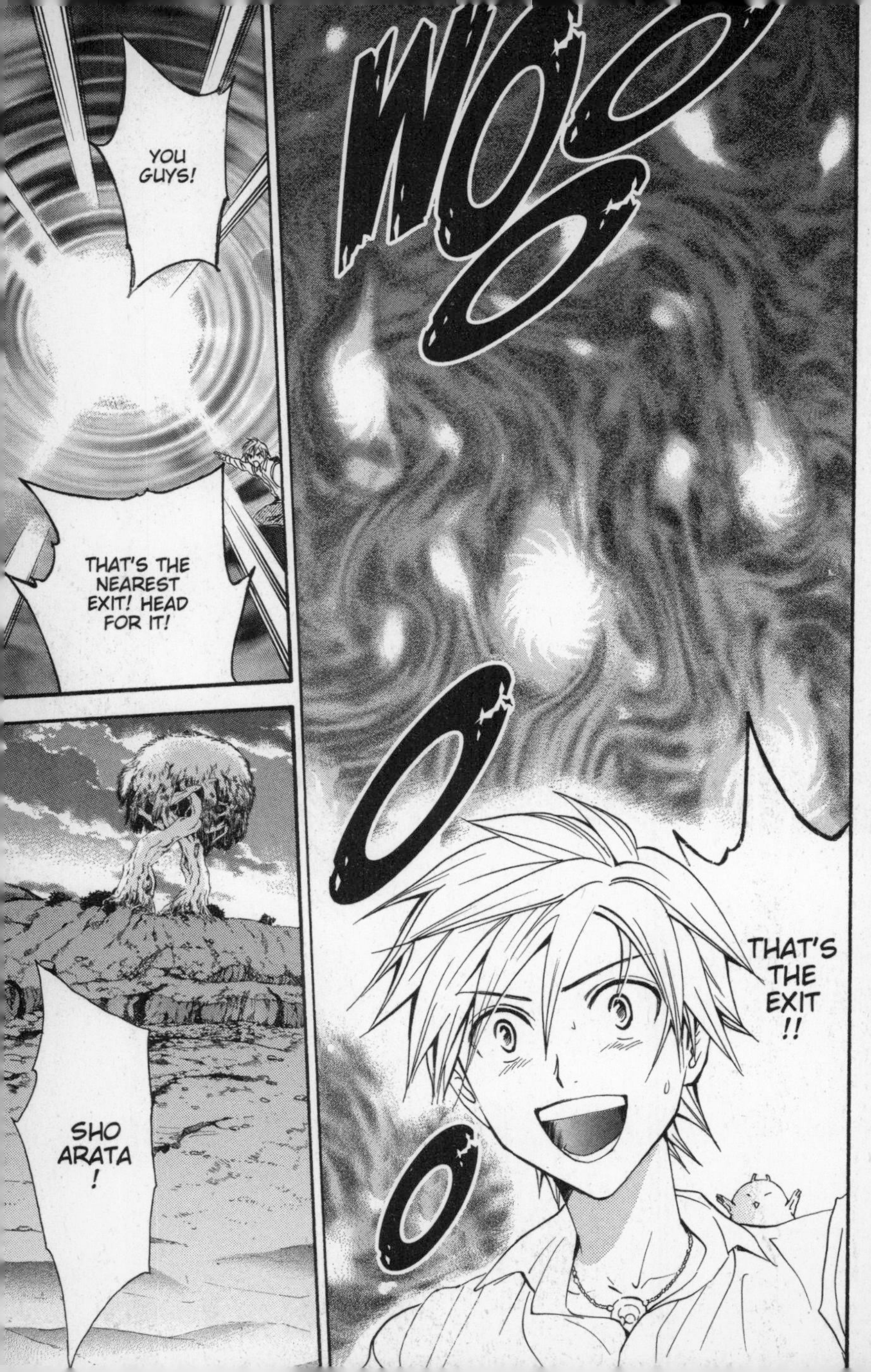
WOOOOOO
THAT'S THE EXIT!!
YOU GUYS!
THAT'S THE NEAREST EXIT! HEAD FOR IT!
SHO ARATA!

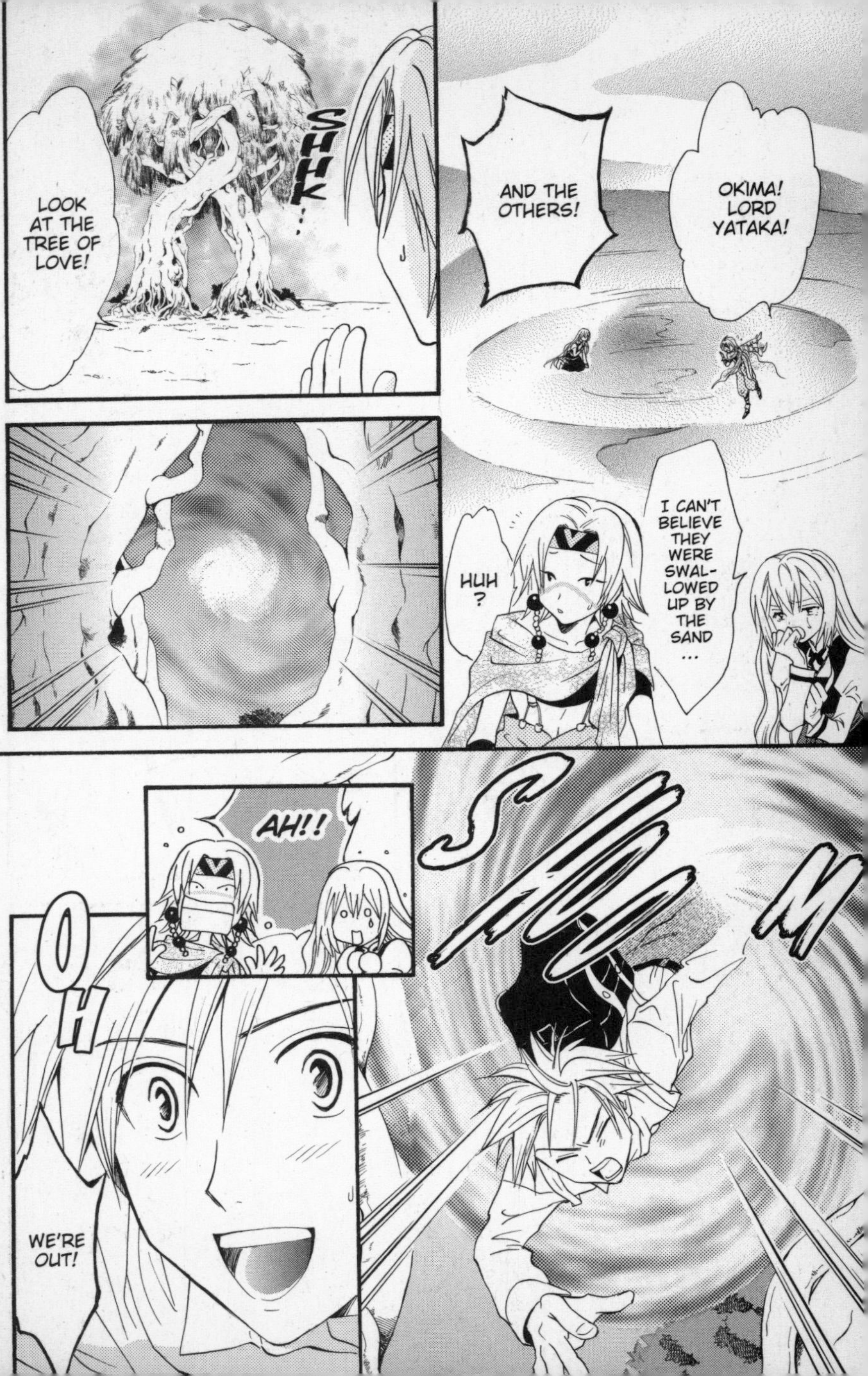
OKIMA! LORD YATAKA!
AND THE OTHERS!
I CAN'T BELIEVE THEY WERE SWAL-LOWED UP BY THE SAND...
HUH?
SHHK...
LOOK AT THE TREE OF LOVE!
SHOOM
AH!!
OH
WE'RE OUT!

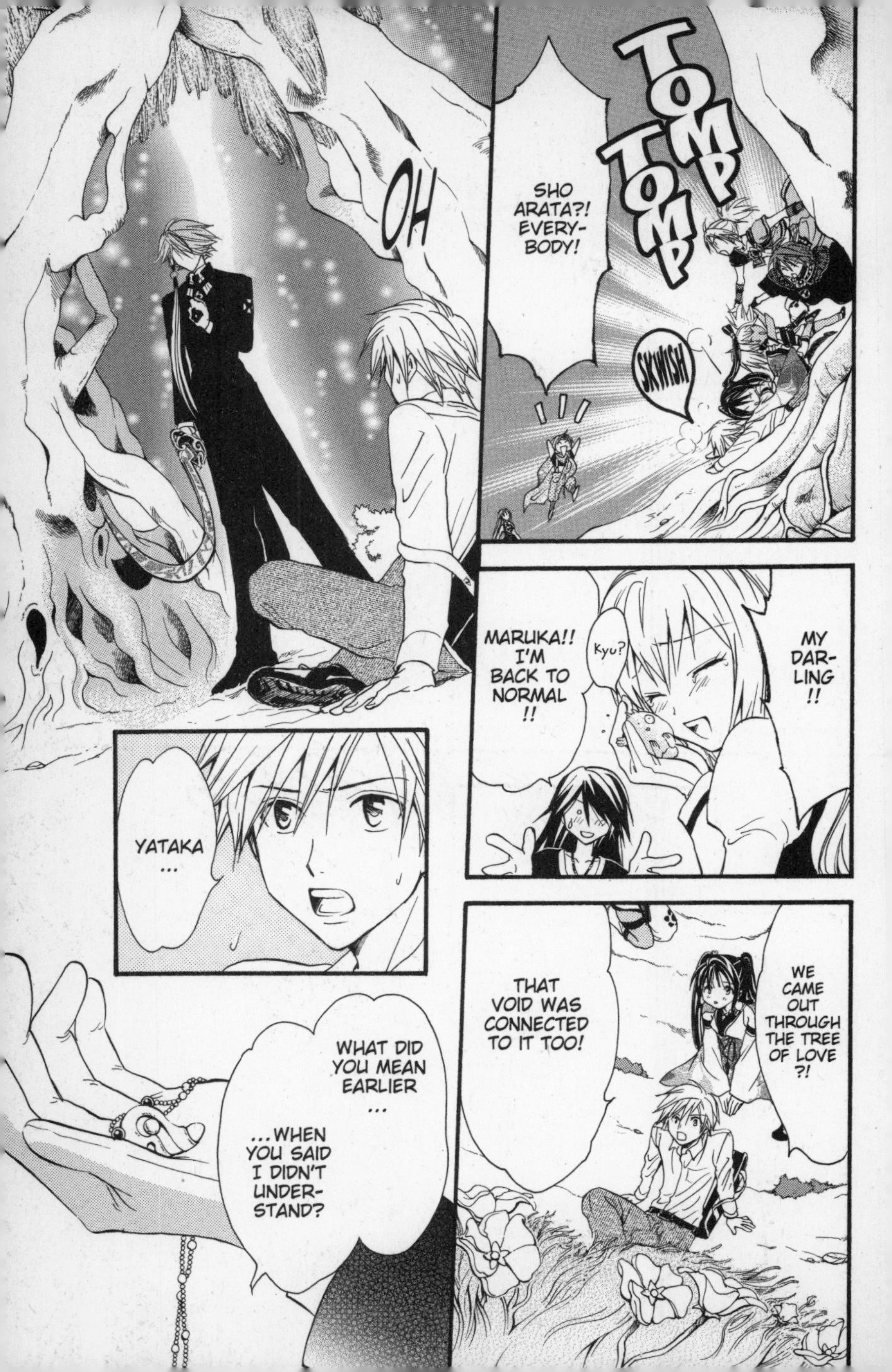
TOMP TOMP
SHO ARATA?! EVERYBODY!
SKWISH
MY DARLING!!
Kyu?
MARUKA!! I'M BACK TO NORMAL!!
OH
WE CAME OUT THROUGH THE TREE OF LOVE?!
THAT VOID WAS CONNECTED TO IT TOO!
YATAKA...
WHAT DID YOU MEAN EARLIER...
...WHEN YOU SAID I DIDN'T UNDERSTAND?

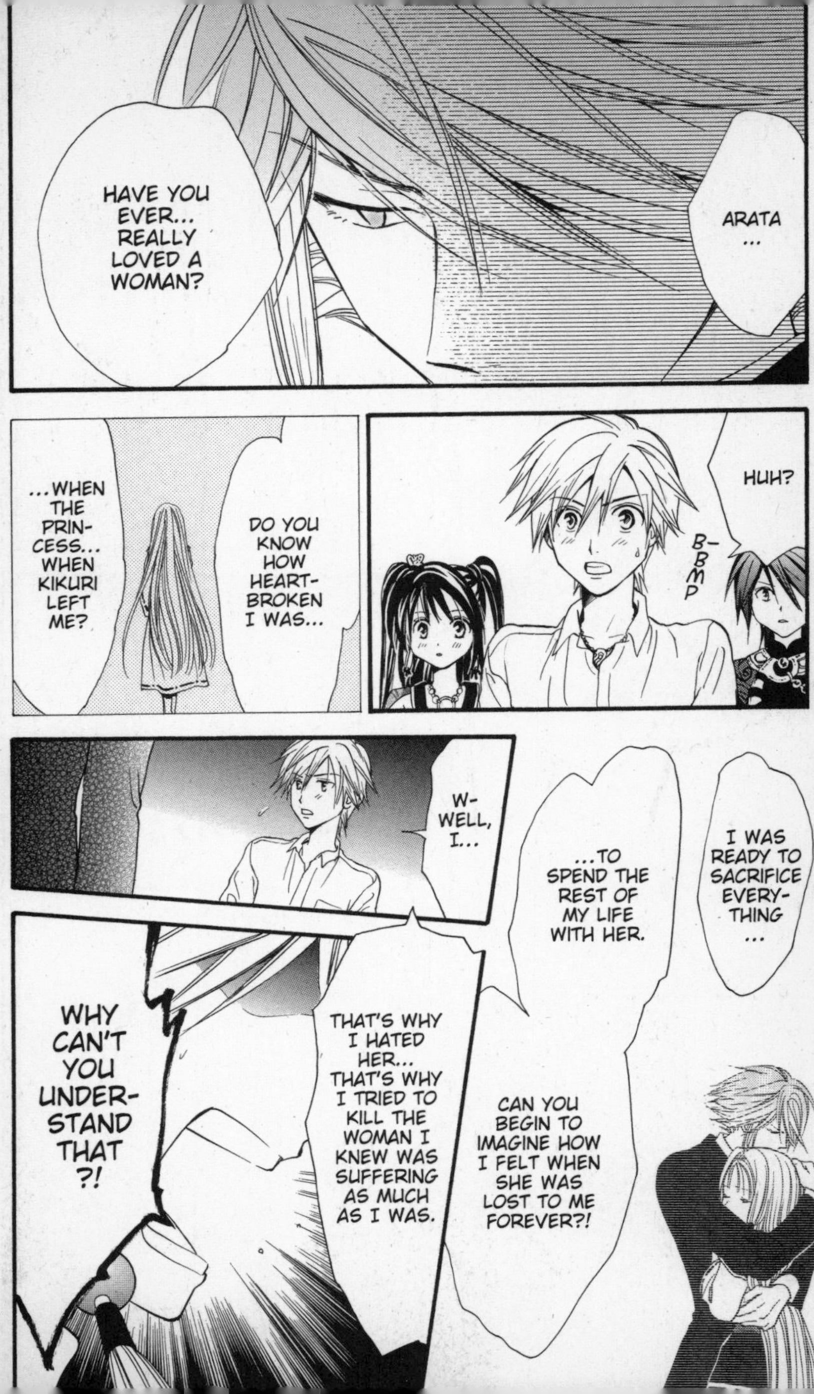
ARATA ...
HAVE YOU EVER... REALLY LOVED A WOMAN?
HUH?
B-BMP
DO YOU KNOW HOW HEART-BROKEN I WAS...
...WHEN THE PRINCESS... WHEN KIKURI LEFT ME?
I WAS READY TO SACRIFICE EVERY-THING ...
...TO SPEND THE REST OF MY LIFE WITH HER.
W-WELL, I...
CAN YOU BEGIN TO IMAGINE HOW I FELT WHEN SHE WAS LOST TO ME FOREVER?!
THAT'S WHY I HATED HER... THAT'S WHY I TRIED TO KILL THE WOMAN I KNEW WAS SUFFERING AS MUCH AS I WAS.
WHY CAN'T YOU UNDER-STAND THAT?!

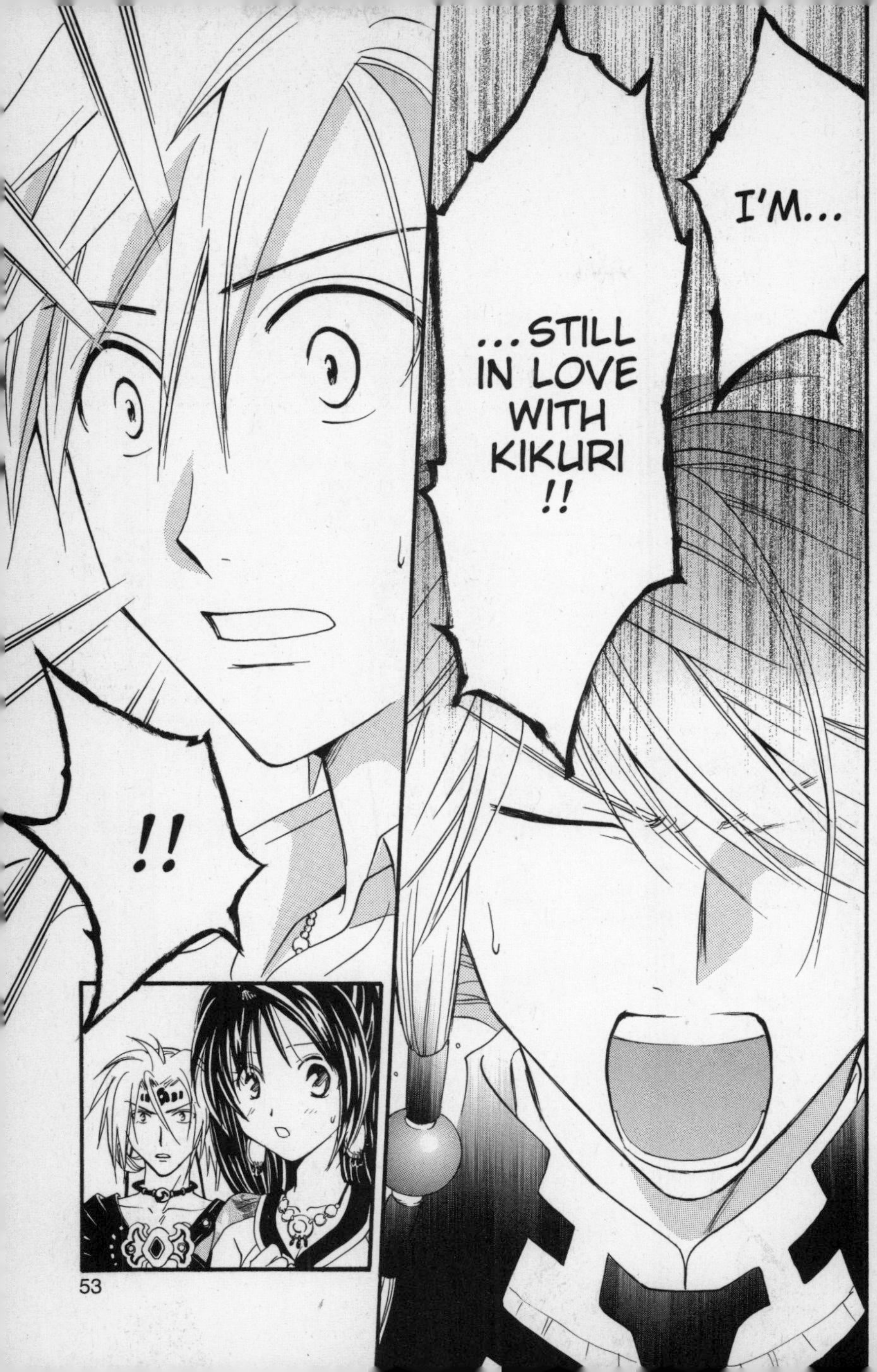
I'M...
...STILL IN LOVE WITH KIKURI !!
!!

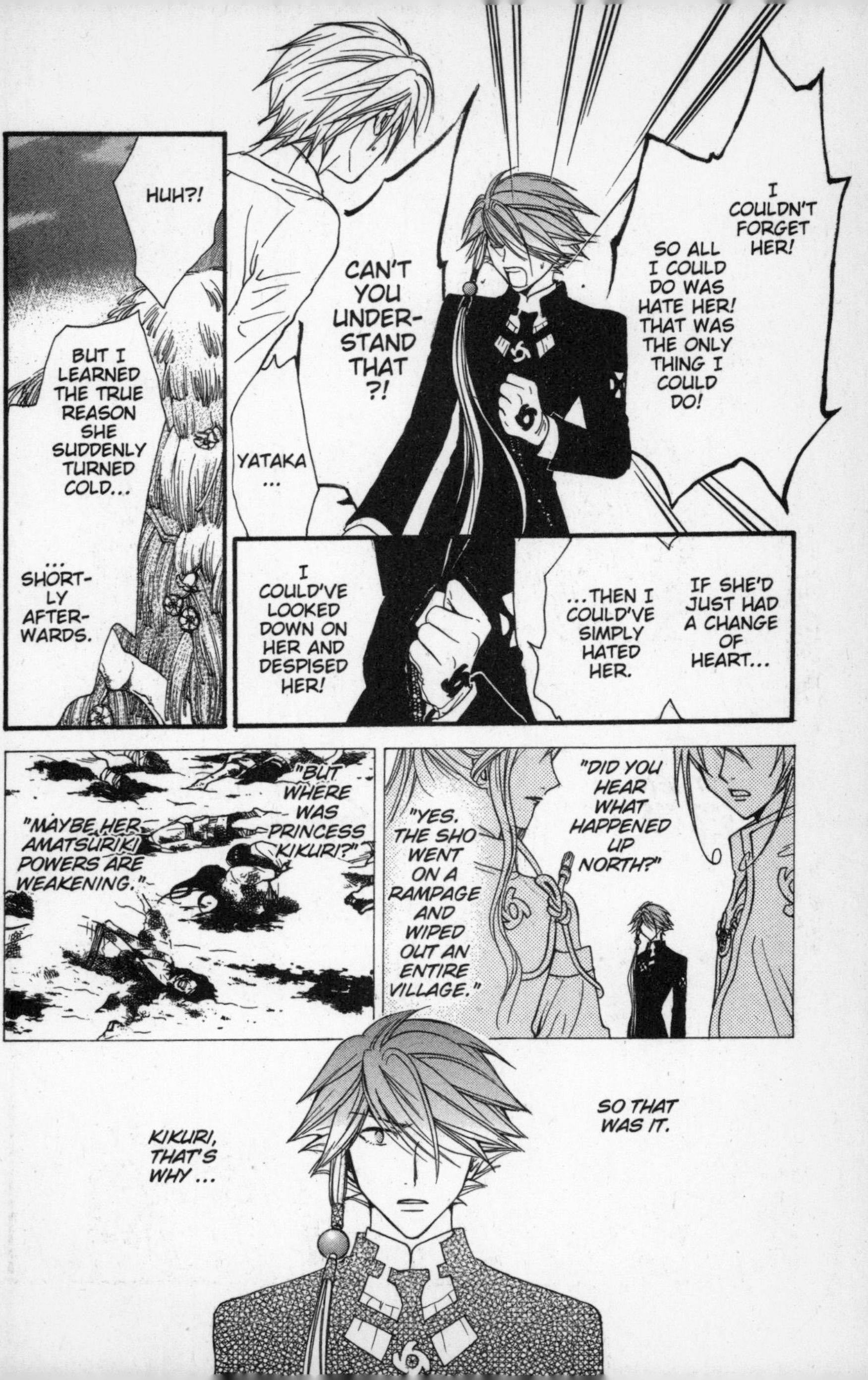

I COULDN'T FORGET HER!
SO ALL I COULD DO WAS HATE HER! THAT WAS THE ONLY THING I COULD DO!
CAN'T YOU UNDER-STAND THAT?!
YATAKA...
IF SHE'D JUST HAD A CHANGE OF HEART...
...THEN I COULD'VE SIMPLY HATED HER.
I COULD'VE LOOKED DOWN ON HER AND DESPISED HER!
HUH?!
BUT I LEARNED THE TRUE REASON SHE SUDDENLY TURNED COLD...
...SHORTLY AFTERWARDS.
"DID YOU HEAR WHAT HAPPENED UP NORTH?"
"YES. THE SHO WENT ON A RAMPAGE AND WIPED OUT AN ENTIRE VILLAGE."
"BUT WHERE WAS PRINCESS KIKURI?"
"MAYBE HER AMATSURIKI POWERS ARE WEAKENING."
SO THAT WAS IT.
KIKURI, THAT'S WHY...

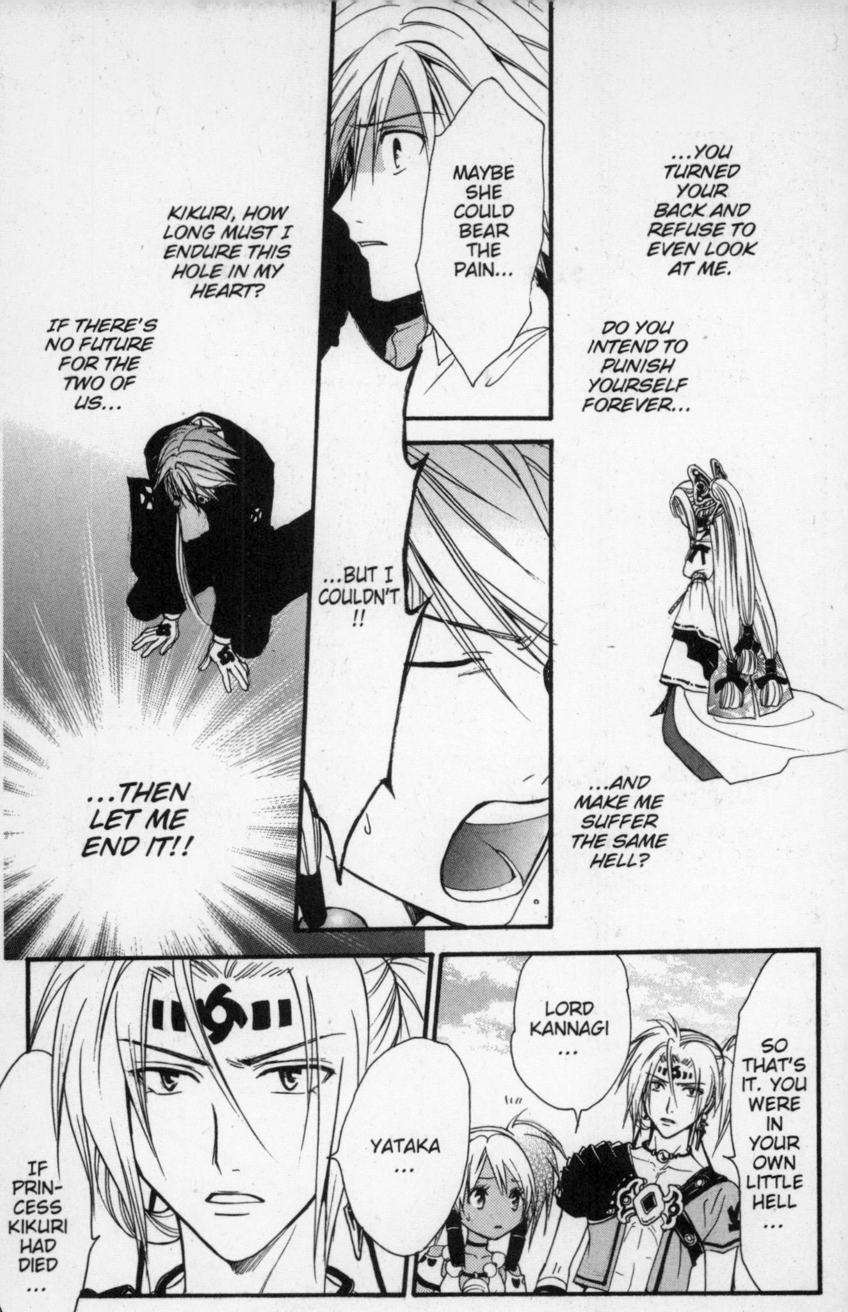
...YOU TURNED YOUR BACK AND REFUSE TO EVEN LOOK AT ME.
DO YOU INTEND TO PUNISH YOURSELF FOREVER...
...AND MAKE ME SUFFER THE SAME HELL?
MAYBE SHE COULD BEAR THE PAIN...
...BUT I COULDN'T !!
KIKURI, HOW LONG MUST I ENDURE THIS HOLE IN MY HEART?
IF THERE'S NO FUTURE FOR THE TWO OF US...
...THEN LET ME END IT!!
SO THAT'S IT. YOU WERE IN YOUR OWN LITTLE HELL...
LORD KANNAGI...
YATAKA...
IF PRINCESS KIKURI HAD DIED...

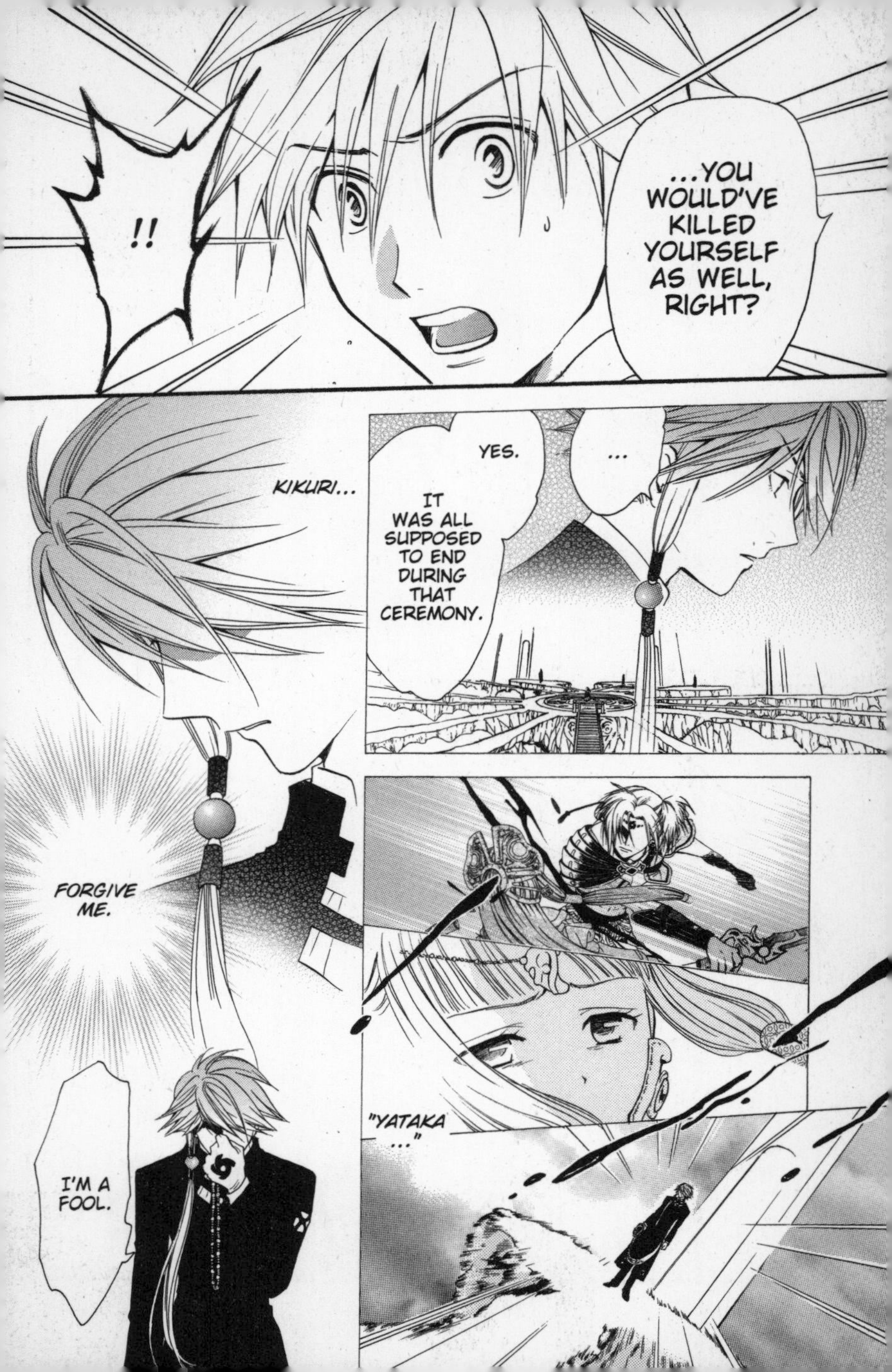

...YOU WOULD'VE KILLED YOURSELF AS WELL, RIGHT?
!!
...
YES.
IT WAS ALL SUPPOSED TO END DURING THAT CEREMONY.
"YATAKA ..."
KIKURI...
FORGIVE ME.
I'M A FOOL.

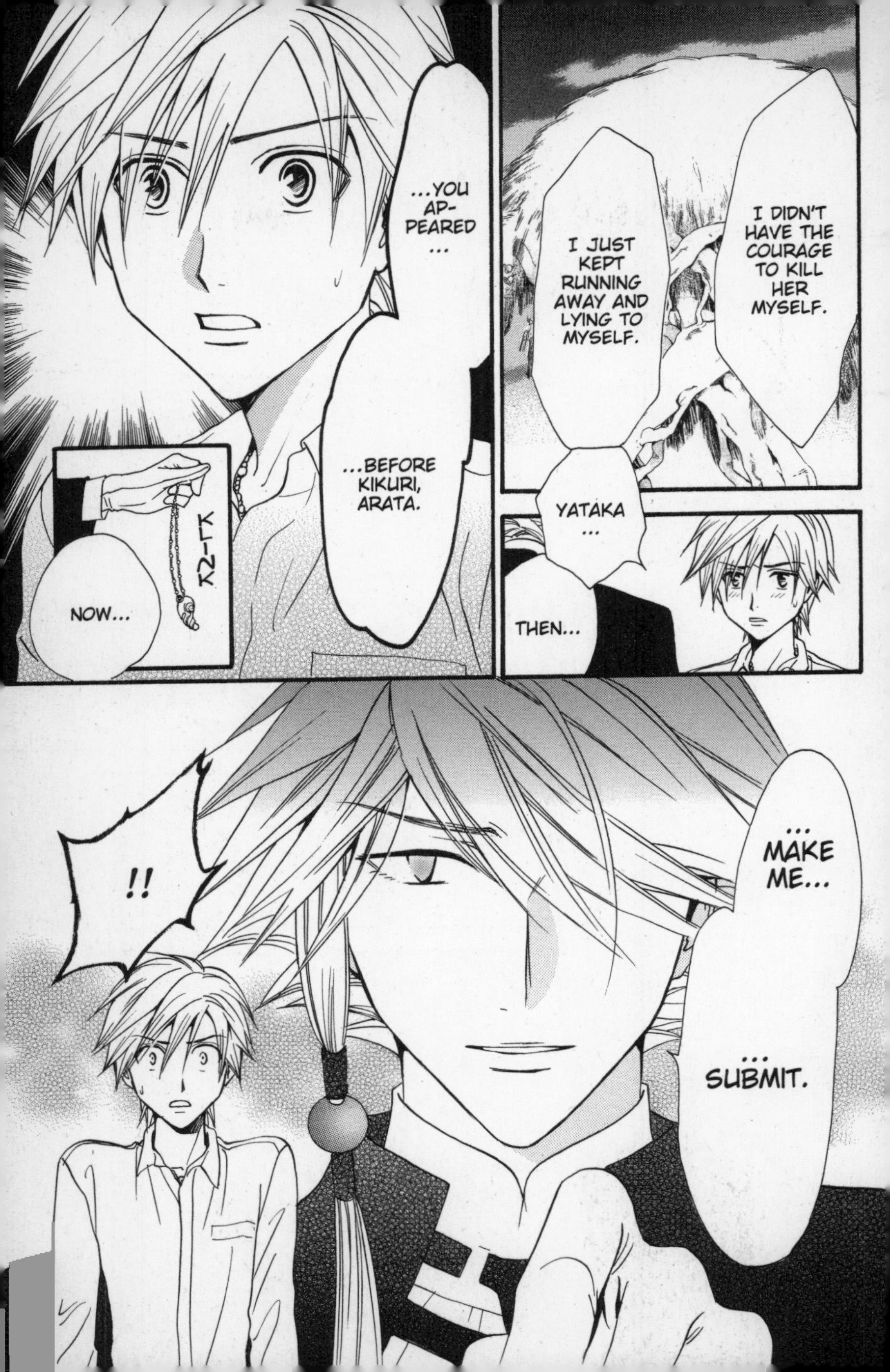
I DIDN'T HAVE THE COURAGE TO KILL HER MYSELF.
I JUST KEPT RUNNING AWAY AND LYING TO MYSELF.
YATAKA...
THEN...
...YOU APPEARED...
...BEFORE KIKURI, ARATA.
KLINK
NOW...
...MAKE ME...
...SUBMIT.
!!

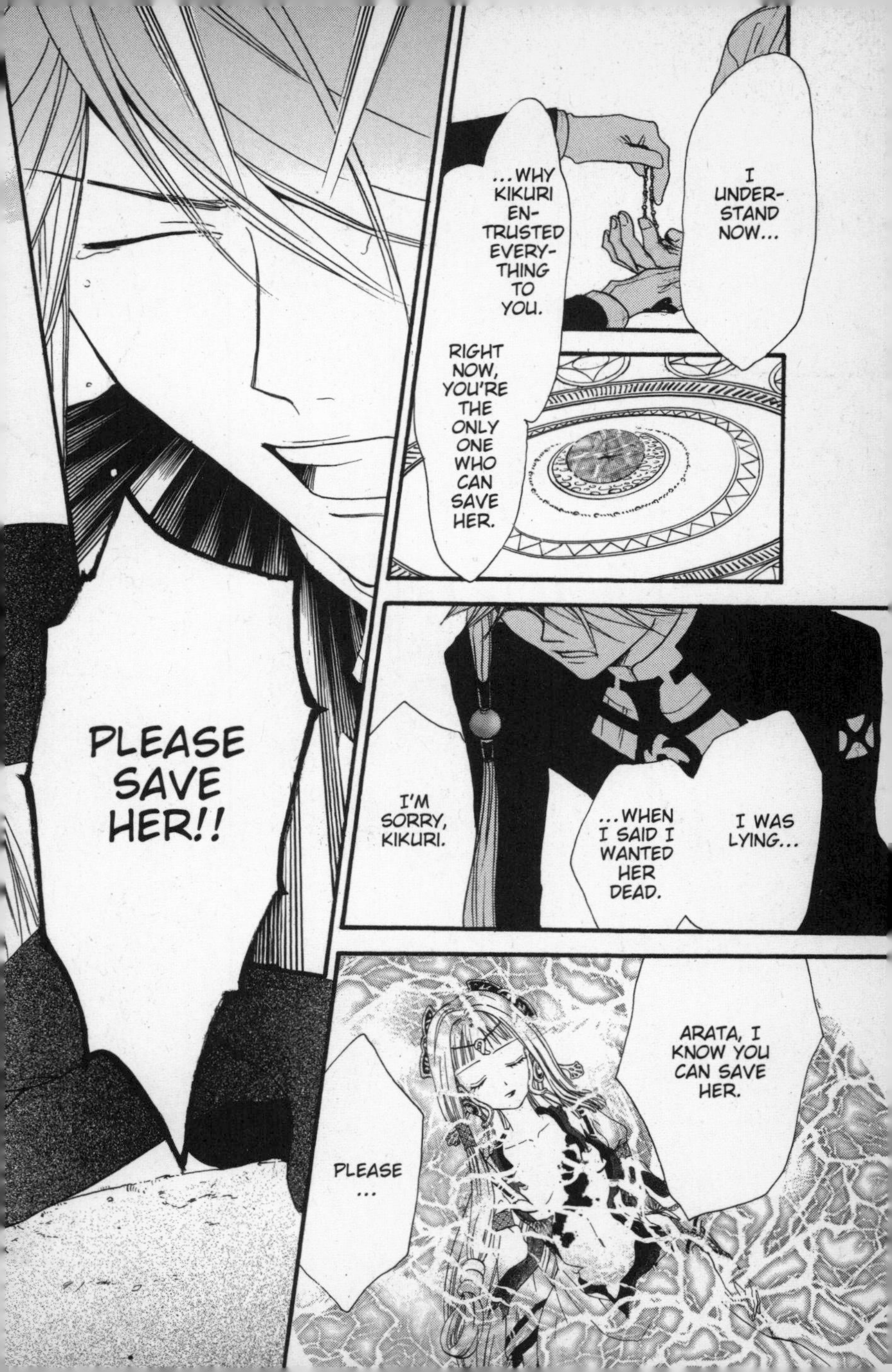

I UNDERSTAND NOW...
...WHY KIKURI ENTRUSTED EVERYTHING TO YOU.
RIGHT NOW, YOU'RE THE ONLY ONE WHO CAN SAVE HER.
I WAS LYING...
...WHEN I SAID I WANTED HER DEAD.
I'M SORRY, KIKURI.
ARATA, I KNOW YOU CAN SAVE HER.
PLEASE ...
PLEASE SAVE HER!!

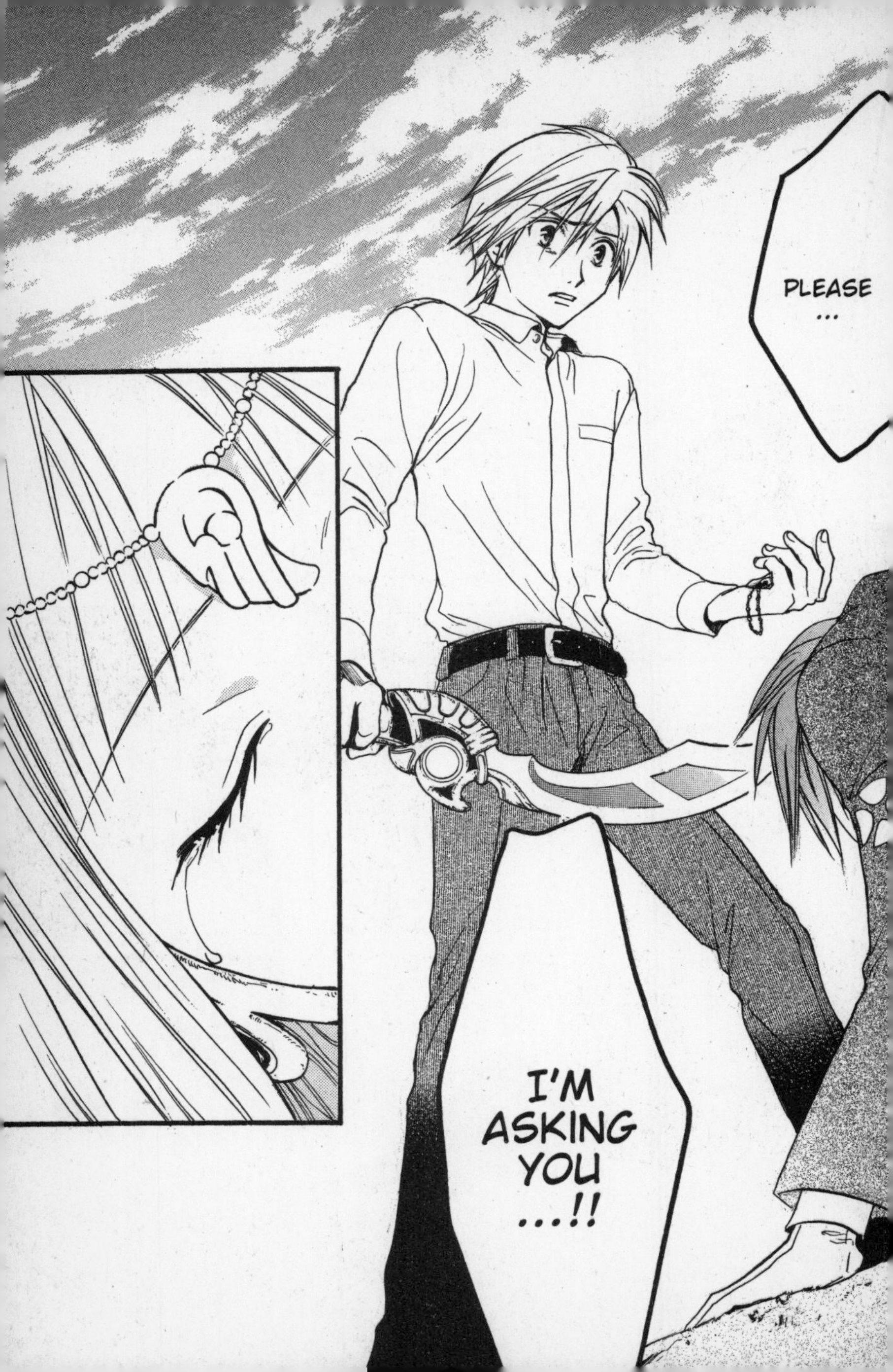
PLEASE ...
I'M ASKING YOU ...!!

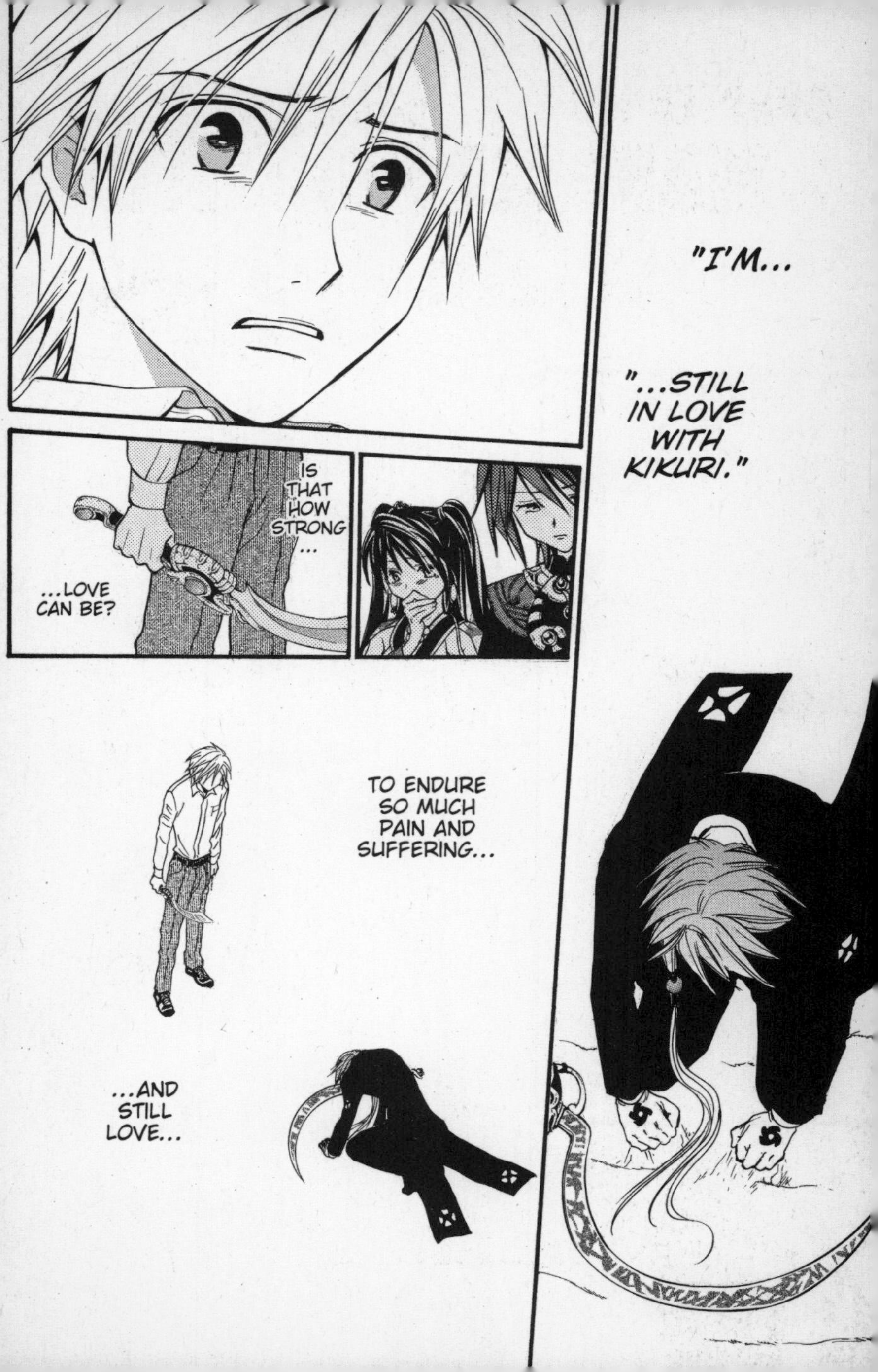
"I'M...
"...STILL IN LOVE WITH KIKURI."
IS THAT HOW STRONG...
...LOVE CAN BE?
TO ENDURE SO MUCH PAIN AND SUFFERING...
...AND STILL LOVE...

CHAPTER 101
MAKE ME SUBMIT!!

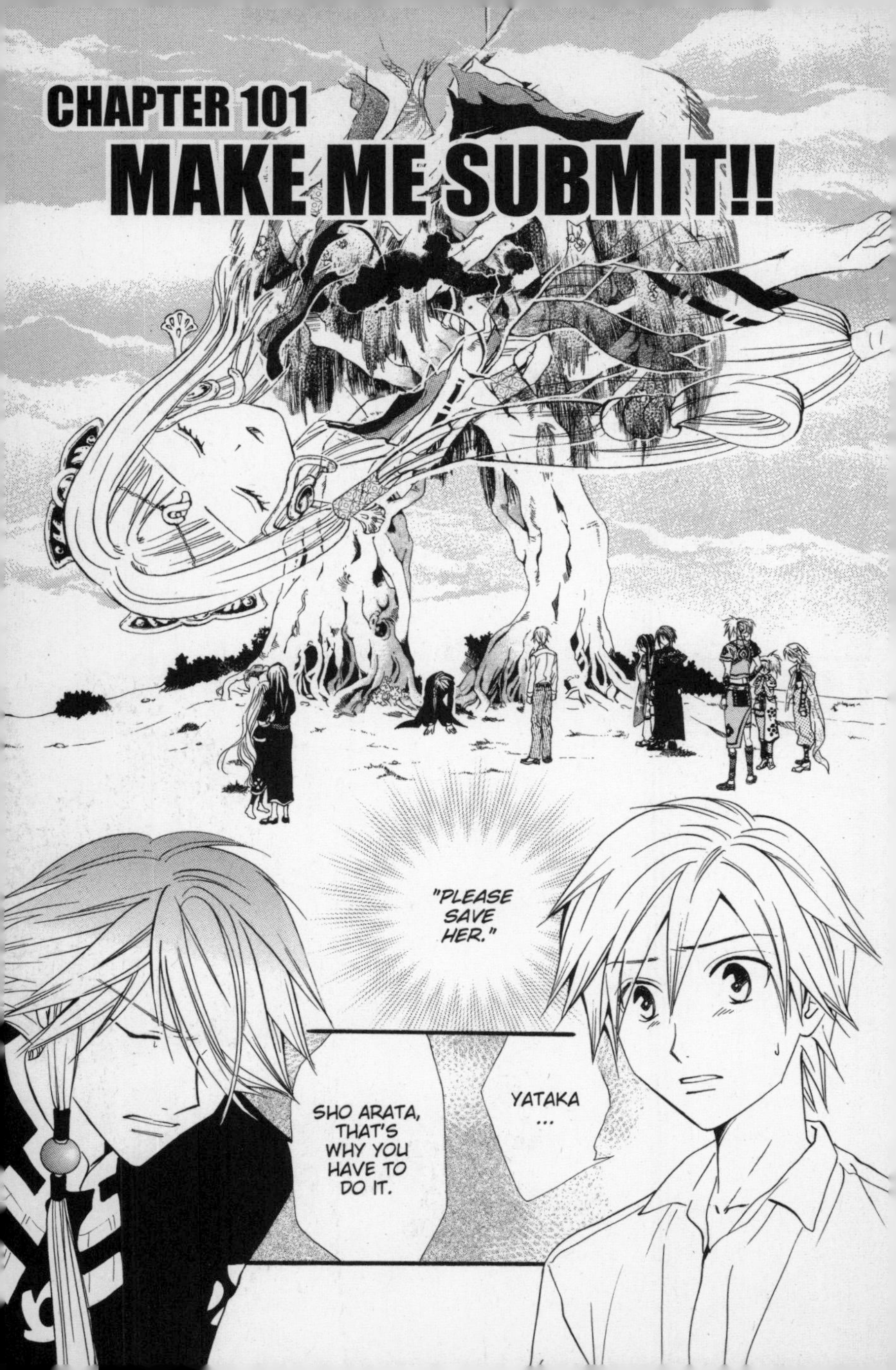
"PLEASE SAVE HER."
YATAKA ...
SHO ARATA, THAT'S WHY YOU HAVE TO DO IT.

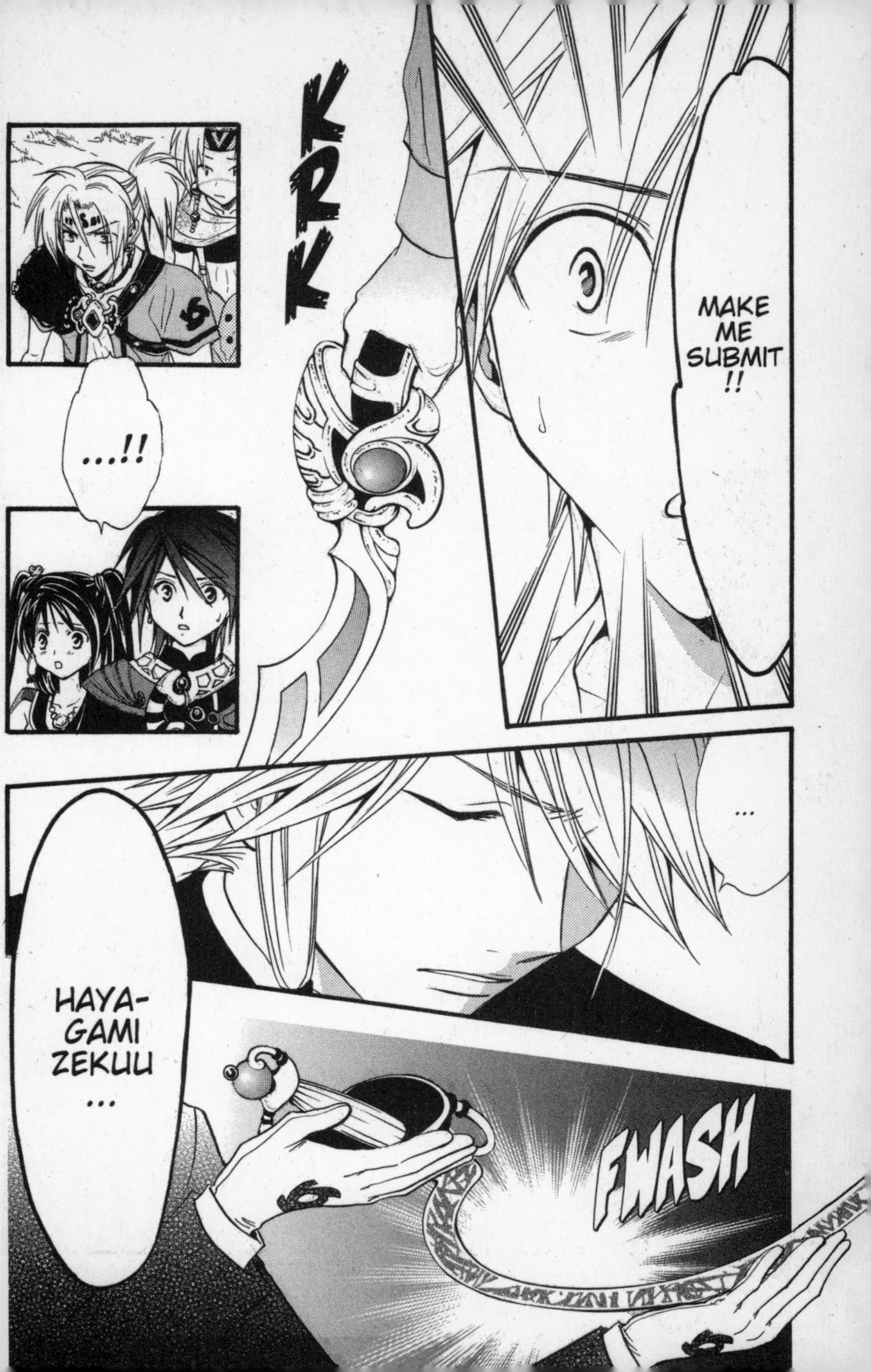
MAKE ME SUBMIT !!
KRK
...!!
...
HAYA-GAMI ZEKUU ...
FWASH

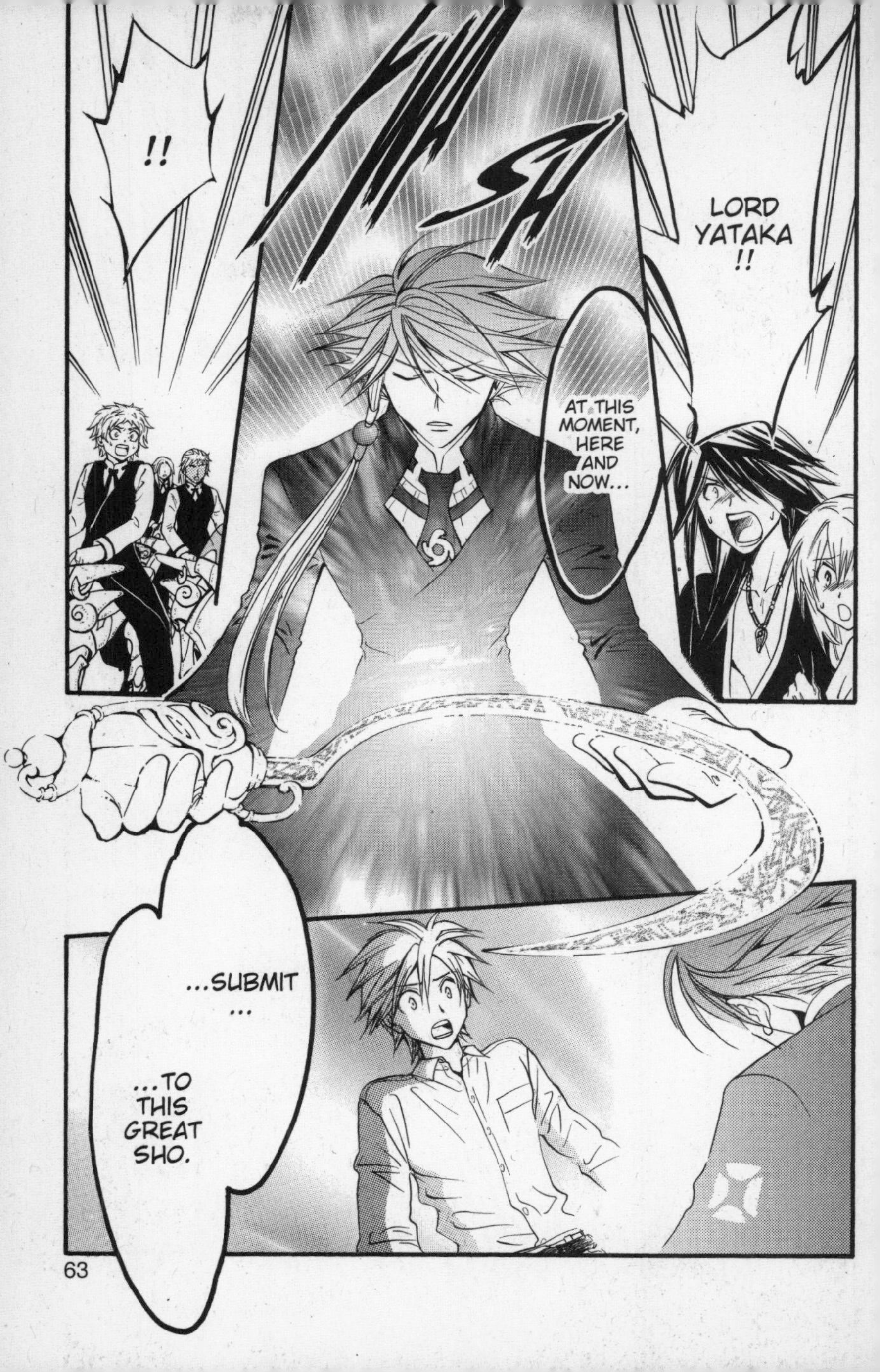
LORD YATAKA !!
AT THIS MOMENT, HERE AND NOW...
!!
...SUBMIT ...
...TO THIS GREAT SHO.

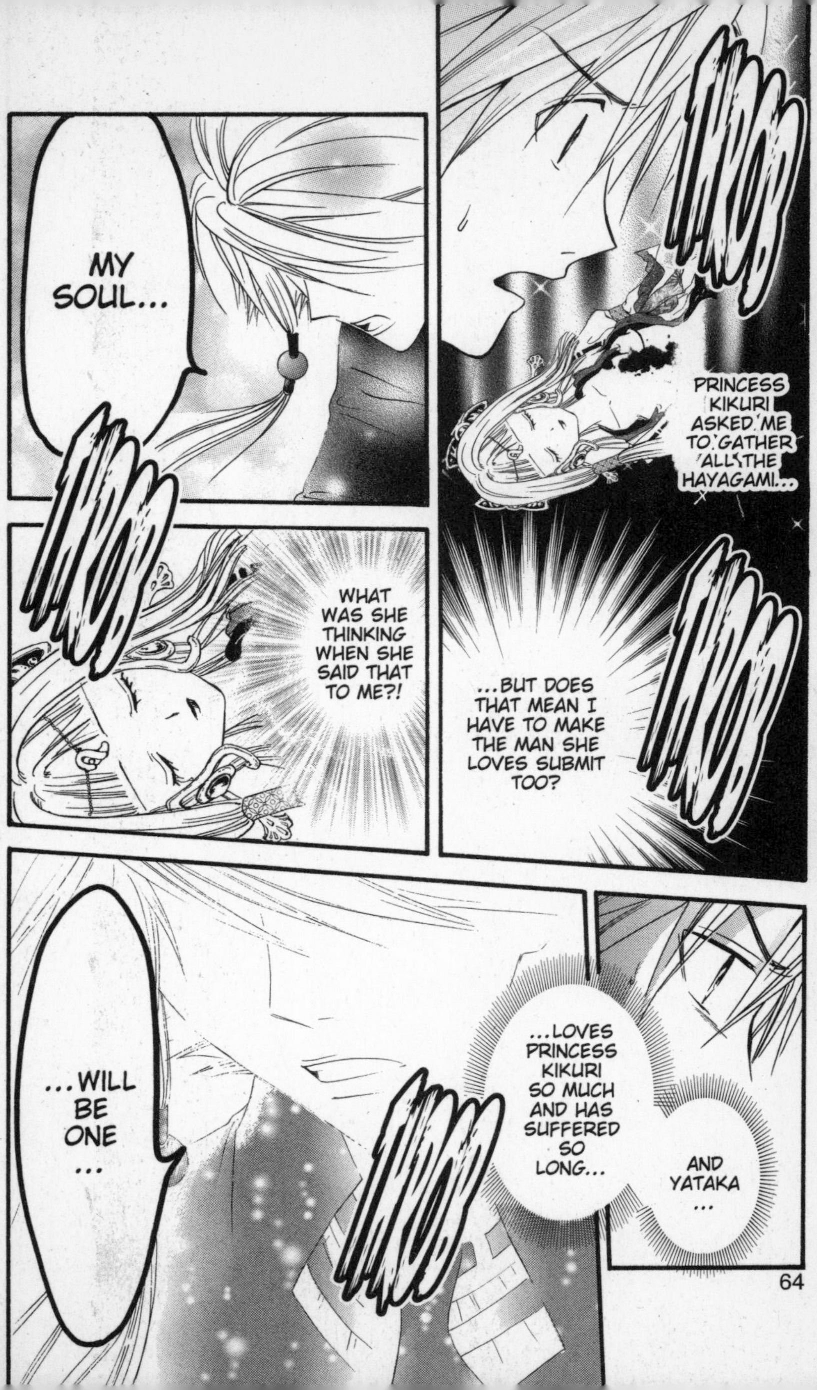
PRINCESS KIKURI ASKED ME TO GATHER ALL THE HAYAGAMI...
...BUT DOES THAT MEAN I HAVE TO MAKE THE MAN SHE LOVES SUBMIT TOO?
MY SOUL...
WHAT WAS SHE THINKING WHEN SHE SAID THAT TO ME?!
AND YATAKA ...
...LOVES PRINCESS KIKURI SO MUCH AND HAS SUFFERED SO LONG...
...WILL BE ONE ...

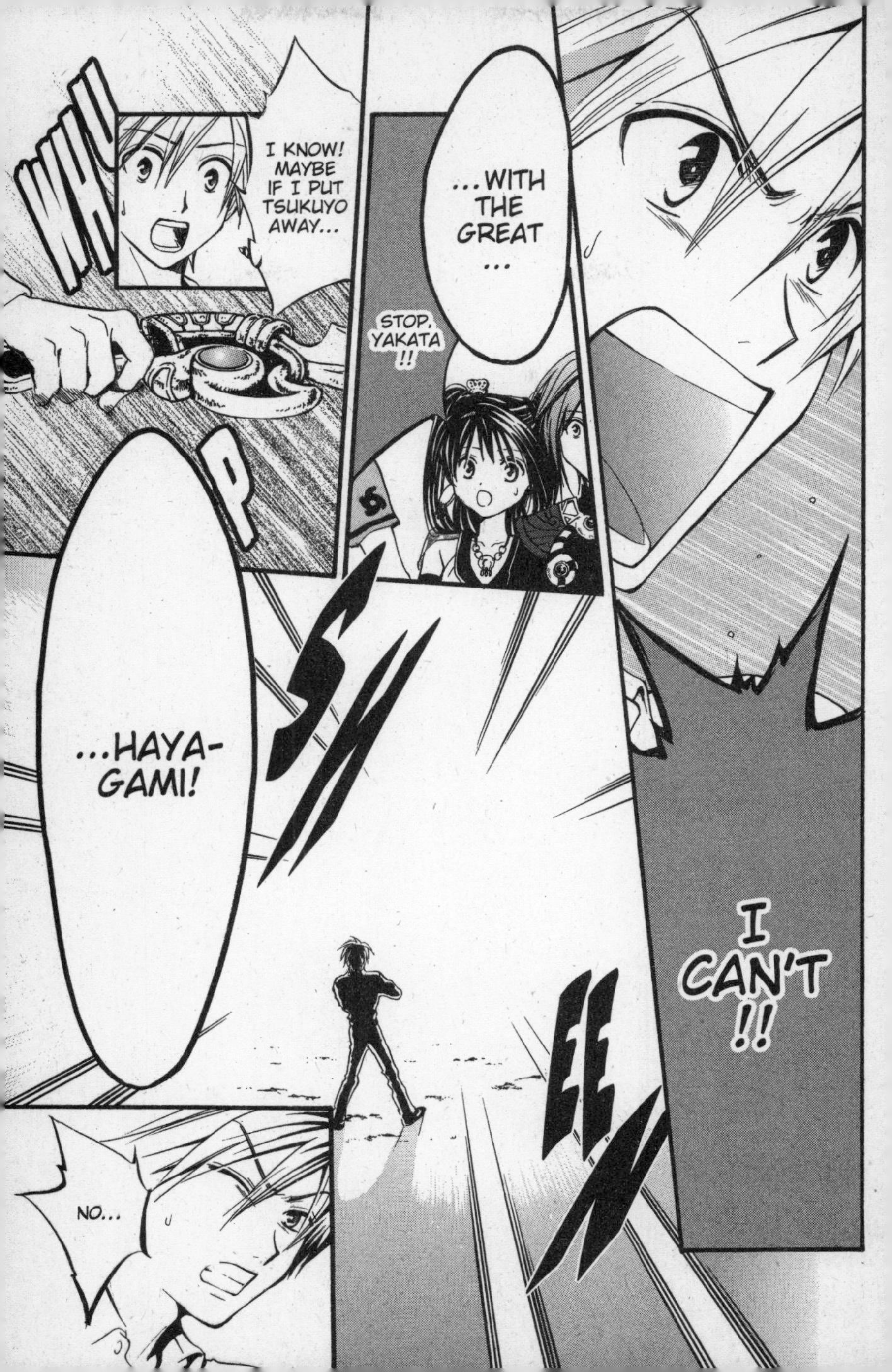

...WITH THE GREAT ...
STOP, YAKATA !!
I KNOW! MAYBE IF I PUT TSUKUYO AWAY...
WHU
P
...HAYA-GAMI!
SH
EEN
NO...
I CAN'T !!

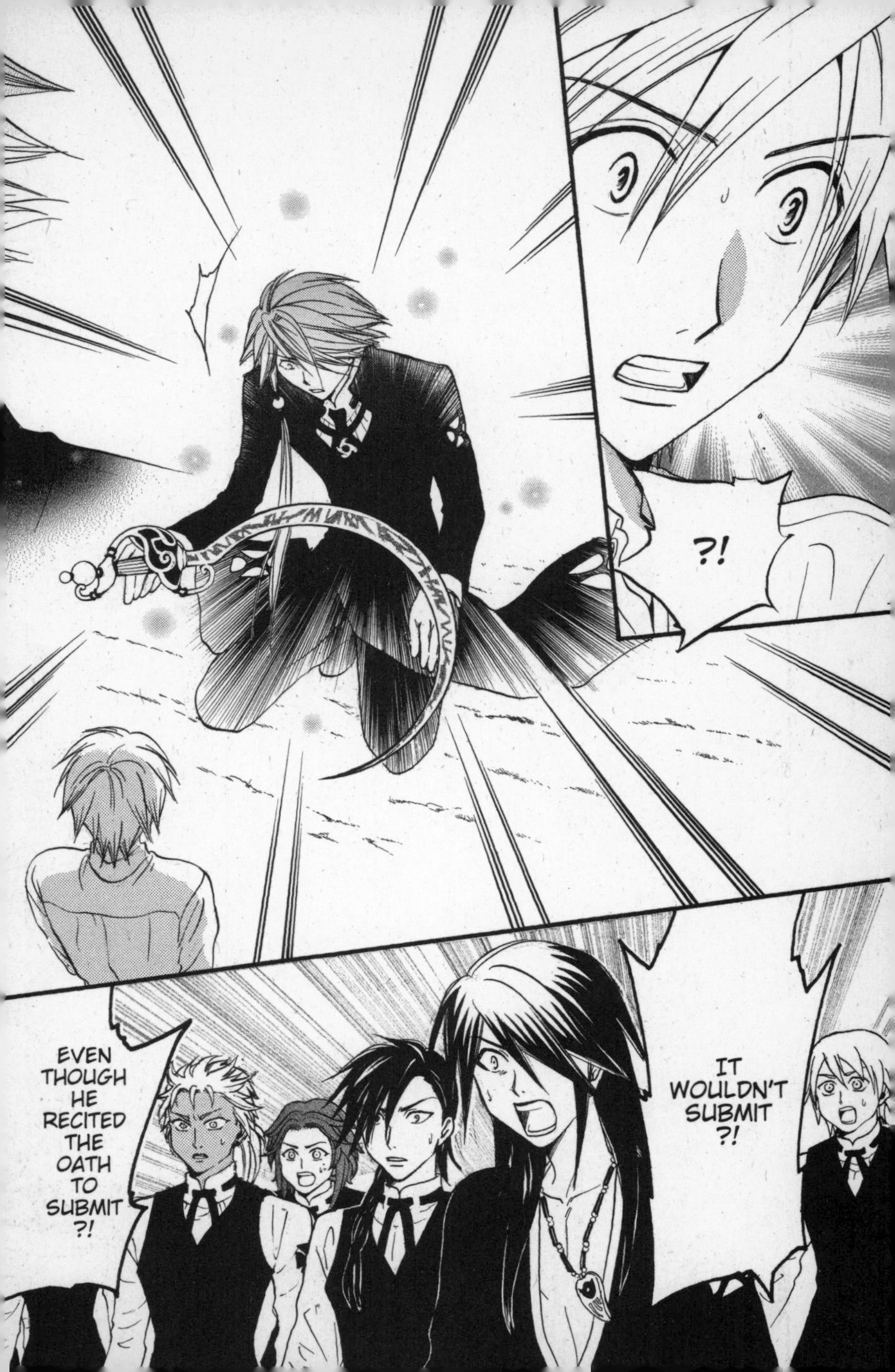
?!
IT WOULDN'T SUBMIT ?!
EVEN THOUGH HE RECITED THE OATH TO SUBMIT ?!

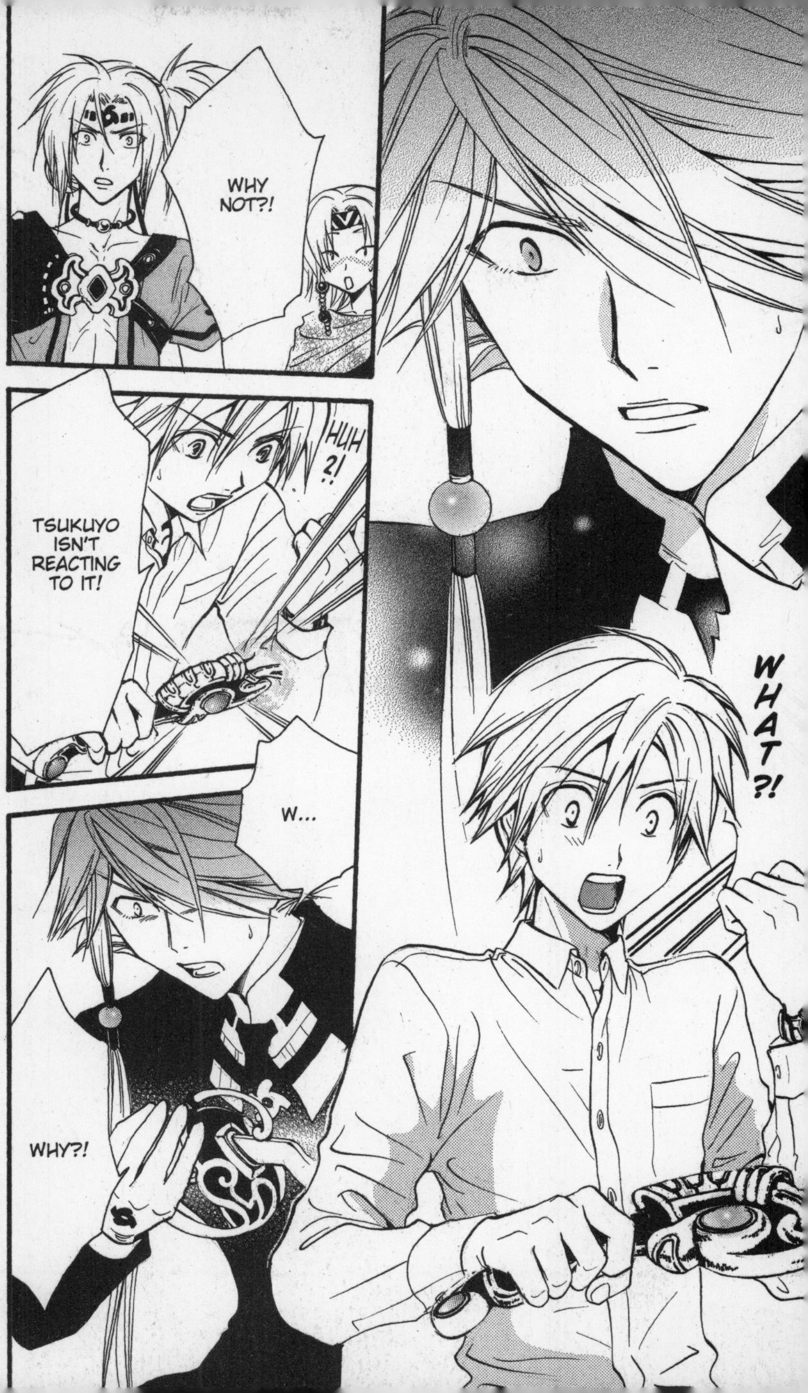
WHAT?!
WHY NOT?!
HUH?!
TSUKUYO ISN'T REACTING TO IT!
W...
WHY?!

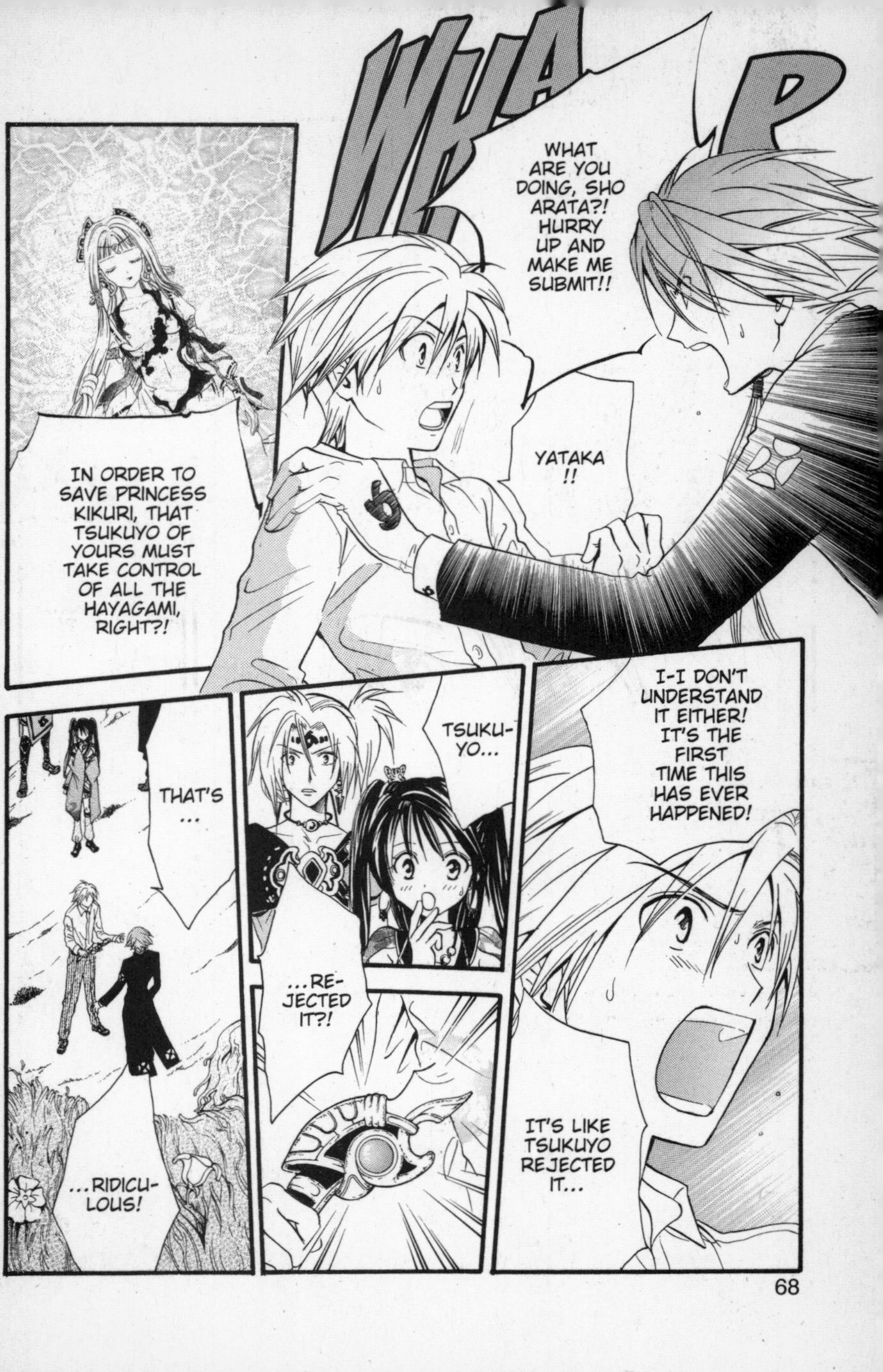
WHAP
WHAT ARE YOU DOING, SHO ARATA?! HURRY UP AND MAKE ME SUBMIT!!
YATAKA !!
IN ORDER TO SAVE PRINCESS KIKURI, THAT TSUKUYO OF YOURS MUST TAKE CONTROL OF ALL THE HAYAGAMI, RIGHT?!
I-I DON'T UNDERSTAND IT EITHER! IT'S THE FIRST TIME THIS HAS EVER HAPPENED!
IT'S LIKE TSUKUYO REJECTED IT...
TSUKU-YO...
...RE-JECTED IT?!
THAT'S ...
...RIDICU-LOUS!

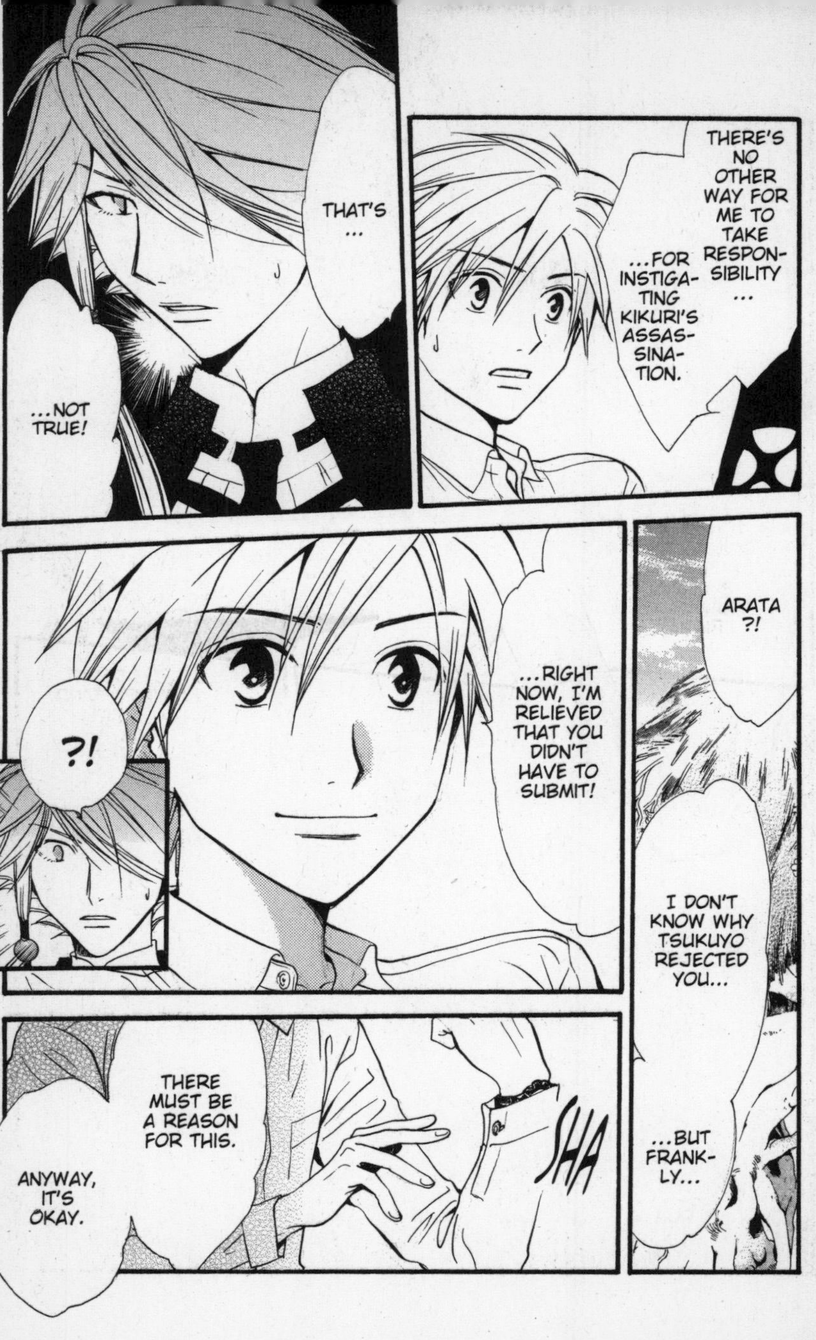
THERE'S NO OTHER WAY FOR ME TO TAKE RESPON-SIBILITY...
...FOR INSTIGA-TING KIKURI'S ASSAS-SINA-TION.
THAT'S...
...NOT TRUE!
ARATA?!
I DON'T KNOW WHY TSUKUYO REJECTED YOU...
...BUT FRANK-LY...
...RIGHT NOW, I'M RELIEVED THAT YOU DIDN'T HAVE TO SUBMIT!
?!
SHA
THERE MUST BE A REASON FOR THIS.
ANYWAY, IT'S OKAY.

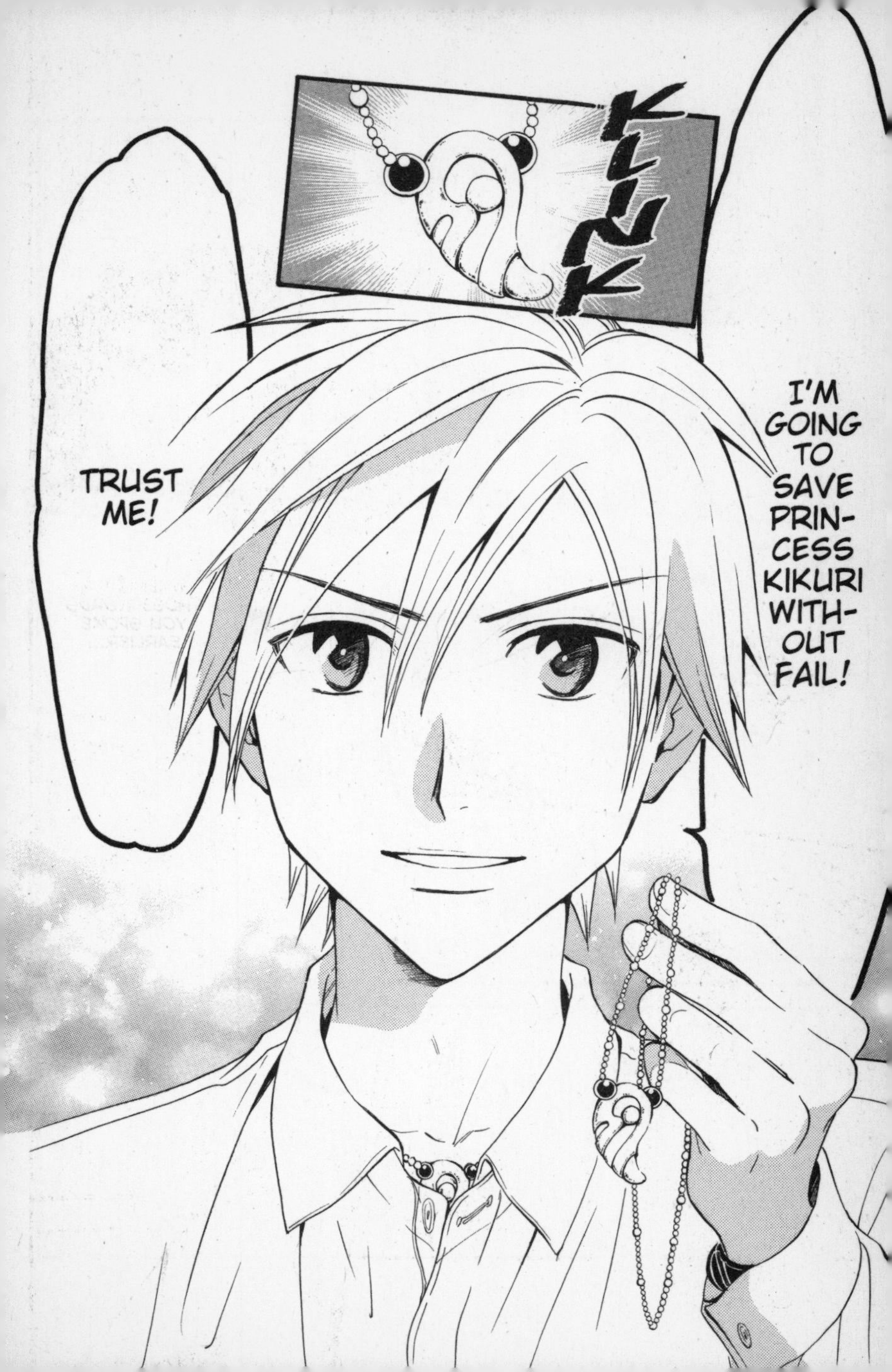
KLINK
I'M GOING TO SAVE PRIN-CESS KIKURI WITH-OUT FAIL!
TRUST ME!

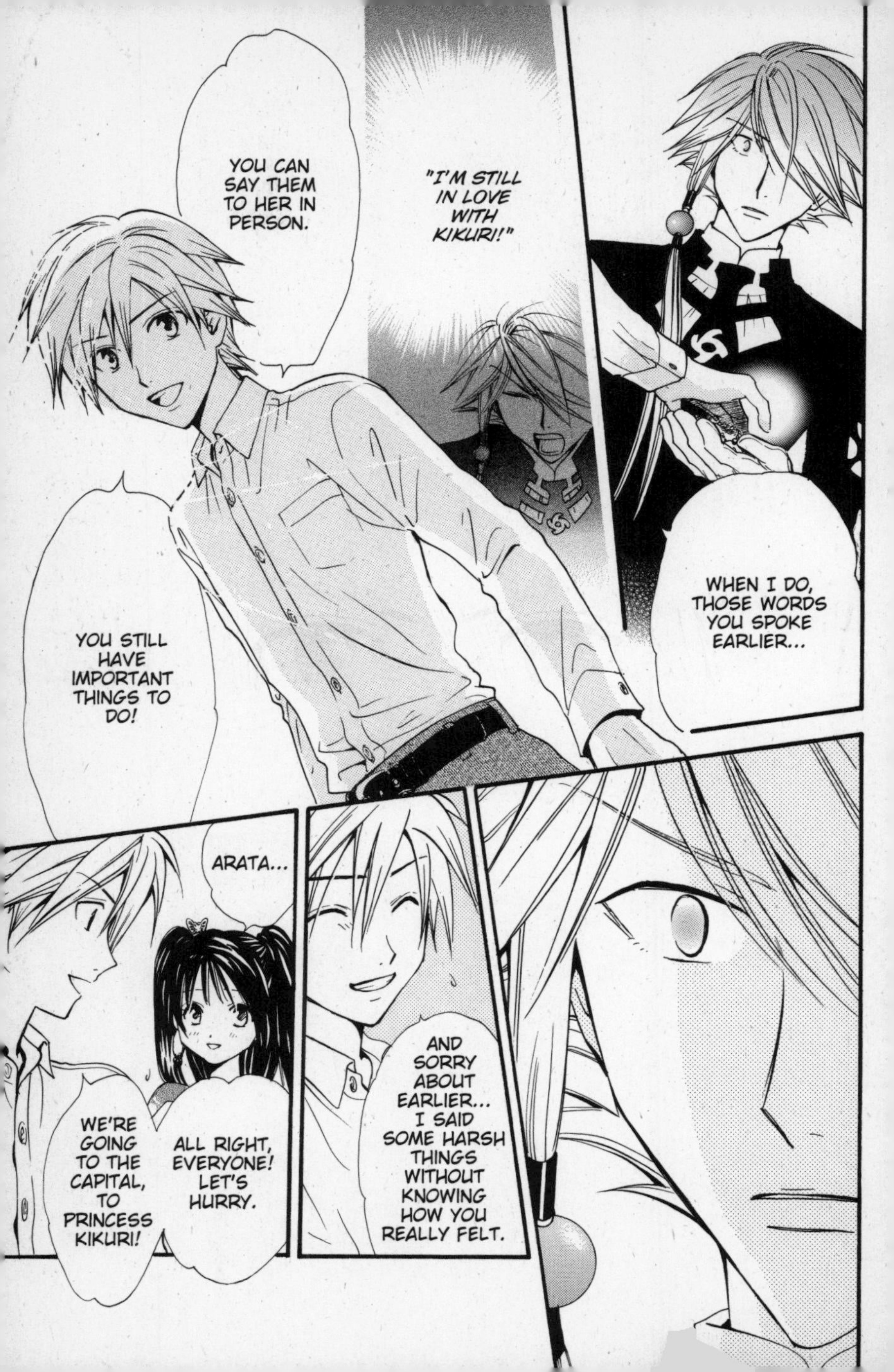
WHEN I DO, THOSE WORDS YOU SPOKE EARLIER...
"I'M STILL IN LOVE WITH KIKURI!"
YOU CAN SAY THEM TO HER IN PERSON.
YOU STILL HAVE IMPORTANT THINGS TO DO!
AND SORRY ABOUT EARLIER... I SAID SOME HARSH THINGS WITHOUT KNOWING HOW YOU REALLY FELT.
ARATA...
ALL RIGHT, EVERYONE! LET'S HURRY.
WE'RE GOING TO THE CAPITAL, TO PRINCESS KIKURI!

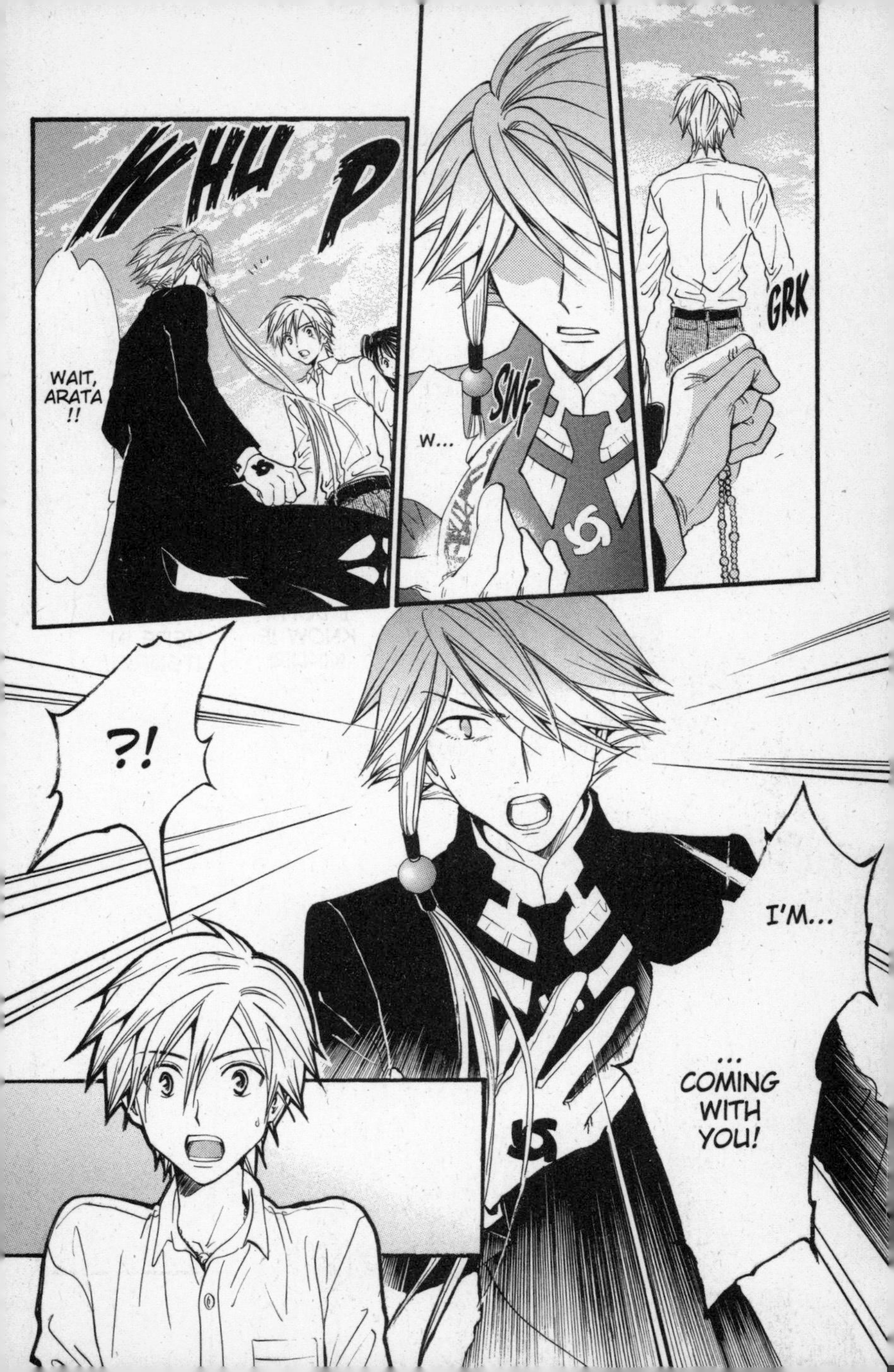
GRK
W...
SWF
WHUP
...
WAIT, ARATA !!
?!
I'M...
... COMING WITH YOU!

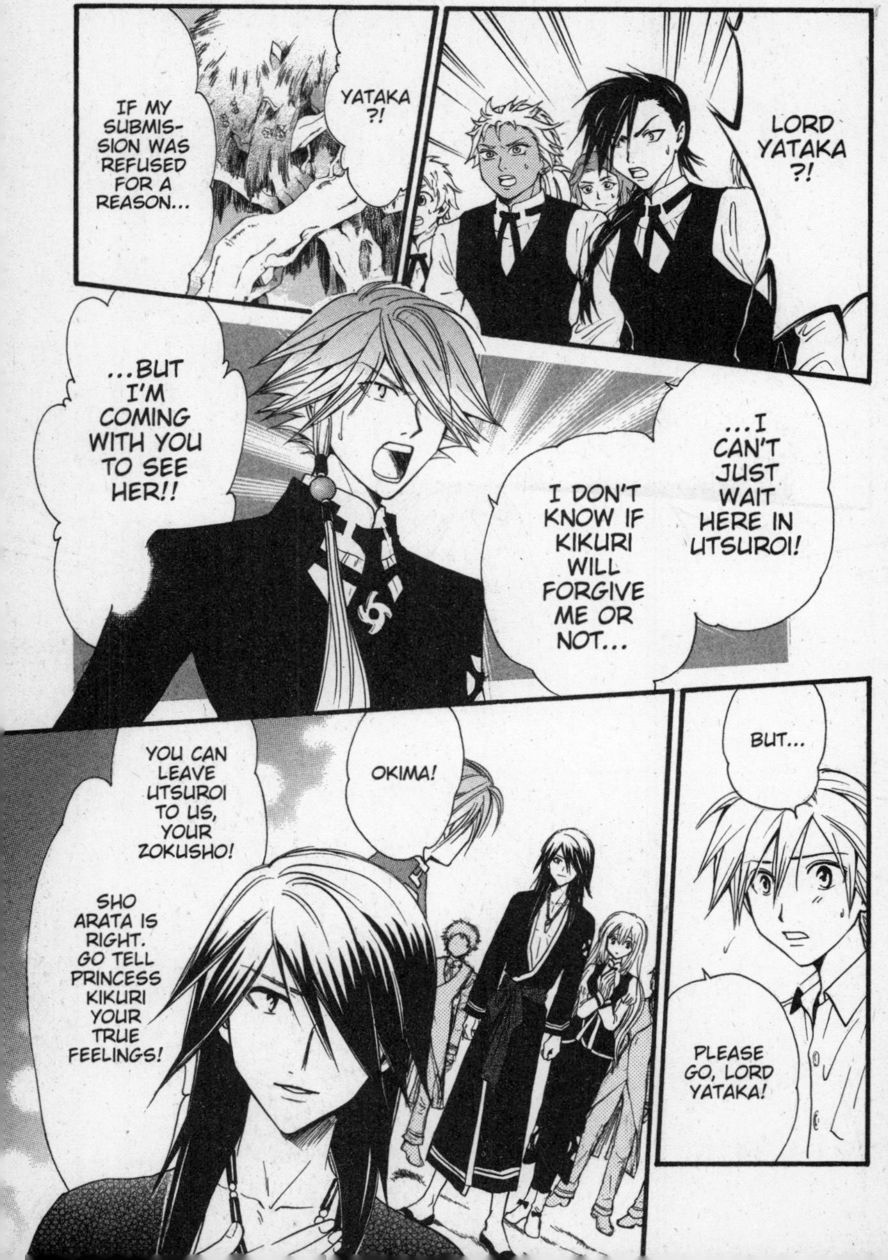
LORD YATAKA ?!
YATAKA ?!
IF MY SUBMISSION WAS REFUSED FOR A REASON...
...I CAN'T JUST WAIT HERE IN UTSUROI!
I DON'T KNOW IF KIKURI WILL FORGIVE ME OR NOT...
...BUT I'M COMING WITH YOU TO SEE HER!!
BUT...
PLEASE GO, LORD YATAKA!
OKIMA!
YOU CAN LEAVE UTSUROI TO US, YOUR ZOKUSHO!
SHO ARATA IS RIGHT. GO TELL PRINCESS KIKURI YOUR TRUE FEELINGS!

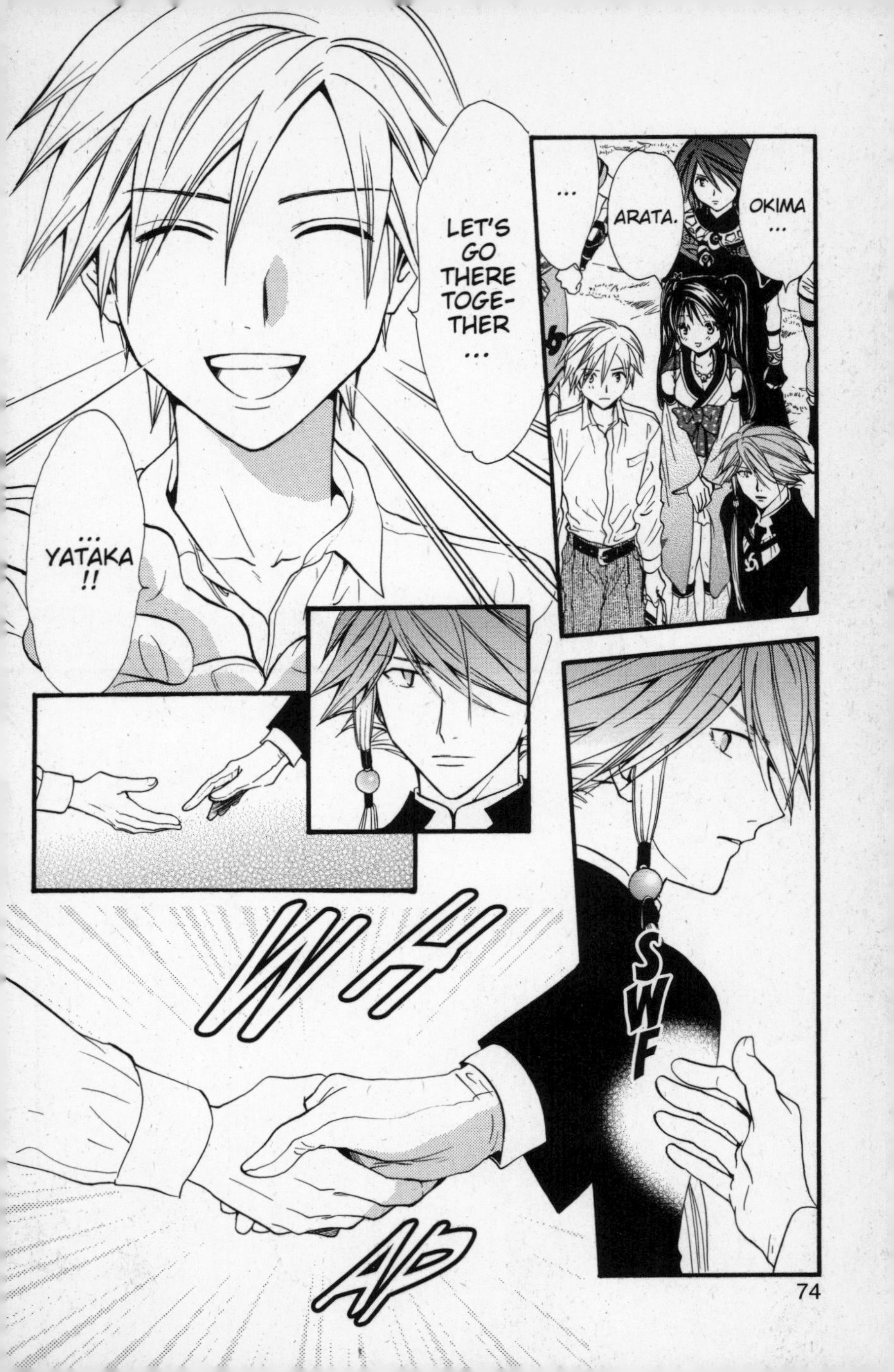
OKIMA ...
ARATA.
...
LET'S GO THERE TOGE-THER ...
... YATAKA !!
SWF
WHAP

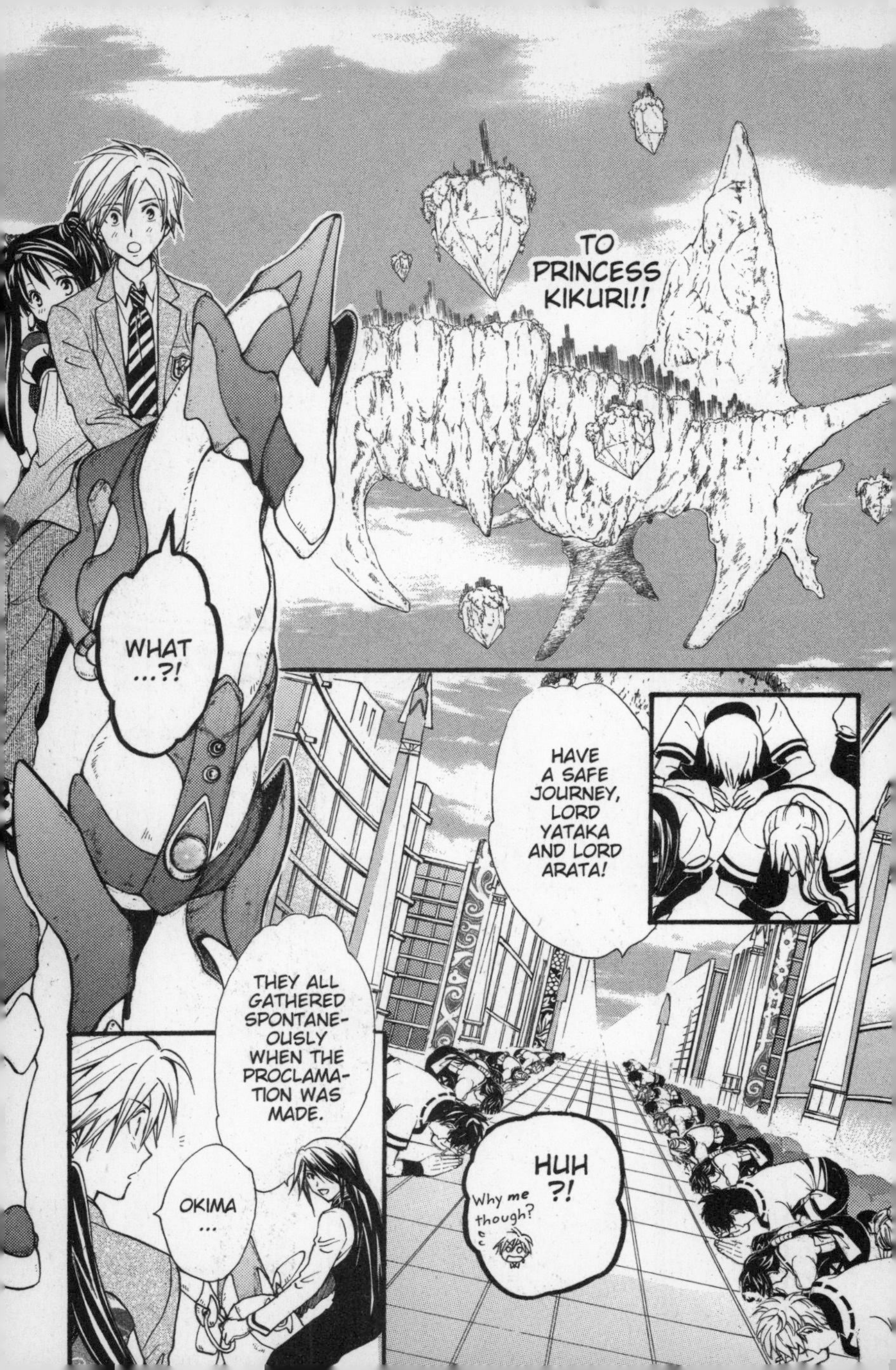
TO PRINCESS KIKURI!!
WHAT ...?!
HAVE A SAFE JOURNEY, LORD YATAKA AND LORD ARATA!
HUH ?!
Why me though?
THEY ALL GATHERED SPONTANE-OUSLY WHEN THE PROCLAMA-TION WAS MADE.
OKIMA ...

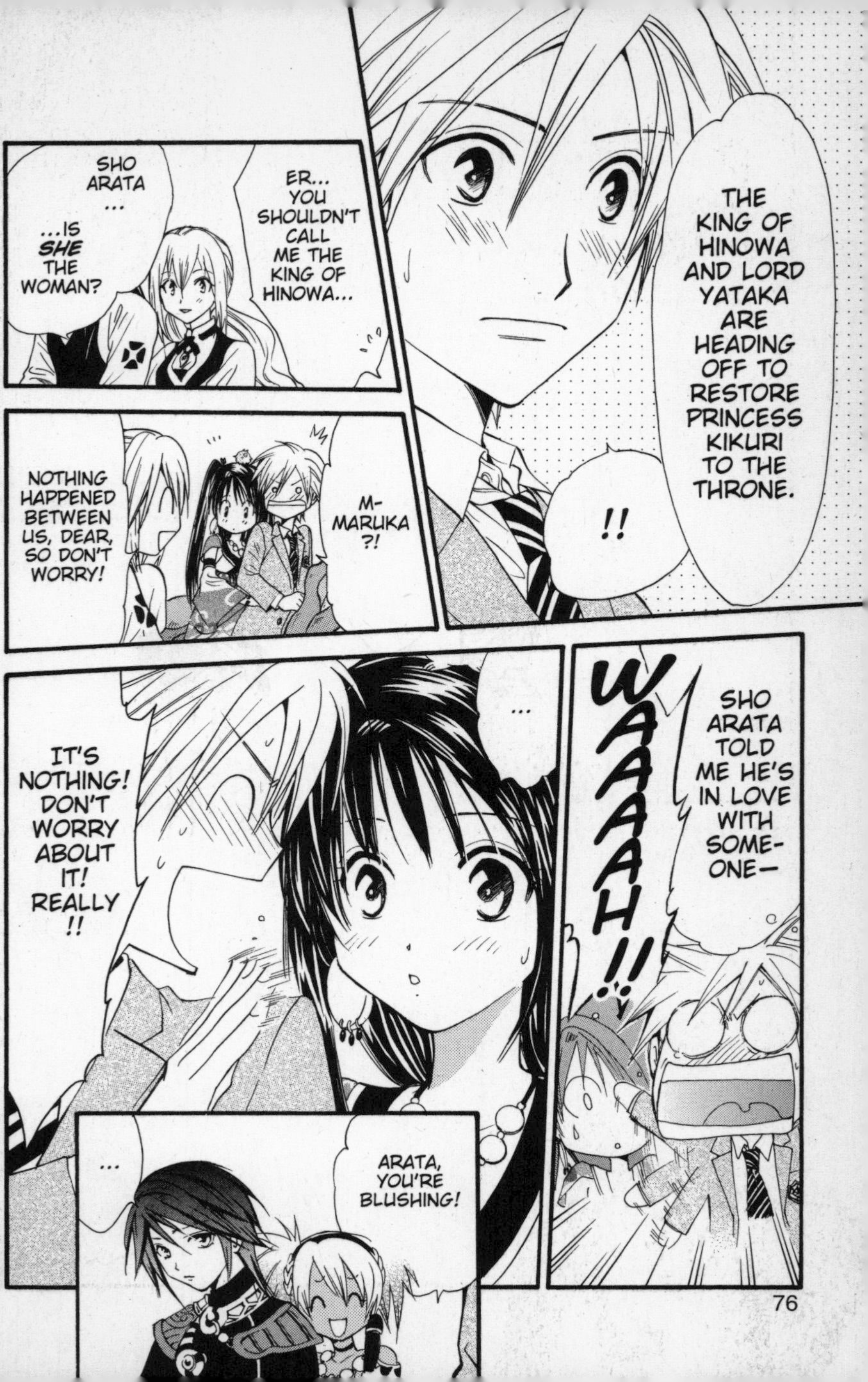
THE KING OF HINOWA AND LORD YATAKA ARE HEADING OFF TO RESTORE PRINCESS KIKURI TO THE THRONE.
!!
ER... YOU SHOULDN'T CALL ME THE KING OF HINOWA...
SHO ARATA... ...IS *SHE* THE WOMAN?
M-MARUKA?!
NOTHING HAPPENED BETWEEN US, DEAR, SO DON'T WORRY!
SHO ARATA TOLD ME HE'S IN LOVE WITH SOME-ONE—
WAAAAAH!!
...
IT'S NOTHING! DON'T WORRY ABOUT IT! REALLY!!
ARATA, YOU'RE BLUSHING!
...

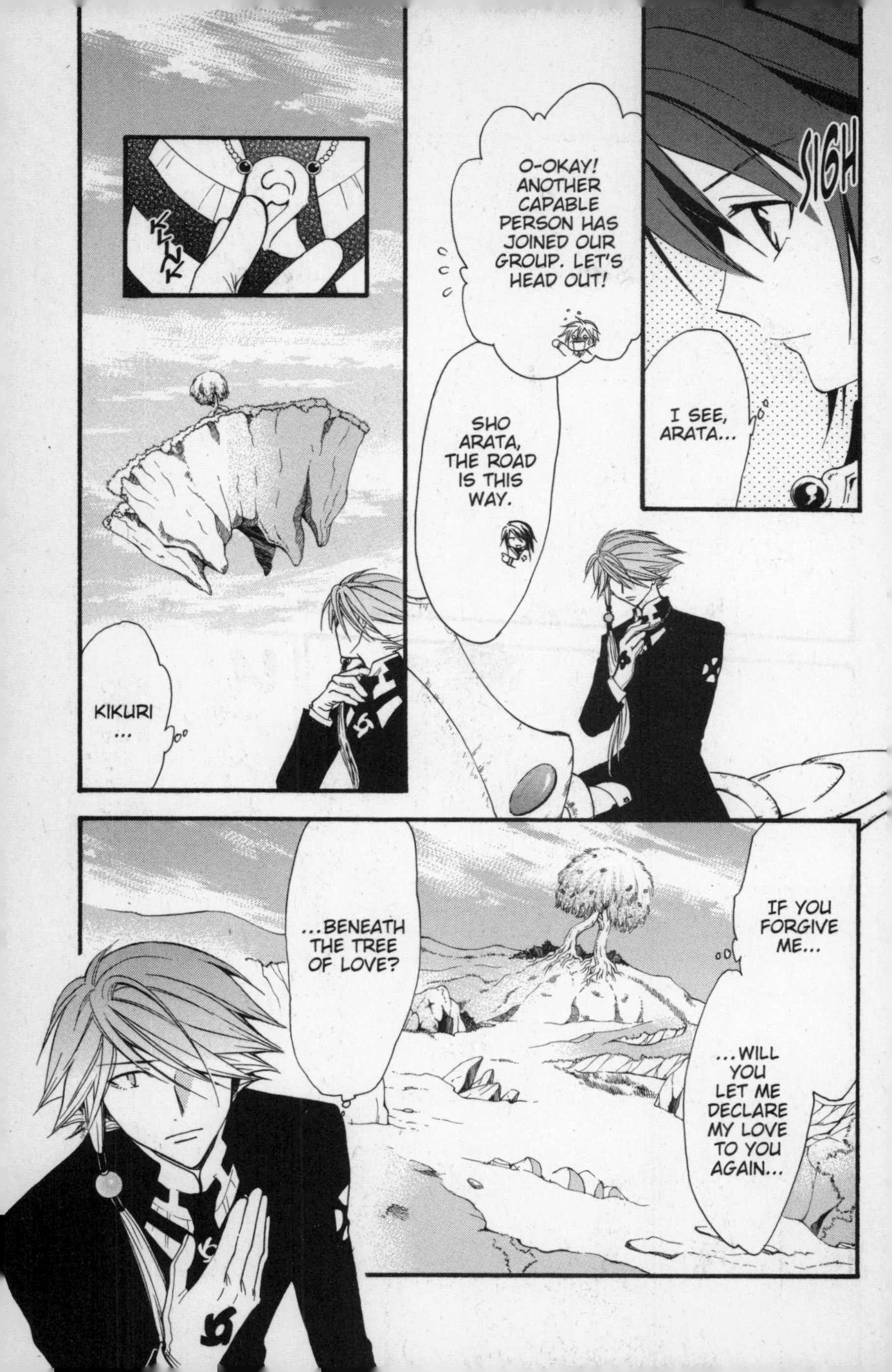
SIGH
I SEE, ARATA...
O-OKAY! ANOTHER CAPABLE PERSON HAS JOINED OUR GROUP. LET'S HEAD OUT!
SHO ARATA, THE ROAD IS THIS WAY.
KLINK
KIKURI ...
IF YOU FORGIVE ME...
...WILL YOU LET ME DECLARE MY LOVE TO YOU AGAIN...
...BENEATH THE TREE OF LOVE?

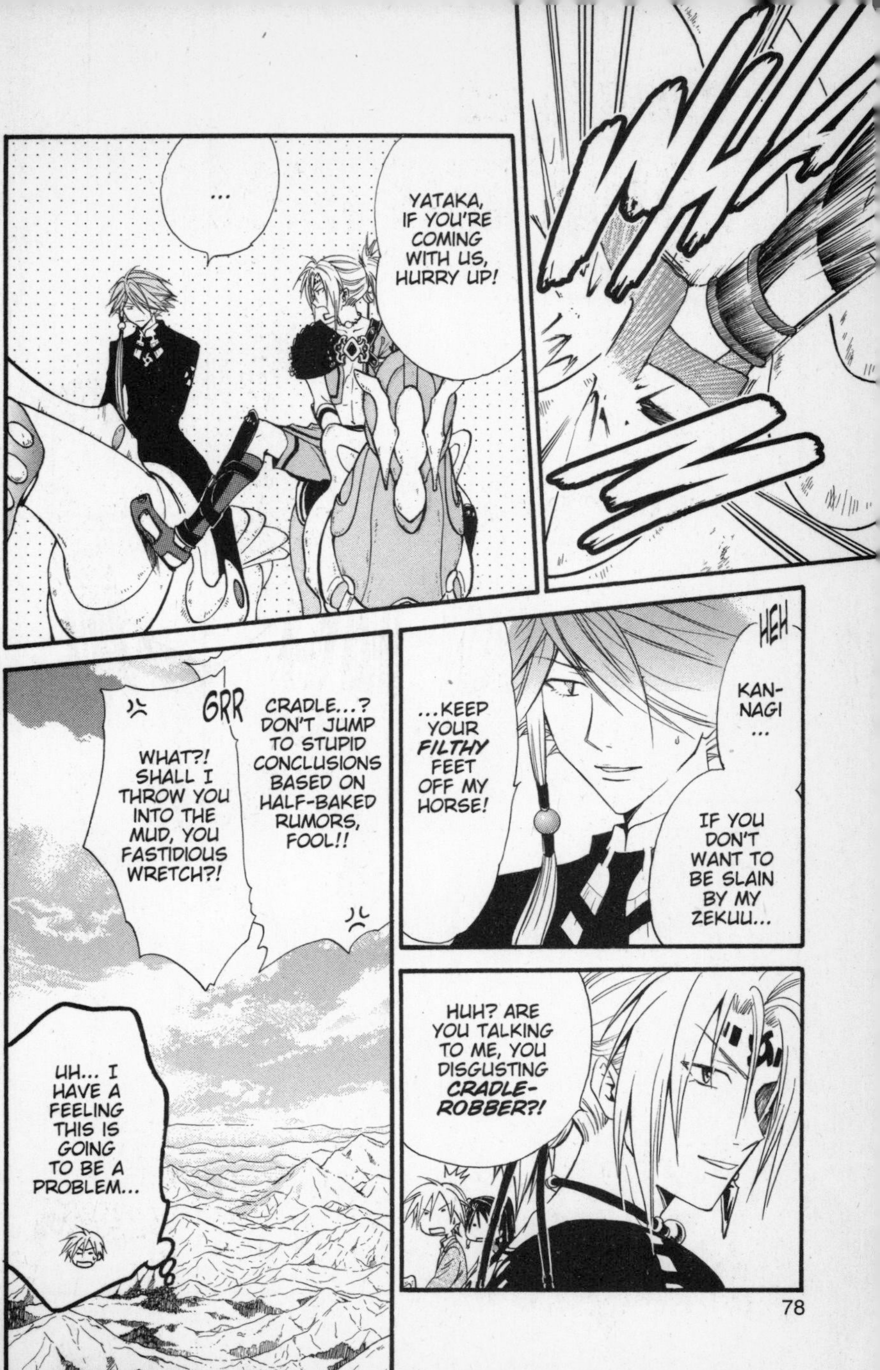
YATAKA, IF YOU'RE COMING WITH US, HURRY UP!
...
HEH
KAN-NAGI...
IF YOU DON'T WANT TO BE SLAIN BY MY ZEKUU...
...KEEP YOUR FILTHY FEET OFF MY HORSE!
HUH? ARE YOU TALKING TO ME, YOU DISGUSTING CRADLE-ROBBER?!
CRADLE...? DON'T JUMP TO STUPID CONCLUSIONS BASED ON HALF-BAKED RUMORS, FOOL!!
GRR
WHAT?! SHALL I THROW YOU INTO THE MUD, YOU FASTIDIOUS WRETCH?!
UH... I HAVE A FEELING THIS IS GOING TO BE A PROBLEM...

CHAPTER 102

ONLY THE GIRLS

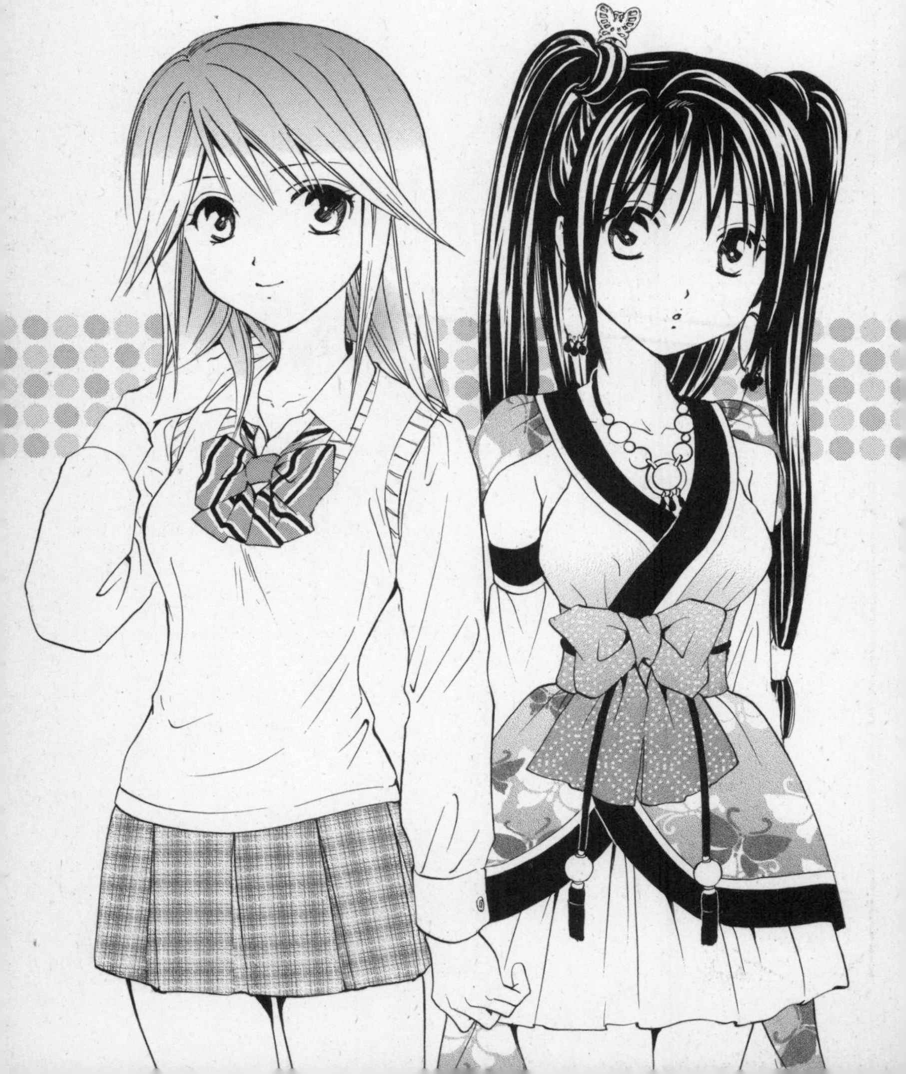

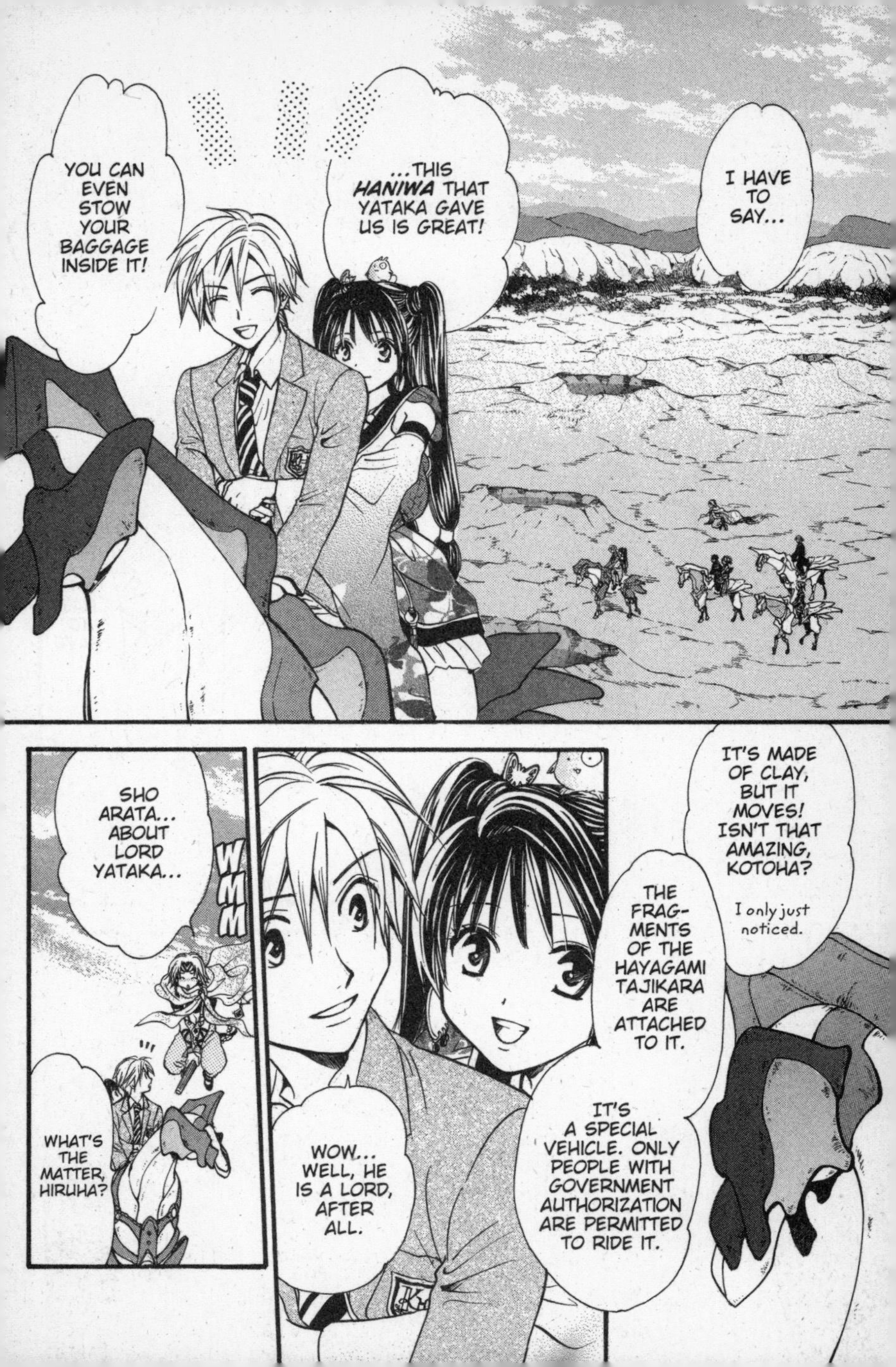
I HAVE TO SAY...
...THIS *HANIWA* THAT YATAKA GAVE US IS GREAT!
YOU CAN EVEN STOW YOUR BAGGAGE INSIDE IT!
IT'S MADE OF CLAY, BUT IT MOVES! ISN'T THAT AMAZING, KOTOHA?
I only just noticed.
THE FRAGMENTS OF THE HAYAGAMI TAJIKARA ARE ATTACHED TO IT.
IT'S A SPECIAL VEHICLE. ONLY PEOPLE WITH GOVERNMENT AUTHORIZATION ARE PERMITTED TO RIDE IT.
WOW... WELL, HE IS A LORD, AFTER ALL.
SHO ARATA... ABOUT LORD YATAKA...
WMM
WHAT'S THE MATTER, HIRUHA?

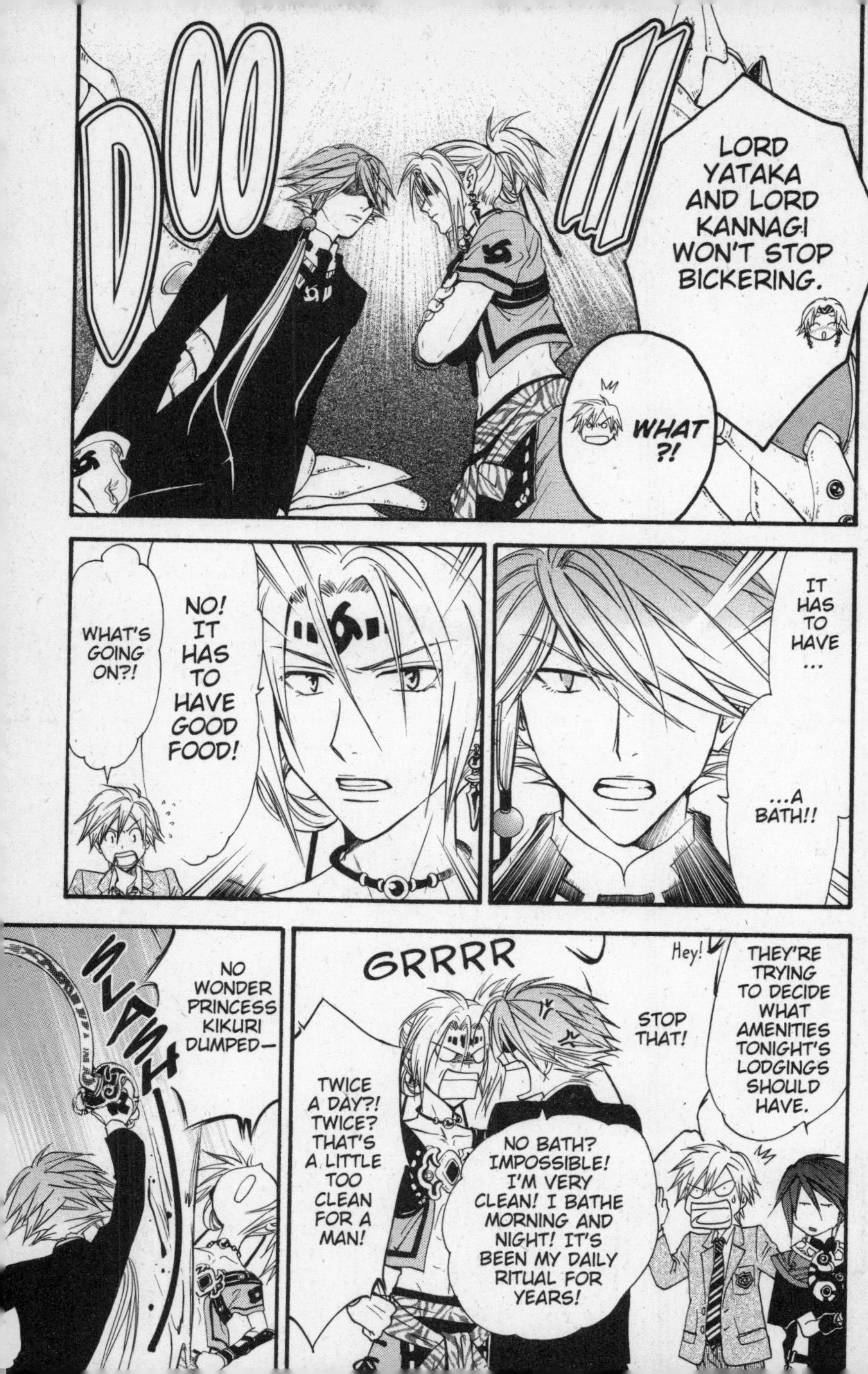

LORD YATAKA AND LORD KANNAGI WON'T STOP BICKERING.
WHAT?!
DOOOM
IT HAS TO HAVE...
...A BATH!!
NO! IT HAS TO HAVE GOOD FOOD!
WHAT'S GOING ON?!
THEY'RE TRYING TO DECIDE WHAT AMENITIES TONIGHT'S LODGINGS SHOULD HAVE.
Hey!
STOP THAT!
GRRRR
NO BATH? IMPOSSIBLE! I'M VERY CLEAN! I BATHE MORNING AND NIGHT! IT'S BEEN MY DAILY RITUAL FOR YEARS!
TWICE A DAY?! TWICE? THAT'S A LITTLE TOO CLEAN FOR A MAN!
SWISH
NO WONDER PRINCESS KIKURI DUMPED—

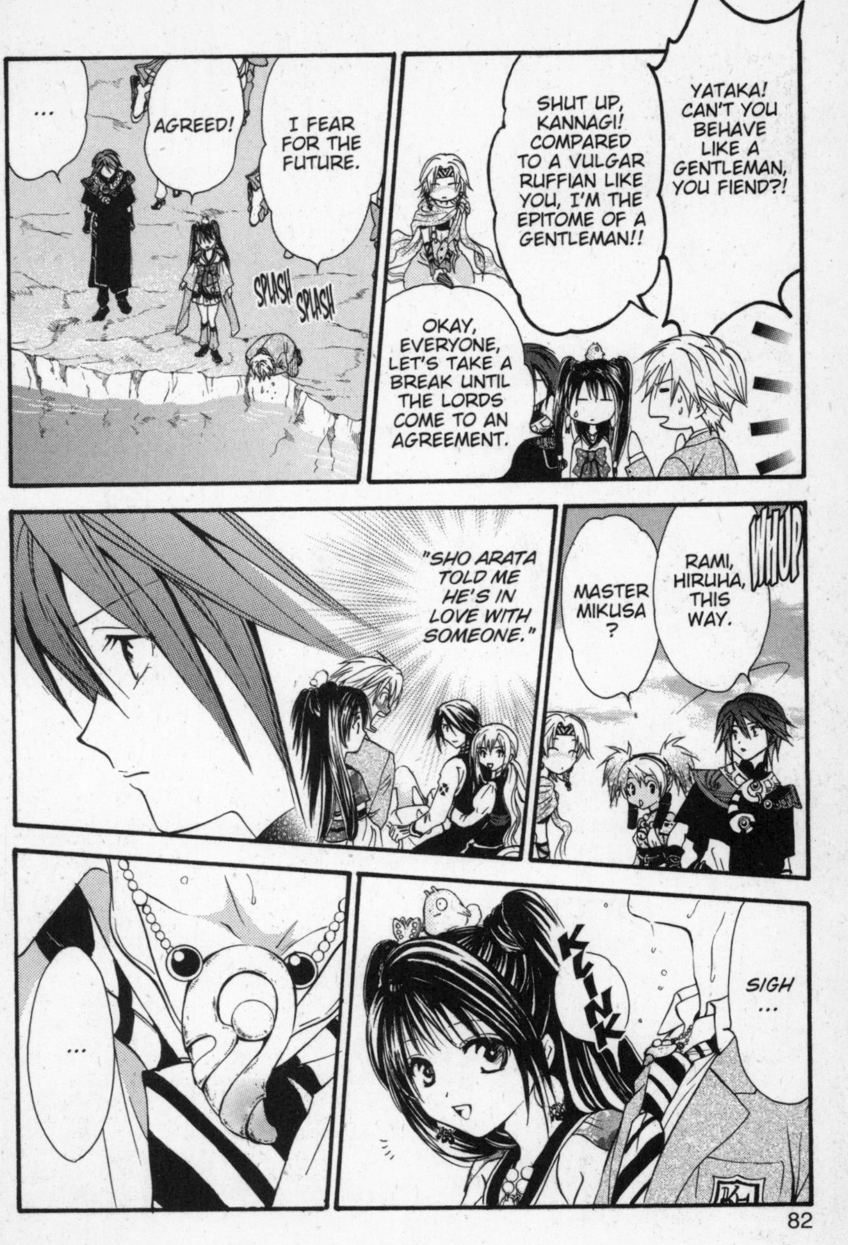
YATAKA! CAN'T YOU BEHAVE LIKE A GENTLEMAN, YOU FIEND?!
SHUT UP, KANNAGI! COMPARED TO A VULGAR RUFFIAN LIKE YOU, I'M THE EPITOME OF A GENTLEMAN!!
OKAY, EVERYONE, LET'S TAKE A BREAK UNTIL THE LORDS COME TO AN AGREEMENT.
I FEAR FOR THE FUTURE.
AGREED!
...
SPLASH
SPLASH
WHOP
RAMI, HIRUHA, THIS WAY.
MASTER MIKUSA ?
"SHO ARATA TOLD ME HE'S IN LOVE WITH SOMEONE."
SIGH ...
KLINK
...

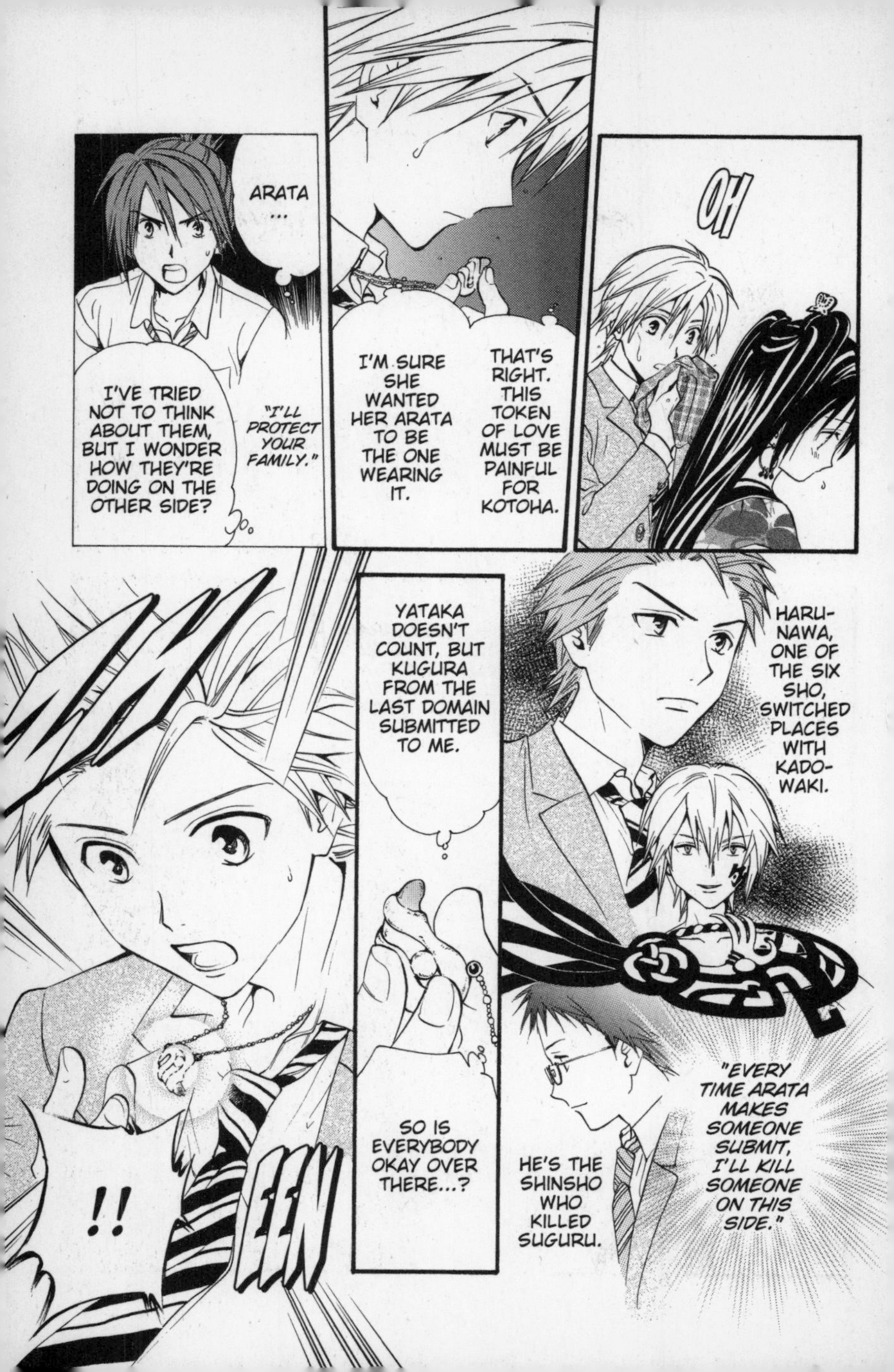
OH
THAT'S RIGHT. THIS TOKEN OF LOVE MUST BE PAINFUL FOR KOTOHA.
I'M SURE SHE WANTED HER ARATA TO BE THE ONE WEARING IT.
ARATA ...
"I'LL PROTECT YOUR FAMILY."
I'VE TRIED NOT TO THINK ABOUT THEM, BUT I WONDER HOW THEY'RE DOING ON THE OTHER SIDE?
HARU-NAWA, ONE OF THE SIX SHO, SWITCHED PLACES WITH KADO-WAKI.
"EVERY TIME ARATA MAKES SOMEONE SUBMIT, I'LL KILL SOMEONE ON THIS SIDE."
HE'S THE SHINSHO WHO KILLED SUGURU.
YATAKA DOESN'T COUNT, BUT KUGURA FROM THE LAST DOMAIN SUBMITTED TO ME.
SO IS EVERYBODY OKAY OVER THERE...?
EEN
!!

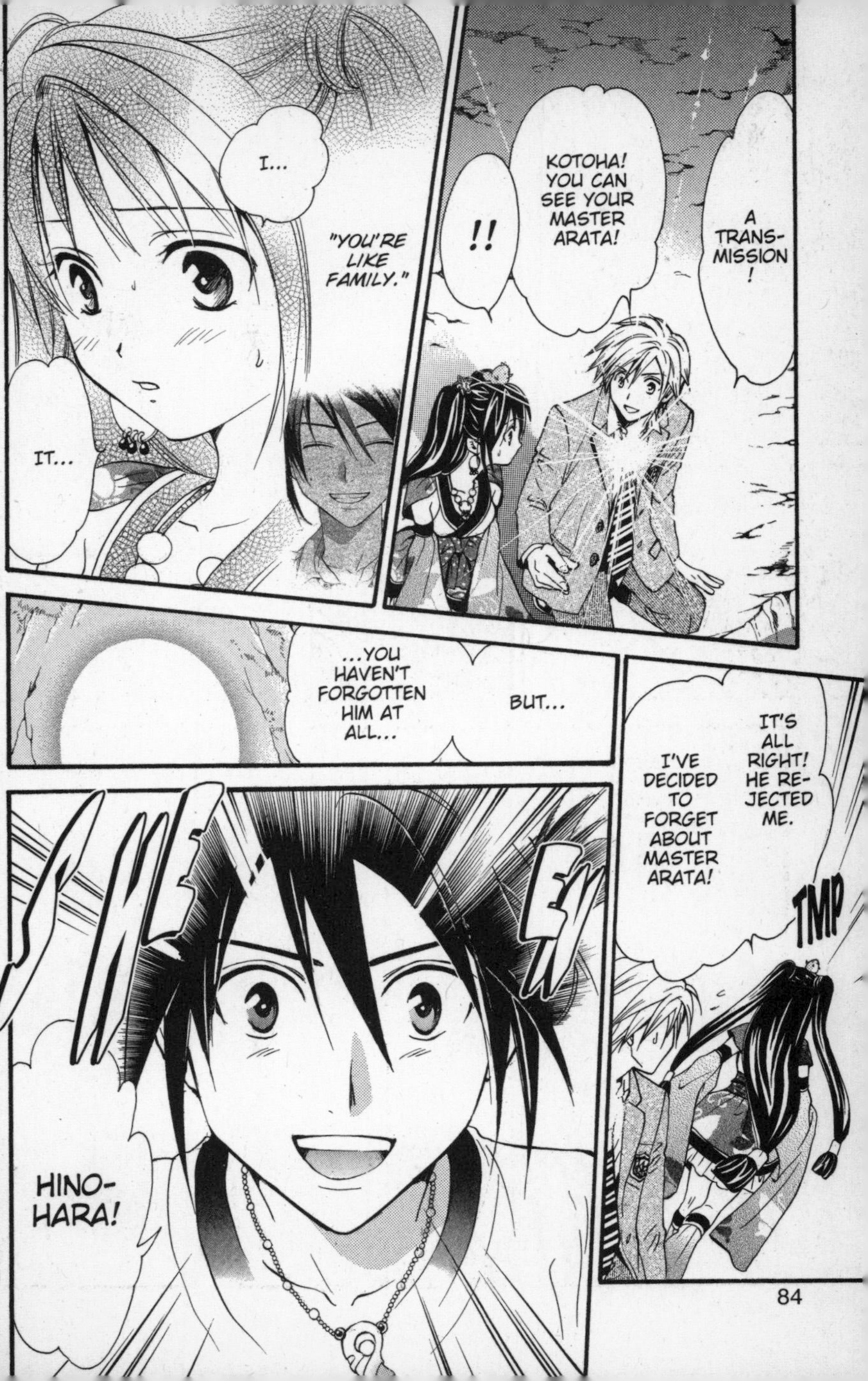
A TRANS-MISSION!
KOTOHA! YOU CAN SEE YOUR MASTER ARATA!
!!
I...
"YOU'RE LIKE FAMILY."
IT...
IT'S ALL RIGHT! HE RE-JECTED ME.
I'VE DECIDED TO FORGET ABOUT MASTER ARATA!
TMP
BUT...
...YOU HAVEN'T FORGOTTEN HIM AT ALL...
HINO-HARA!

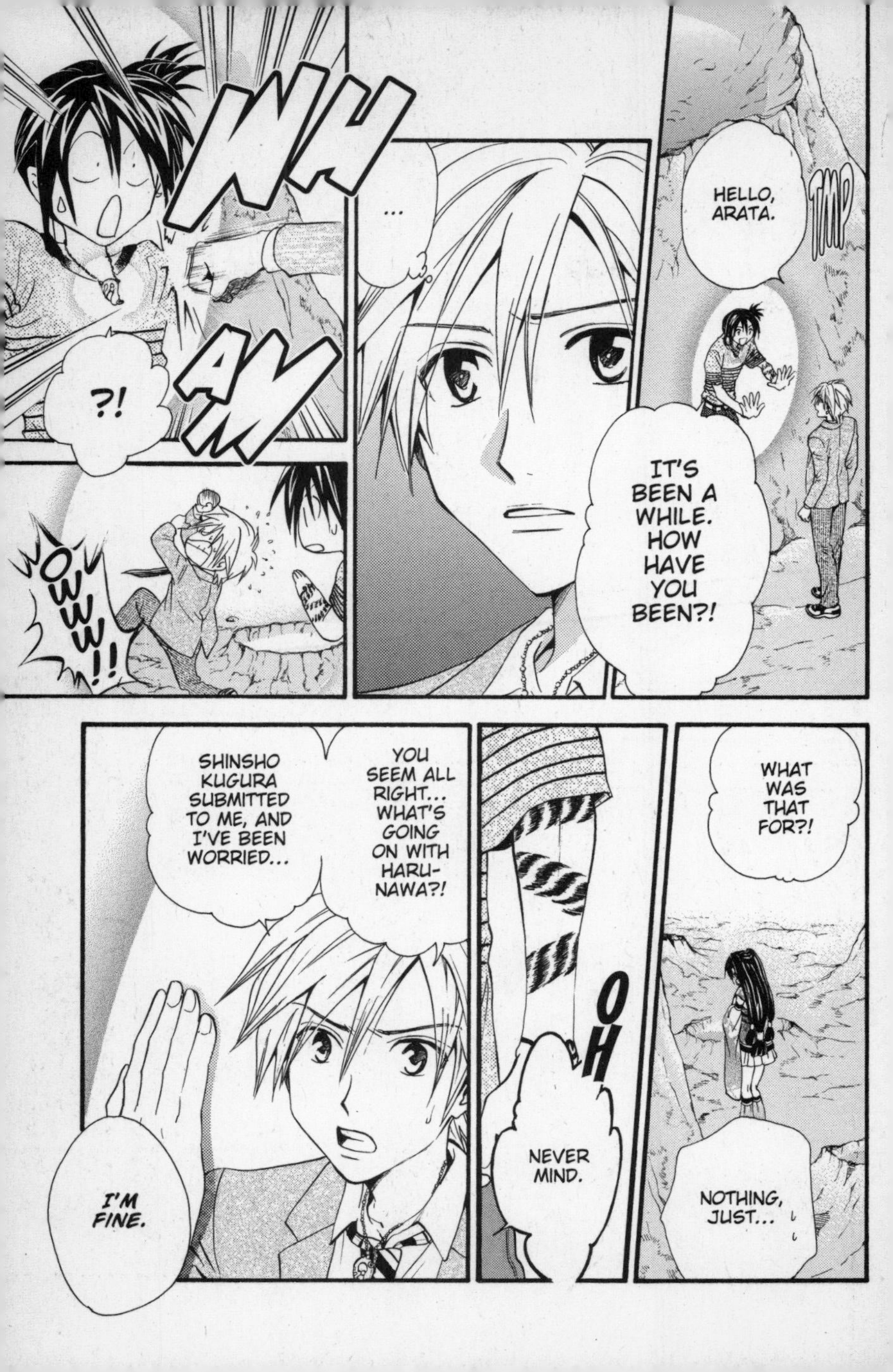
TMP
HELLO, ARATA.
IT'S BEEN A WHILE. HOW HAVE YOU BEEN?!
...
WHAM
?!
OWWW!!
WHAT WAS THAT FOR?!
NOTHING, JUST...
OH
NEVER MIND.
YOU SEEM ALL RIGHT... WHAT'S GOING ON WITH HARU-NAWA?!
SHINSHO KUGURA SUBMITTED TO ME, AND I'VE BEEN WORRIED...
I'M FINE.

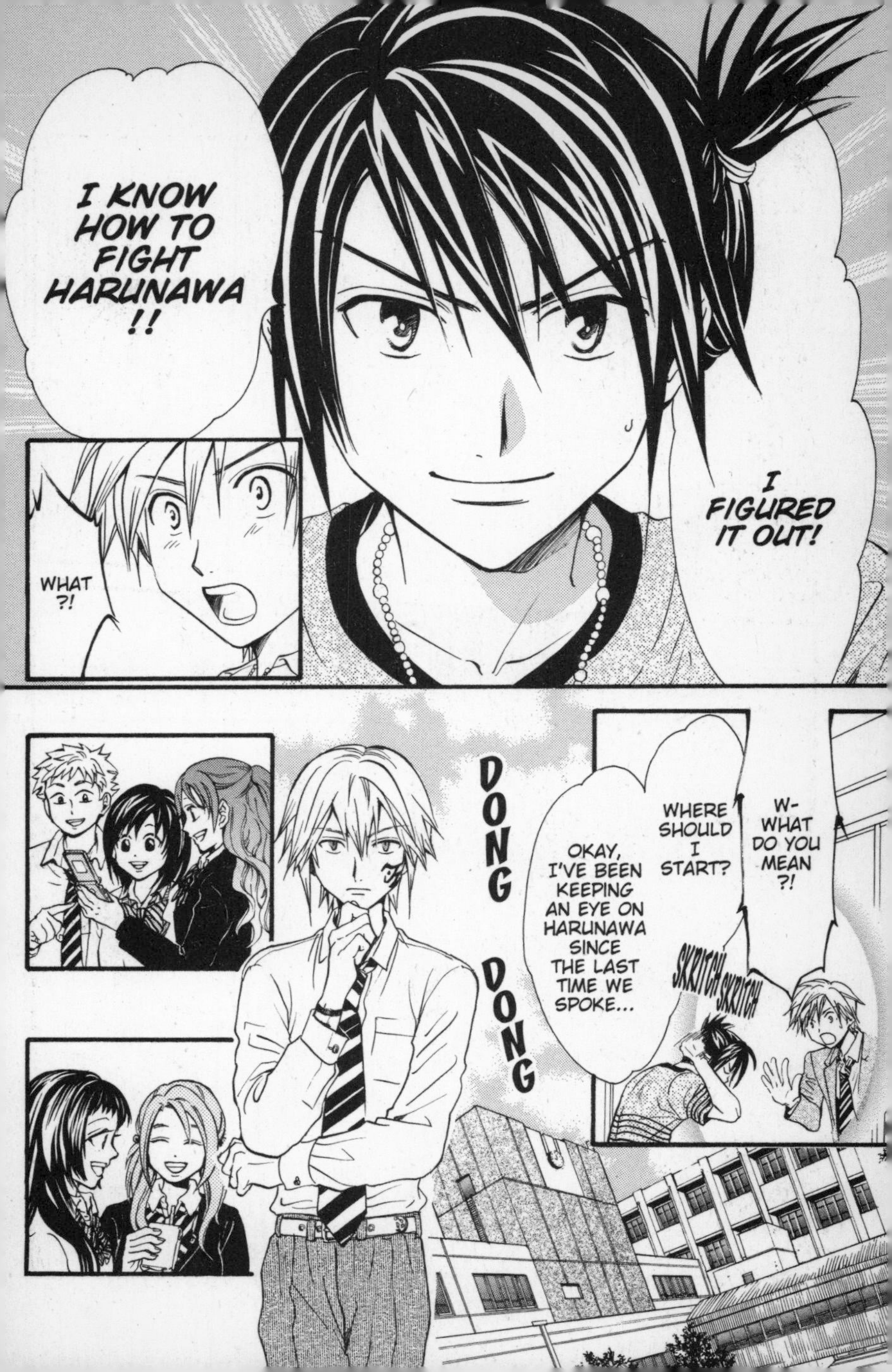
I FIGURED IT OUT!
I KNOW HOW TO FIGHT HARUNAWA!!
WHAT?!
W-WHAT DO YOU MEAN?!
SKRITCH SKRITCH
WHERE SHOULD I START?
OKAY, I'VE BEEN KEEPING AN EYE ON HARUNAWA SINCE THE LAST TIME WE SPOKE...
DONG DONG DONG

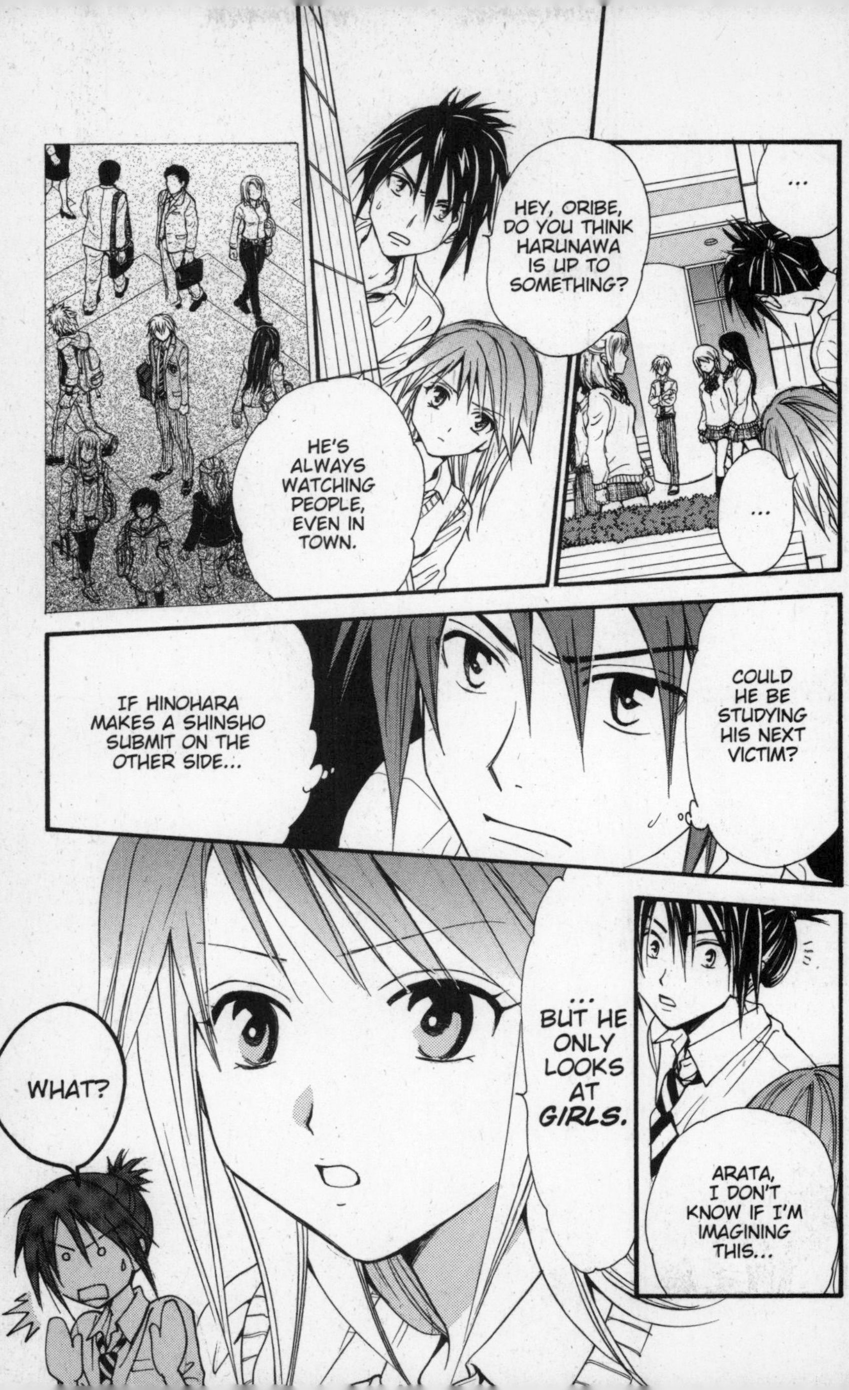
...
...
HEY, ORIBE, DO YOU THINK HARUNAWA IS UP TO SOMETHING?
HE'S ALWAYS WATCHING PEOPLE, EVEN IN TOWN.
COULD HE BE STUDYING HIS NEXT VICTIM?
IF HINOHARA MAKES A SHINSHO SUBMIT ON THE OTHER SIDE...
ARATA, I DON'T KNOW IF I'M IMAGINING THIS...
... BUT HE ONLY LOOKS AT *GIRLS*.
WHAT?

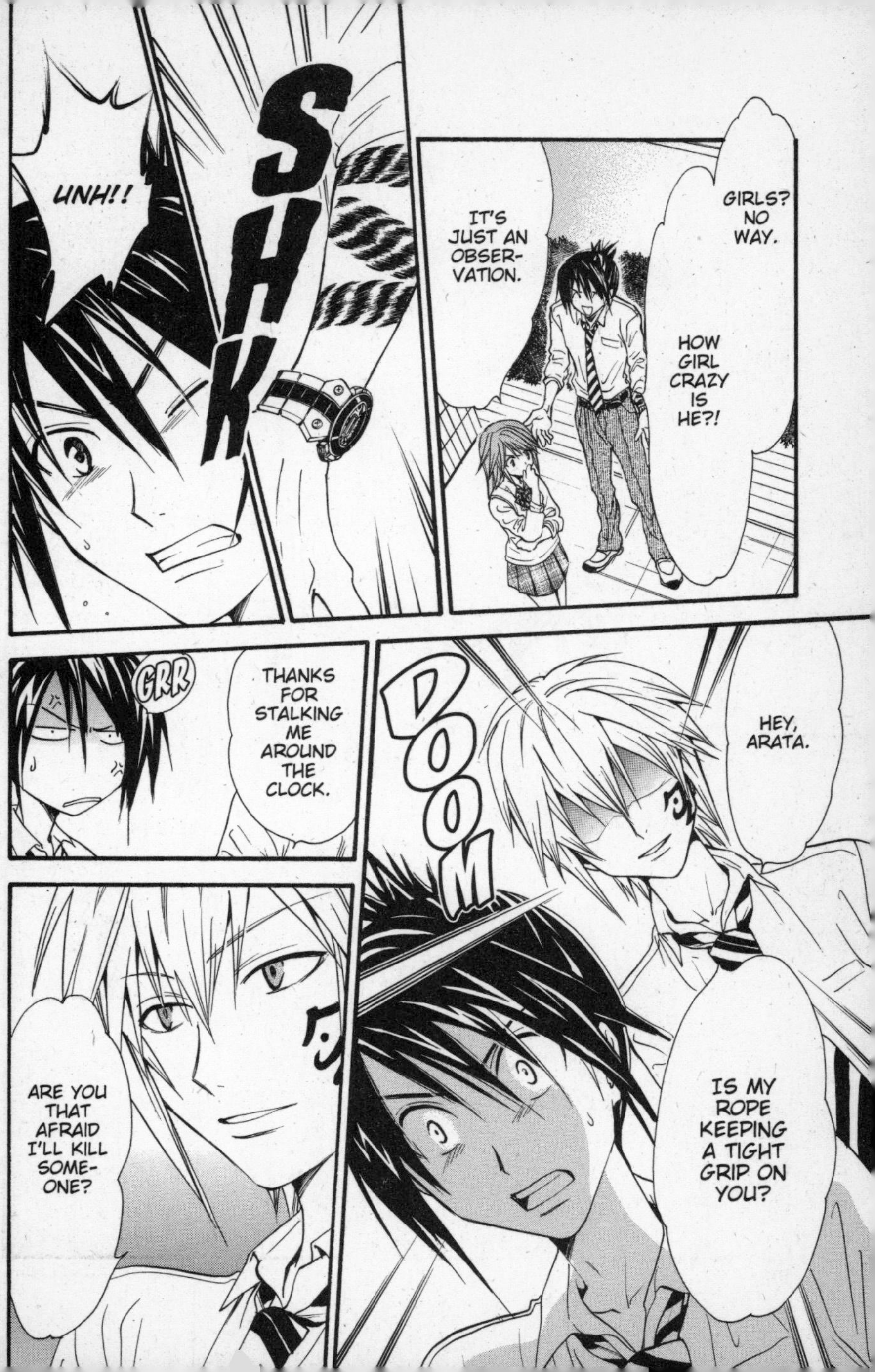
GIRLS? NO WAY.
HOW GIRL CRAZY IS HE?!
IT'S JUST AN OBSERVATION.
SHK
UNH!!
DOOM
HEY, ARATA.
GRR
THANKS FOR STALKING ME AROUND THE CLOCK.
IS MY ROPE KEEPING A TIGHT GRIP ON YOU?
ARE YOU THAT AFRAID I'LL KILL SOMEONE?

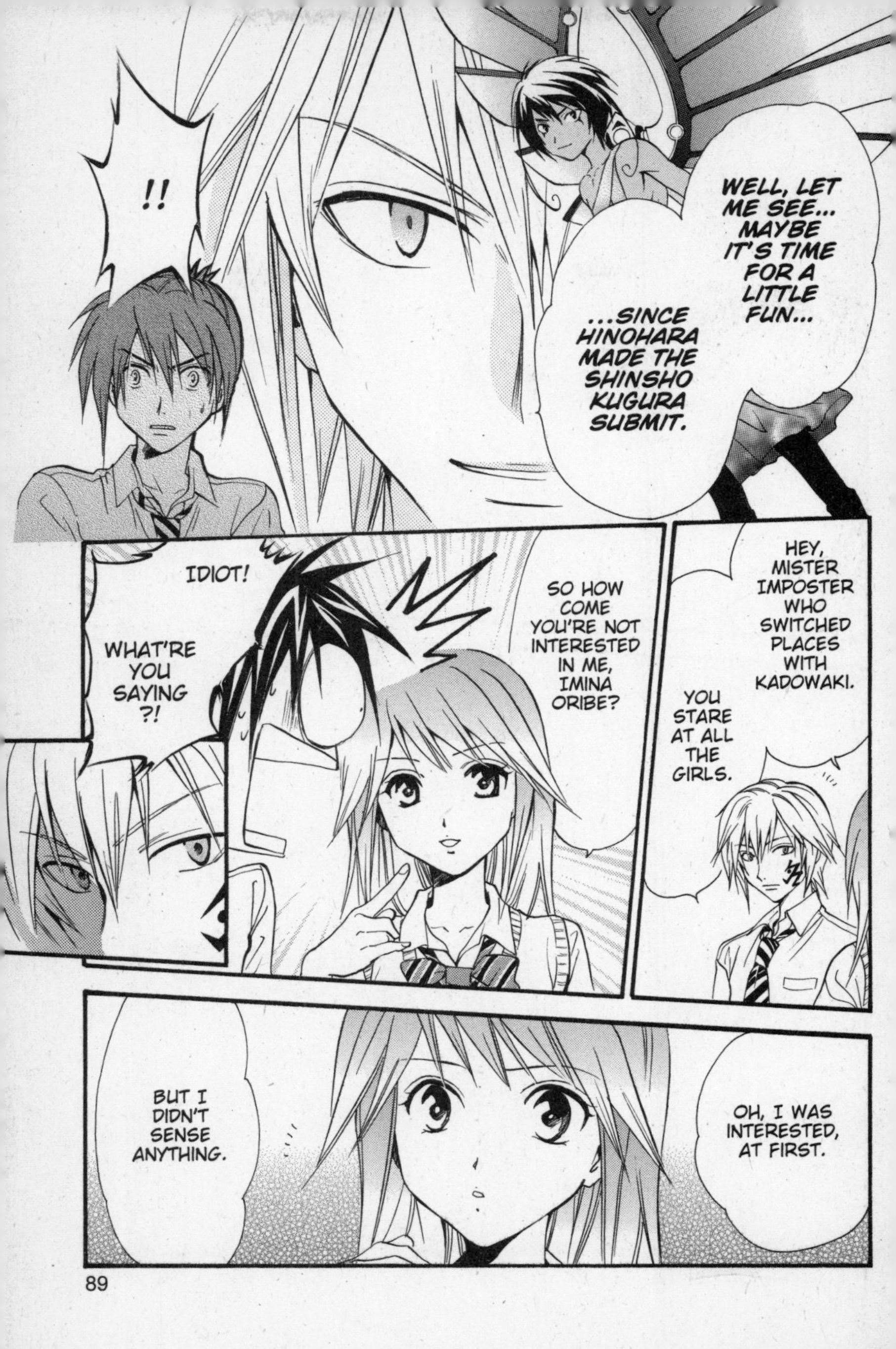
WELL, LET ME SEE... MAYBE IT'S TIME FOR A LITTLE FUN...
...SINCE HINOHARA MADE THE SHINSHO KUGURA SUBMIT.
!!
HEY, MISTER IMPOSTER WHO SWITCHED PLACES WITH KADOWAKI.
YOU STARE AT ALL THE GIRLS.
SO HOW COME YOU'RE NOT INTERESTED IN ME, IMINA ORIBE?
IDIOT!
WHAT'RE YOU SAYING ?!
OH, I WAS INTERESTED, AT FIRST.
BUT I DIDN'T SENSE ANYTHING.

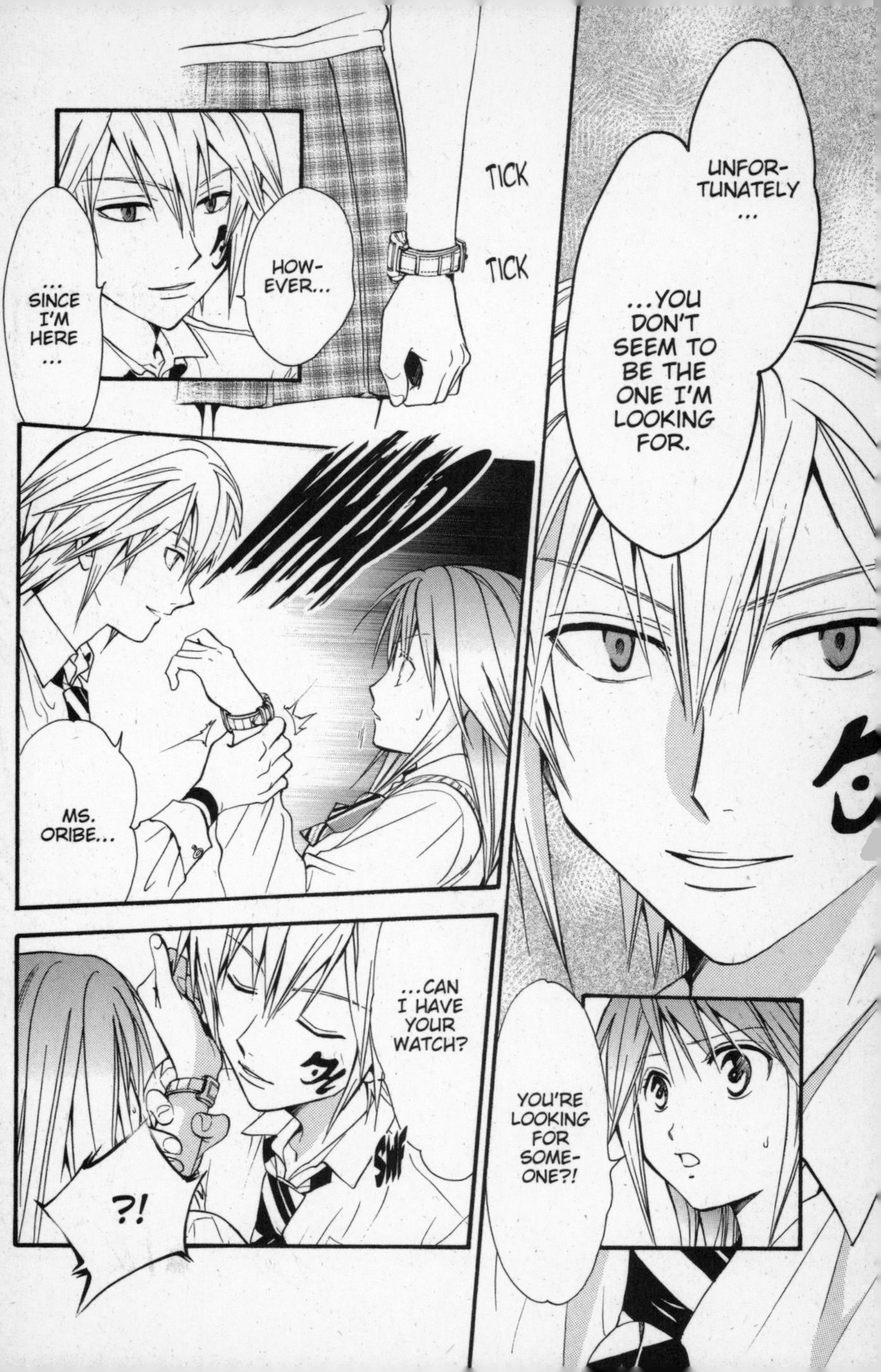
UNFOR-TUNATELY ...
...YOU DON'T SEEM TO BE THE ONE I'M LOOKING FOR.
YOU'RE LOOKING FOR SOME-ONE?!
TICK
TICK
HOW-EVER...
... SINCE I'M HERE ...
MS. ORIBE...
...CAN I HAVE YOUR WATCH?
SMF
?!

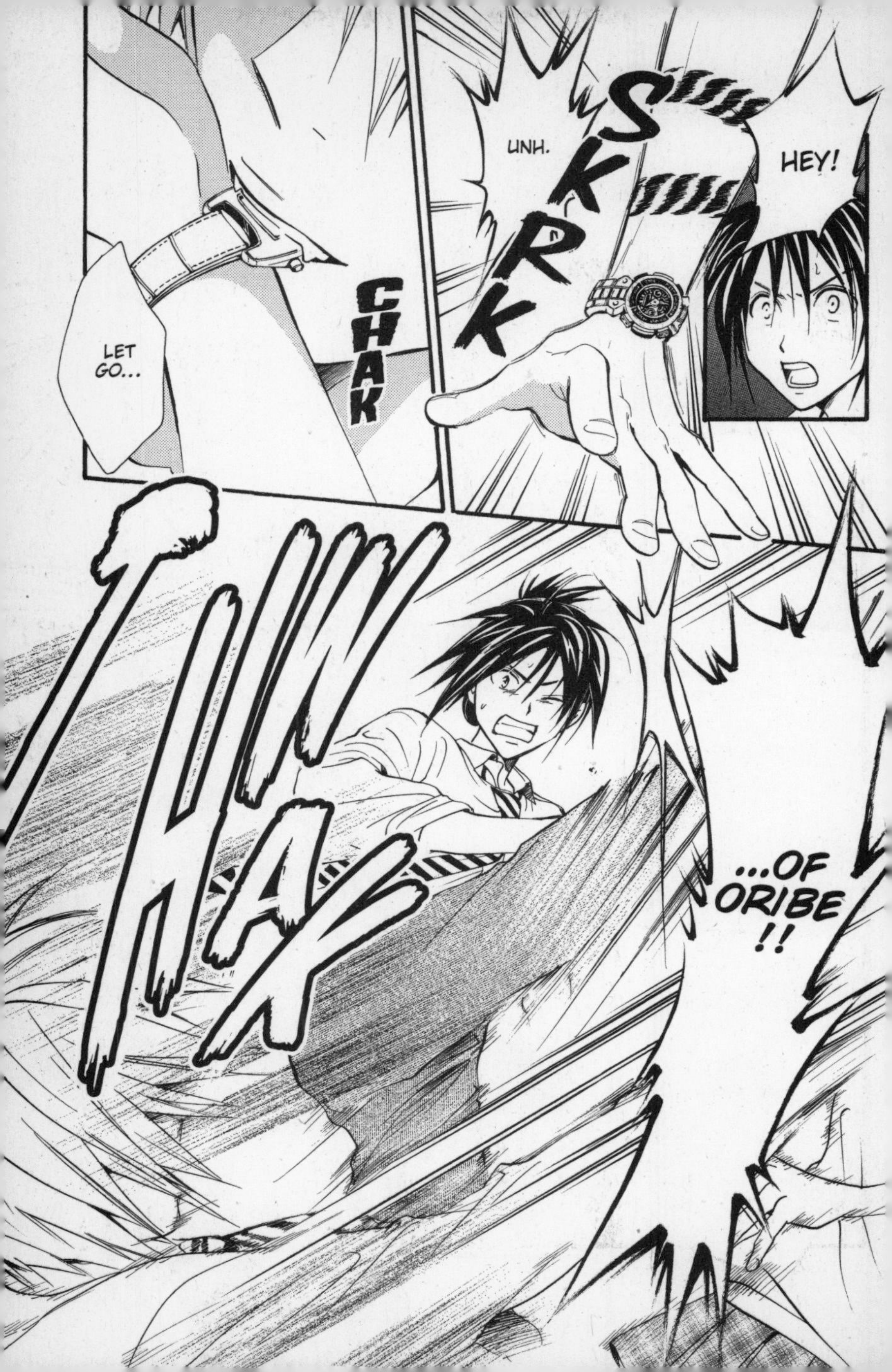
HEY!
SKRRK
UNH.
CHAK
LET GO...
...OF ORIBE!!

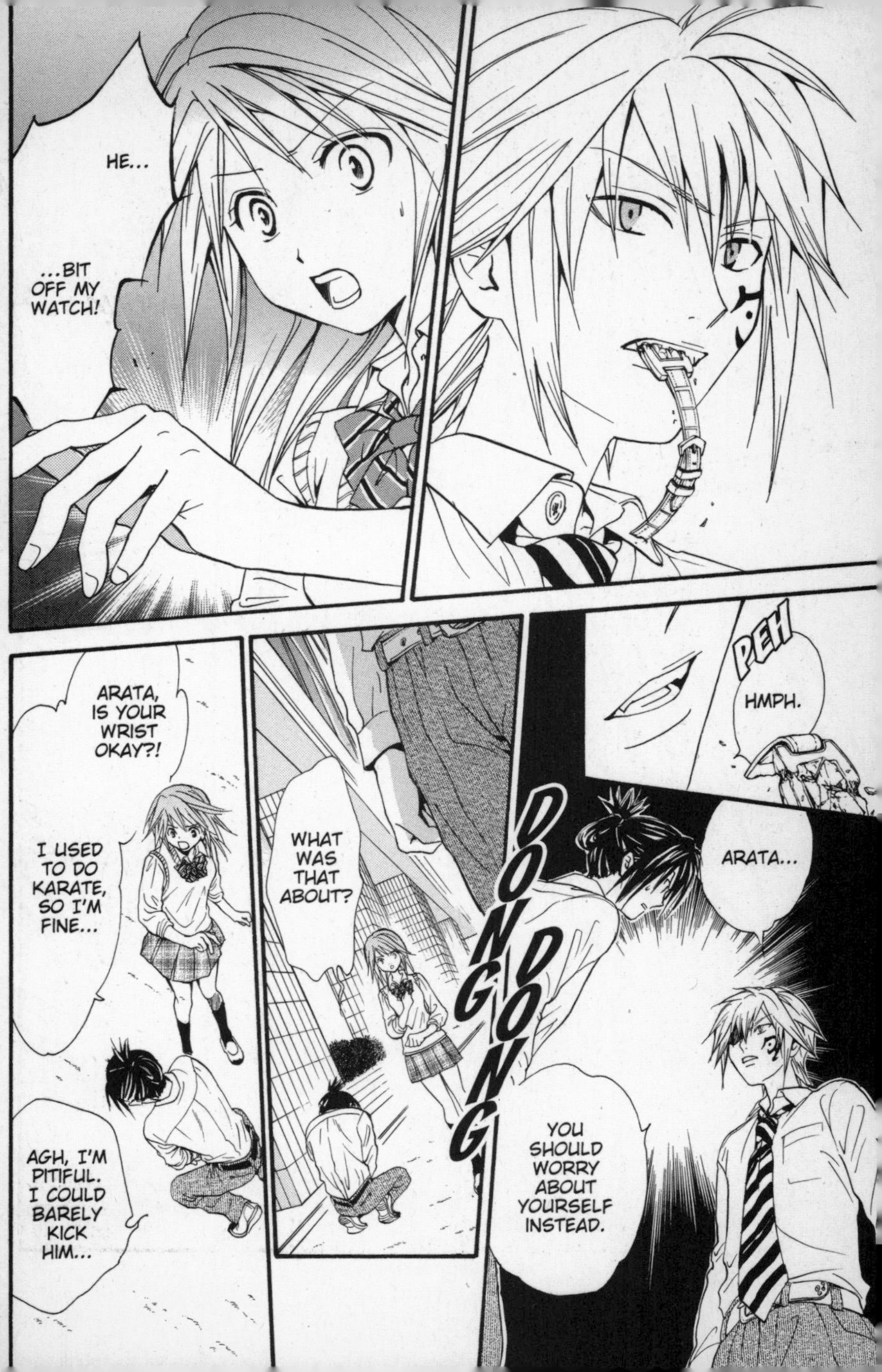
HE...
...BIT OFF MY WATCH!
PEH
HMPH.
ARATA...
DONG DONG
YOU SHOULD WORRY ABOUT YOURSELF INSTEAD.
WHAT WAS THAT ABOUT?
ARATA, IS YOUR WRIST OKAY?!
I USED TO DO KARATE, SO I'M FINE...
AGH, I'M PITIFUL. I COULD BARELY KICK HIM...

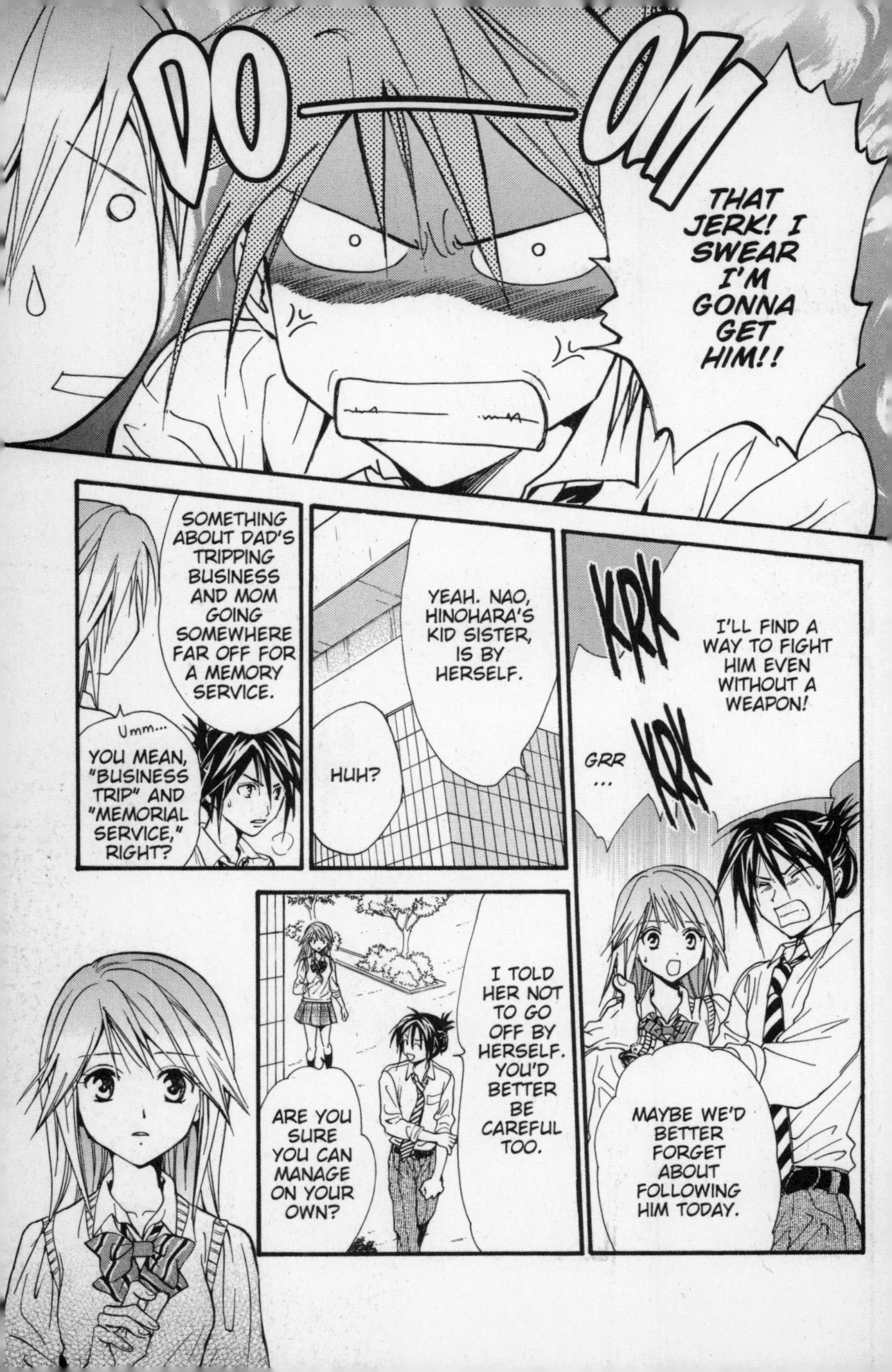
DO—OM
THAT JERK! I SWEAR I'M GONNA GET HIM!!
I'LL FIND A WAY TO FIGHT HIM EVEN WITHOUT A WEAPON!
KRK
KRK
GRR...
MAYBE WE'D BETTER FORGET ABOUT FOLLOWING HIM TODAY.
YEAH. NAO, HINOHARA'S KID SISTER, IS BY HERSELF.
HUH?
SOMETHING ABOUT DAD'S TRIPPING BUSINESS AND MOM GOING SOMEWHERE FAR OFF FOR A MEMORY SERVICE.
Umm...
YOU MEAN, "BUSINESS TRIP" AND "MEMORIAL SERVICE," RIGHT?
I TOLD HER NOT TO GO OFF BY HERSELF. YOU'D BETTER BE CAREFUL TOO.
ARE YOU SURE YOU CAN MANAGE ON YOUR OWN?

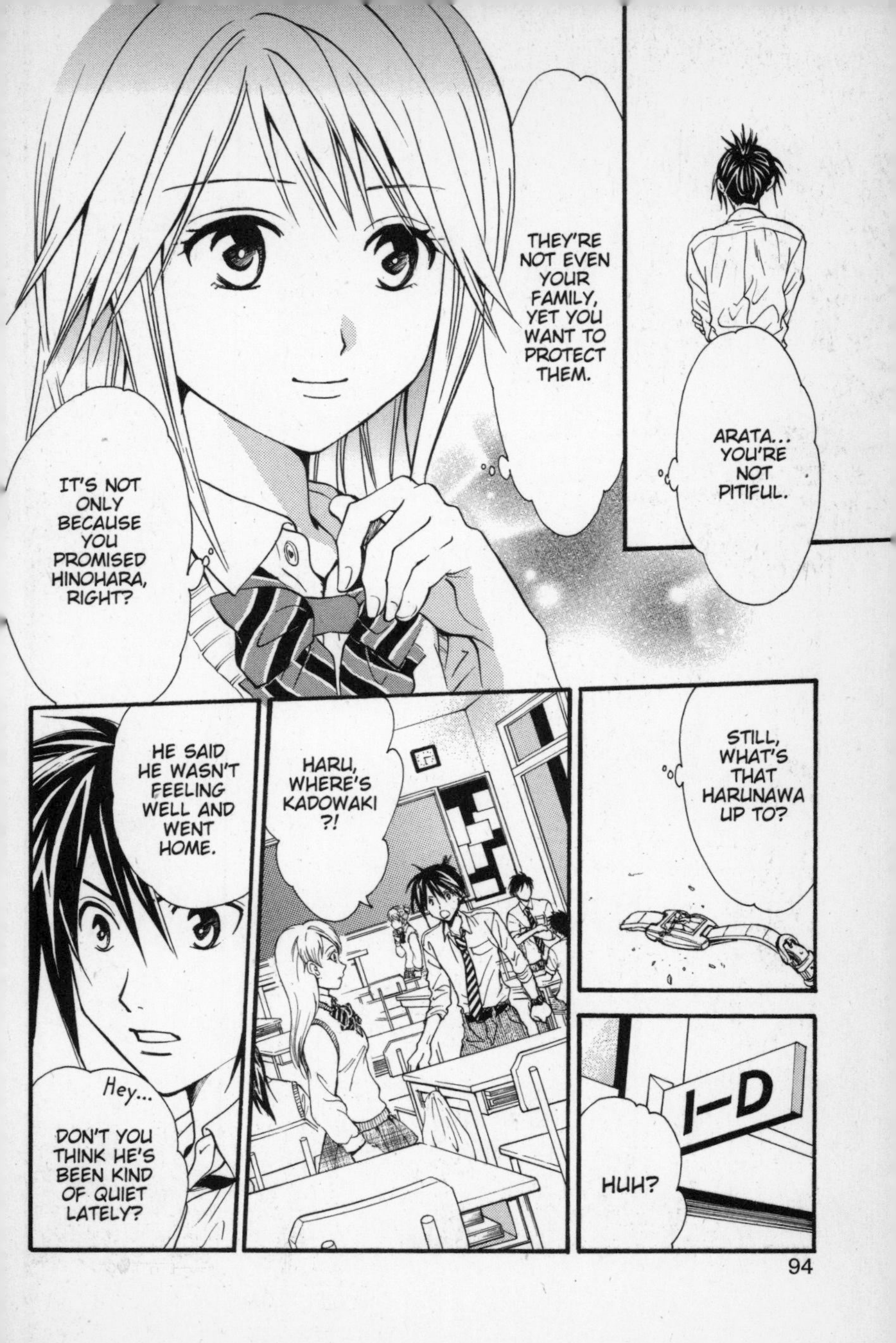
ARATA... YOU'RE NOT PITIFUL.
THEY'RE NOT EVEN YOUR FAMILY, YET YOU WANT TO PROTECT THEM.
IT'S NOT ONLY BECAUSE YOU PROMISED HINOHARA, RIGHT?
STILL, WHAT'S THAT HARUNAWA UP TO?
I-D
HUH?
HARU, WHERE'S KADOWAKI ?!
HE SAID HE WASN'T FEELING WELL AND WENT HOME.
Hey...
DON'T YOU THINK HE'S BEEN KIND OF QUIET LATELY?

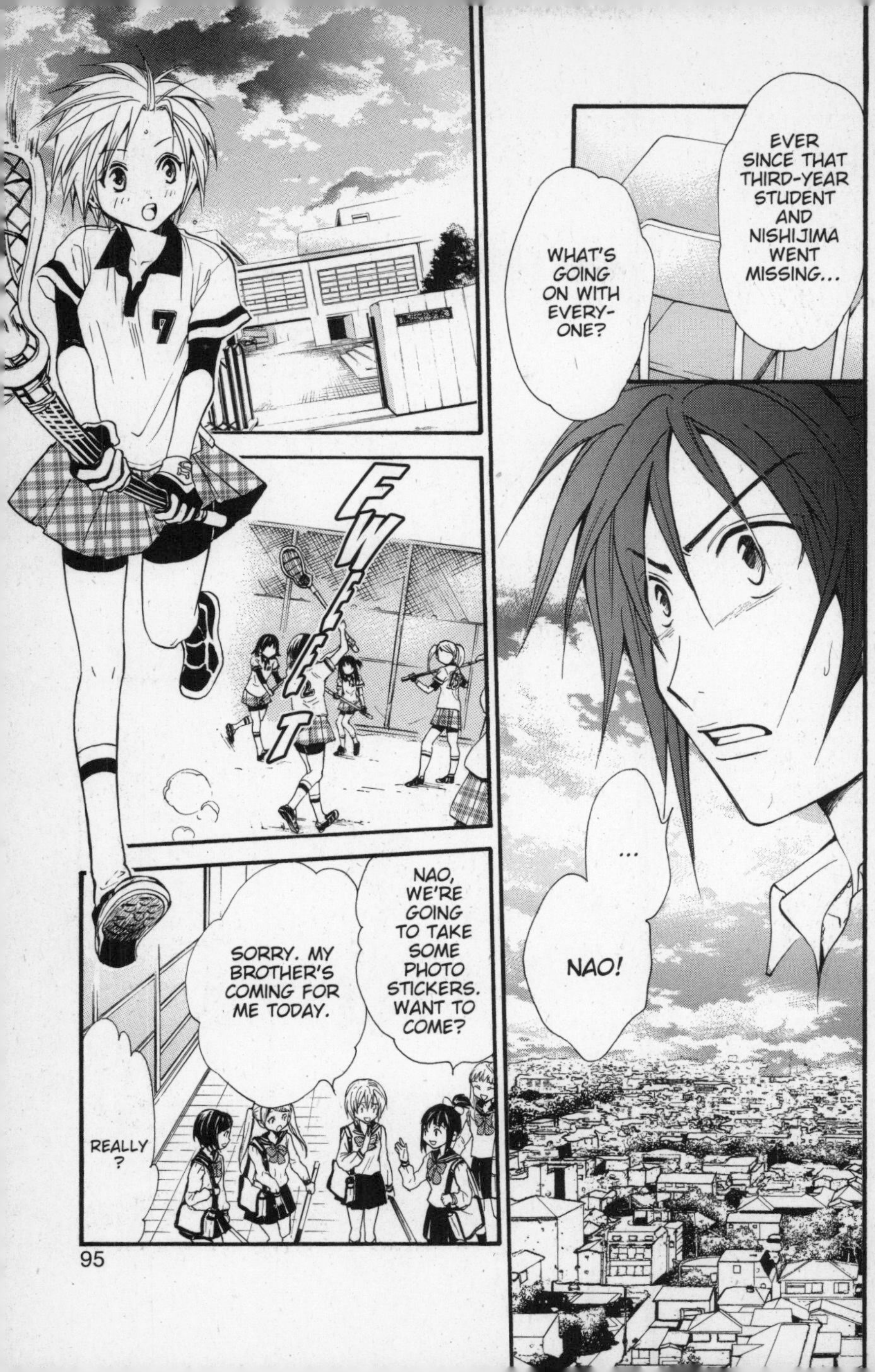
EVER SINCE THAT THIRD-YEAR STUDENT AND NISHIJIMA WENT MISSING...
WHAT'S GOING ON WITH EVERY-ONE?
...
NAO!
FWEEEET
NAO, WE'RE GOING TO TAKE SOME PHOTO STICKERS. WANT TO COME?
SORRY. MY BROTHER'S COMING FOR ME TODAY.
REALLY?

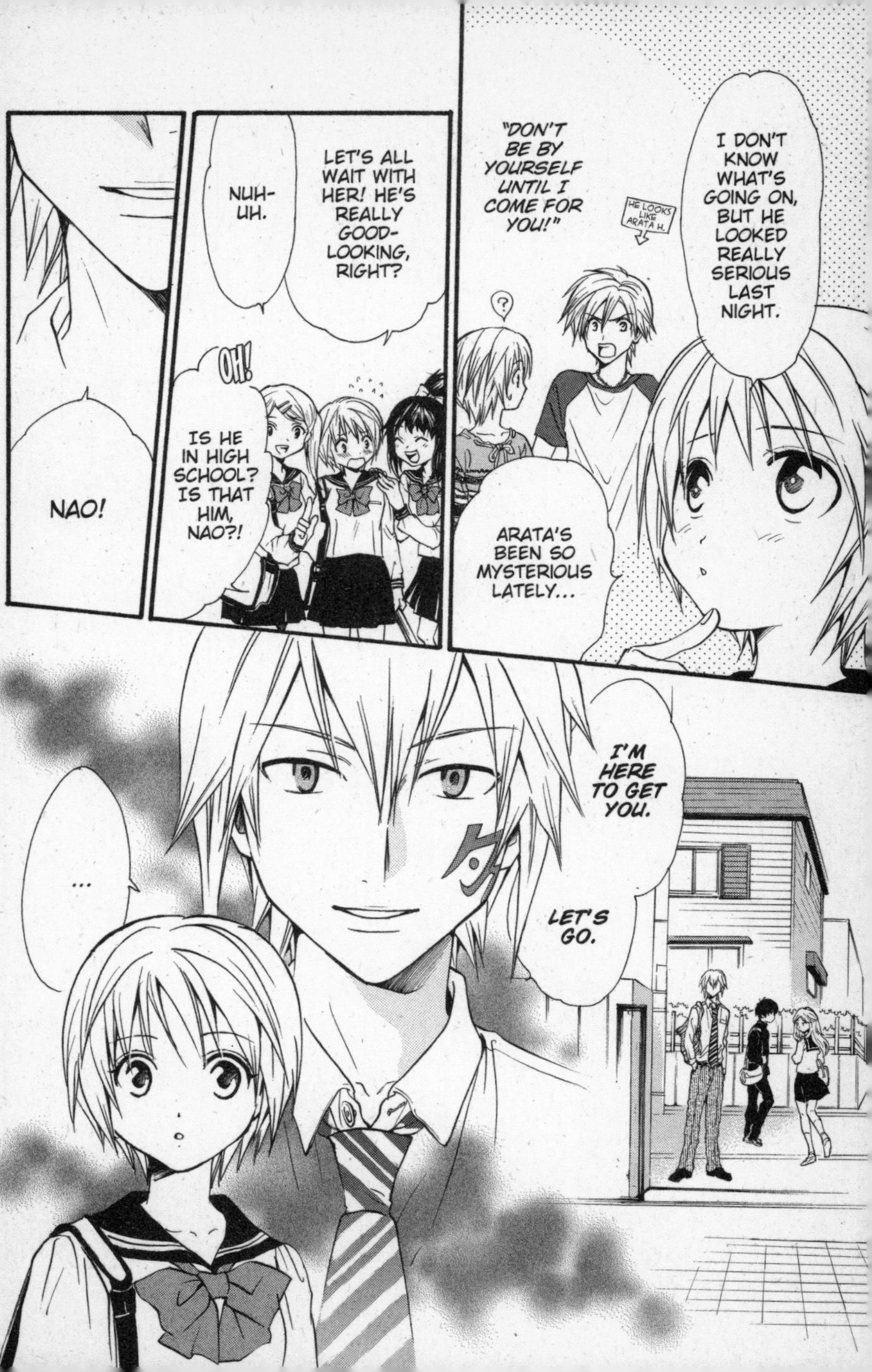

I DON'T KNOW WHAT'S GOING ON, BUT HE LOOKED REALLY SERIOUS LAST NIGHT.
"DON'T BE BY YOURSELF UNTIL I COME FOR YOU!"
HE LOOKS LIKE ARATA H.
ARATA'S BEEN SO MYSTERIOUS LATELY...
LET'S ALL WAIT WITH HER! HE'S REALLY GOOD-LOOKING, RIGHT?
NUH-UH.
OH!
IS HE IN HIGH SCHOOL? IS THAT HIM, NAO?!
NAO!
I'M HERE TO GET YOU.
LET'S GO.
...

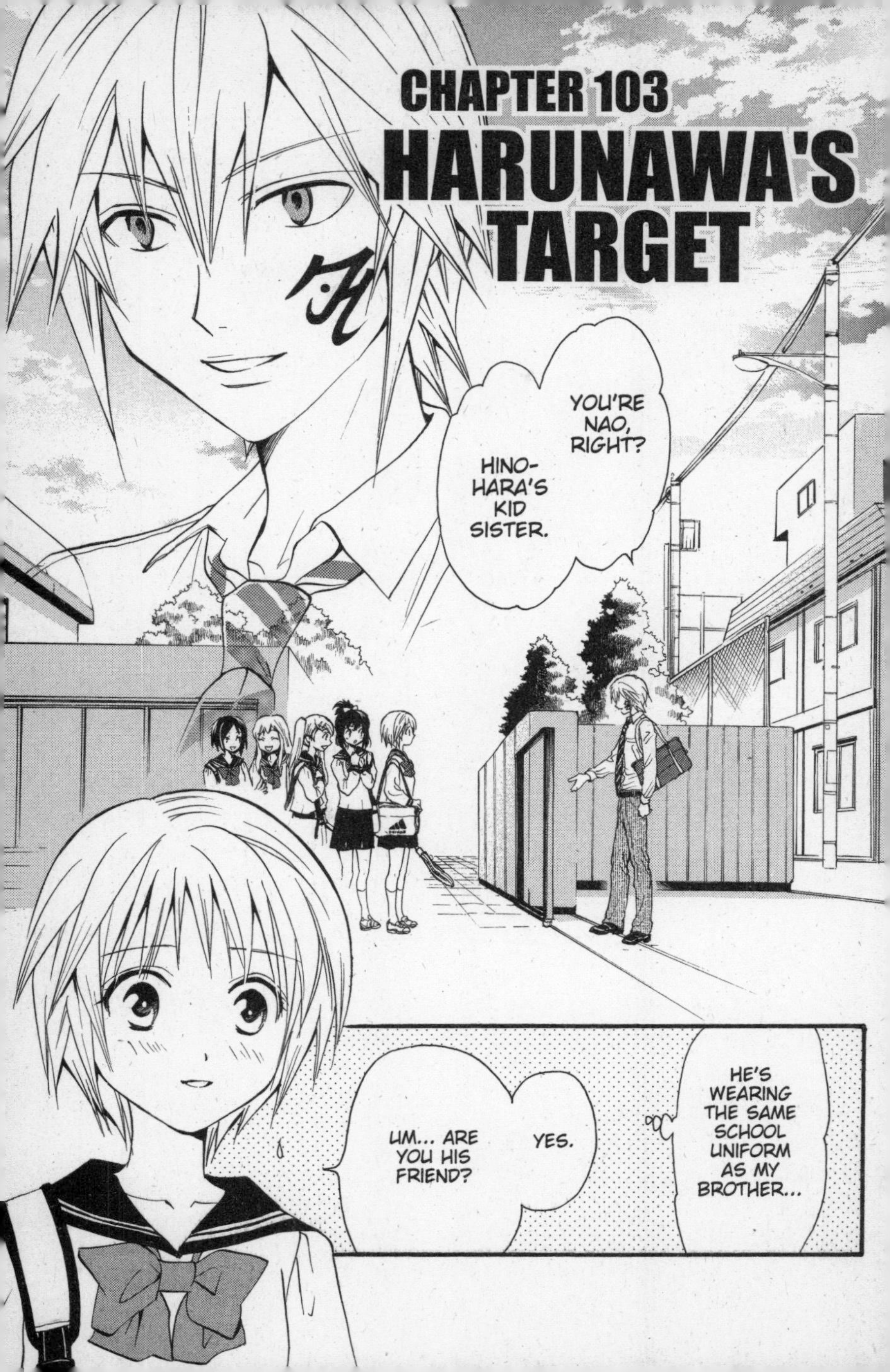
CHAPTER 103
HARUNAWA'S TARGET
YOU'RE NAO, RIGHT?
HINO-HARA'S KID SISTER.
HE'S WEARING THE SAME SCHOOL UNIFORM AS MY BROTHER...
YES.
UM... ARE YOU HIS FRIEND?

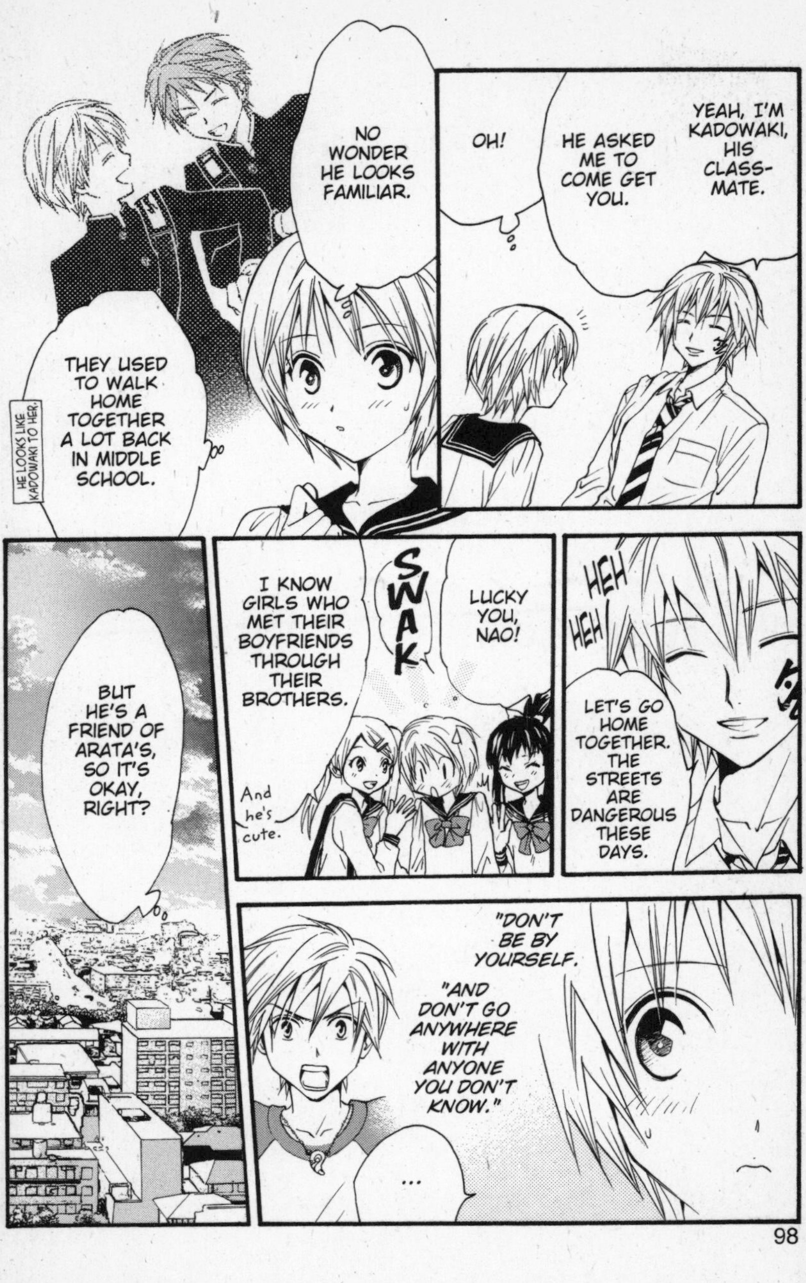
YEAH, I'M KADOWAKI, HIS CLASSMATE.
HE ASKED ME TO COME GET YOU.
OH!
NO WONDER HE LOOKS FAMILIAR.
THEY USED TO WALK HOME TOGETHER A LOT BACK IN MIDDLE SCHOOL.
HE LOOKS LIKE KADOWAKI TO HER.
HEH HEH
LET'S GO HOME TOGETHER. THE STREETS ARE DANGEROUS THESE DAYS.
LUCKY YOU, NAO!
SWAK
I KNOW GIRLS WHO MET THEIR BOYFRIENDS THROUGH THEIR BROTHERS.
And he's cute.
"DON'T BE BY YOURSELF.
"AND DON'T GO ANYWHERE WITH ANYONE YOU DON'T KNOW."
...
BUT HE'S A FRIEND OF ARATA'S, SO IT'S OKAY, RIGHT?

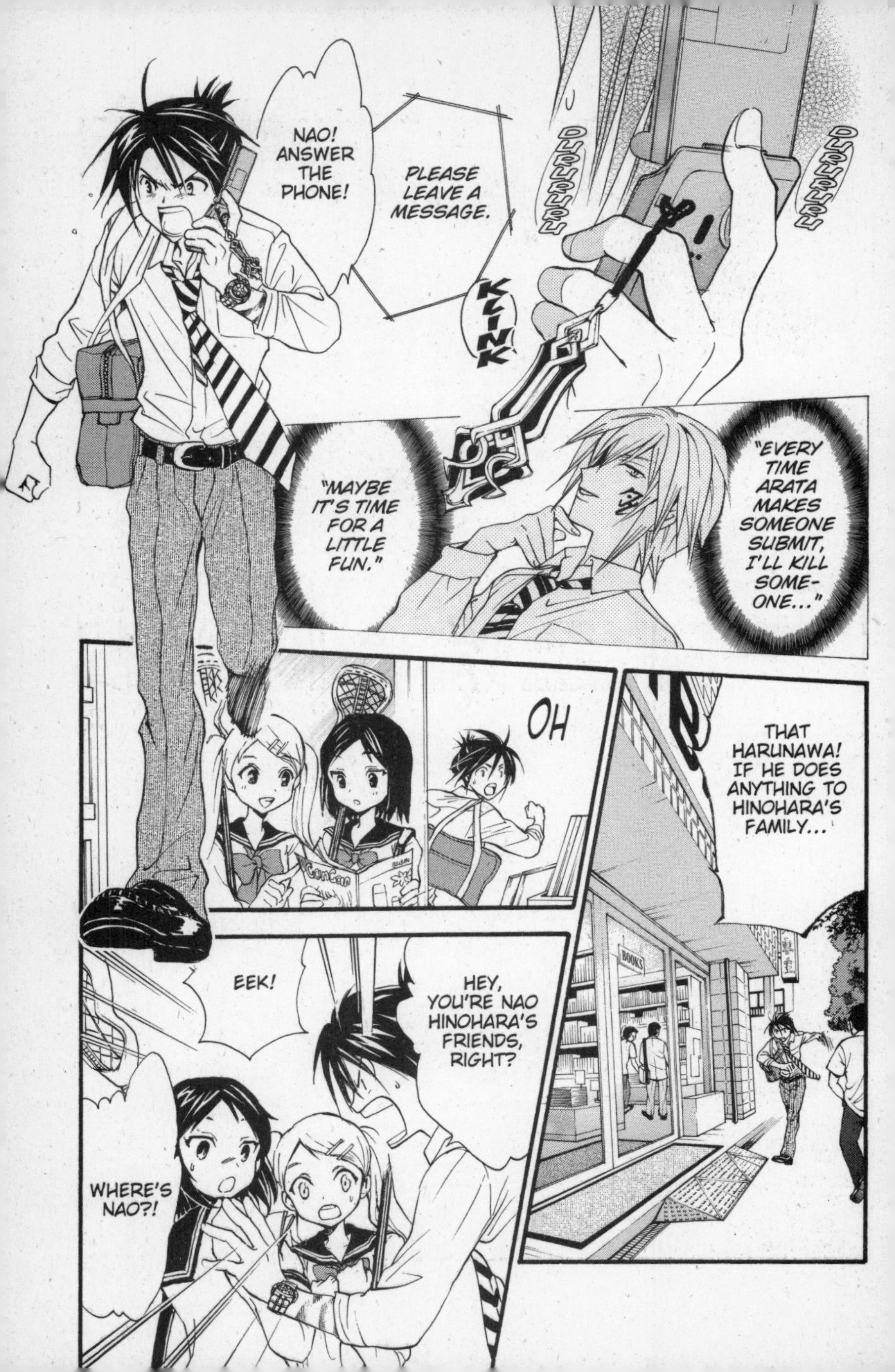
DURURURU
DURURURU
PLEASE LEAVE A MESSAGE.
KLINK
NAO! ANSWER THE PHONE!
"EVERY TIME ARATA MAKES SOMEONE SUBMIT, I'LL KILL SOME-ONE..."
"MAYBE IT'S TIME FOR A LITTLE FUN."
THAT HARUNAWA! IF HE DOES ANYTHING TO HINOHARA'S FAMILY...
OH
HEY, YOU'RE NAO HINOHARA'S FRIENDS, RIGHT?
EEK!
WHERE'S NAO?!

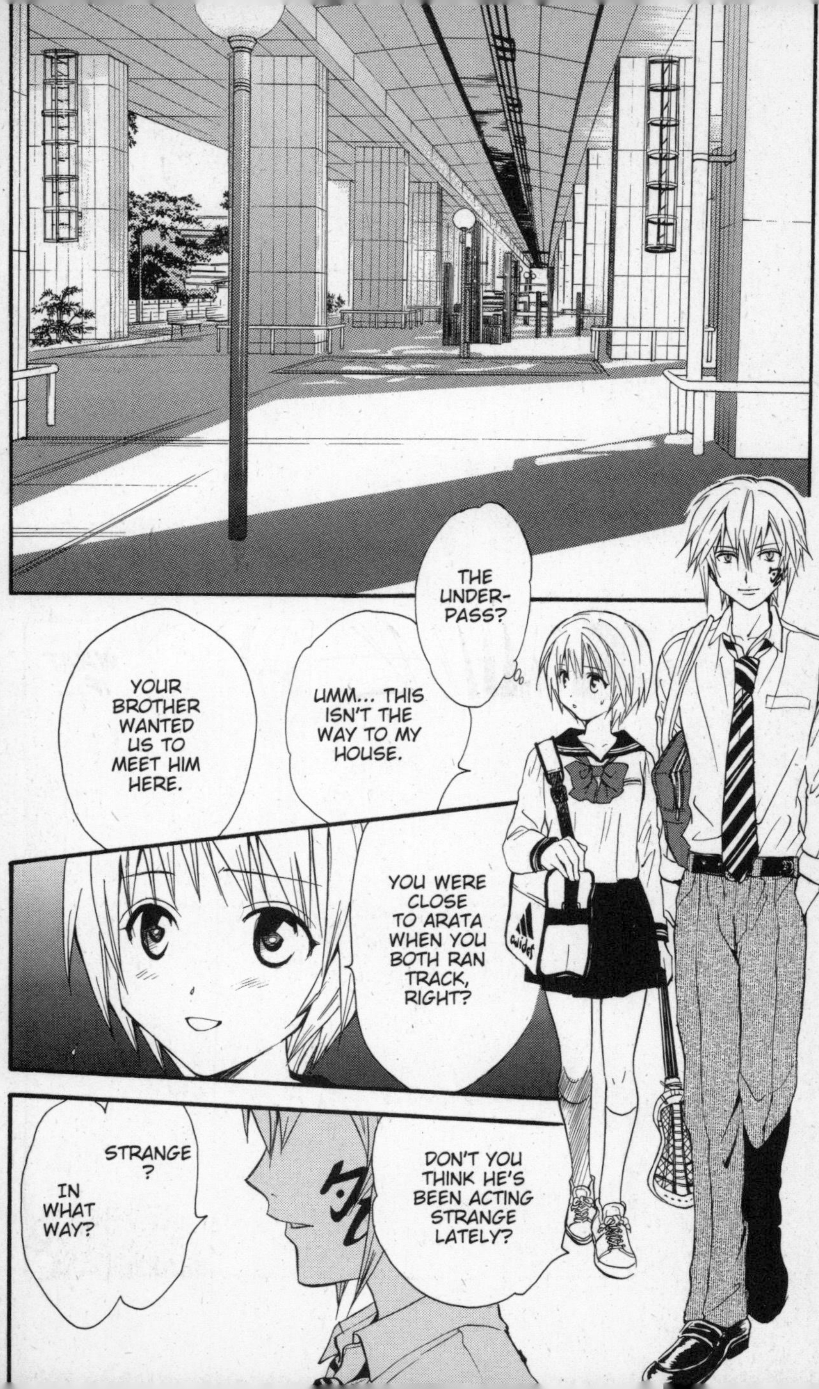
THE UNDER-PASS?
UMM... THIS ISN'T THE WAY TO MY HOUSE.
YOUR BROTHER WANTED US TO MEET HIM HERE.
YOU WERE CLOSE TO ARATA WHEN YOU BOTH RAN TRACK, RIGHT?
DON'T YOU THINK HE'S BEEN ACTING STRANGE LATELY?
STRANGE?
IN WHAT WAY?

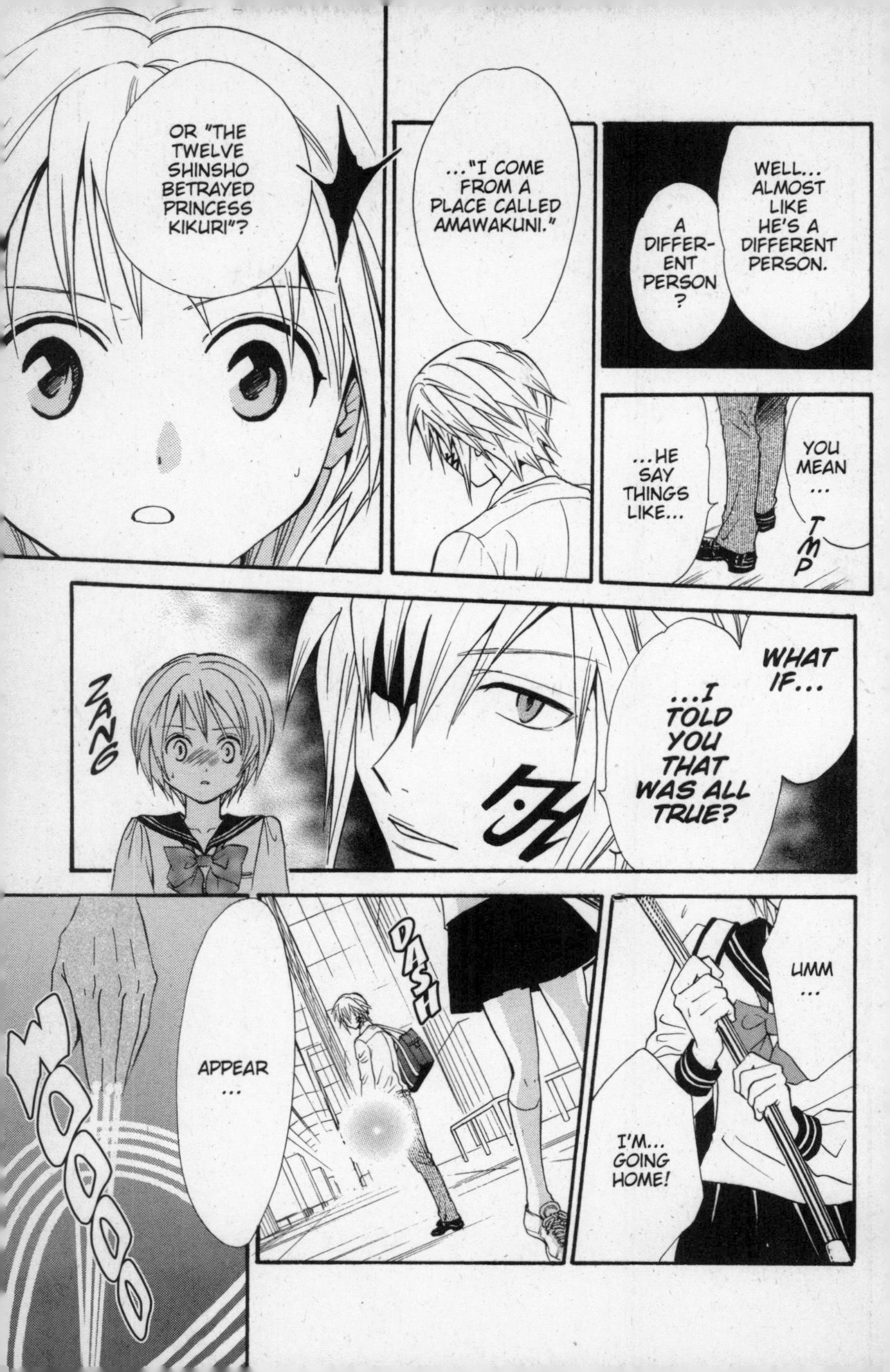
WELL... ALMOST LIKE HE'S A DIFFERENT PERSON.
A DIFFER-ENT PERSON?
YOU MEAN...
...HE SAY THINGS LIKE...
TMP
..."I COME FROM A PLACE CALLED AMAWAKUNI."
OR "THE TWELVE SHINSHO BETRAYED PRINCESS KIKURI"?
WHAT IF...
...I TOLD YOU THAT WAS ALL TRUE?
ZANG
UMM...
I'M... GOING HOME!
DASH
APPEAR...

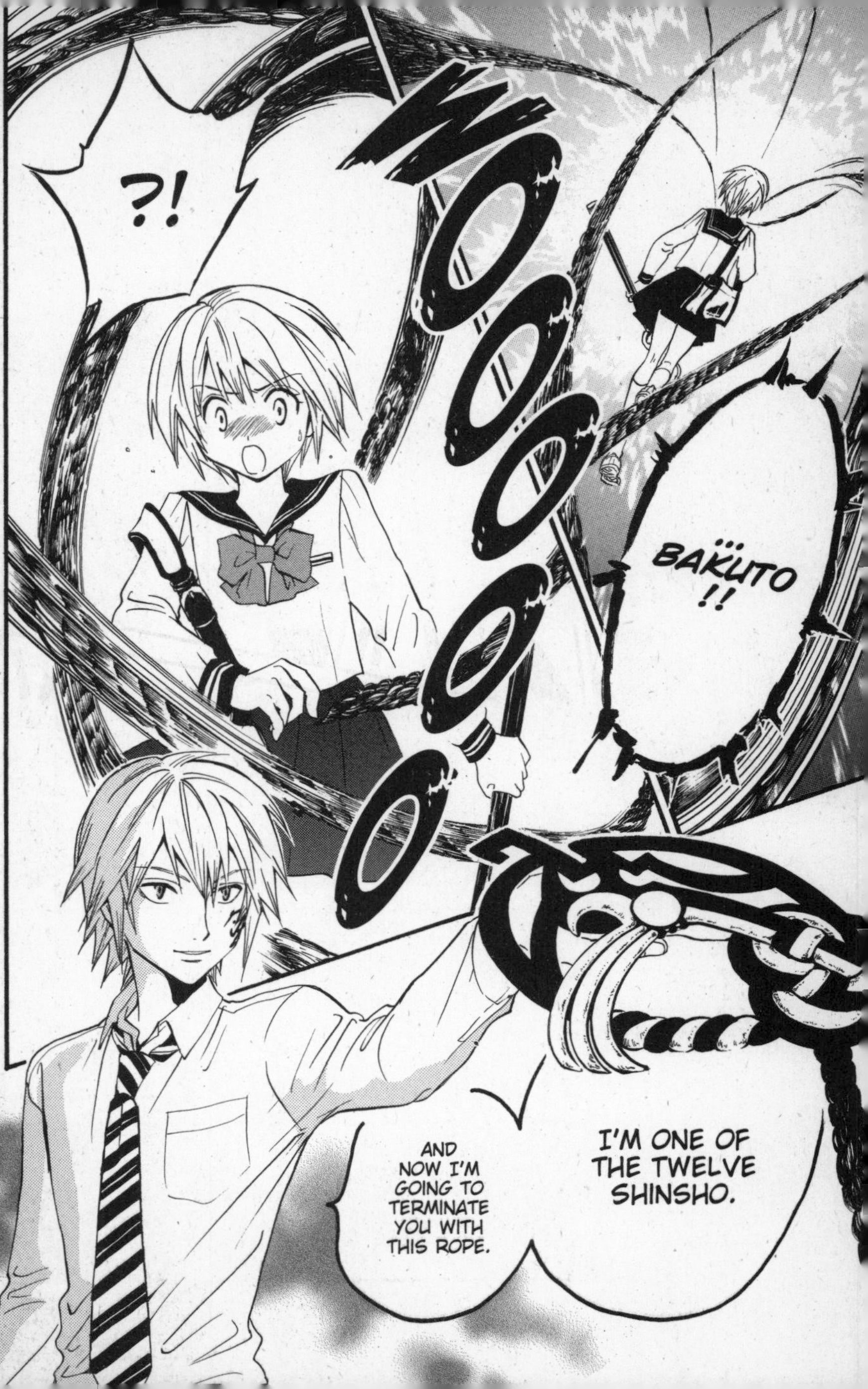
...BAKUTO!!
WOOOOOOO
?!
I'M ONE OF THE TWELVE SHINSHO.
AND NOW I'M GOING TO TERMINATE YOU WITH THIS ROPE.

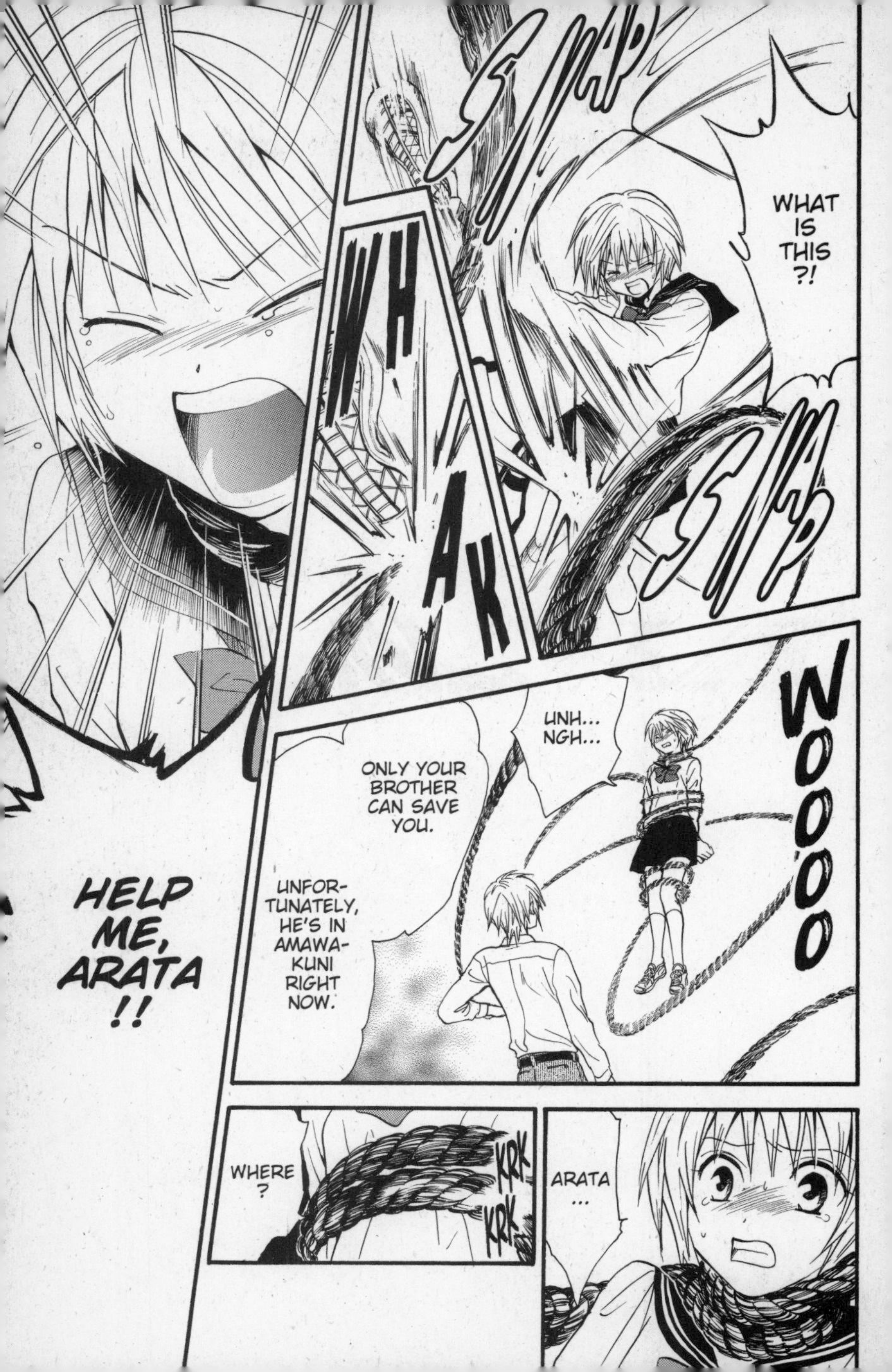

WHAT IS THIS ?!
WHAK
WOOOOO
UNH... NGH...
ONLY YOUR BROTHER CAN SAVE YOU.
UNFORTUNATELY, HE'S IN AMAWAKUNI RIGHT NOW.
ARATA ...
WHERE ?
KRK KRK
HELP ME, ARATA !!

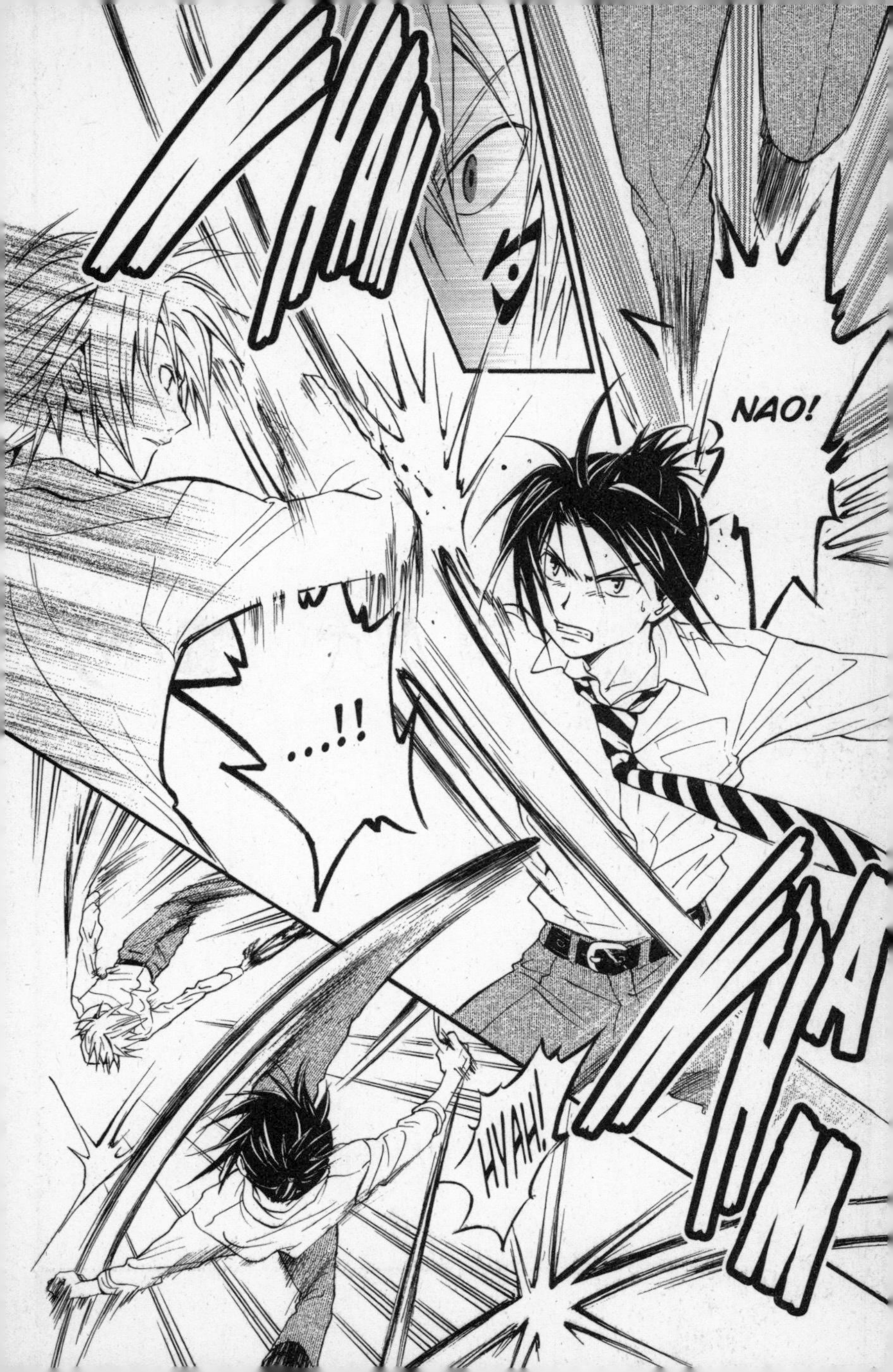
NAO!
...!!
HYAH!

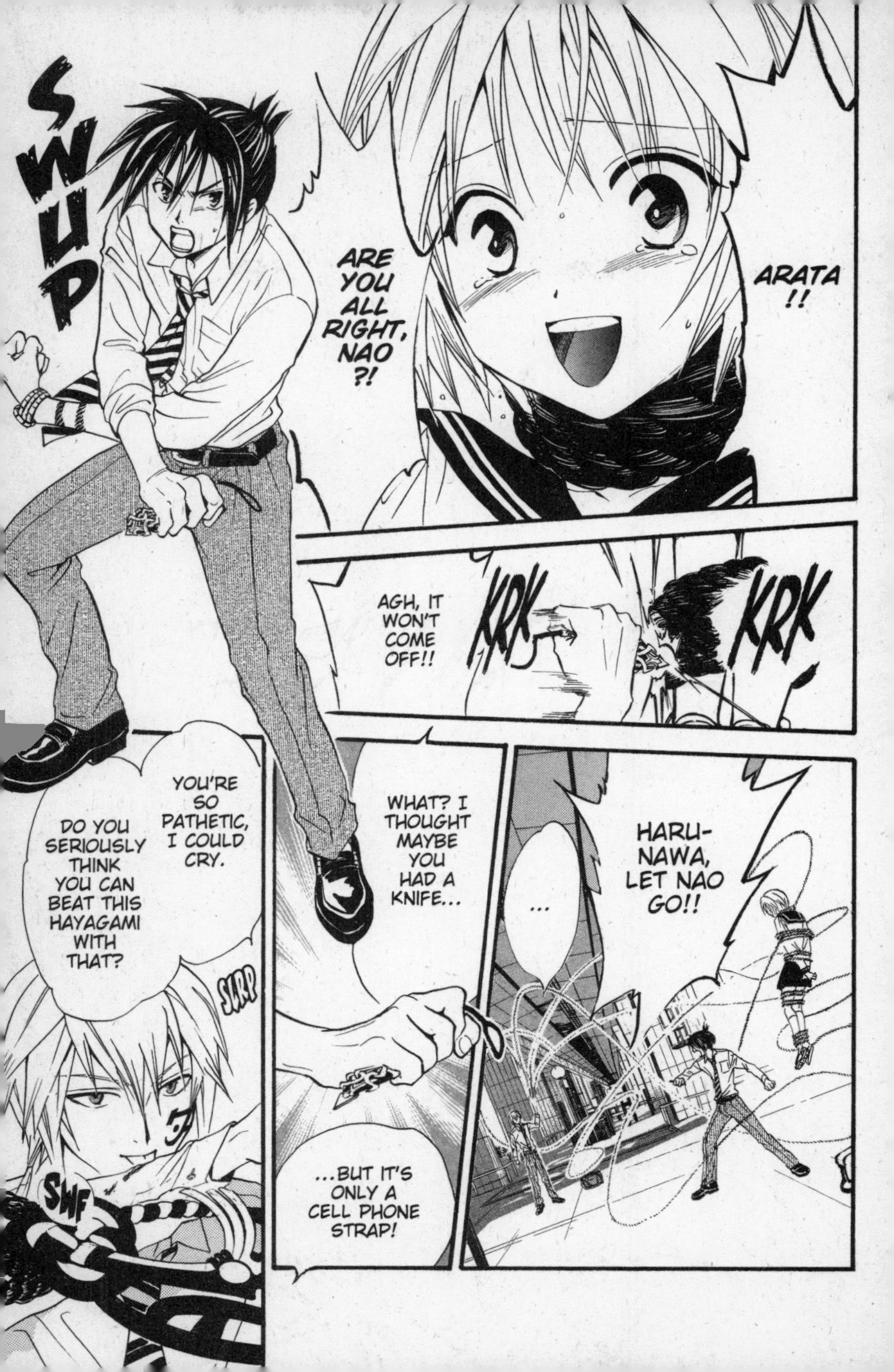
ARATA!!
ARE YOU ALL RIGHT, NAO?!
SWUP
KRK
KRK
AGH, IT WON'T COME OFF!!
HARU-NAWA, LET NAO GO!!
...
WHAT? I THOUGHT MAYBE YOU HAD A KNIFE...
...BUT IT'S ONLY A CELL PHONE STRAP!
YOU'RE SO PATHETIC, I COULD CRY.
DO YOU SERIOUSLY THINK YOU CAN BEAT THIS HAYAGAMI WITH THAT?
SLRP
SWF

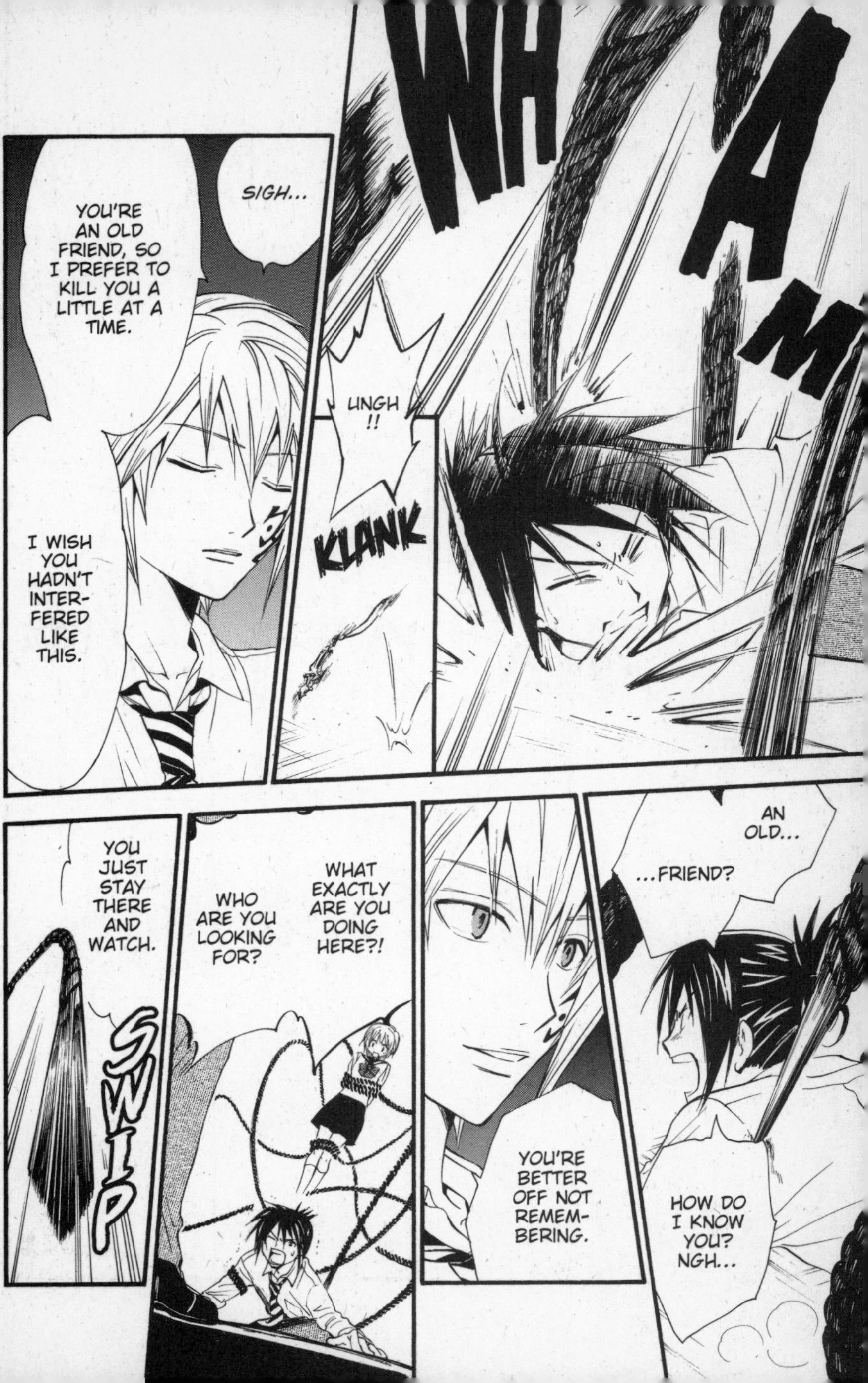
WHAAM
UNGH !!
KLANK
SIGH...
YOU'RE AN OLD FRIEND, SO I PREFER TO KILL YOU A LITTLE AT A TIME.
I WISH YOU HADN'T INTER-FERED LIKE THIS.
AN OLD...
...FRIEND?
HOW DO I KNOW YOU? NGH...
YOU'RE BETTER OFF NOT REMEM-BERING.
WHAT EXACTLY ARE YOU DOING HERE?!
WHO ARE YOU LOOKING FOR?
YOU JUST STAY THERE AND WATCH.
SWIP

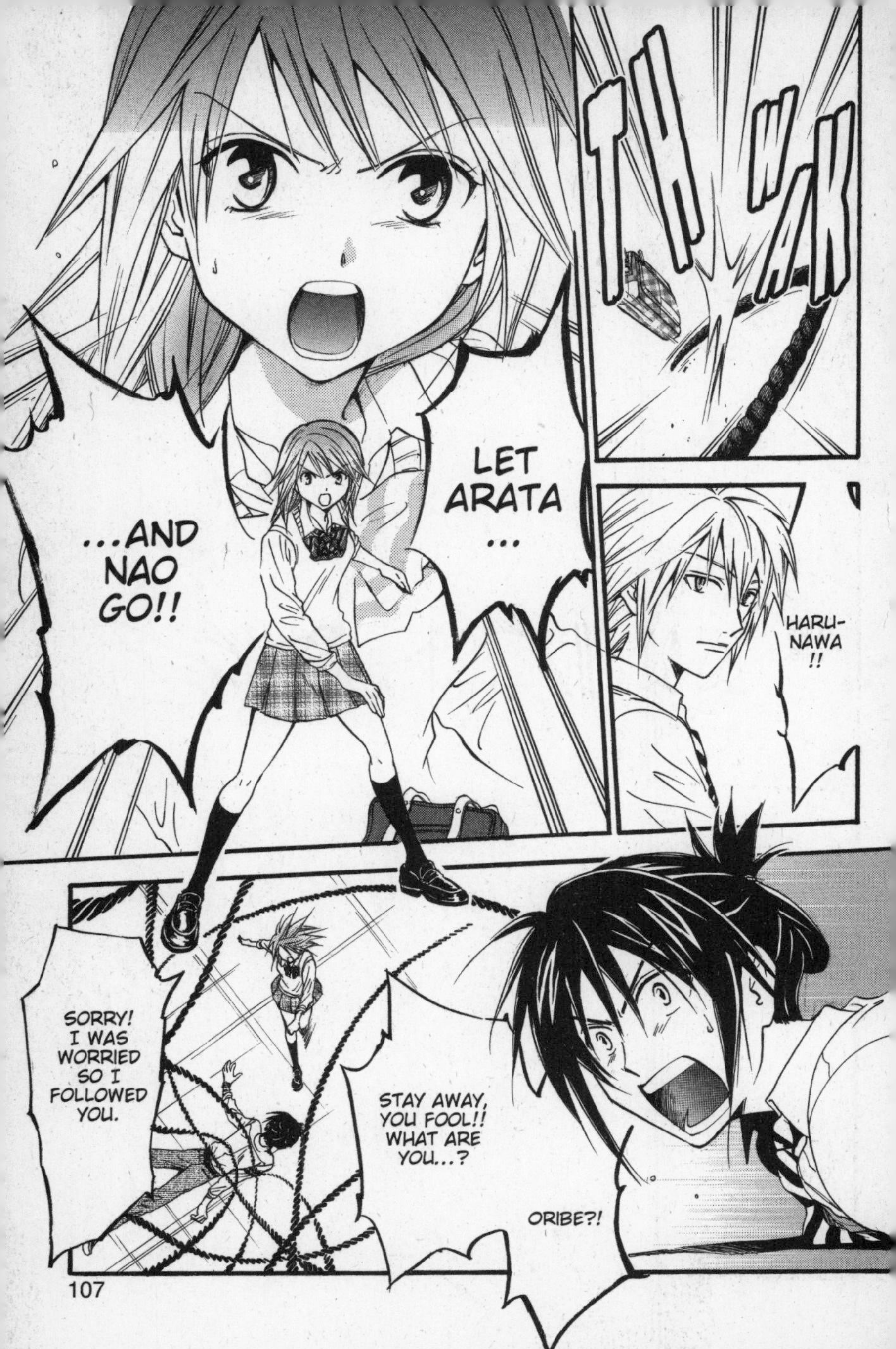
THWAK
HARU-NAWA!!
LET ARATA...
...AND NAO GO!!
ORIBE?!
STAY AWAY, YOU FOOL!! WHAT ARE YOU...?
SORRY! I WAS WORRIED SO I FOLLOWED YOU.

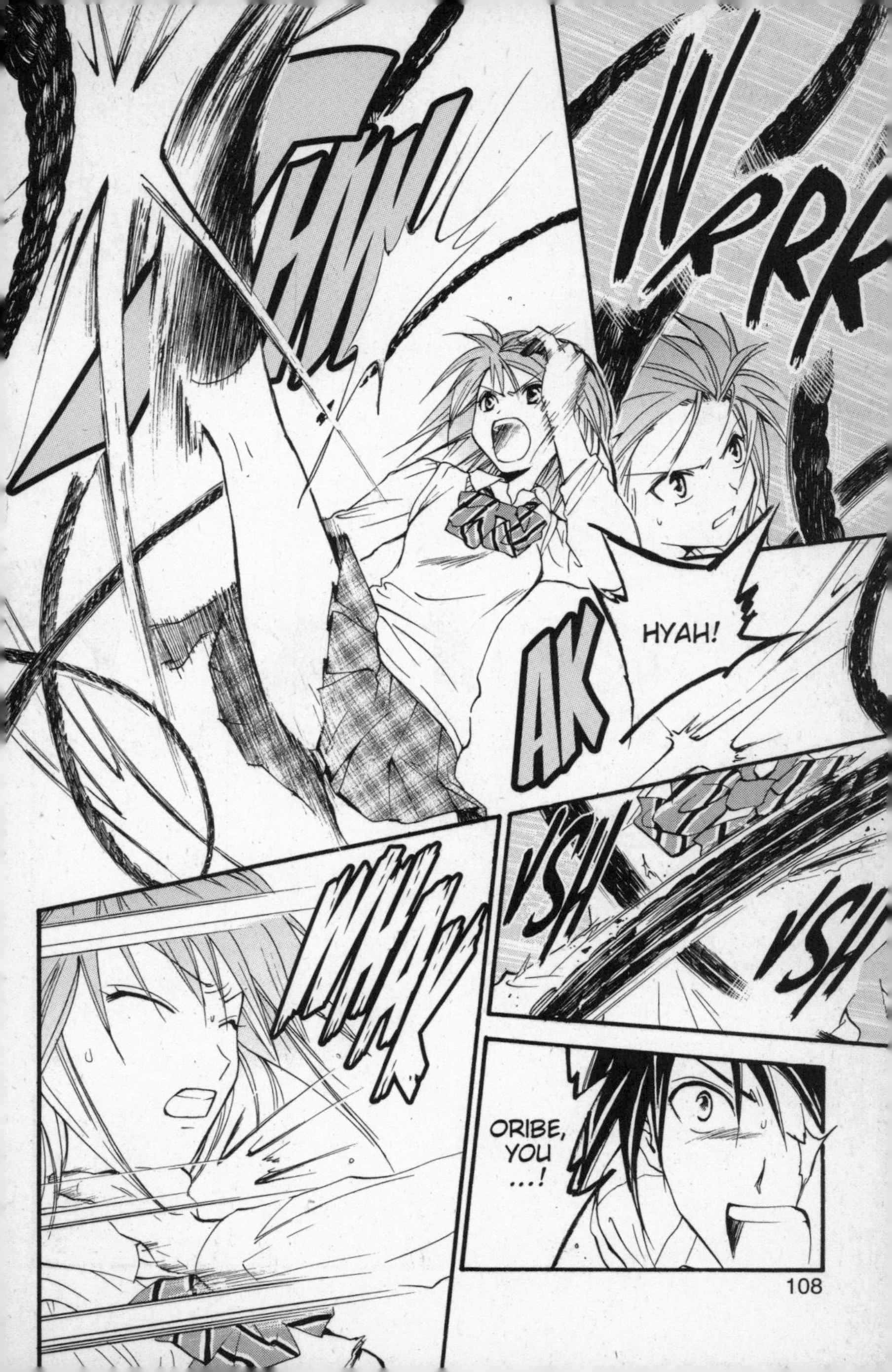
HYAH!
AK
VSH
VSH
ORIBE, YOU ...!

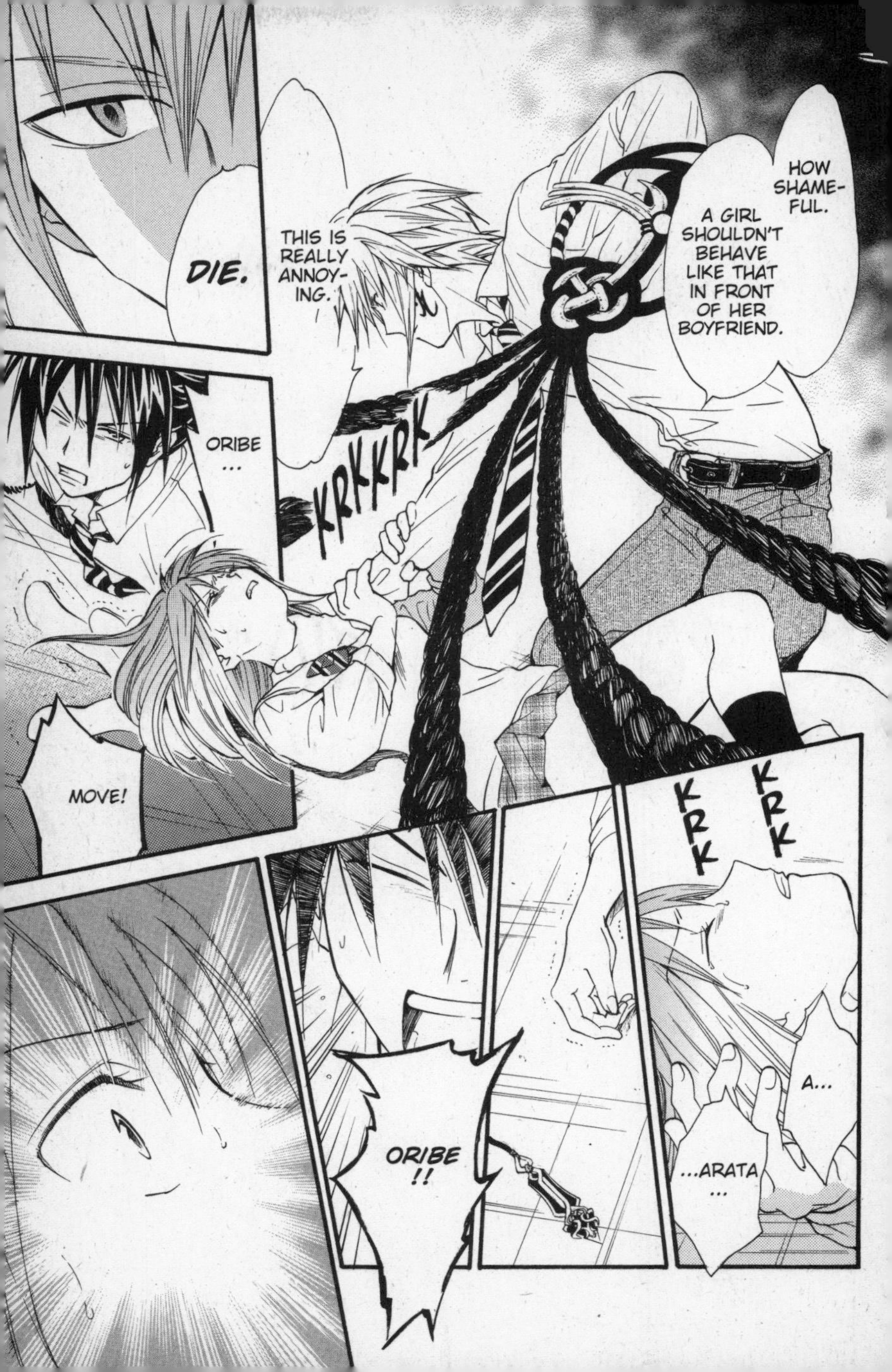

HOW SHAME-FUL.
A GIRL SHOULDN'T BEHAVE LIKE THAT IN FRONT OF HER BOYFRIEND.
THIS IS REALLY ANNOY-ING.
KRKKRK
DIE.
ORIBE ...
MOVE!
KRK KRK
A...
...ARATA ...
ORIBE !!

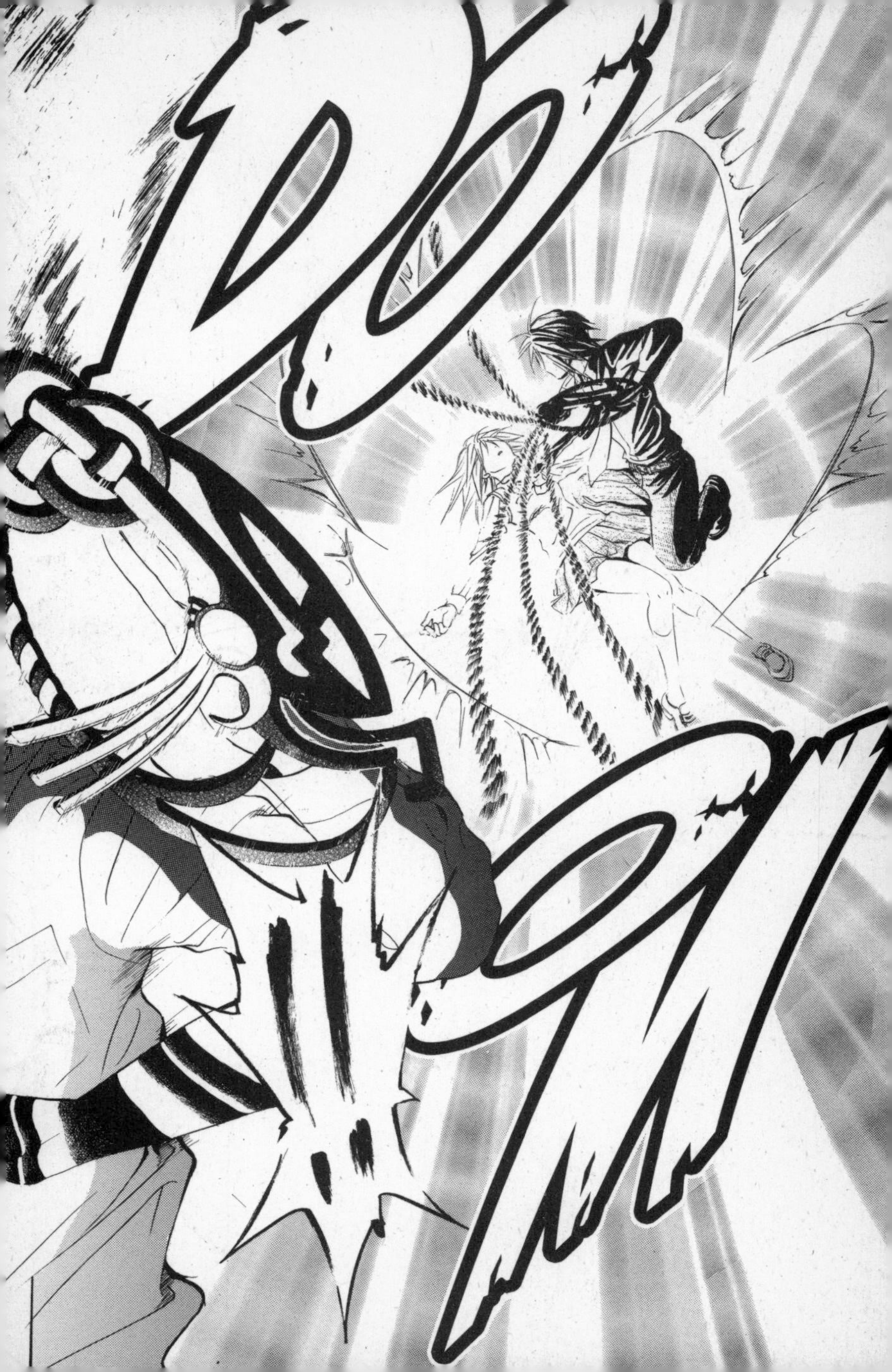

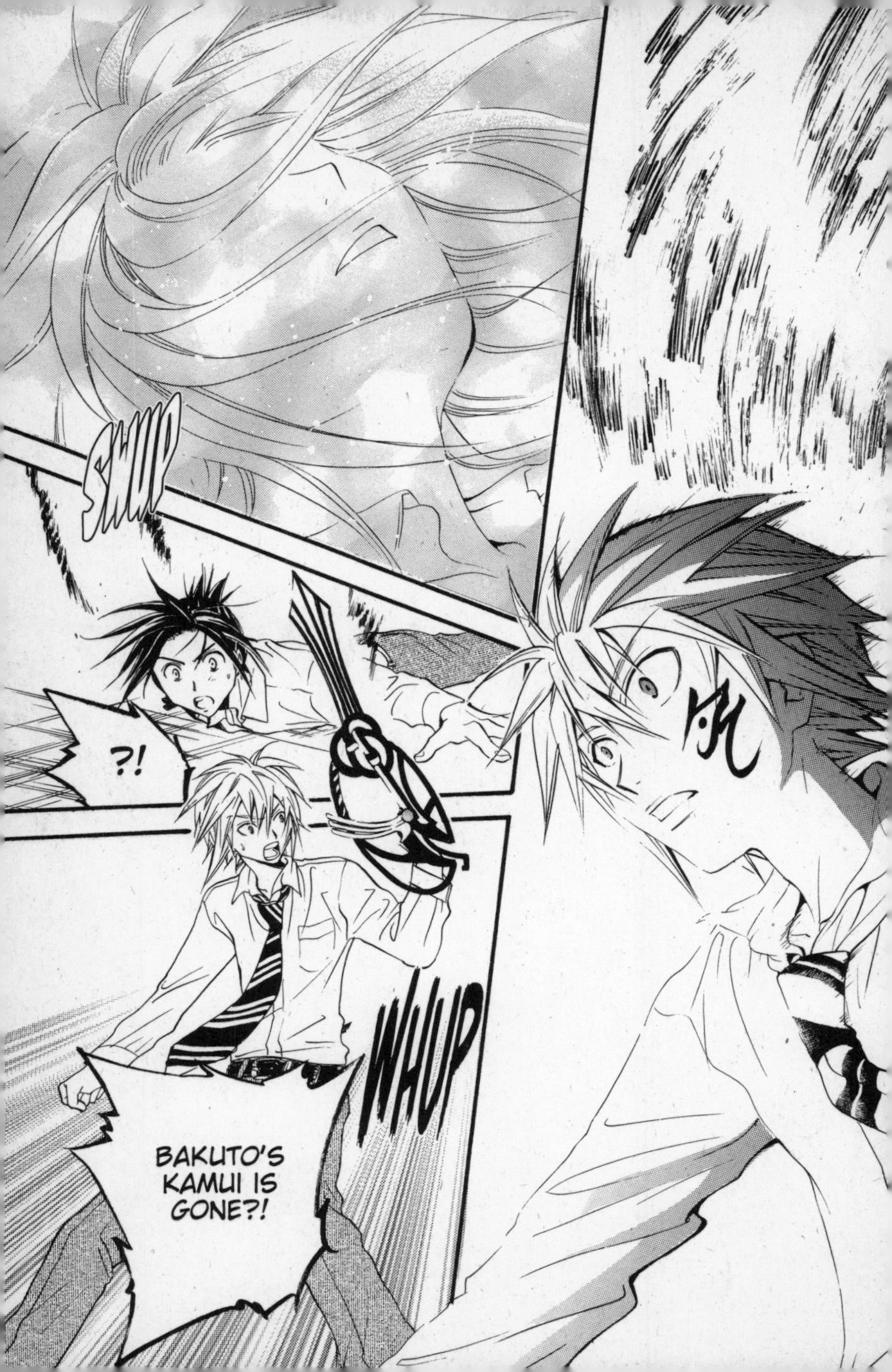
SHUP
?!
WHUP
BAKUTO'S KAMUI IS GONE?!

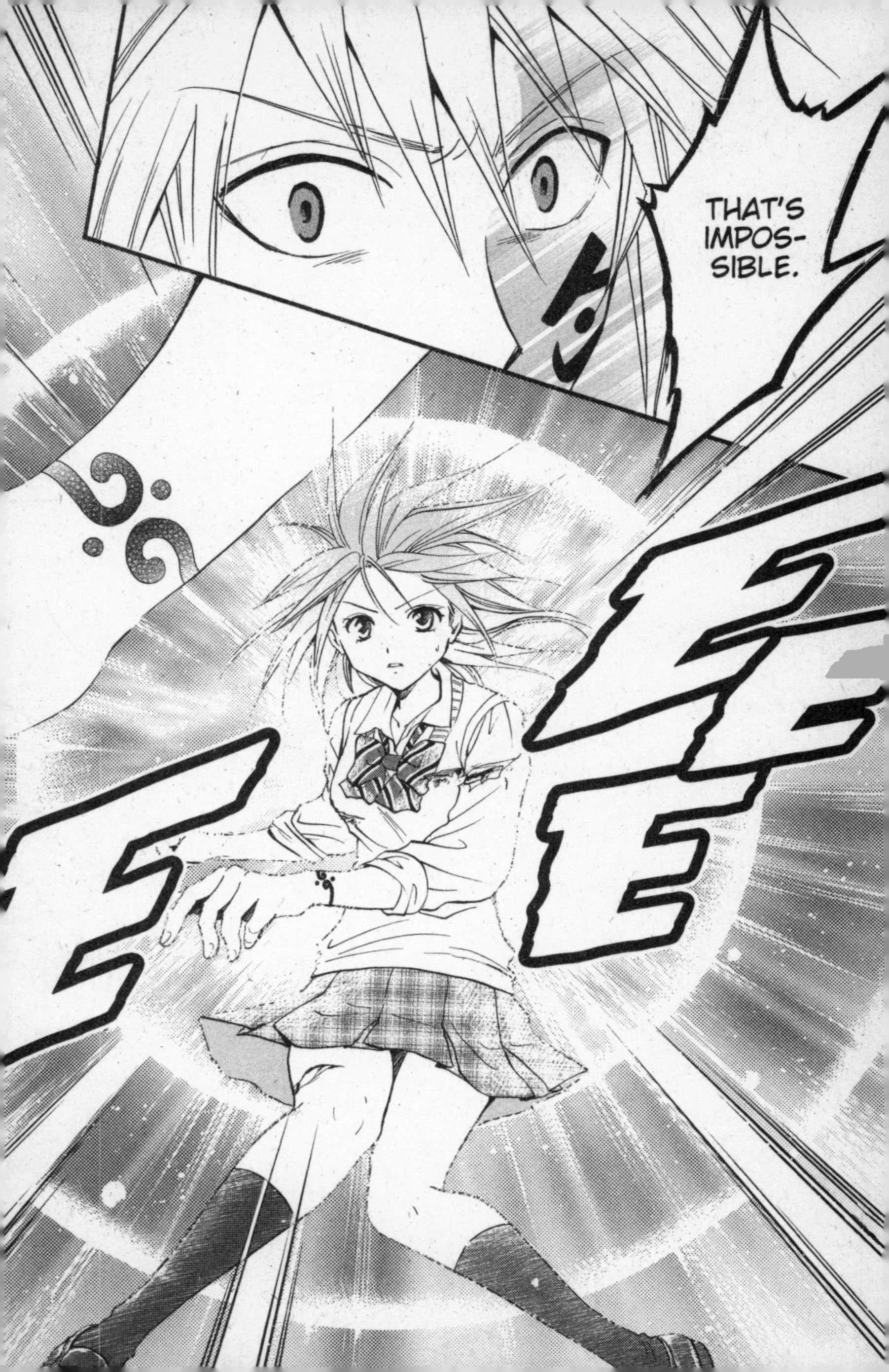
THAT'S IMPOSSIBLE.

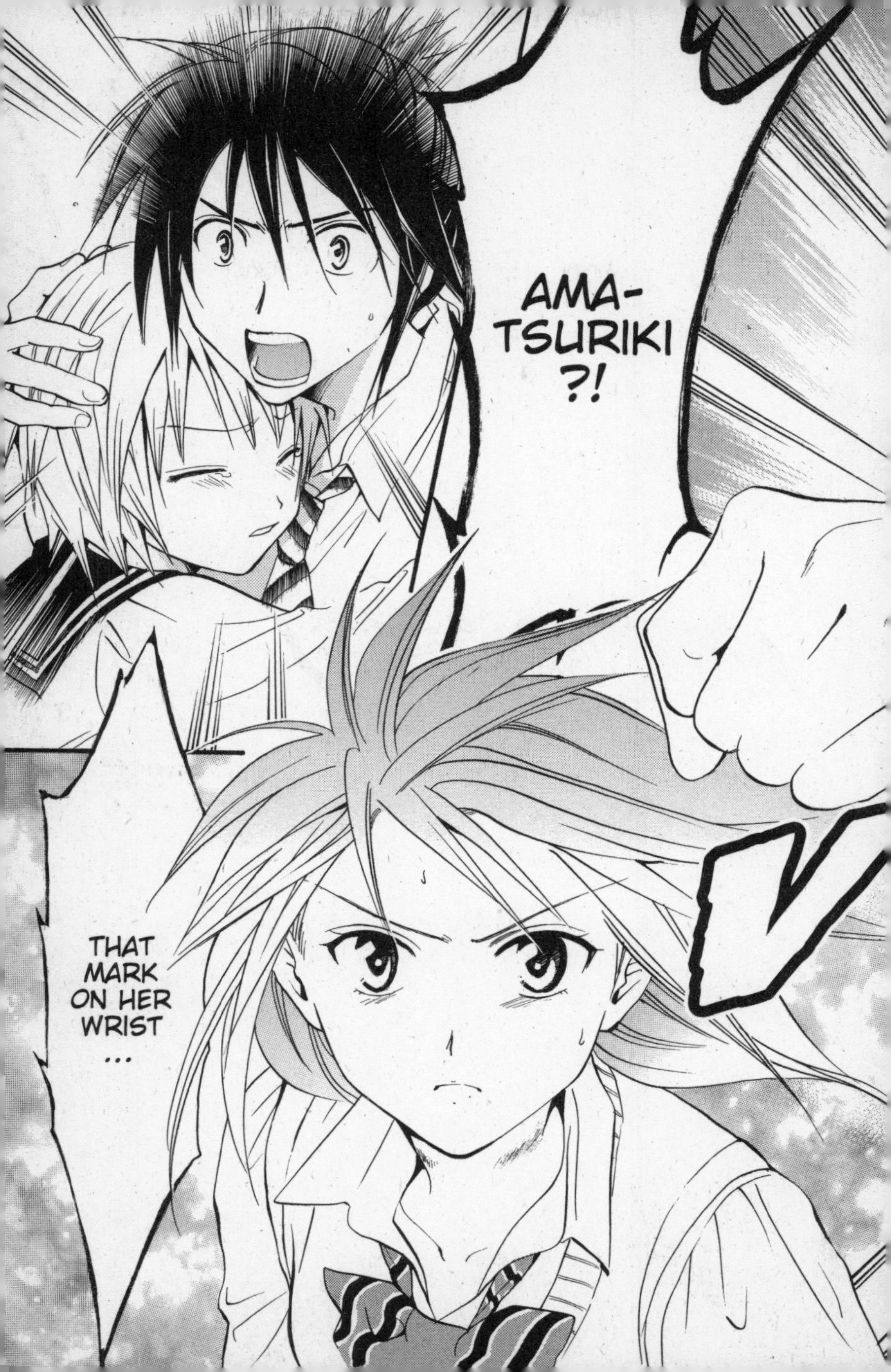
AMA-TSURIKI ?!
THAT MARK ON HER WRIST ...

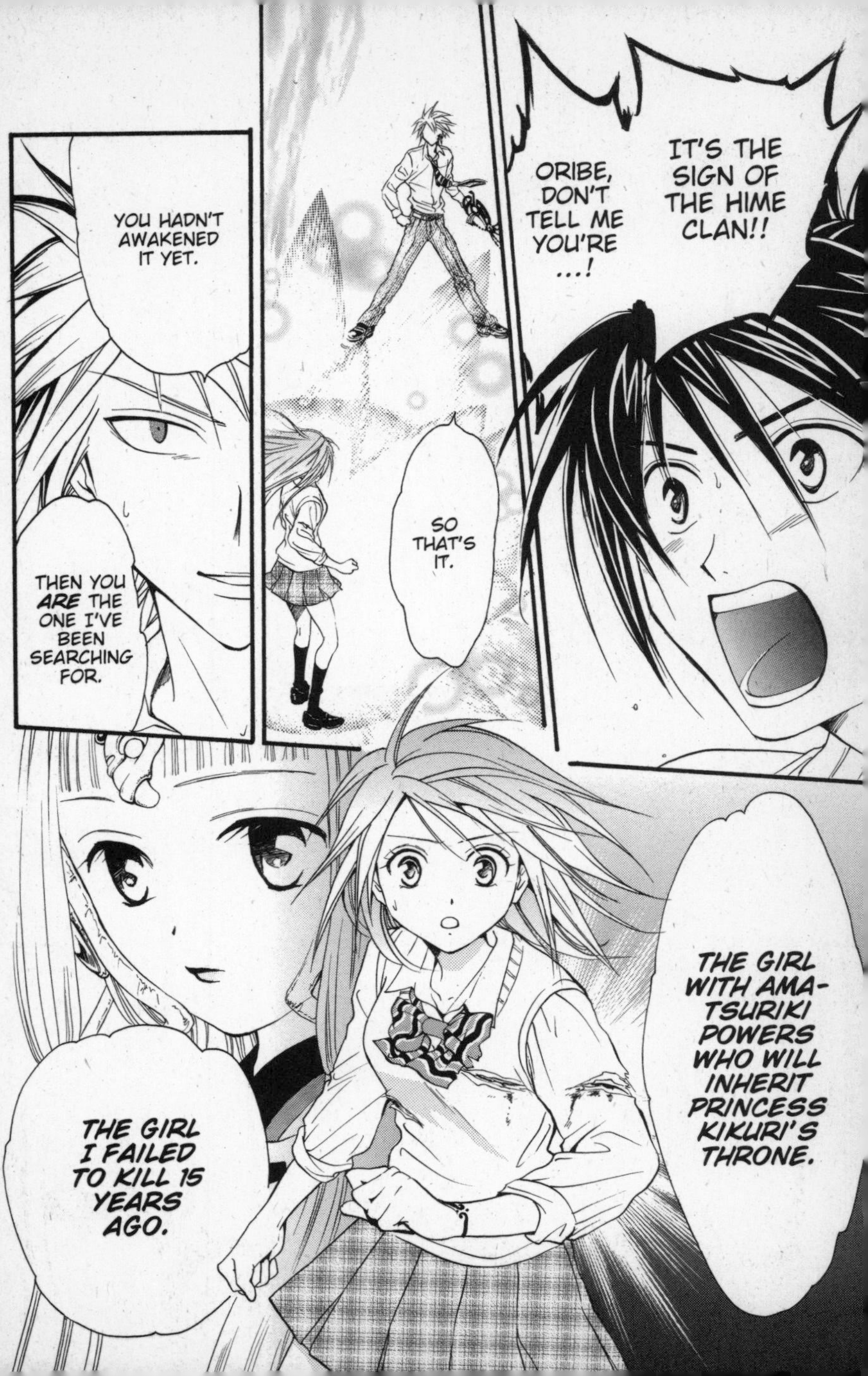
IT'S THE SIGN OF THE HIME CLAN!!
ORIBE, DON'T TELL ME YOU'RE ...!
SO THAT'S IT.
YOU HADN'T AWAKENED IT YET.
THEN YOU ARE THE ONE I'VE BEEN SEARCHING FOR.
THE GIRL WITH AMA-TSURIKI POWERS WHO WILL INHERIT PRINCESS KIKURI'S THRONE.
THE GIRL I FAILED TO KILL 15 YEARS AGO.

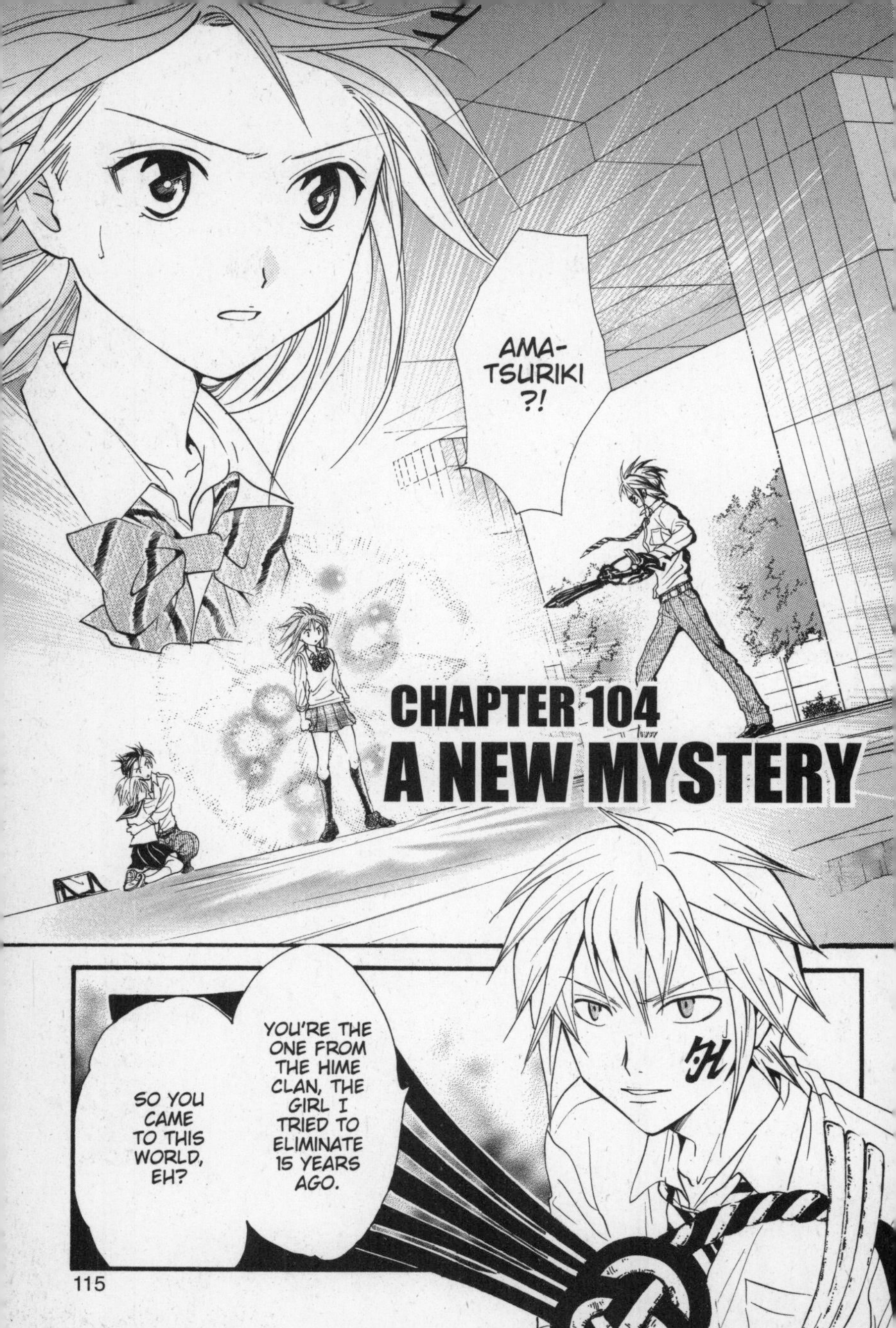
AMA-TSURIKI ?!
CHAPTER 104
A NEW MYSTERY
YOU'RE THE ONE FROM THE HIME CLAN, THE GIRL I TRIED TO ELIMINATE 15 YEARS AGO.
SO YOU CAME TO THIS WORLD, EH?

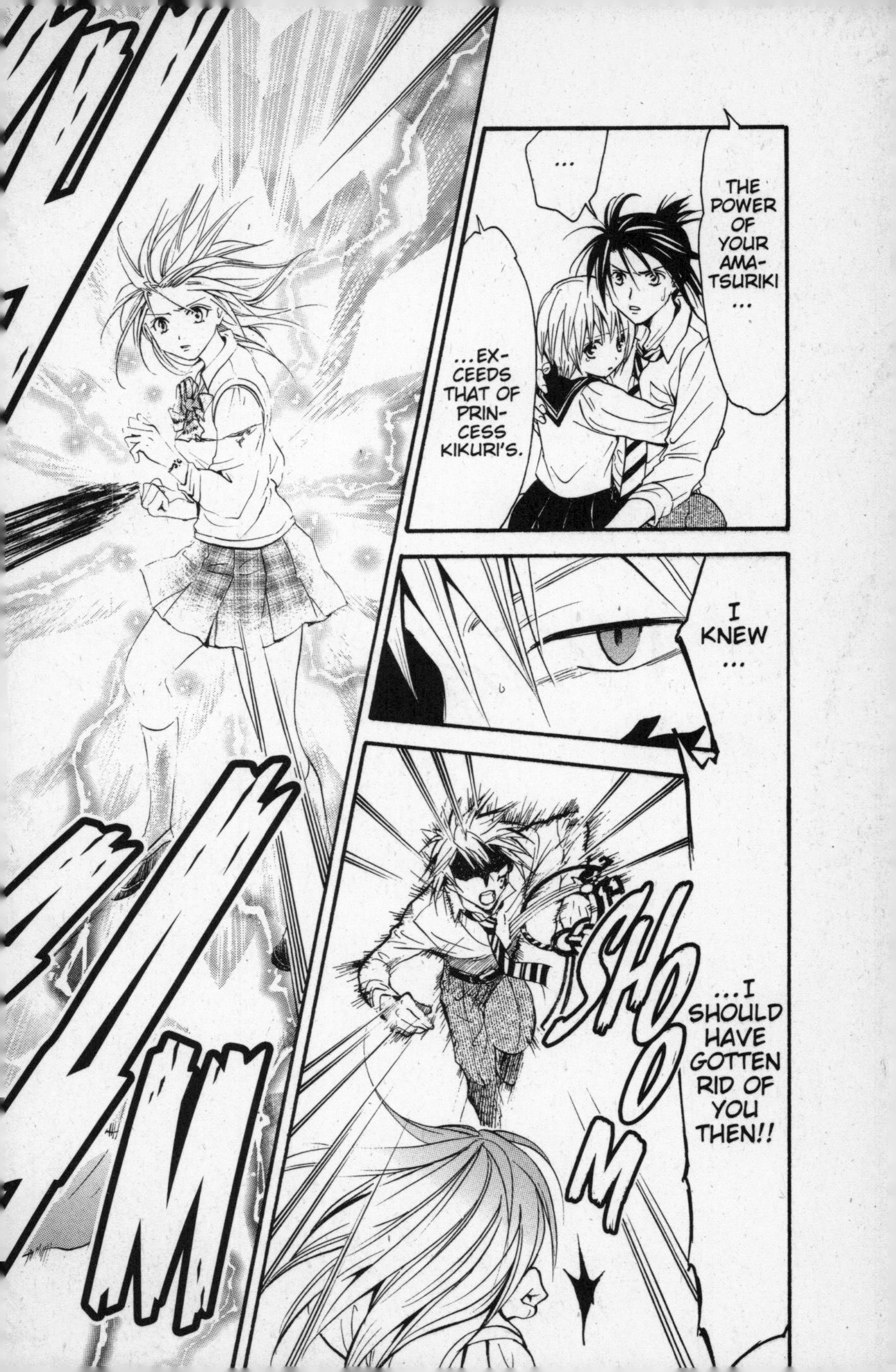
THE POWER OF YOUR AMA-TSURIKI ...
...
...EX-CEEDS THAT OF PRIN-CESS KIKURI'S.
I KNEW ...
SHOOM
...I SHOULD HAVE GOTTEN RID OF YOU THEN!!

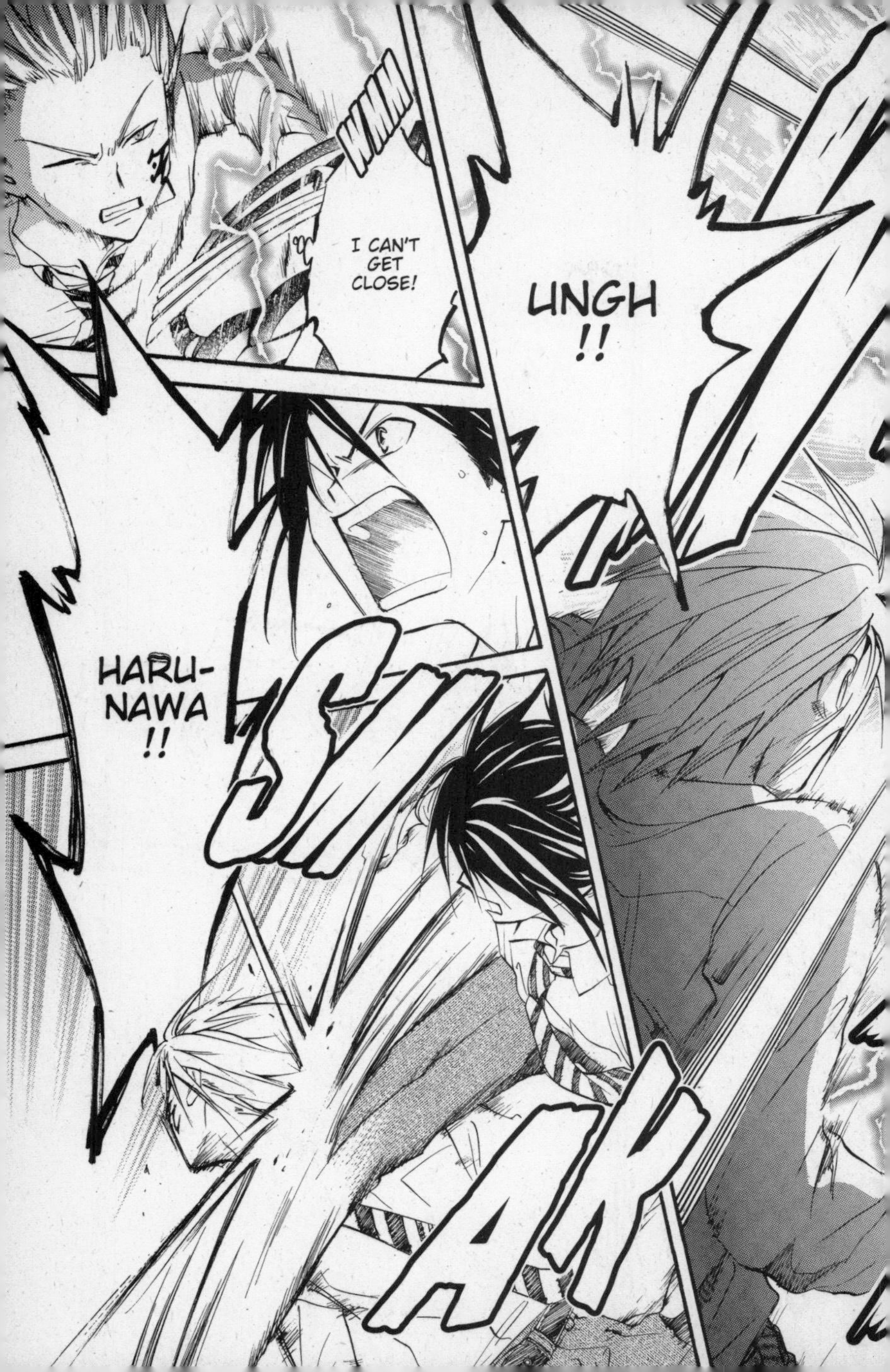
I CAN'T GET CLOSE!
UNGH!!
HARU-NAWA!!
SWAK

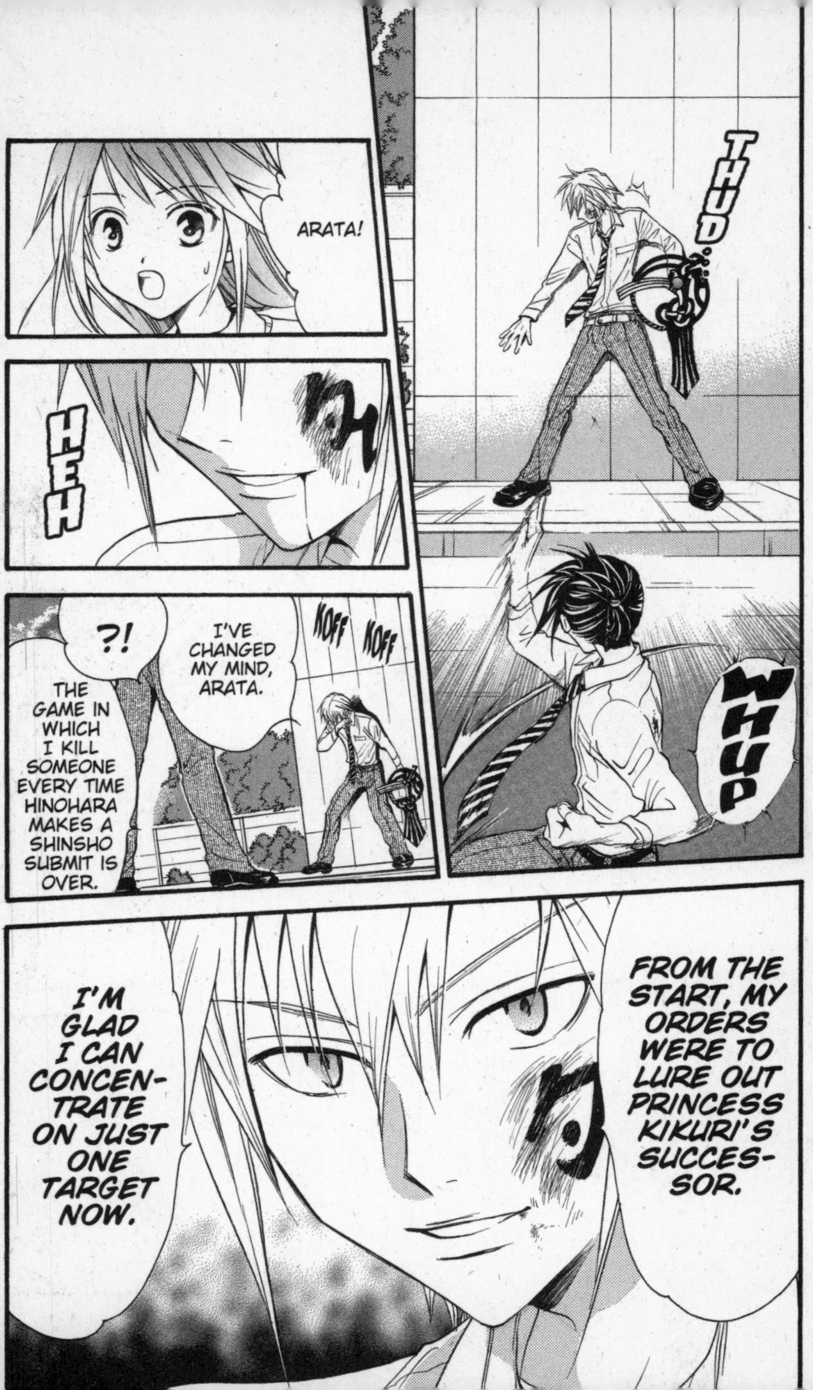
THUD
WHUP
ARATA!
HEH
KOFF KOFF
I'VE CHANGED MY MIND, ARATA.
?!
THE GAME IN WHICH I KILL SOMEONE EVERY TIME HINOHARA MAKES A SHINSHO SUBMIT IS OVER.
FROM THE START, MY ORDERS WERE TO LURE OUT PRINCESS KIKURI'S SUCCESSOR.
I'M GLAD I CAN CONCENTRATE ON JUST ONE TARGET NOW.

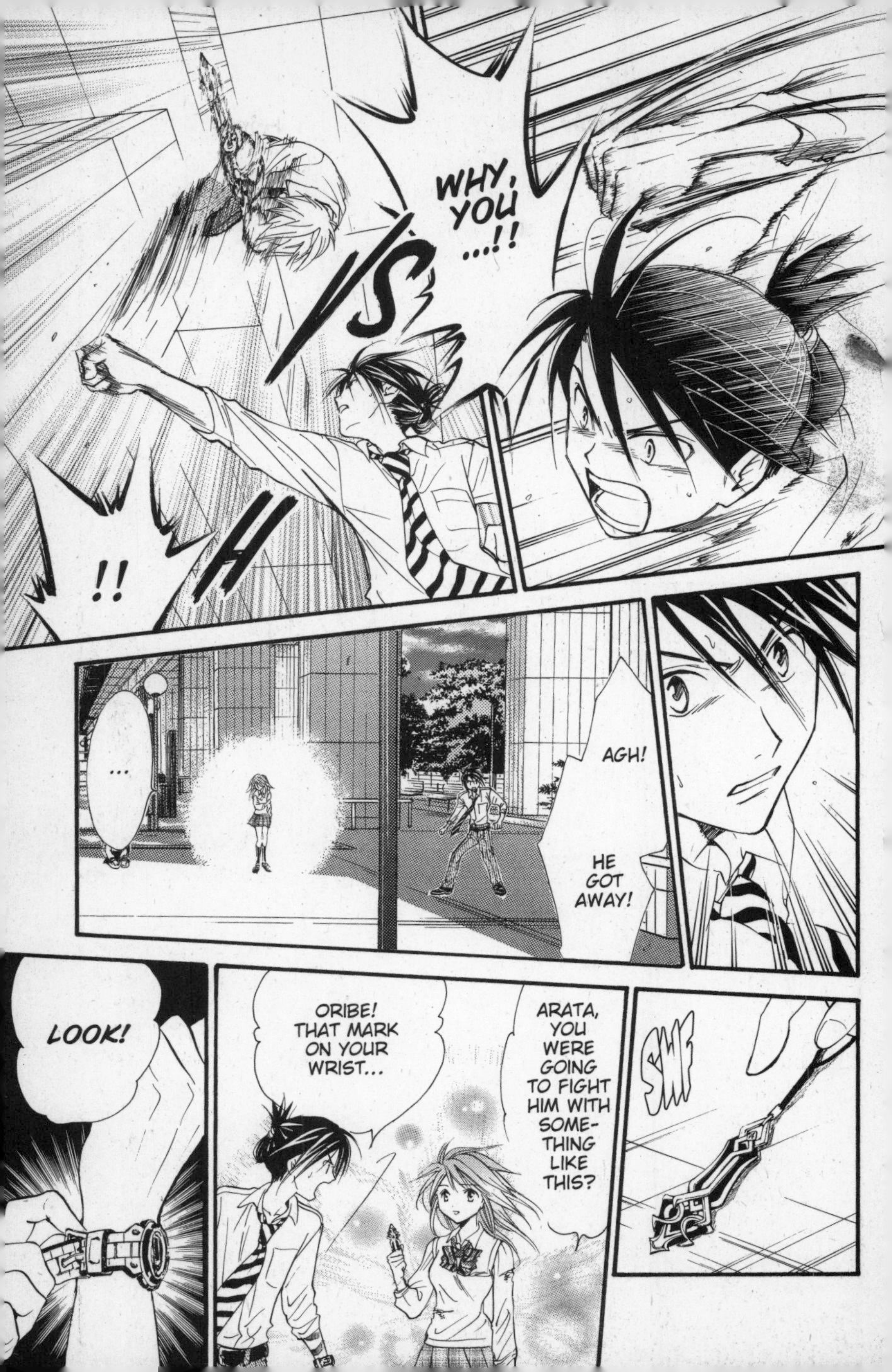
WHY, YOU ...!!
!!
AGH!
HE GOT AWAY!
...
ARATA, YOU WERE GOING TO FIGHT HIM WITH SOME-THING LIKE THIS?
ORIBE! THAT MARK ON YOUR WRIST...
LOOK!

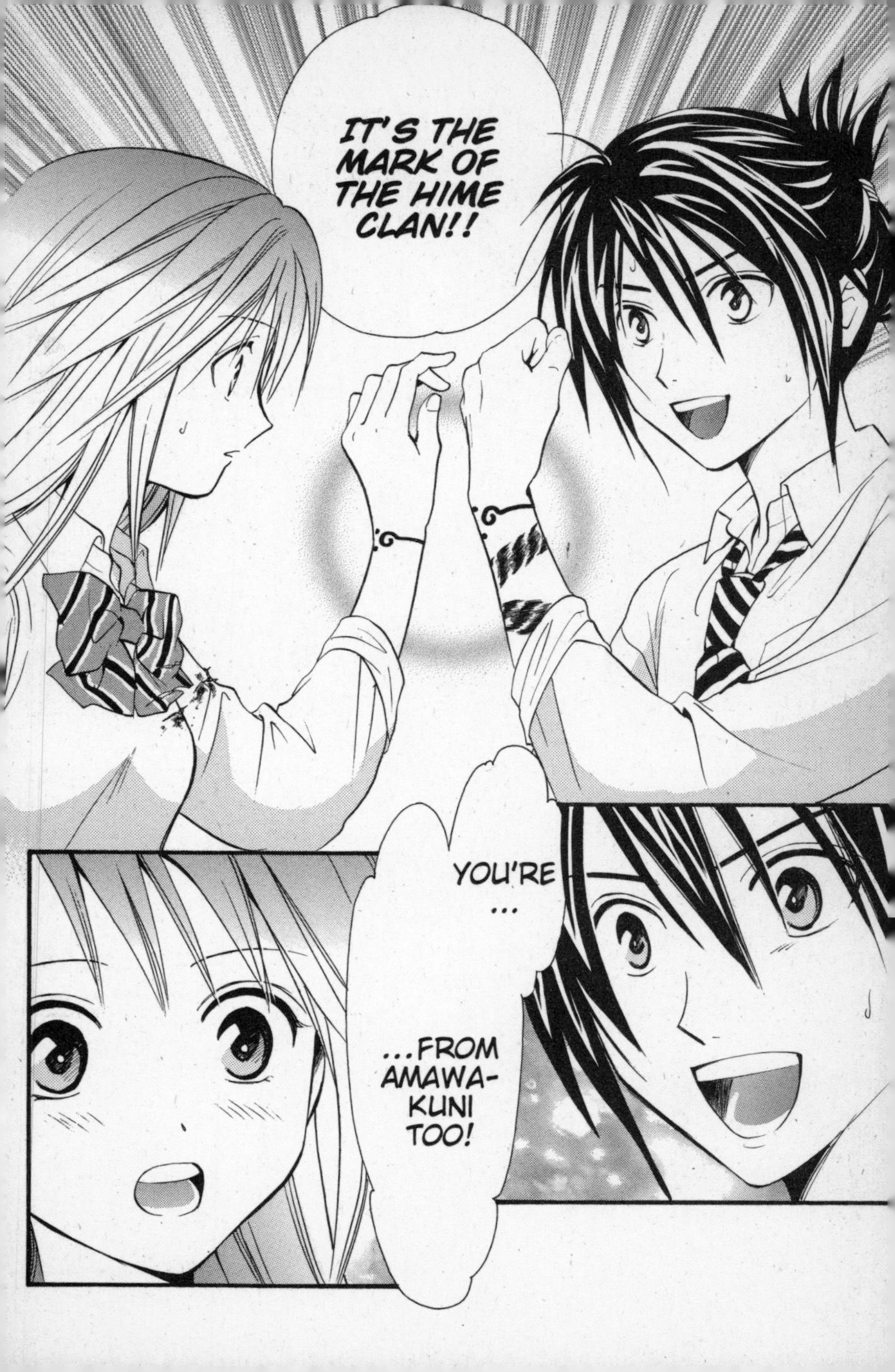
IT'S THE MARK OF THE HIME CLAN!!
YOU'RE ...
...FROM AMAWA-KUNI TOO!

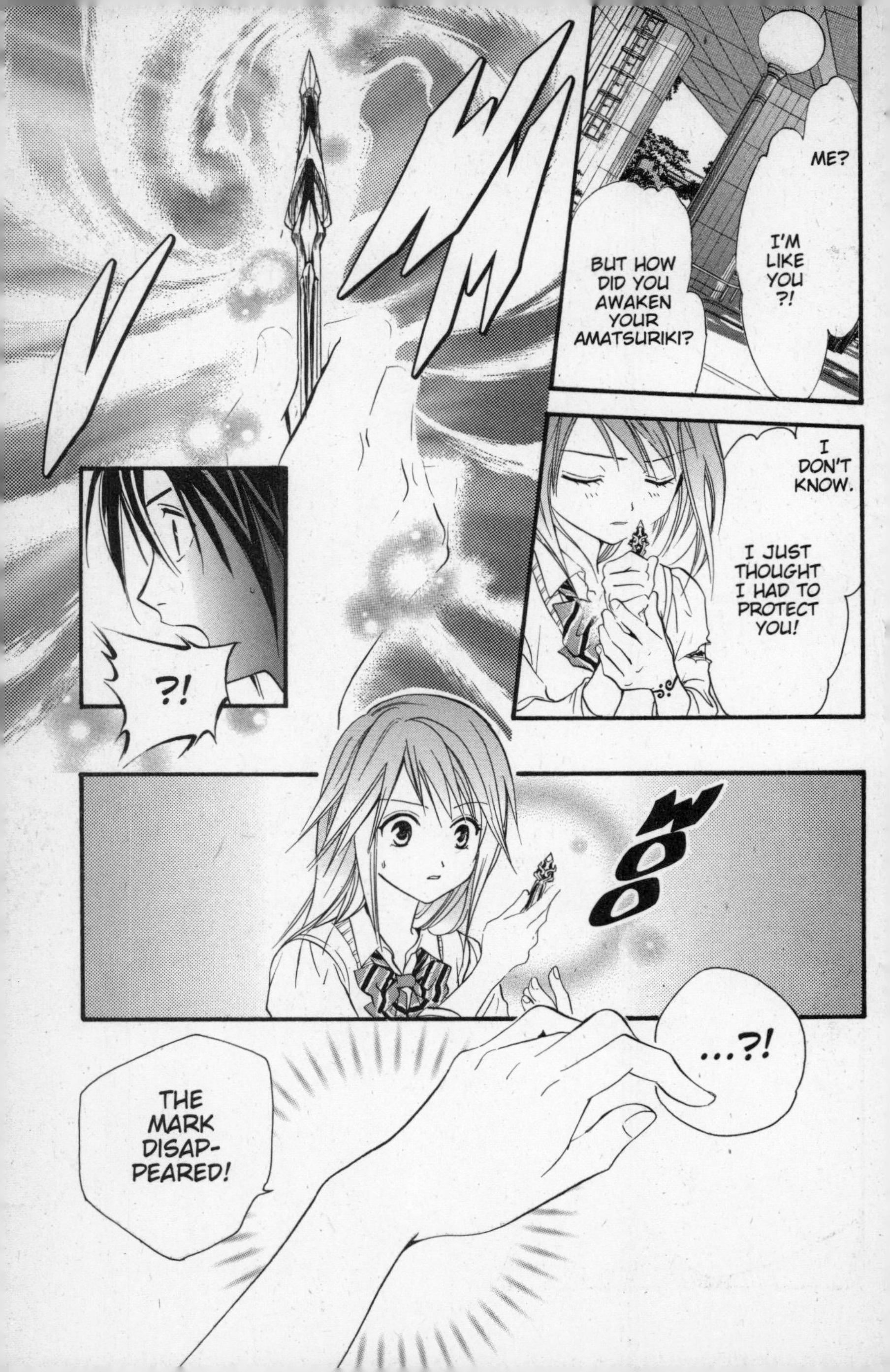
ME?
I'M LIKE YOU ?!
BUT HOW DID YOU AWAKEN YOUR AMATSURIKI?
I DON'T KNOW.
I JUST THOUGHT I HAD TO PROTECT YOU!
?!
WOO
...?!
THE MARK DISAP-PEARED!

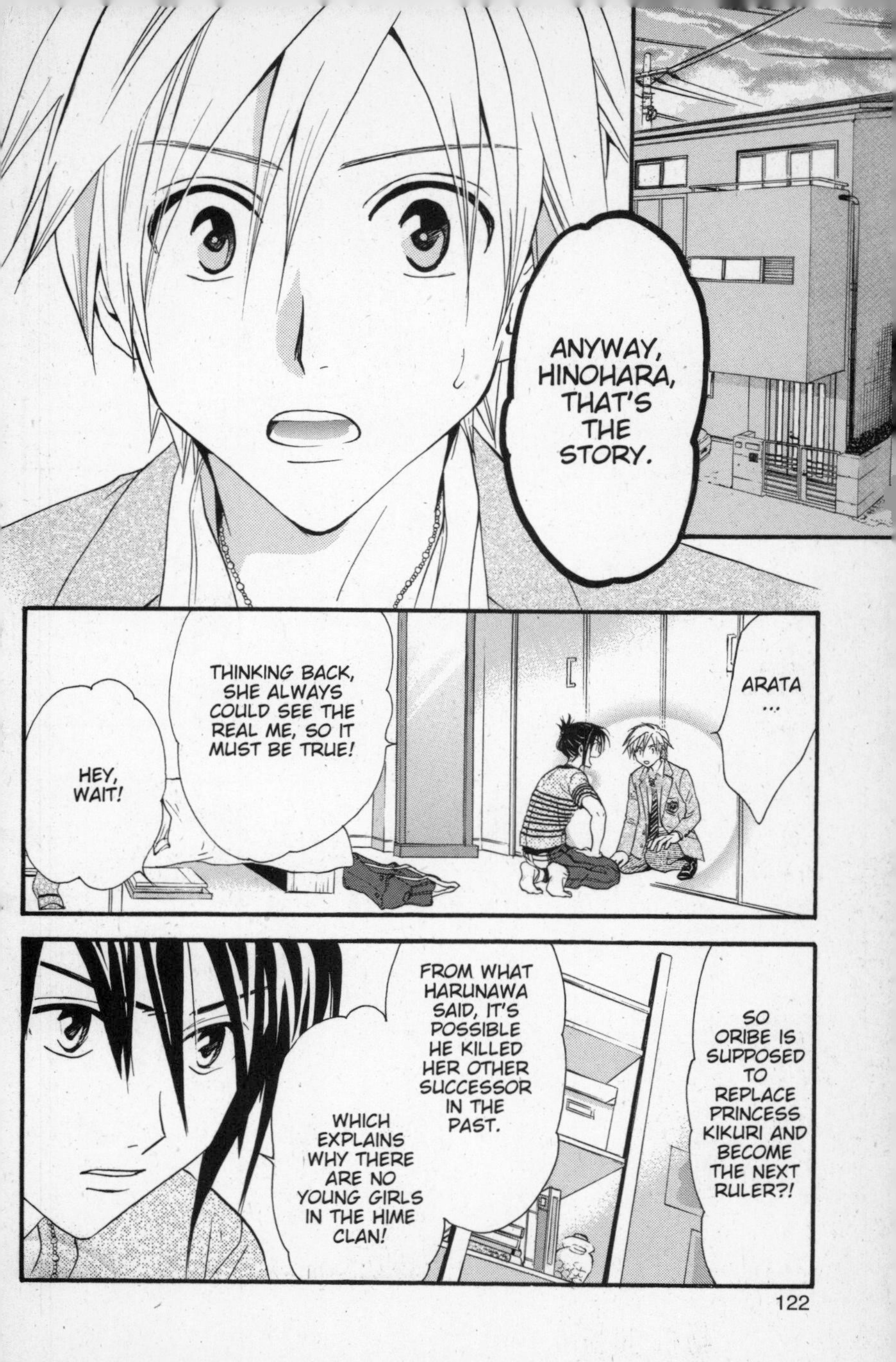
ANYWAY, HINOHARA, THAT'S THE STORY.
ARATA ...
THINKING BACK, SHE ALWAYS COULD SEE THE REAL ME, SO IT MUST BE TRUE!
HEY, WAIT!
SO ORIBE IS SUPPOSED TO REPLACE PRINCESS KIKURI AND BECOME THE NEXT RULER?!
FROM WHAT HARUNAWA SAID, IT'S POSSIBLE HE KILLED HER OTHER SUCCESSOR IN THE PAST.
WHICH EXPLAINS WHY THERE ARE NO YOUNG GIRLS IN THE HIME CLAN!

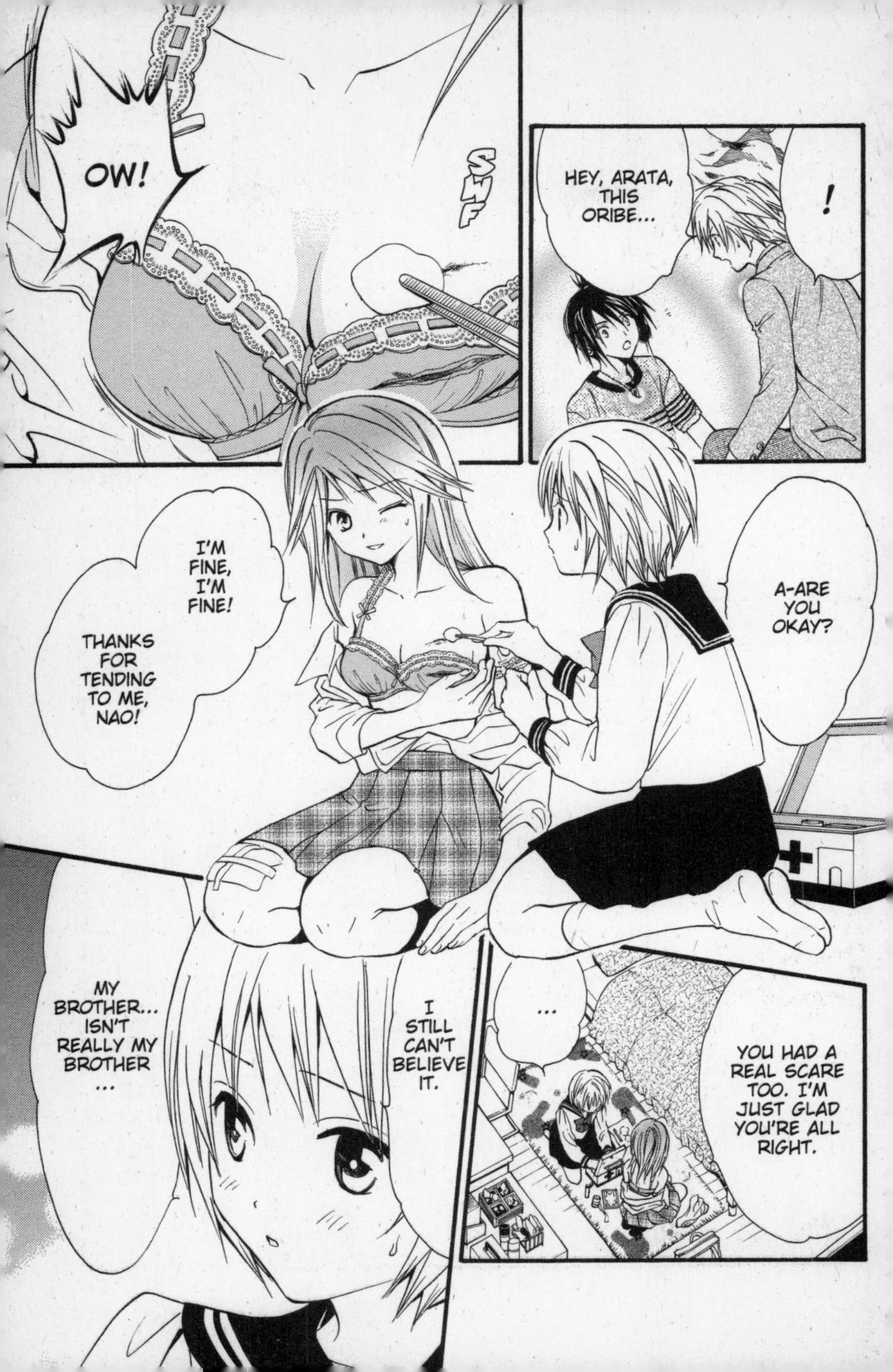
HEY, ARATA, THIS ORIBE...
!
SWF
OW!
A-ARE YOU OKAY?
I'M FINE, I'M FINE!
THANKS FOR TENDING TO ME, NAO!
YOU HAD A REAL SCARE TOO. I'M JUST GLAD YOU'RE ALL RIGHT.
...
I STILL CAN'T BELIEVE IT.
MY BROTHER... ISN'T REALLY MY BROTHER ...

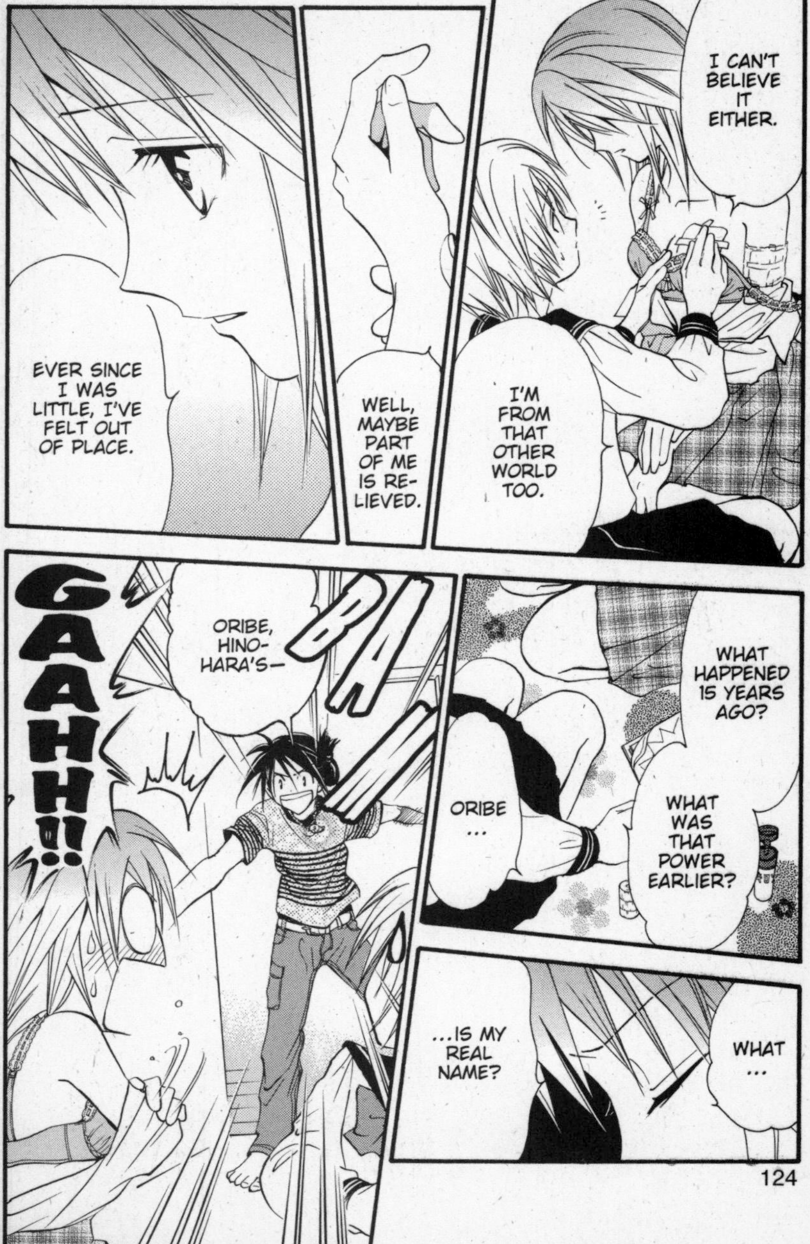
I CAN'T BELIEVE IT EITHER.
I'M FROM THAT OTHER WORLD TOO.
WELL, MAYBE PART OF ME IS RE-LIEVED.
EVER SINCE I WAS LITTLE, I'VE FELT OUT OF PLACE.
WHAT HAPPENED 15 YEARS AGO?
WHAT WAS THAT POWER EARLIER?
ORIBE ...
WHAT ...
...IS MY REAL NAME?
BA
ORIBE, HINO-HARA'S—
GAAHH!!

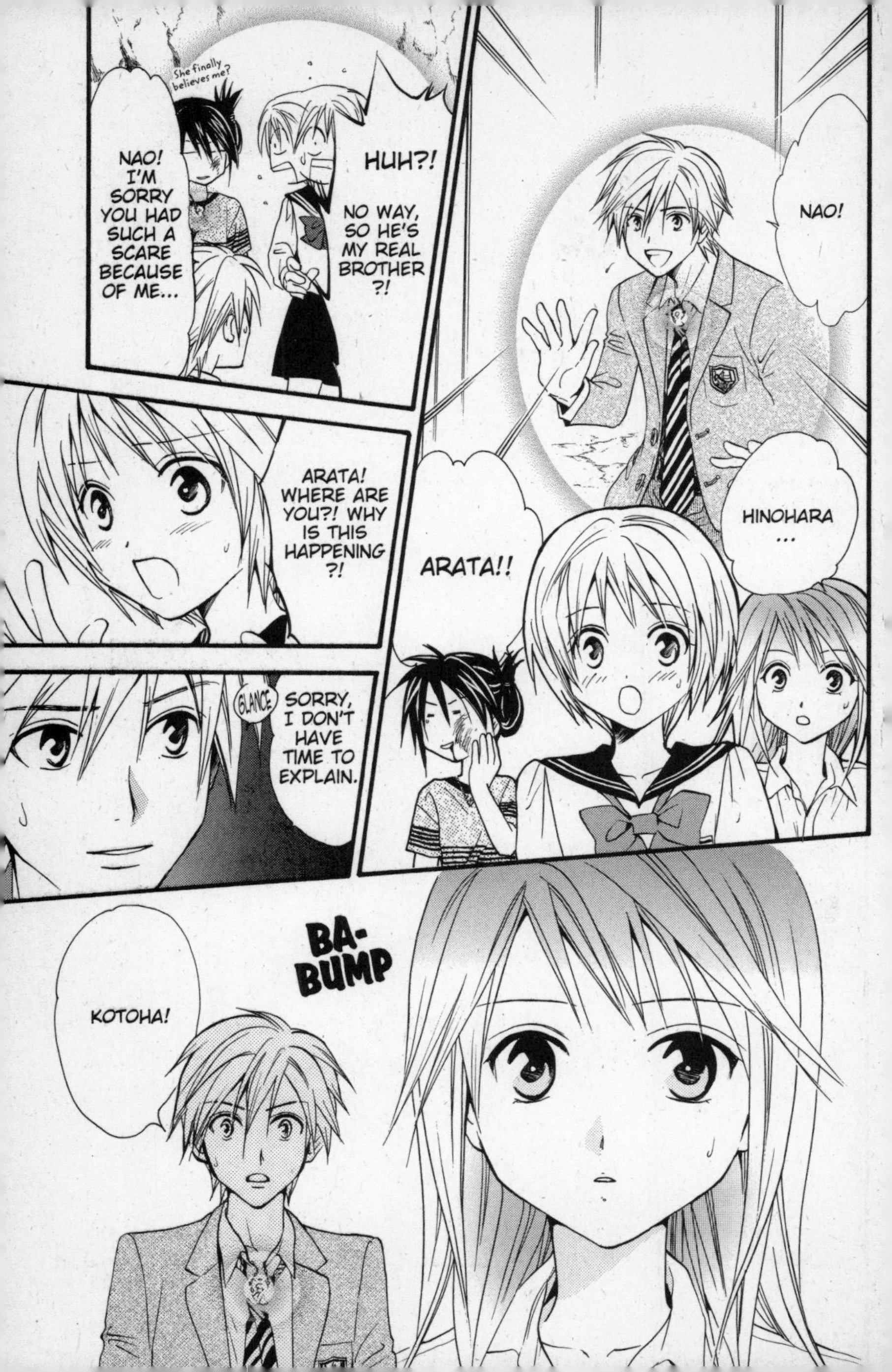
NAO!
HINOHARA ...
ARATA!!
HUH?!
NO WAY, SO HE'S MY REAL BROTHER ?!
She finally believes me?
NAO! I'M SORRY YOU HAD SUCH A SCARE BECAUSE OF ME...
ARATA! WHERE ARE YOU?! WHY IS THIS HAPPENING ?!
SORRY, I DON'T HAVE TIME TO EXPLAIN.
GLANCE
BA-BUMP
KOTOHA!

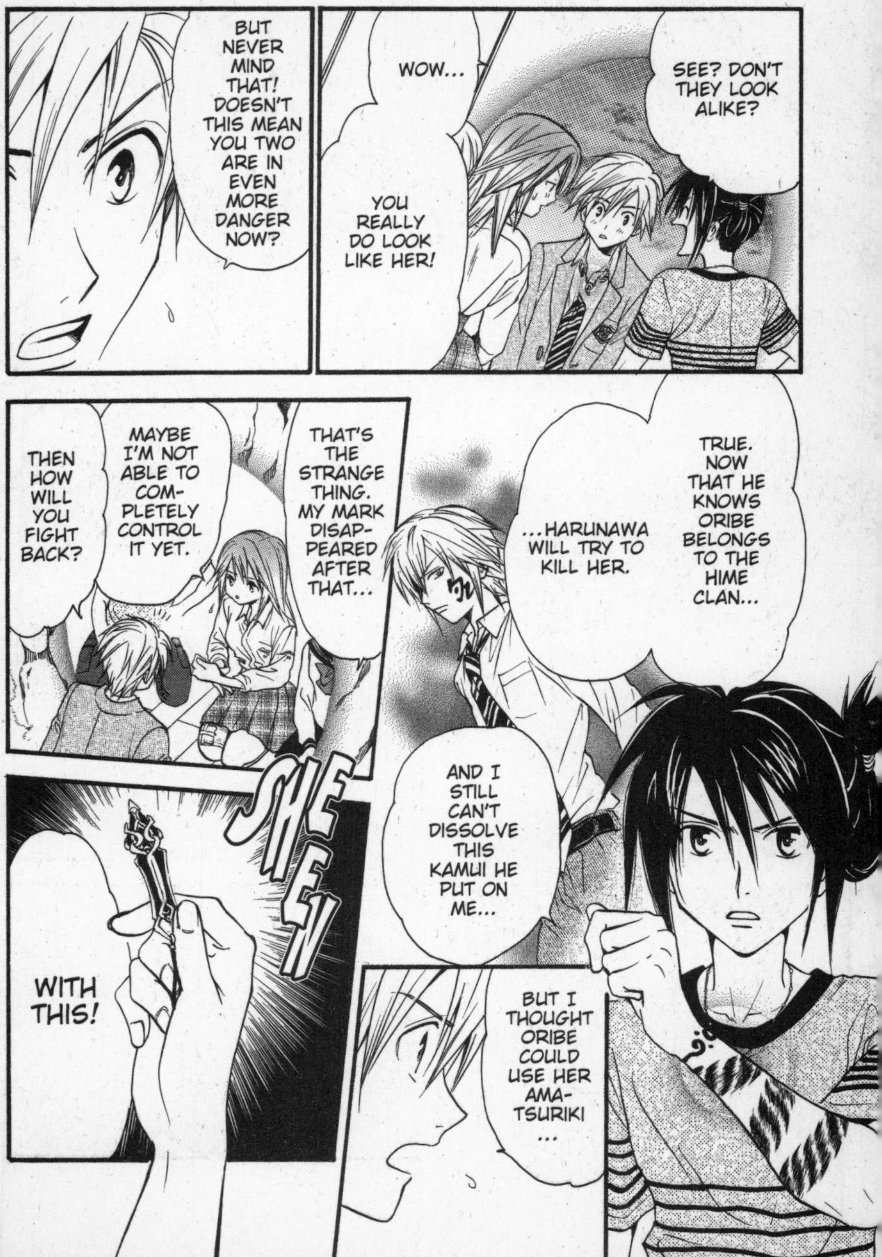
SEE? DON'T THEY LOOK ALIKE?
WOW...
YOU REALLY DO LOOK LIKE HER!
BUT NEVER MIND THAT! DOESN'T THIS MEAN YOU TWO ARE IN EVEN MORE DANGER NOW?
TRUE. NOW THAT HE KNOWS ORIBE BELONGS TO THE HIME CLAN...
...HARUNAWA WILL TRY TO KILL HER.
AND I STILL CAN'T DISSOLVE THIS KAMUI HE PUT ON ME...
THAT'S THE STRANGE THING. MY MARK DISAP-PEARED AFTER THAT...
MAYBE I'M NOT ABLE TO COM-PLETELY CONTROL IT YET.
THEN HOW WILL YOU FIGHT BACK?
BUT I THOUGHT ORIBE COULD USE HER AMA-TSURIKI ...
SHEEN
WITH THIS!

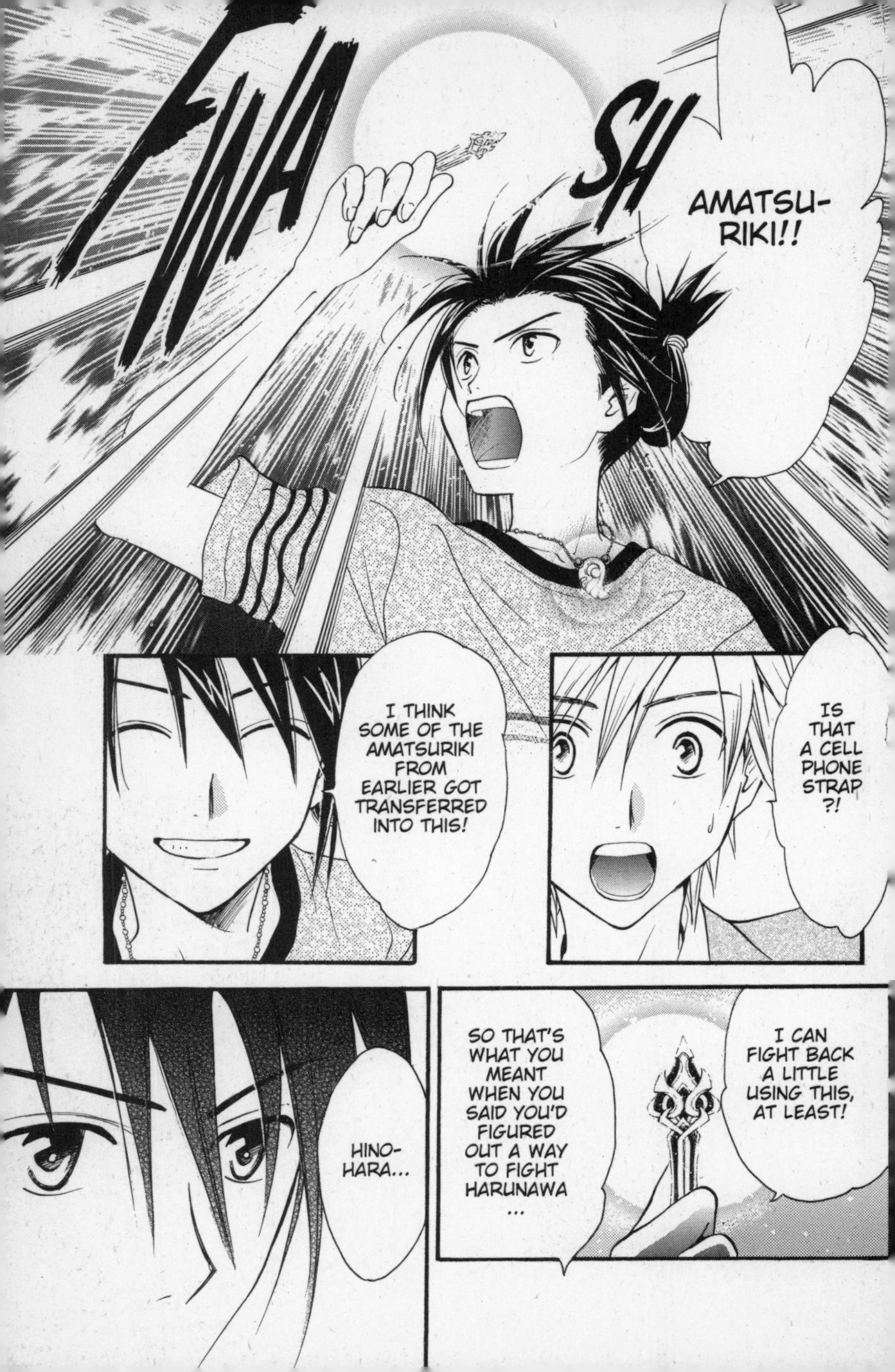
FLASH
AMATSU-RIKI!!
IS THAT A CELL PHONE STRAP?!
I THINK SOME OF THE AMATSURIKI FROM EARLIER GOT TRANSFERRED INTO THIS!
I CAN FIGHT BACK A LITTLE USING THIS, AT LEAST!
SO THAT'S WHAT YOU MEANT WHEN YOU SAID YOU'D FIGURED OUT A WAY TO FIGHT HARUNAWA...
HINO-HARA...

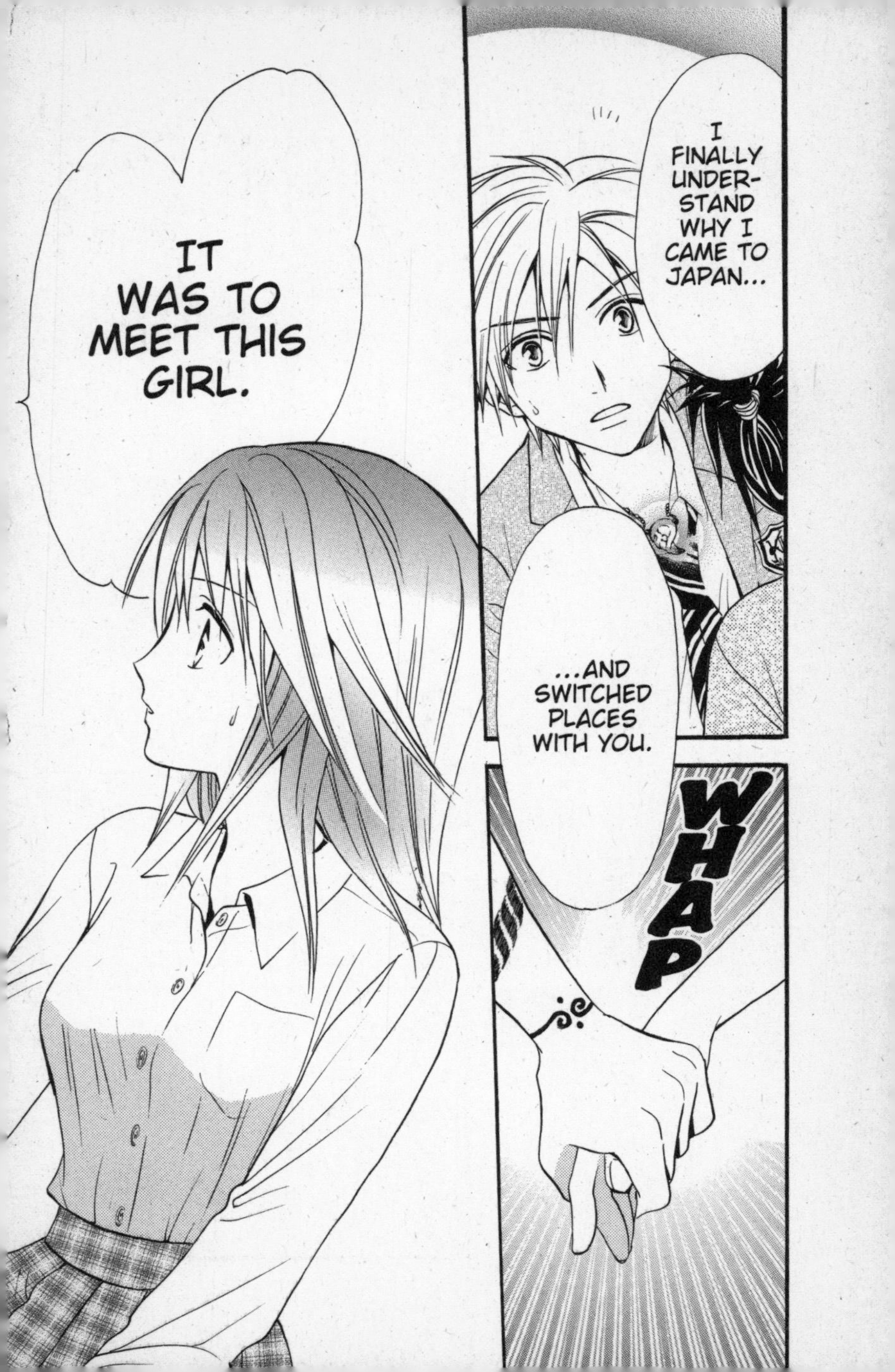
I FINALLY UNDER-STAND WHY I CAME TO JAPAN...
...AND SWITCHED PLACES WITH YOU.
WHAP
IT WAS TO MEET THIS GIRL.

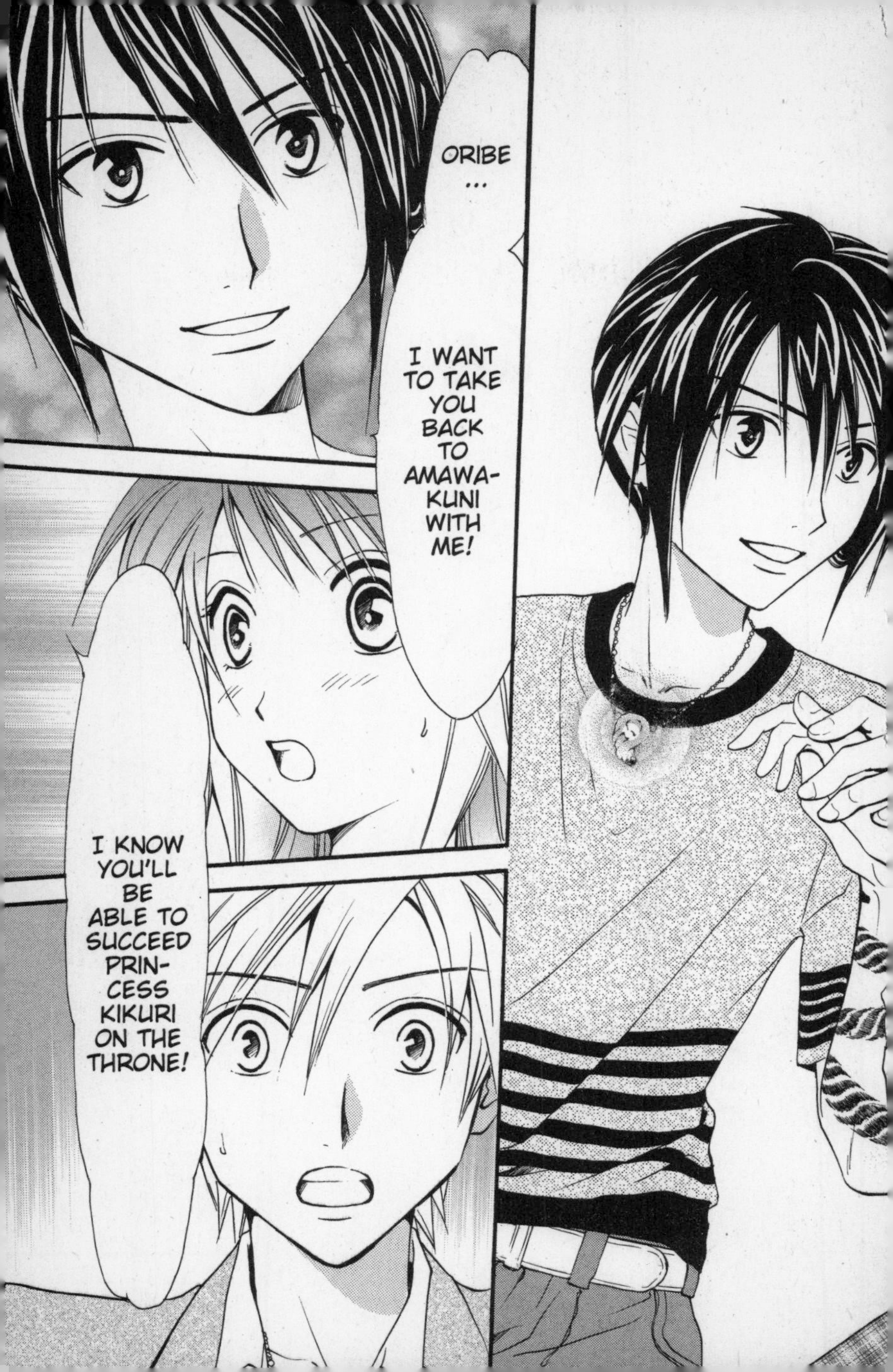
ORIBE ...
I WANT TO TAKE YOU BACK TO AMAWA-KUNI WITH ME!
I KNOW YOU'LL BE ABLE TO SUCCEED PRIN-CESS KIKURI ON THE THRONE!

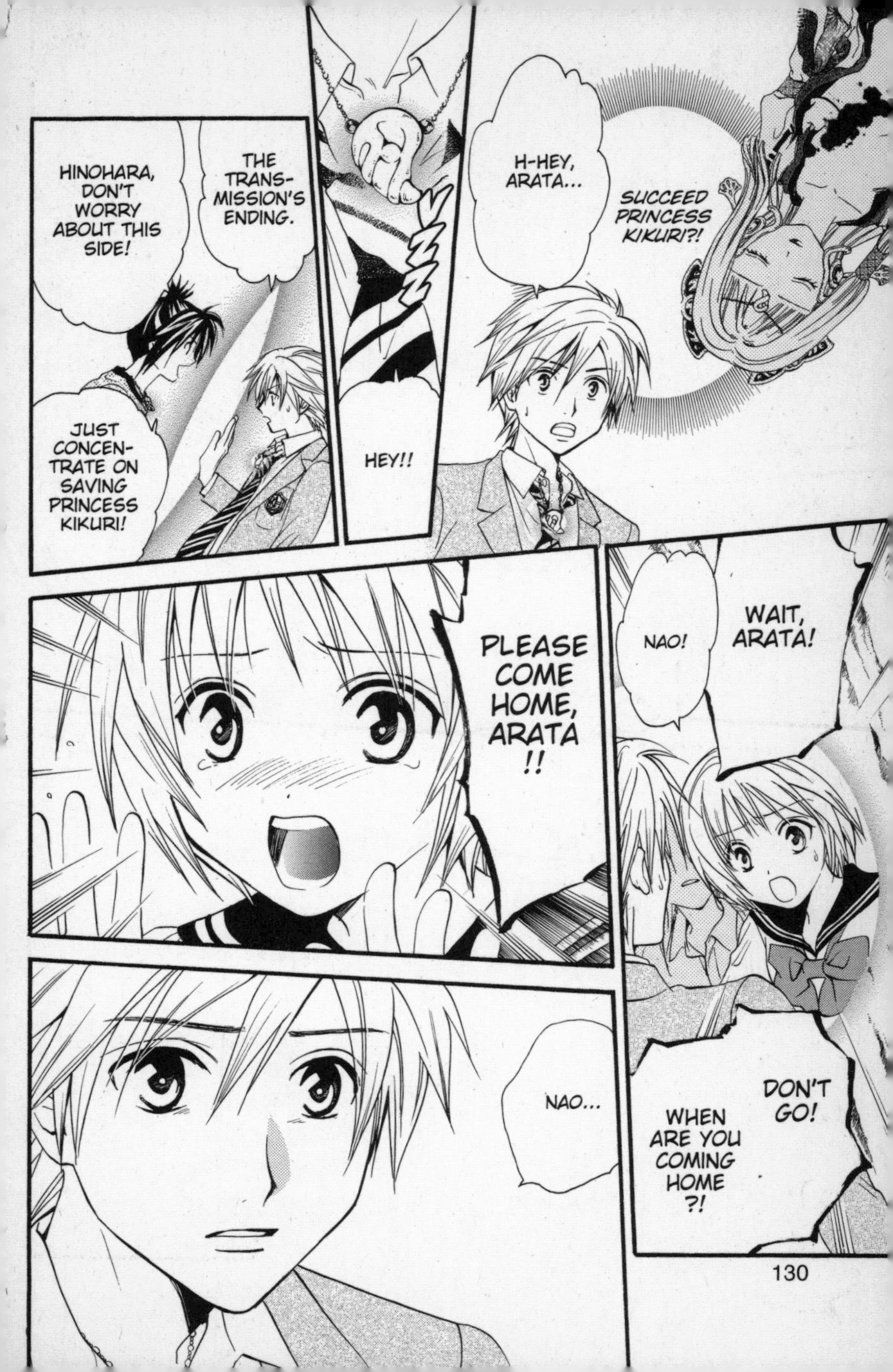
SUCCEED PRINCESS KIKURI?!
H-HEY, ARATA...
HEY!!
THE TRANS-MISSION'S ENDING.
HINOHARA, DON'T WORRY ABOUT THIS SIDE!
JUST CONCEN-TRATE ON SAVING PRINCESS KIKURI!
WAIT, ARATA!
NAO!
DON'T GO!
WHEN ARE YOU COMING HOME ?!
PLEASE COME HOME, ARATA !!
NAO...

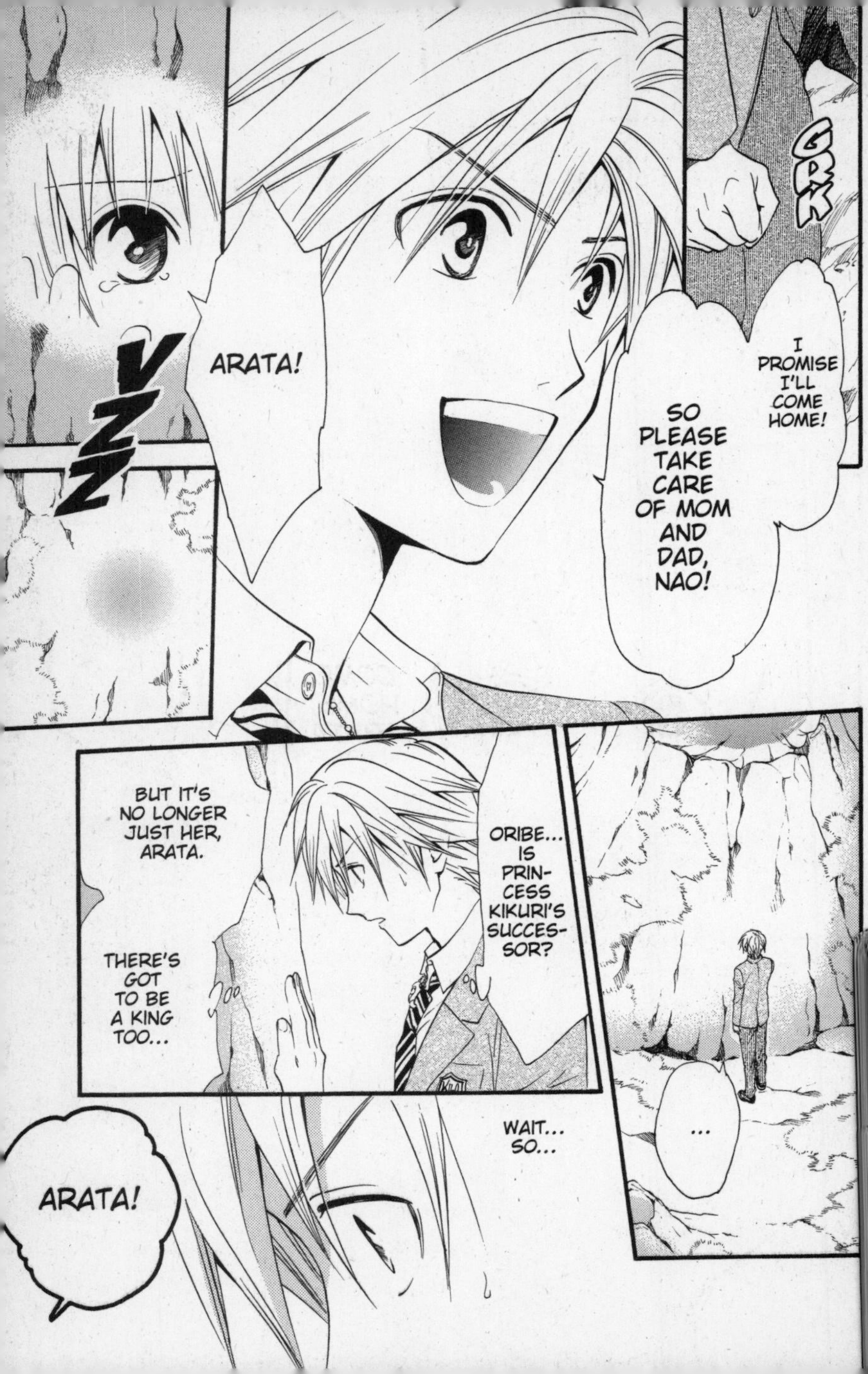
GRK
I PROMISE I'LL COME HOME!
SO PLEASE TAKE CARE OF MOM AND DAD, NAO!
ARATA!
VZZ
...
ORIBE... IS PRIN-CESS KIKURI'S SUCCES-SOR?
BUT IT'S NO LONGER JUST HER, ARATA.
THERE'S GOT TO BE A KING TOO...
WAIT... SO...
ARATA!

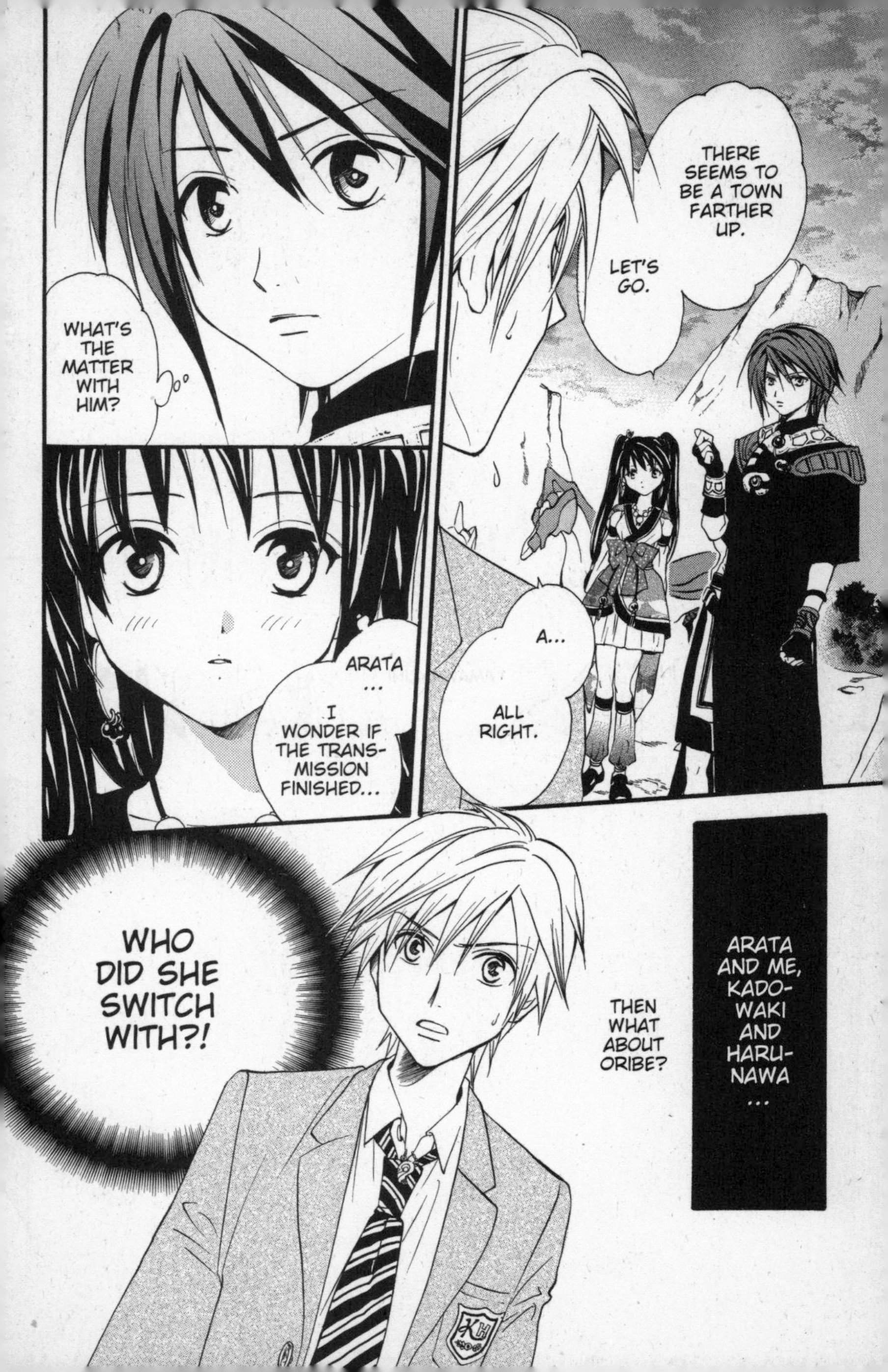

THERE SEEMS TO BE A TOWN FARTHER UP.
LET'S GO.
A... ALL RIGHT.
WHAT'S THE MATTER WITH HIM?
ARATA... I WONDER IF THE TRANS-MISSION FINISHED...
ARATA AND ME, KADO-WAKI AND HARU-NAWA...
THEN WHAT ABOUT ORIBE?
WHO DID SHE SWITCH WITH?!

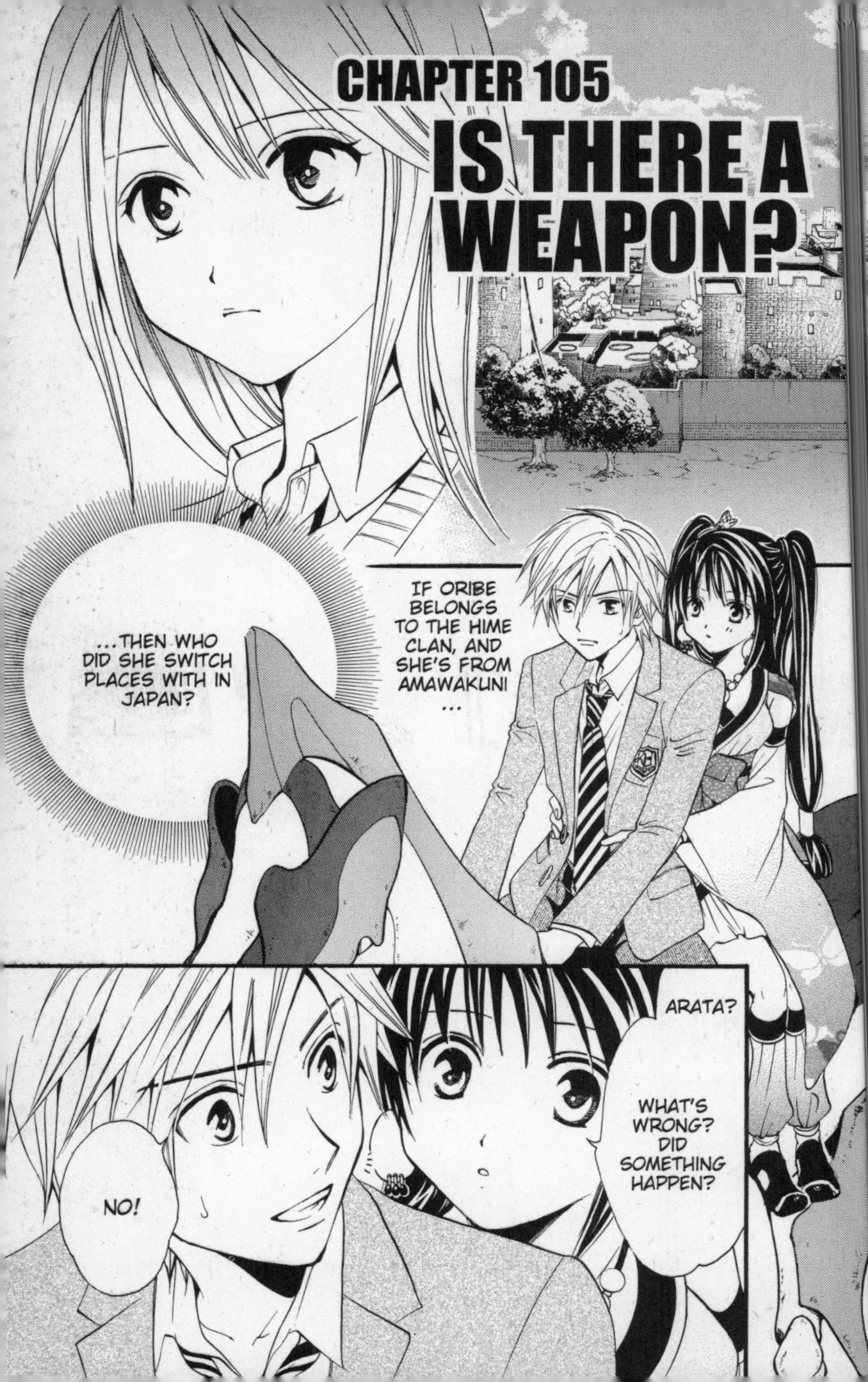
CHAPTER 105
IS THERE A WEAPON?
IF ORIBE BELONGS TO THE HIME CLAN, AND SHE'S FROM AMAWAKUNI ...
...THEN WHO DID SHE SWITCH PLACES WITH IN JAPAN?
ARATA?
WHAT'S WRONG? DID SOMETHING HAPPEN?
NO!

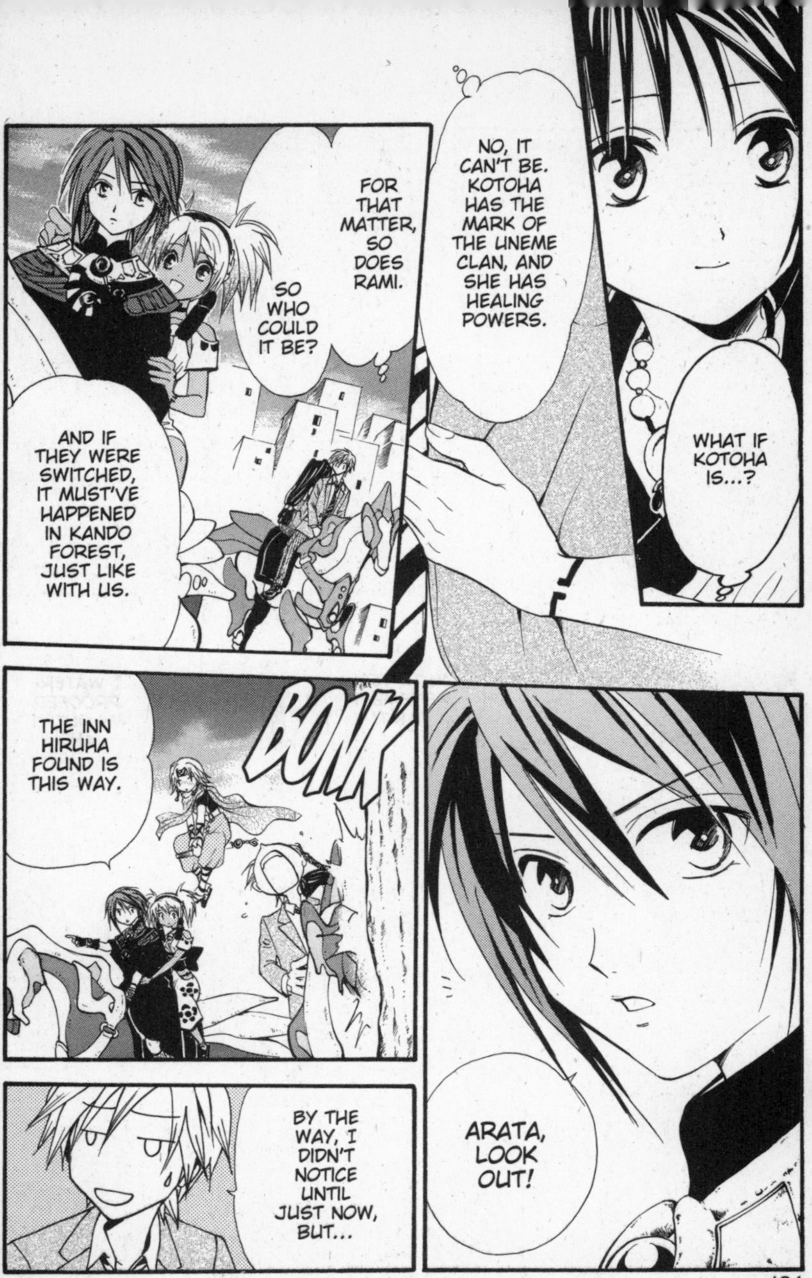
WHAT IF KOTOHA IS...?
NO, IT CAN'T BE. KOTOHA HAS THE MARK OF THE UNEME CLAN, AND SHE HAS HEALING POWERS.
FOR THAT MATTER, SO DOES RAMI.
SO WHO COULD IT BE?
AND IF THEY WERE SWITCHED, IT MUST'VE HAPPENED IN KANDO FOREST, JUST LIKE WITH US.
ARATA, LOOK OUT!
BONK
THE INN HIRUHA FOUND IS THIS WAY.
BY THE WAY, I DIDN'T NOTICE UNTIL JUST NOW, BUT...

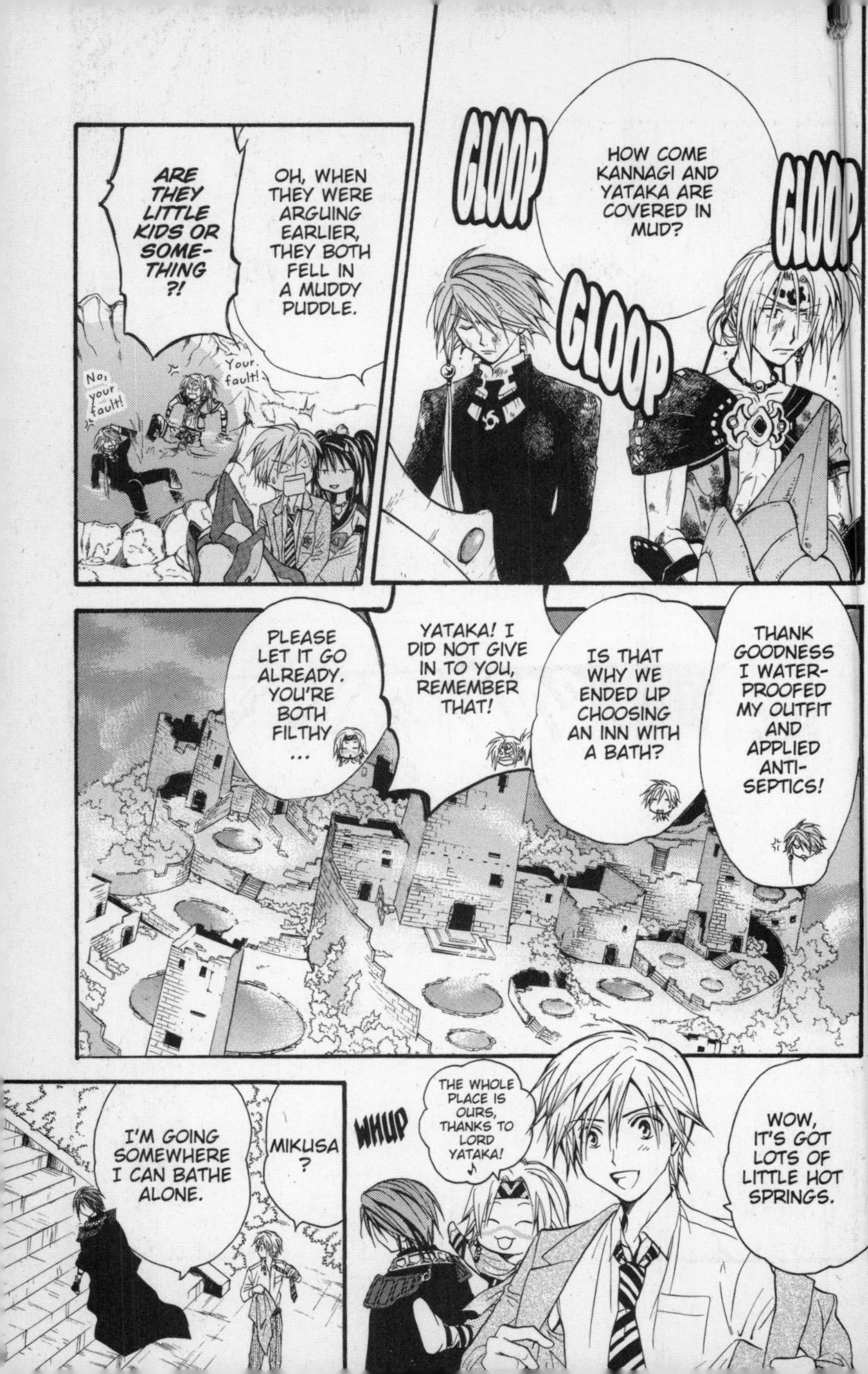
GLOOP
HOW COME KANNAGI AND YATAKA ARE COVERED IN MUD?
GLOOP
GLOOP
OH, WHEN THEY WERE ARGUING EARLIER, THEY BOTH FELL IN A MUDDY PUDDLE.
ARE THEY LITTLE KIDS OR SOME-THING?!
Your fault!
No, your fault!
THANK GOODNESS I WATER-PROOFED MY OUTFIT AND APPLIED ANTI-SEPTICS!
IS THAT WHY WE ENDED UP CHOOSING AN INN WITH A BATH?
YATAKA! I DID NOT GIVE IN TO YOU, REMEMBER THAT!
PLEASE LET IT GO ALREADY. YOU'RE BOTH FILTHY...
WOW, IT'S GOT LOTS OF LITTLE HOT SPRINGS.
THE WHOLE PLACE IS OURS, THANKS TO LORD YATAKA! ♪
WHUP
MIKUSA?
I'M GOING SOMEWHERE I CAN BATHE ALONE.

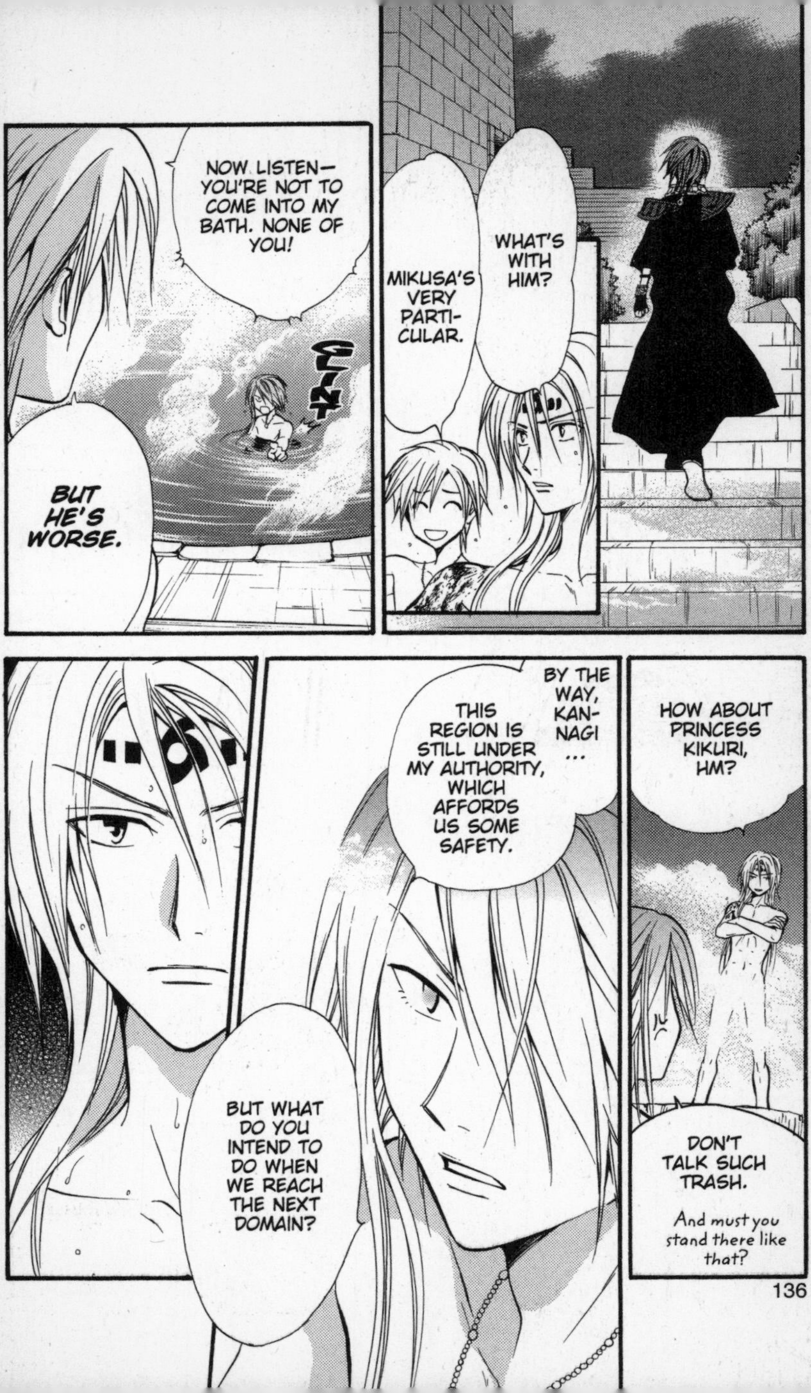
WHAT'S WITH HIM?
MIKUSA'S VERY PARTI-CULAR.
NOW LISTEN—YOU'RE NOT TO COME INTO MY BATH. NONE OF YOU!
GLINT
BUT HE'S WORSE.
HOW ABOUT PRINCESS KIKURI, HM?
DON'T TALK SUCH TRASH.
And must you stand there like that?
BY THE WAY, KAN-NAGI...
THIS REGION IS STILL UNDER MY AUTHORITY, WHICH AFFORDS US SOME SAFETY.
BUT WHAT DO YOU INTEND TO DO WHEN WE REACH THE NEXT DOMAIN?

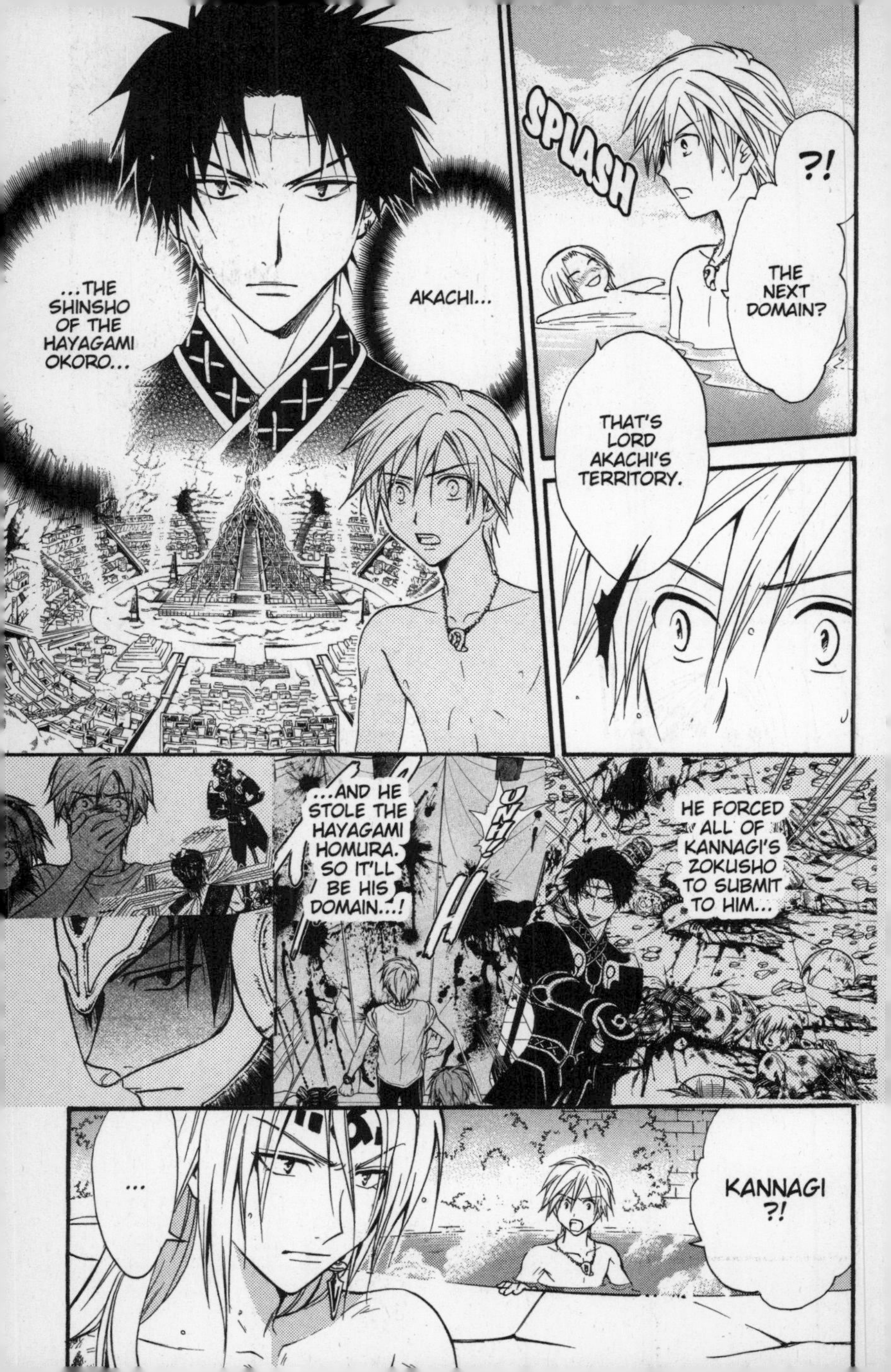
SPLASH
?!
THE NEXT DOMAIN?
THAT'S LORD AKACHI'S TERRITORY.
AKACHI...
...THE SHINSHO OF THE HAYAGAMI OKORO...
HE FORCED ALL OF KANNAGI'S ZOKUSHO TO SUBMIT TO HIM...
...AND HE STOLE THE HAYAGAMI HOMURA. SO IT'LL BE HIS DOMAIN...!
KANNAGI ?!
...

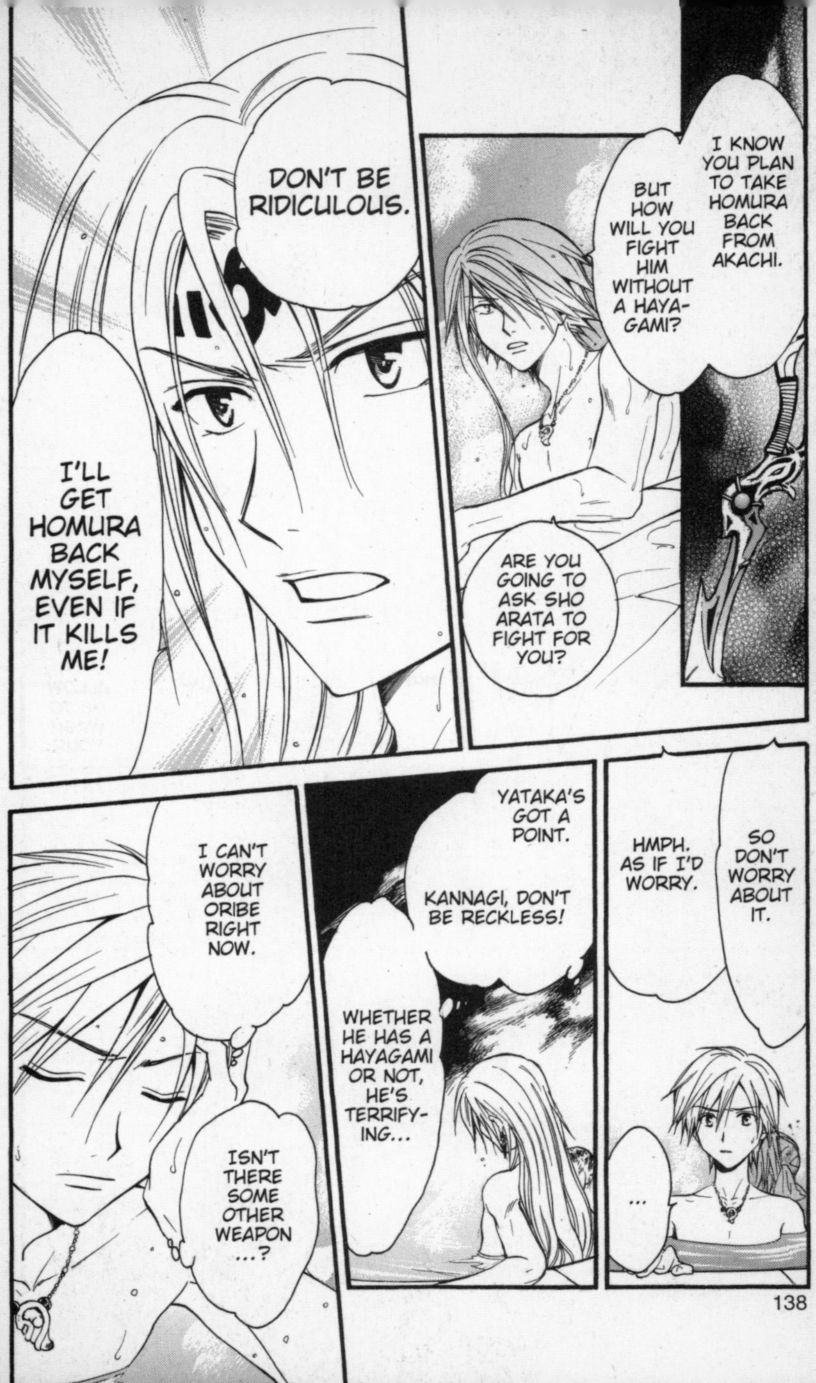

I KNOW YOU PLAN TO TAKE HOMURA BACK FROM AKACHI.
BUT HOW WILL YOU FIGHT HIM WITHOUT A HAYA-GAMI?
ARE YOU GOING TO ASK SHO ARATA TO FIGHT FOR YOU?
DON'T BE RIDICULOUS.
I'LL GET HOMURA BACK MYSELF, EVEN IF IT KILLS ME!
SO DON'T WORRY ABOUT IT.
HMPH. AS IF I'D WORRY.
...
YATAKA'S GOT A POINT.
KANNAGI, DON'T BE RECKLESS!
WHETHER HE HAS A HAYAGAMI OR NOT, HE'S TERRIFY-ING...
I CAN'T WORRY ABOUT ORIBE RIGHT NOW.
ISN'T THERE SOME OTHER WEAPON...?

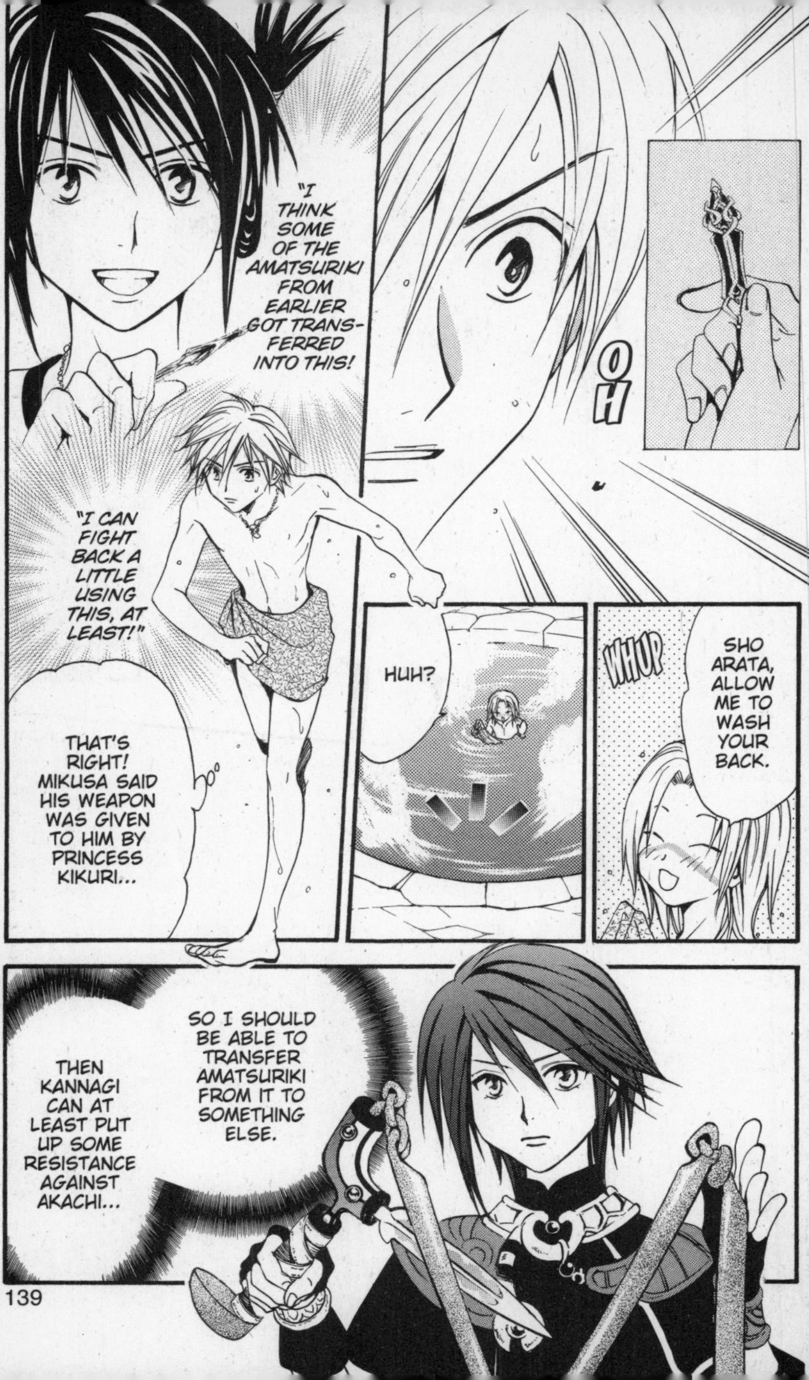

OH
WHUP
SHO ARATA, ALLOW ME TO WASH YOUR BACK.
HUH?
"I THINK SOME OF THE AMATSURIKI FROM EARLIER GOT TRANSFERRED INTO THIS!
"I CAN FIGHT BACK A LITTLE USING THIS, AT LEAST!"
THAT'S RIGHT! MIKUSA SAID HIS WEAPON WAS GIVEN TO HIM BY PRINCESS KIKURI...
SO I SHOULD BE ABLE TO TRANSFER AMATSURIKI FROM IT TO SOMETHING ELSE.
THEN KANNAGI CAN AT LEAST PUT UP SOME RESISTANCE AGAINST AKACHI...

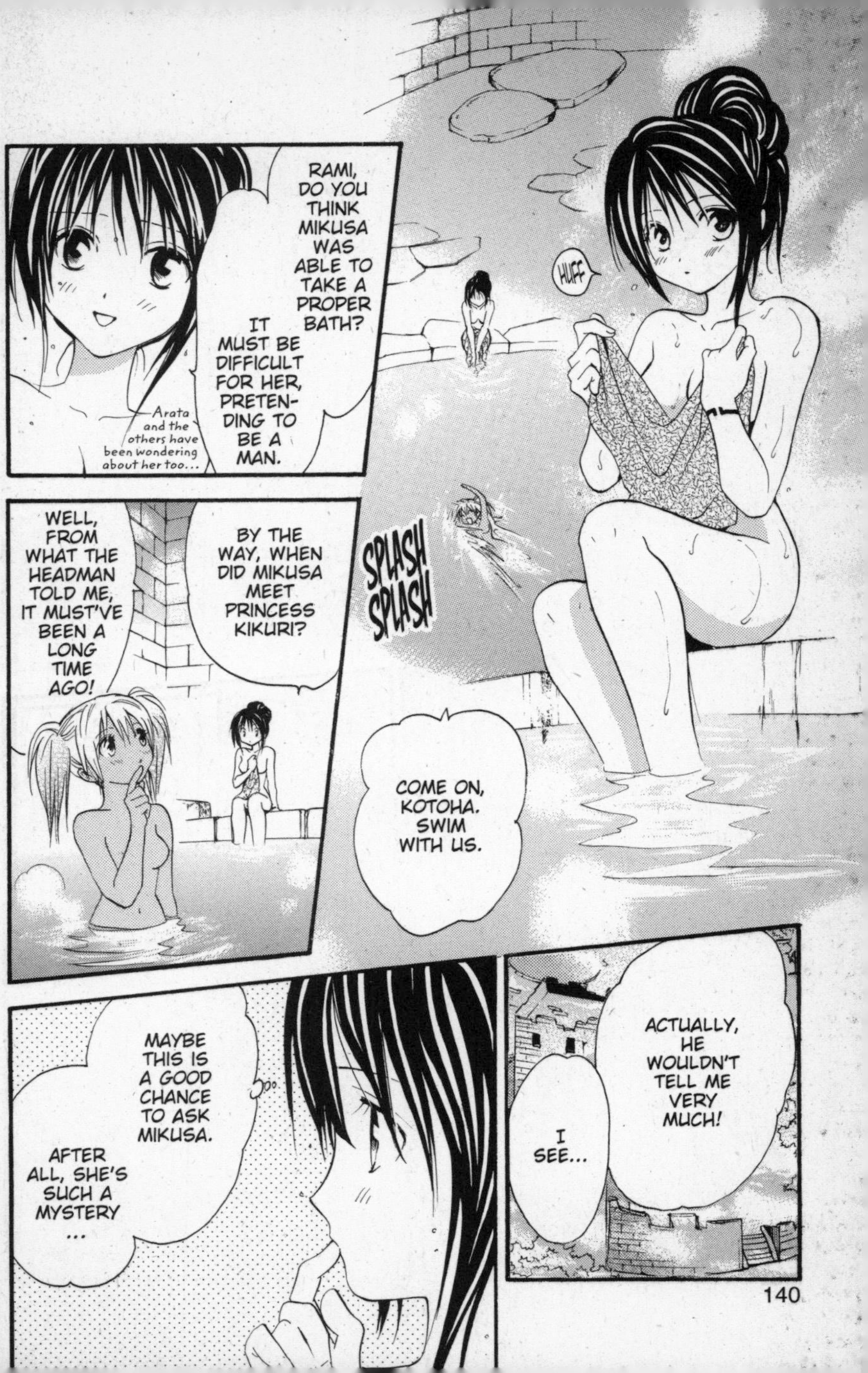
HUFF
SPLASH SPLASH
COME ON, KOTOHA. SWIM WITH US.
RAMI, DO YOU THINK MIKUSA WAS ABLE TO TAKE A PROPER BATH?
IT MUST BE DIFFICULT FOR HER, PRETENDING TO BE A MAN.
Arata and the others have been wondering about her too...
BY THE WAY, WHEN DID MIKUSA MEET PRINCESS KIKURI?
WELL, FROM WHAT THE HEADMAN TOLD ME, IT MUST'VE BEEN A LONG TIME AGO!
ACTUALLY, HE WOULDN'T TELL ME VERY MUCH!
I SEE...
MAYBE THIS IS A GOOD CHANCE TO ASK MIKUSA.
AFTER ALL, SHE'S SUCH A MYSTERY...

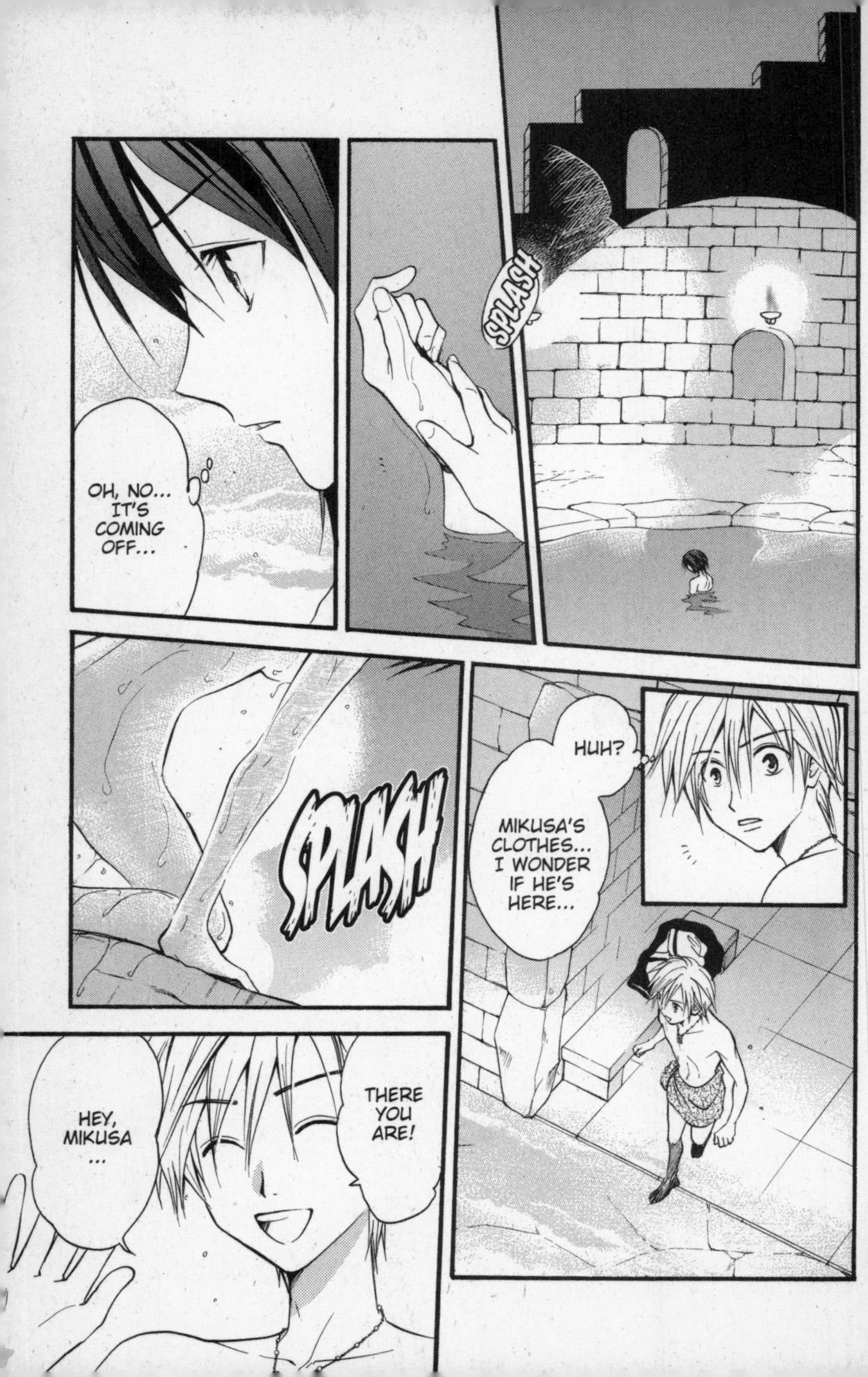
SPLASH
OH, NO... IT'S COMING OFF...
HUH?
MIKUSA'S CLOTHES... I WONDER IF HE'S HERE...
SPLASH
THERE YOU ARE!
HEY, MIKUSA ...

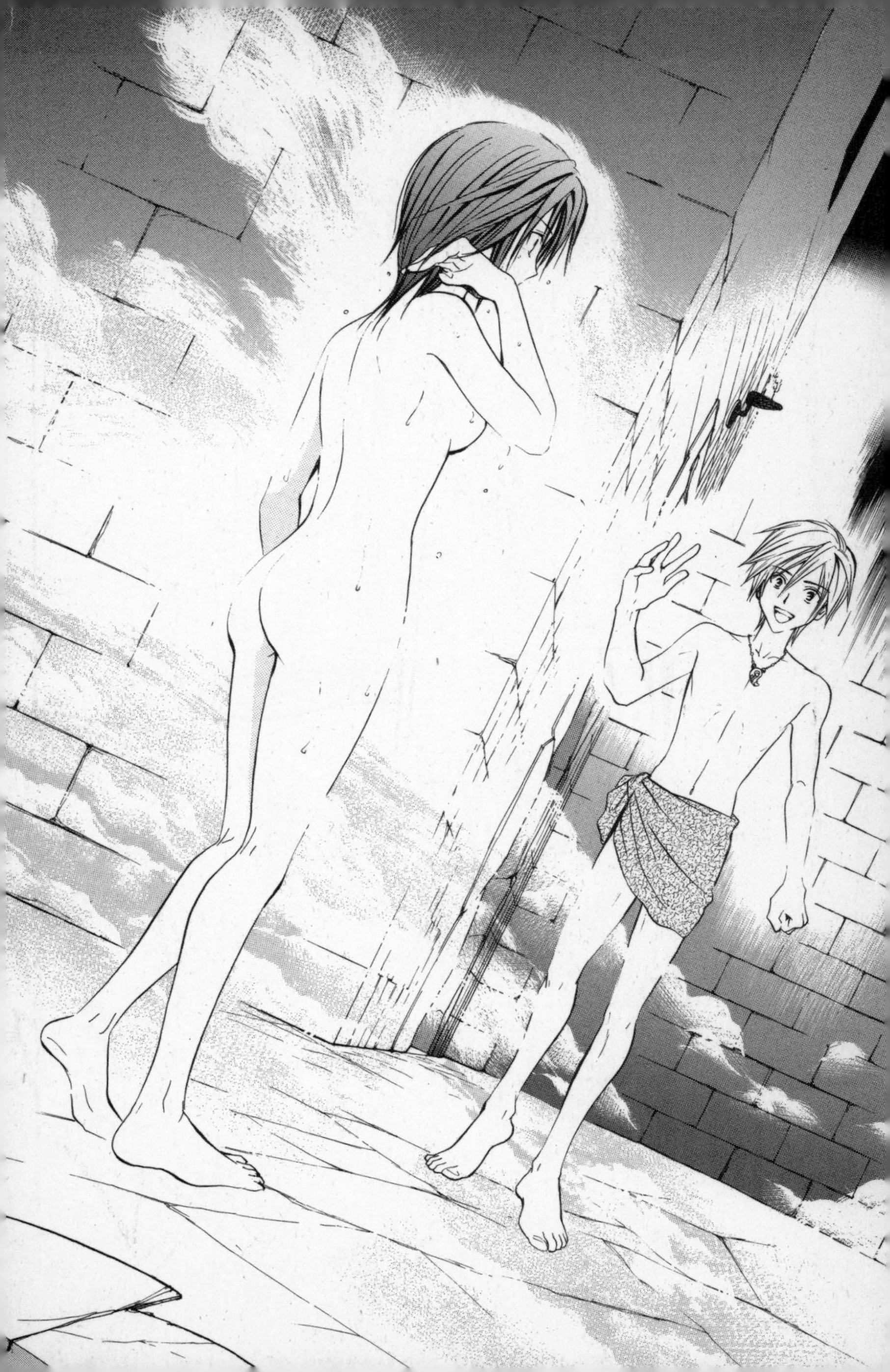

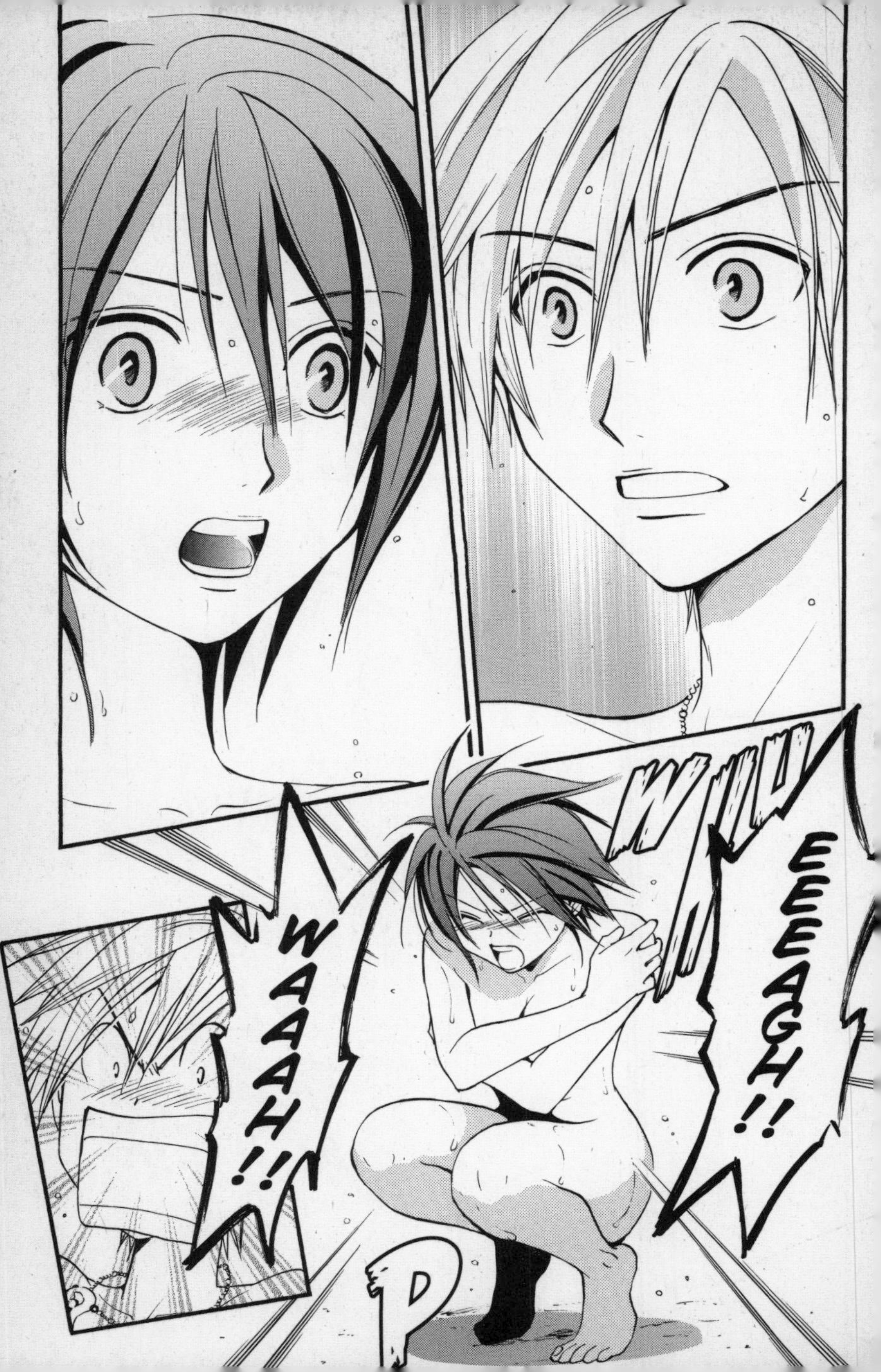
WHO
EEEAGH!!
WAAAAH!!
P

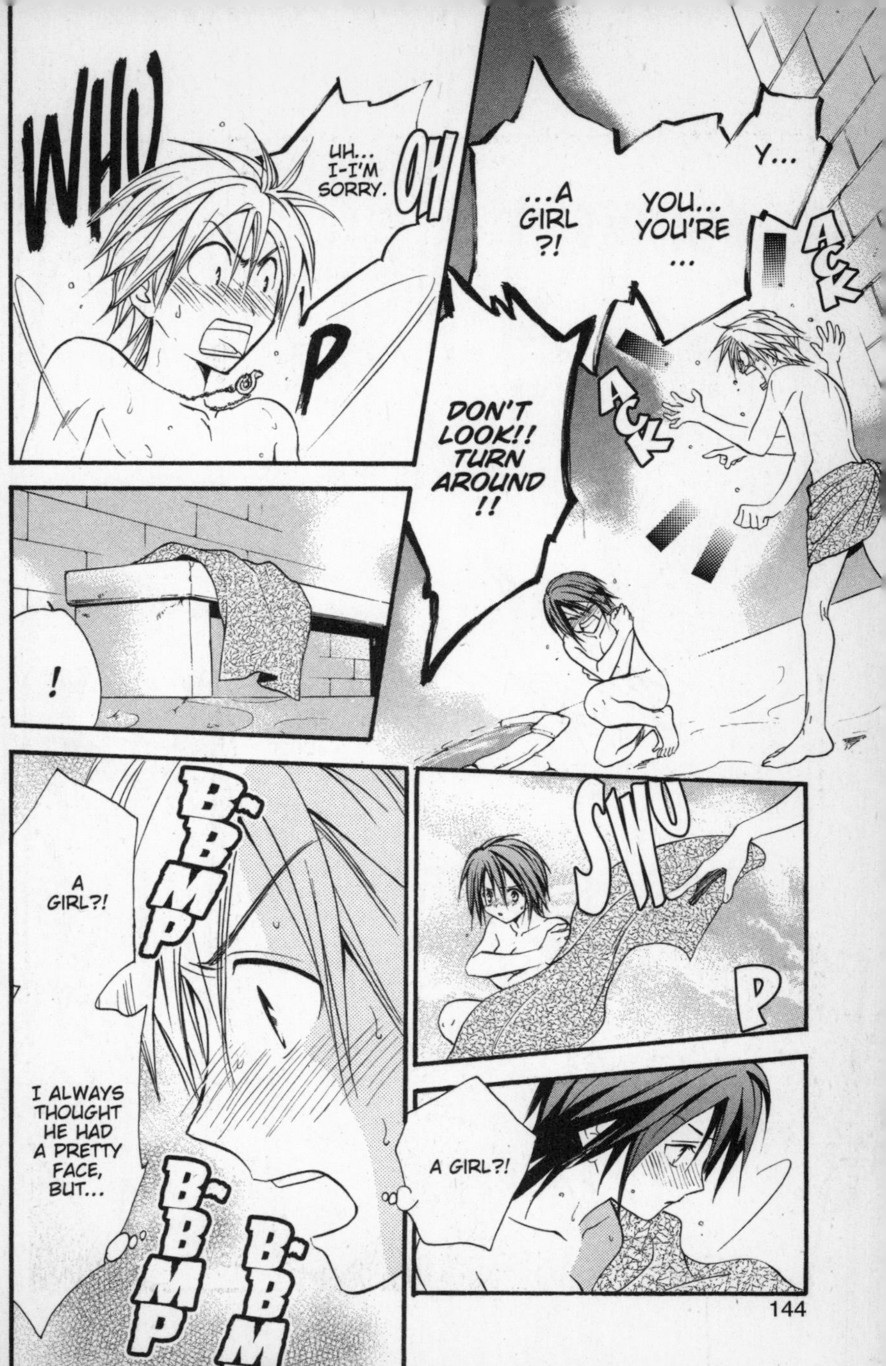
Y...
YOU... YOU'RE ...
...A GIRL?!
ACK
ACK
DON'T LOOK!! TURN AROUND!!
WHU
UH... I-I'M SORRY.
OH
P
!
SWU
P
A GIRL?!
A GIRL?!
B-BMP
I ALWAYS THOUGHT HE HAD A PRETTY FACE, BUT...
B-BMP
B-BMP

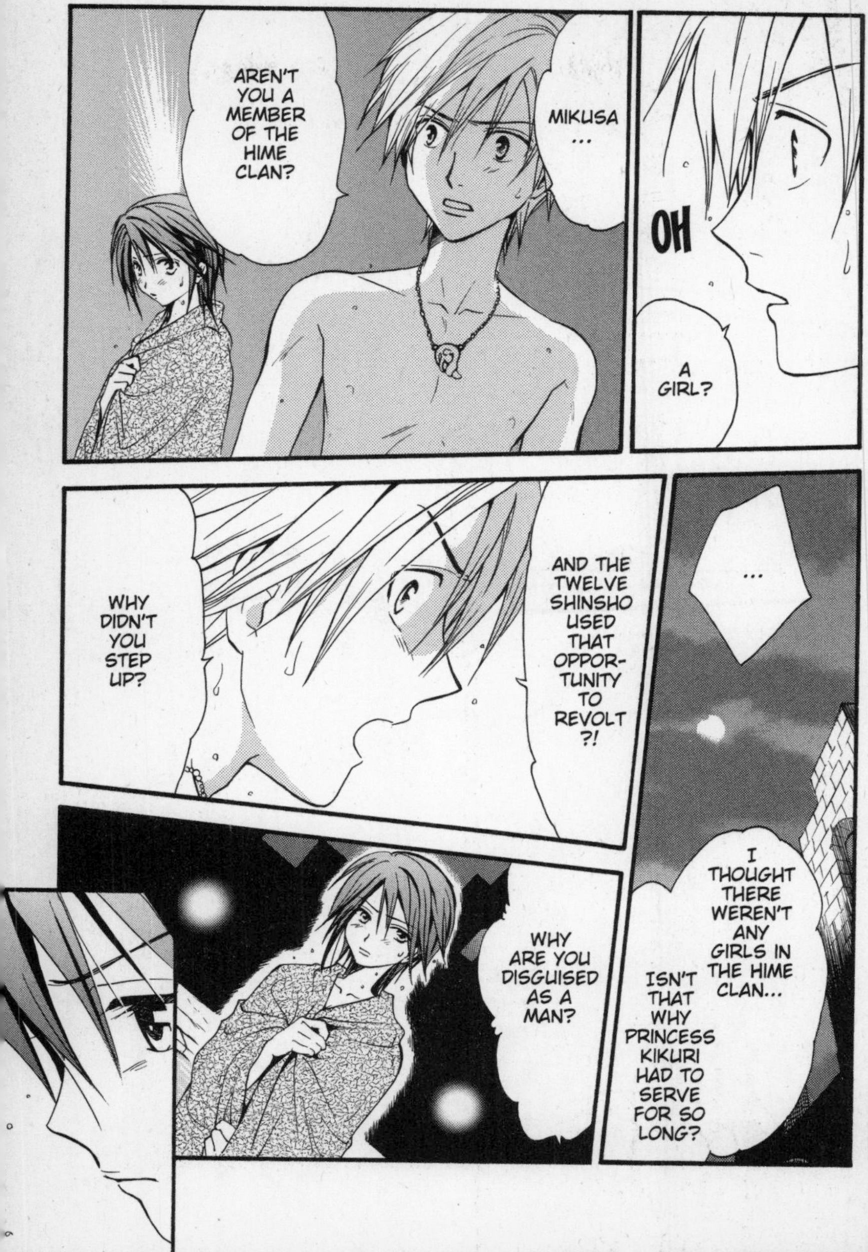
OH
A GIRL?
MIKUSA ...
AREN'T YOU A MEMBER OF THE HIME CLAN?
...
AND THE TWELVE SHINSHO USED THAT OPPORTUNITY TO REVOLT?!
WHY DIDN'T YOU STEP UP?
I THOUGHT THERE WEREN'T ANY GIRLS IN THE HIME CLAN...
ISN'T THAT WHY PRINCESS KIKURI HAD TO SERVE FOR SO LONG?
WHY ARE YOU DISGUISED AS A MAN?

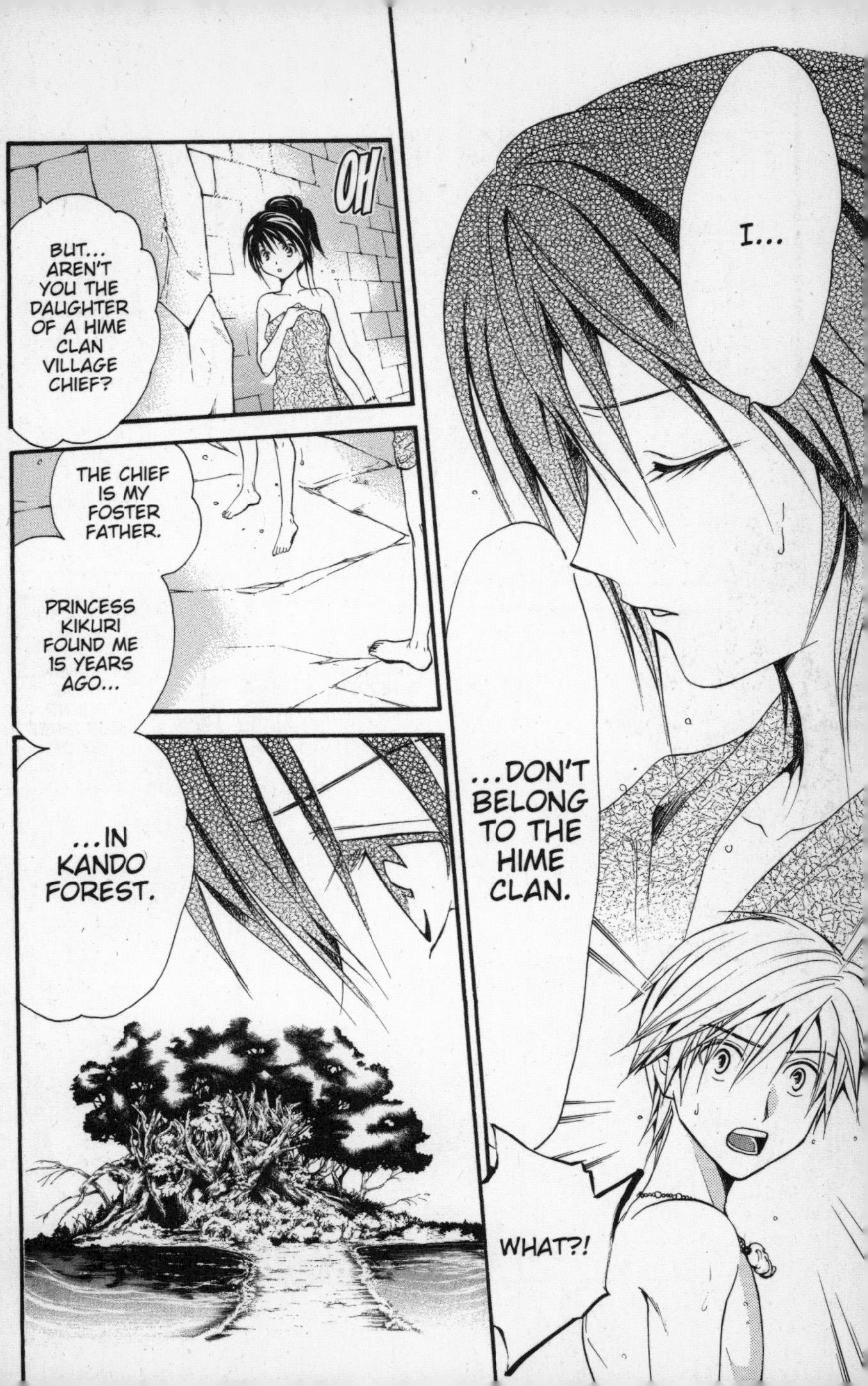
I...
...DON'T BELONG TO THE HIME CLAN.
WHAT?!
OH
BUT... AREN'T YOU THE DAUGHTER OF A HIME CLAN VILLAGE CHIEF?
THE CHIEF IS MY FOSTER FATHER.
PRINCESS KIKURI FOUND ME 15 YEARS AGO...
...IN KANDO FOREST.

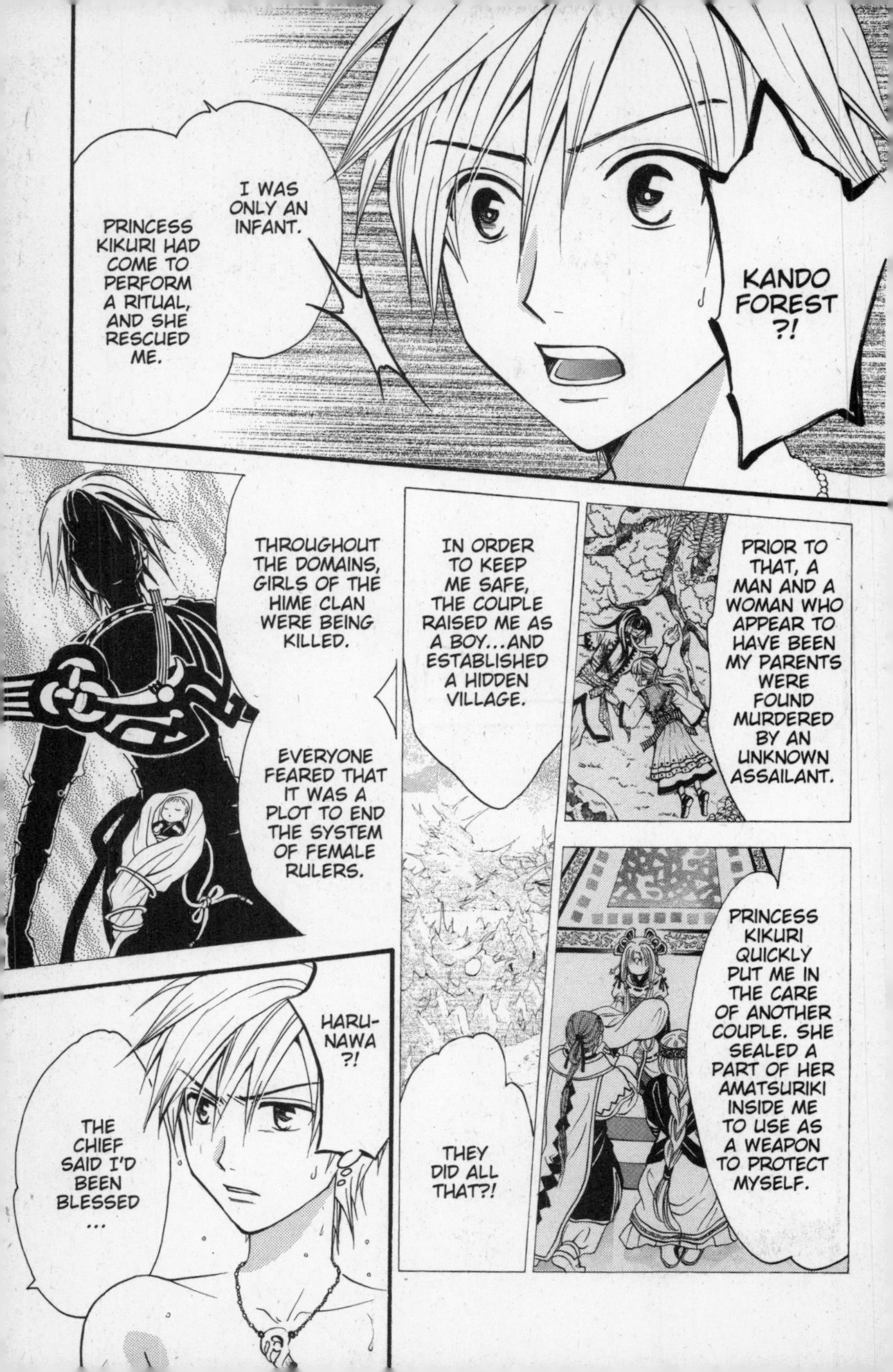
KANDO FOREST ?!
I WAS ONLY AN INFANT.
PRINCESS KIKURI HAD COME TO PERFORM A RITUAL, AND SHE RESCUED ME.
PRIOR TO THAT, A MAN AND A WOMAN WHO APPEAR TO HAVE BEEN MY PARENTS WERE FOUND MURDERED BY AN UNKNOWN ASSAILANT.
PRINCESS KIKURI QUICKLY PUT ME IN THE CARE OF ANOTHER COUPLE. SHE SEALED A PART OF HER AMATSURIKI INSIDE ME TO USE AS A WEAPON TO PROTECT MYSELF.
IN ORDER TO KEEP ME SAFE, THE COUPLE RAISED ME AS A BOY...AND ESTABLISHED A HIDDEN VILLAGE.
THEY DID ALL THAT?!
THROUGHOUT THE DOMAINS, GIRLS OF THE HIME CLAN WERE BEING KILLED.
EVERYONE FEARED THAT IT WAS A PLOT TO END THE SYSTEM OF FEMALE RULERS.
HARU-NAWA ?!
THE CHIEF SAID I'D BEEN BLESSED ...

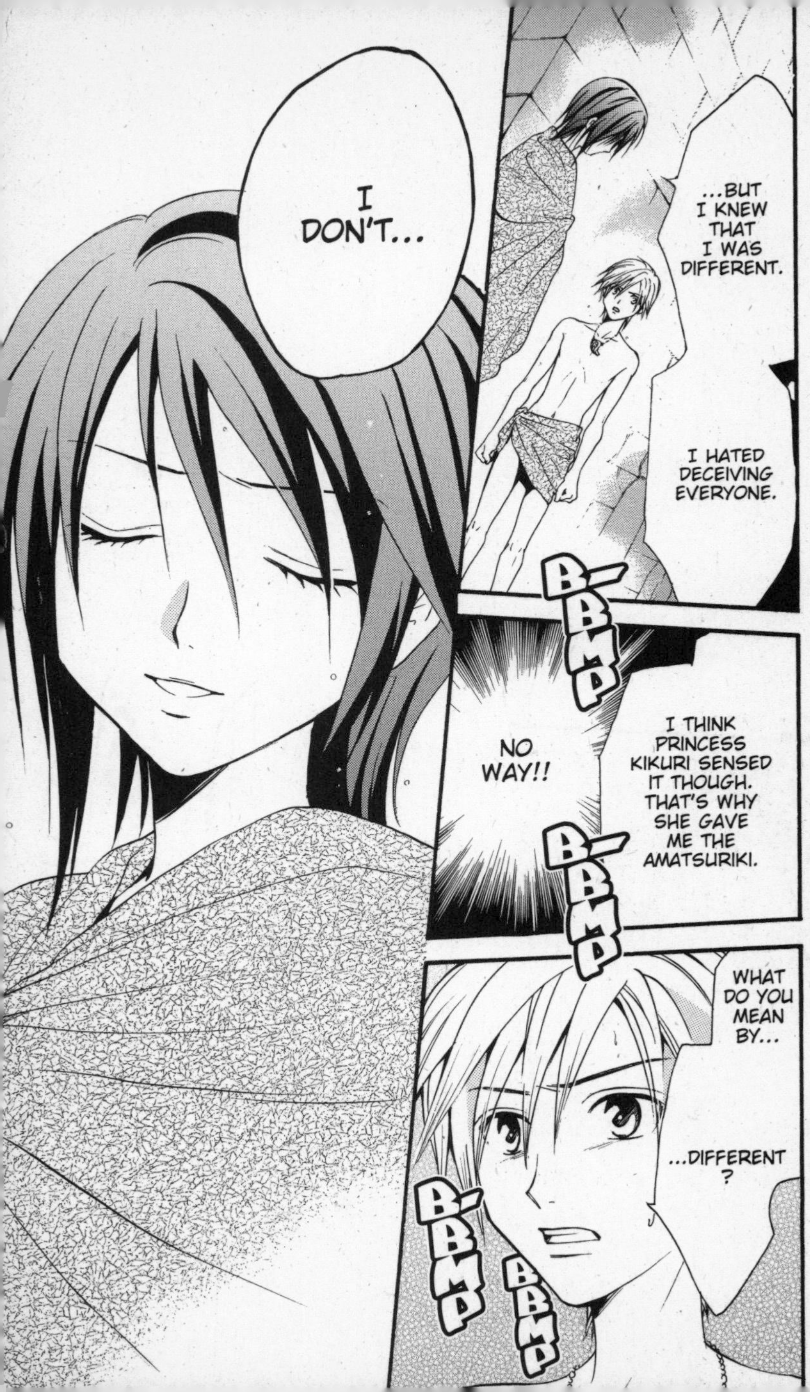
...BUT I KNEW THAT I WAS DIFFERENT.
I HATED DECEIVING EVERYONE.
B-BMP
I THINK PRINCESS KIKURI SENSED IT THOUGH. THAT'S WHY SHE GAVE ME THE AMATSURIKI.
NO WAY!!
B-BMP
B-BMP
WHAT DO YOU MEAN BY...
...DIFFERENT?
B-BMP
BBMP
I DON'T...

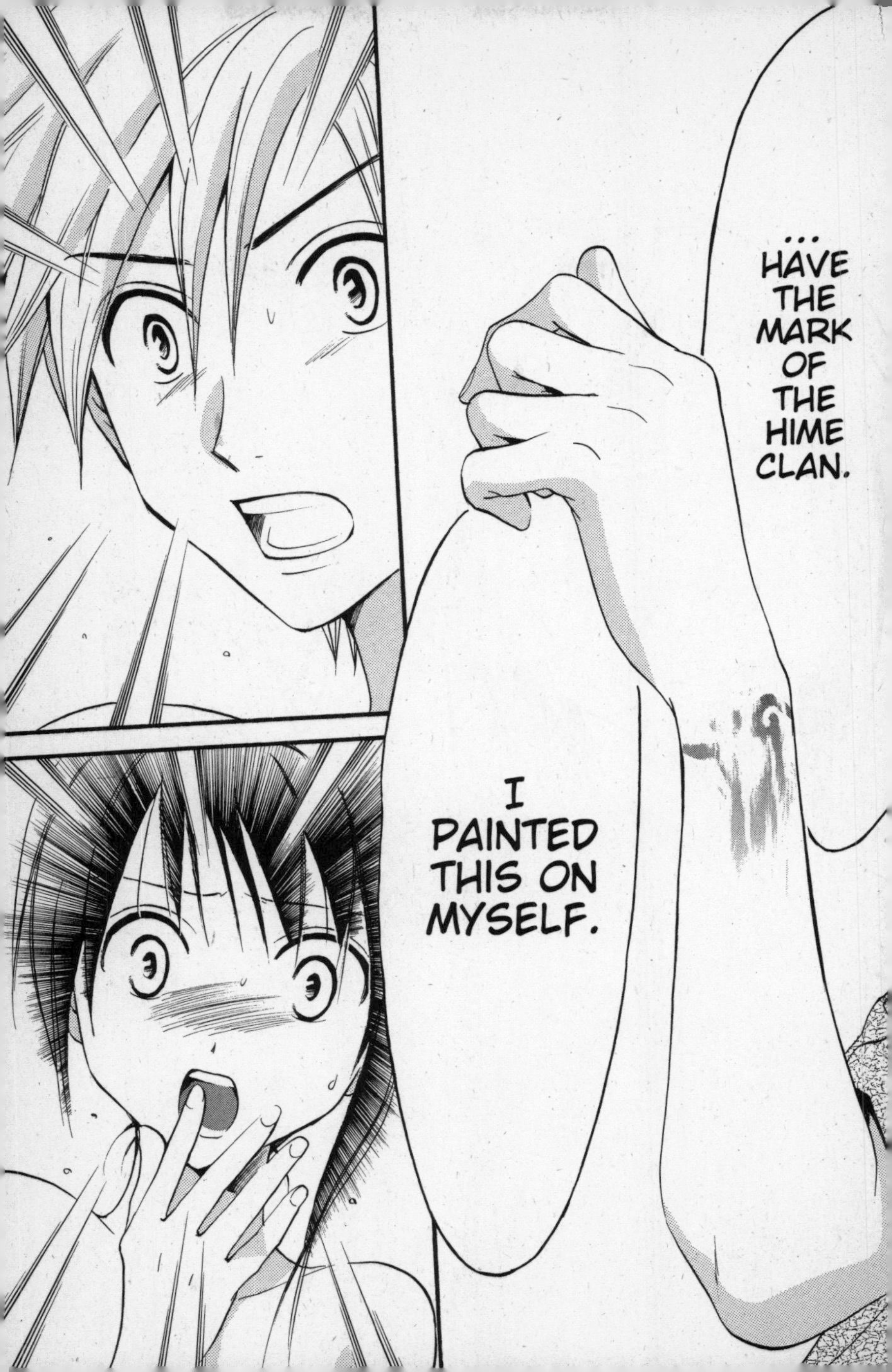
...HAVE THE MARK OF THE HIME CLAN.
I PAINTED THIS ON MYSELF.

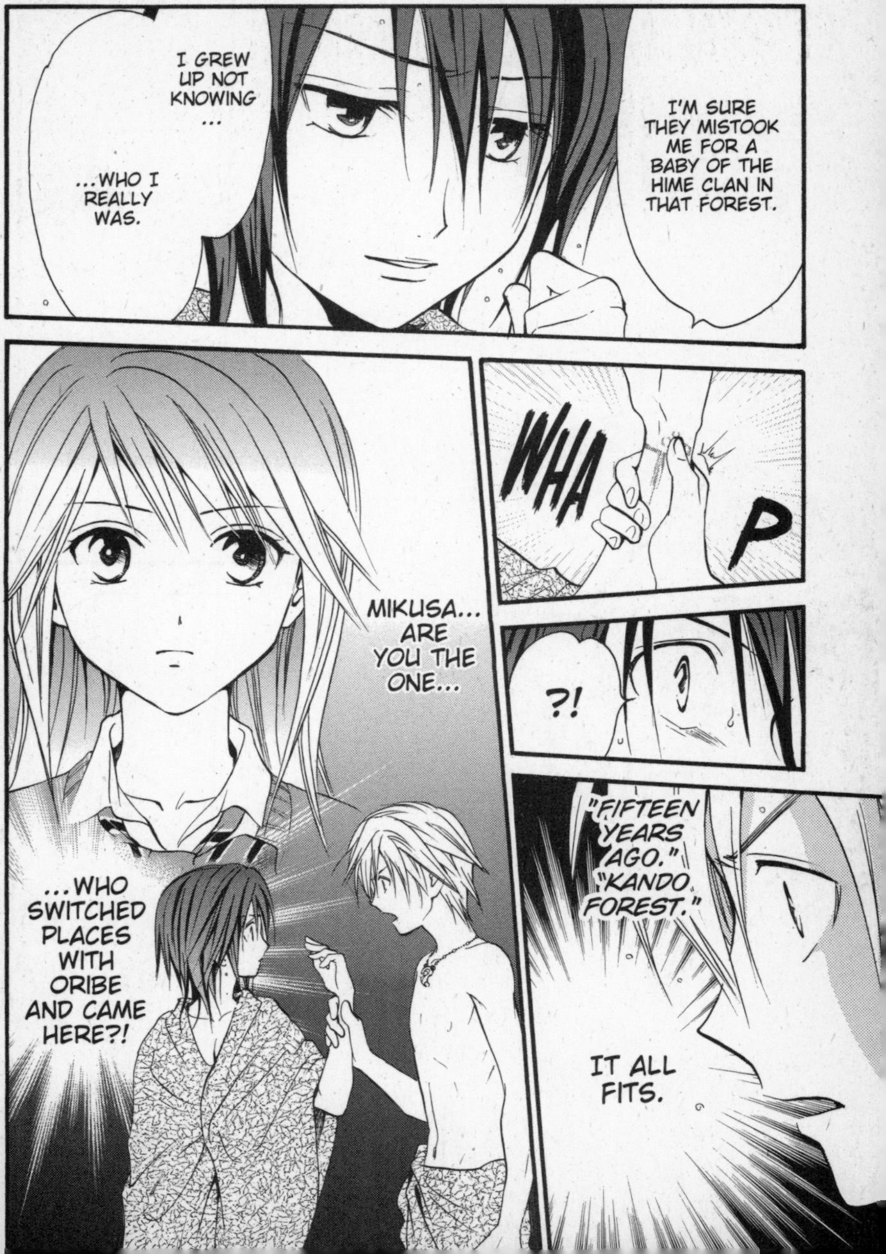
I'M SURE THEY MISTOOK ME FOR A BABY OF THE HIME CLAN IN THAT FOREST.
I GREW UP NOT KNOWING ...
...WHO I REALLY WAS.
WHAP
?!
"FIFTEEN YEARS AGO." "KANDO FOREST."
IT ALL FITS.
MIKUSA... ARE YOU THE ONE...
...WHO SWITCHED PLACES WITH ORIBE AND CAME HERE?!

CHAPTER 106
TWO CHILDHOOD FRIENDS

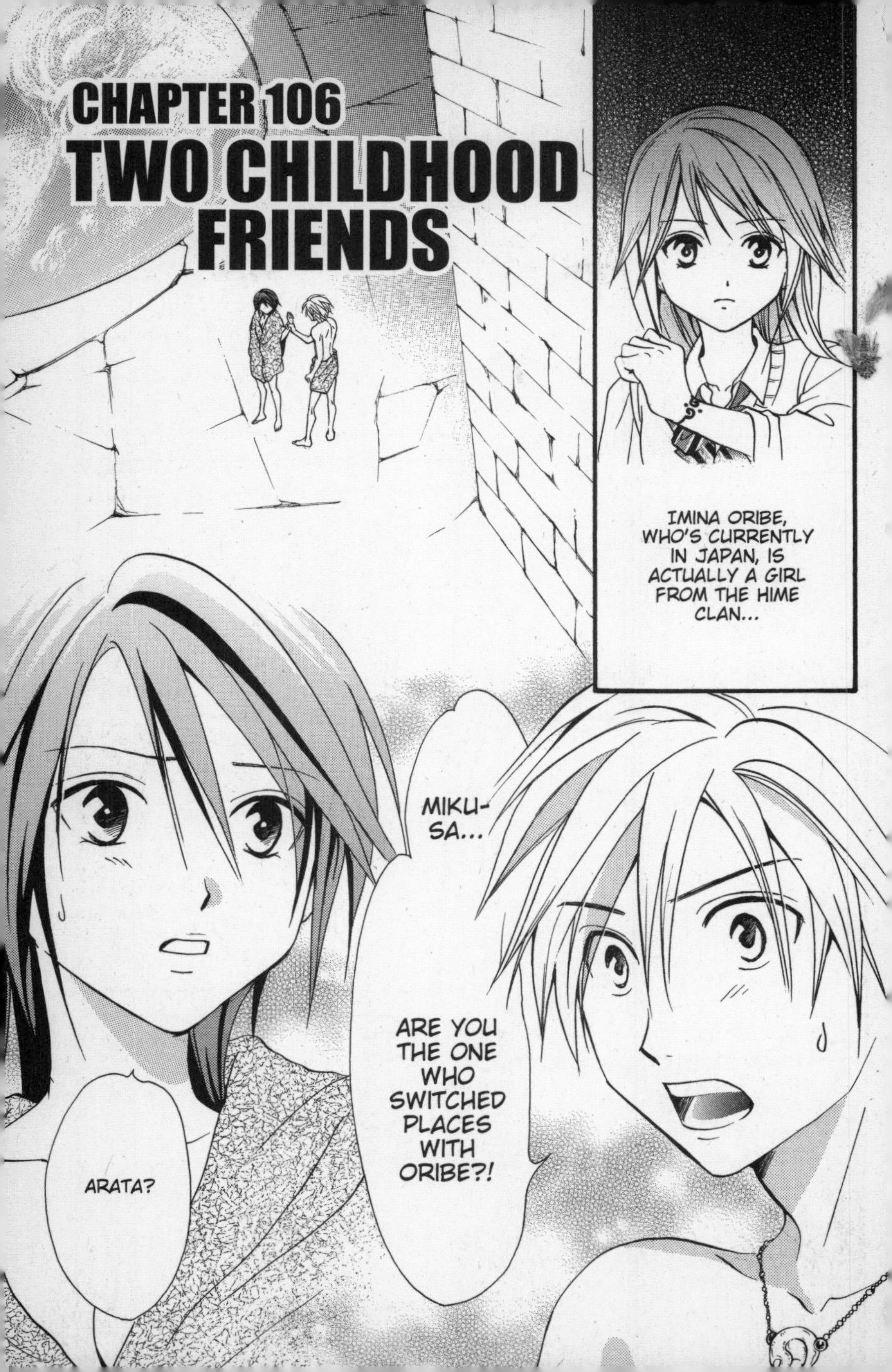
IMINA ORIBE, WHO'S CURRENTLY IN JAPAN, IS ACTUALLY A GIRL FROM THE HIME CLAN...
MIKU-SA...
ARE YOU THE ONE WHO SWITCHED PLACES WITH ORIBE?!
ARATA?

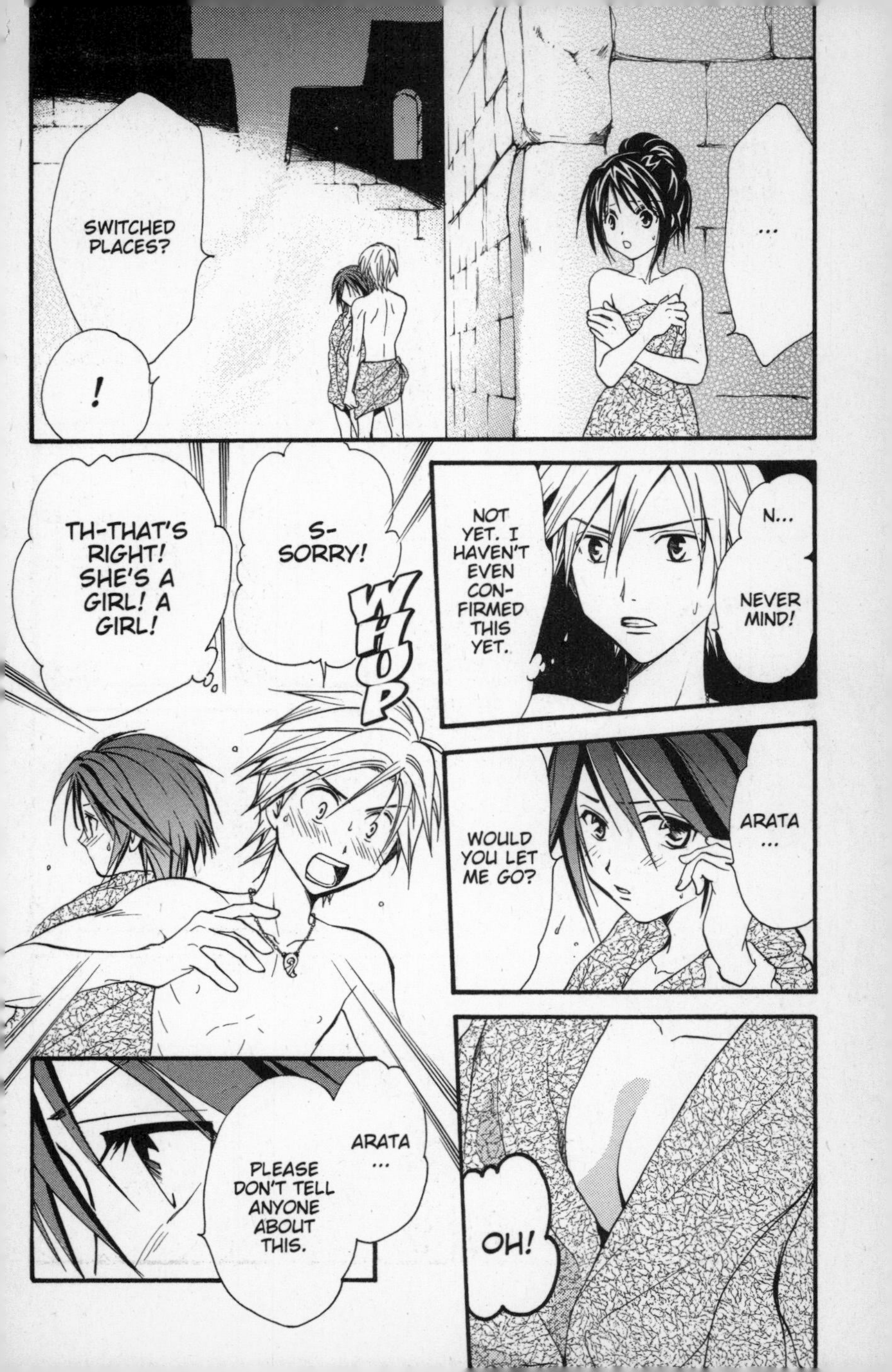
...
SWITCHED PLACES?
!
N... NEVER MIND!
NOT YET. I HAVEN'T EVEN CON-FIRMED THIS YET.
ARATA ...
WOULD YOU LET ME GO?
OH!
S-SORRY!
WHOP
TH-THAT'S RIGHT! SHE'S A GIRL! A GIRL!
ARATA ...
PLEASE DON'T TELL ANYONE ABOUT THIS.

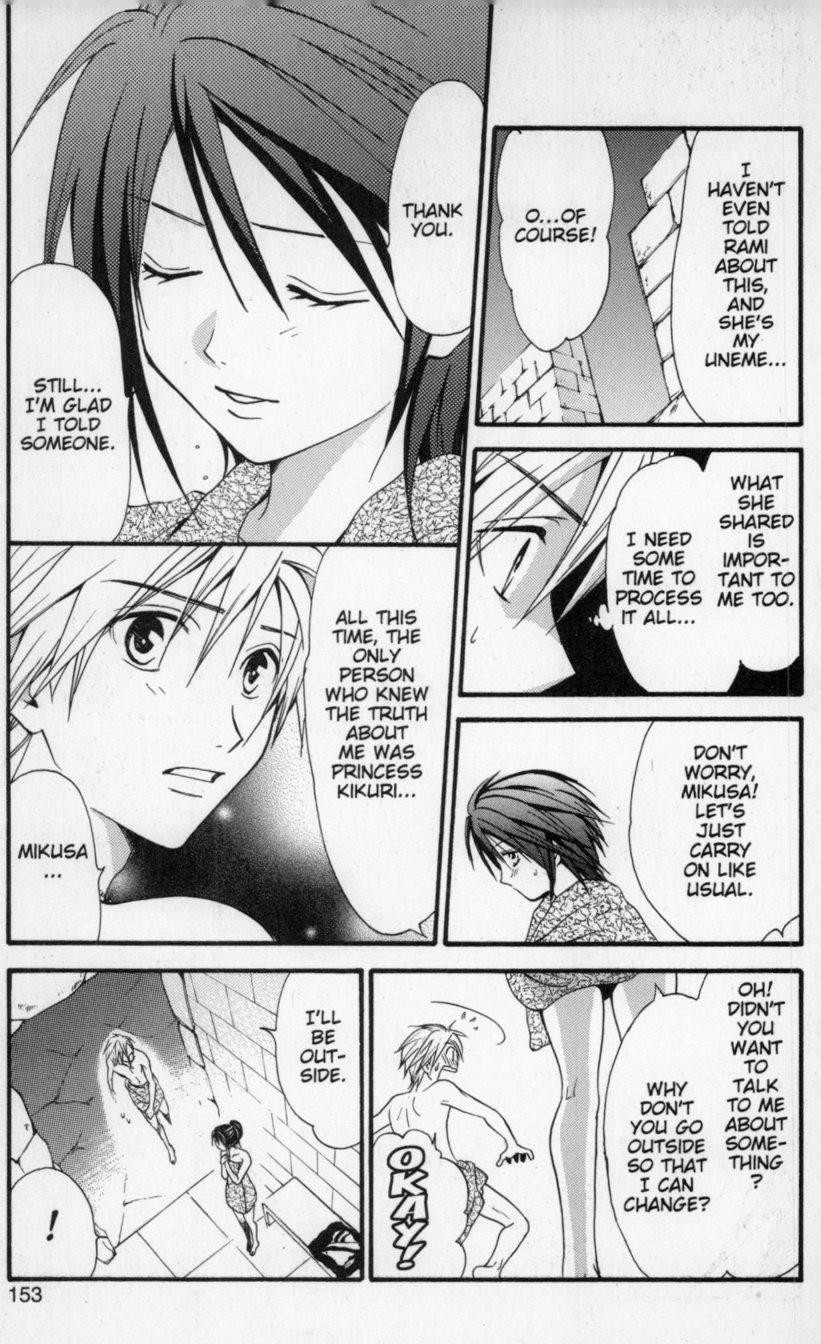

I HAVEN'T EVEN TOLD RAMI ABOUT THIS, AND SHE'S MY UNEME...
O...OF COURSE!
THANK YOU.
STILL... I'M GLAD I TOLD SOMEONE.
WHAT SHE SHARED IS IMPORTANT TO ME TOO.
I NEED SOME TIME TO PROCESS IT ALL...
ALL THIS TIME, THE ONLY PERSON WHO KNEW THE TRUTH ABOUT ME WAS PRINCESS KIKURI...
MIKUSA ...
DON'T WORRY, MIKUSA! LET'S JUST CARRY ON LIKE USUAL.
OH! DIDN'T YOU WANT TO TALK TO ME ABOUT SOME-THING?
WHY DON'T YOU GO OUTSIDE SO THAT I CAN CHANGE?
OKAY!
I'LL BE OUT-SIDE.
!

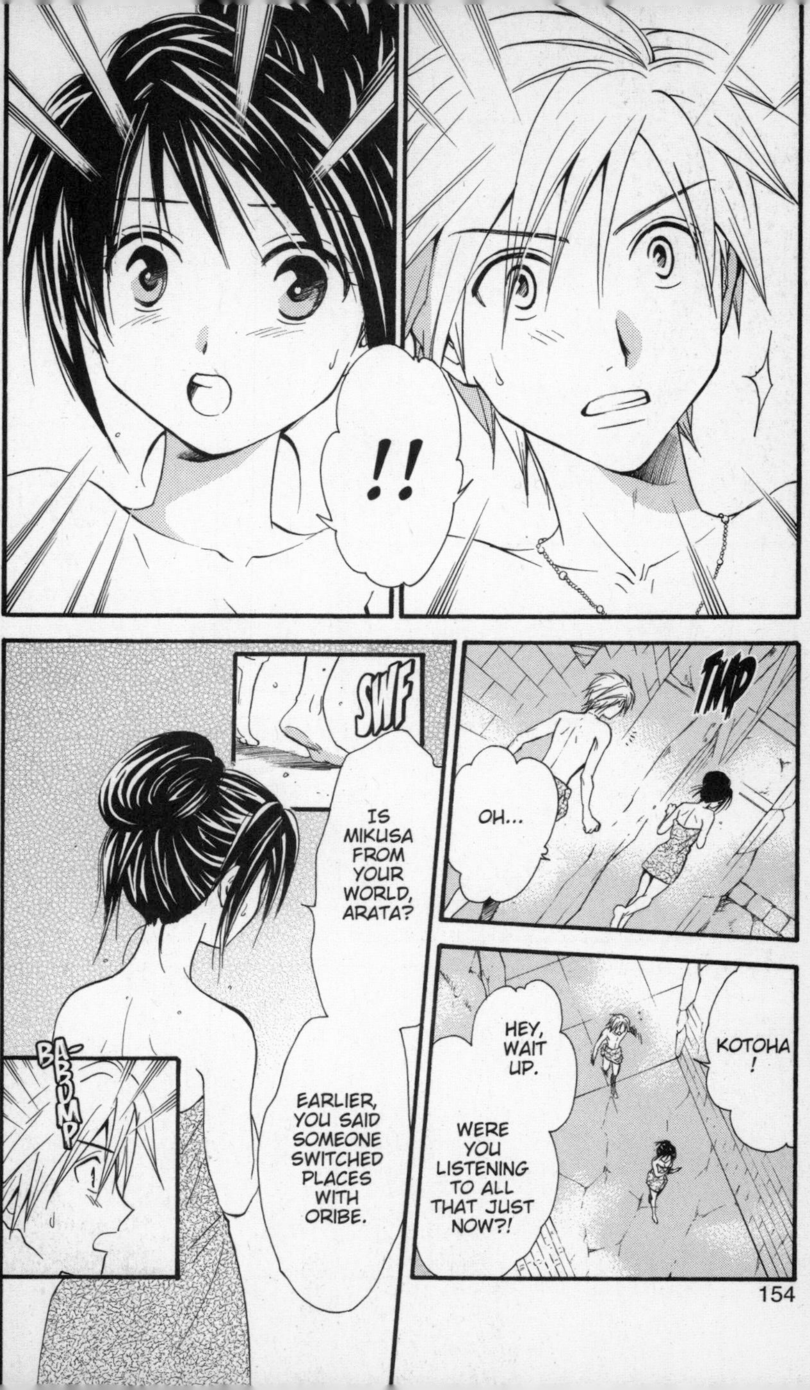
!!
TMP
OH...
KOTOHA!
HEY, WAIT UP.
WERE YOU LISTENING TO ALL THAT JUST NOW?!
SWF
IS MIKUSA FROM YOUR WORLD, ARATA?
EARLIER, YOU SAID SOMEONE SWITCHED PLACES WITH ORIBE.
BA-BUMP

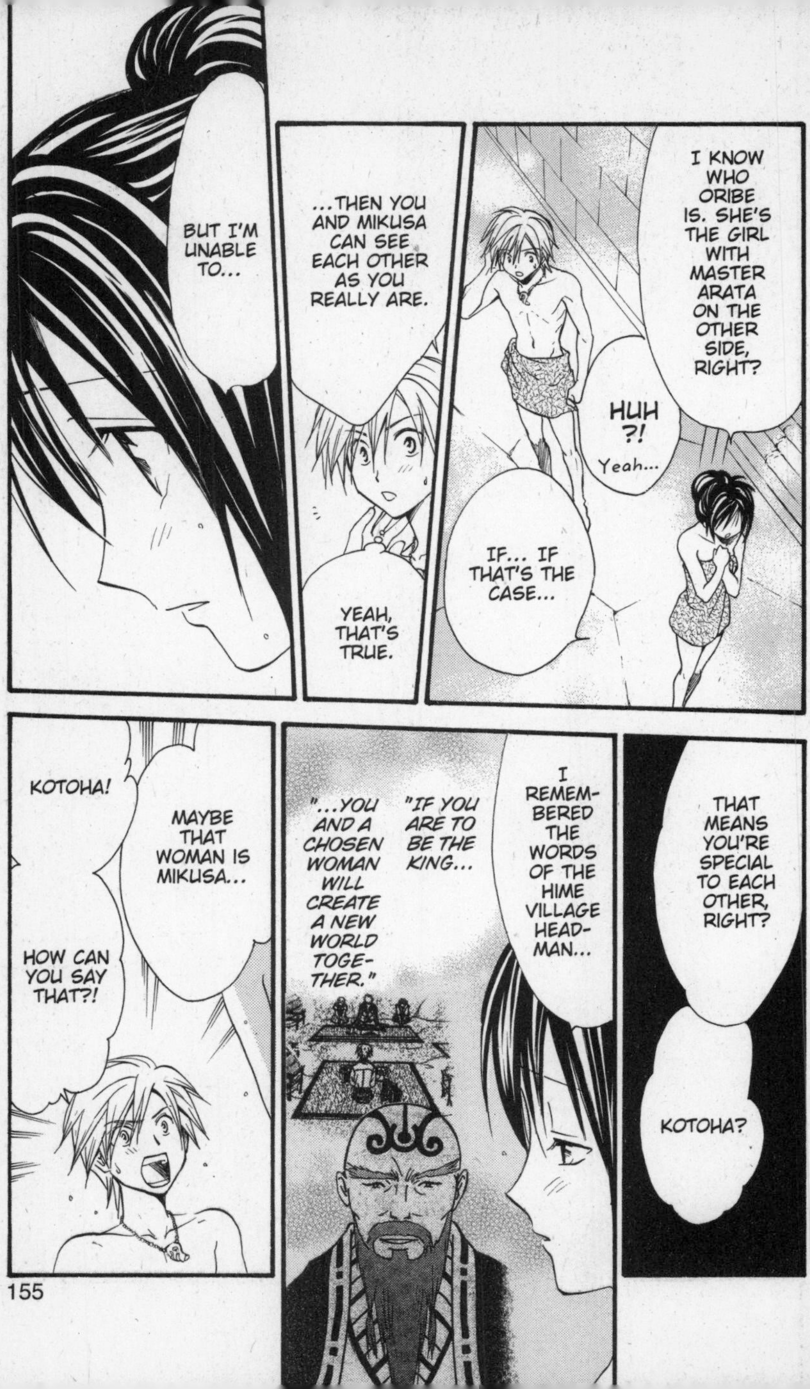
I KNOW WHO ORIBE IS. SHE'S THE GIRL WITH MASTER ARATA ON THE OTHER SIDE, RIGHT?
HUH ?!
Yeah...
IF... IF THAT'S THE CASE...
...THEN YOU AND MIKUSA CAN SEE EACH OTHER AS YOU REALLY ARE.
YEAH, THAT'S TRUE.
BUT I'M UNABLE TO...
THAT MEANS YOU'RE SPECIAL TO EACH OTHER, RIGHT?
KOTOHA?
I REMEMBERED THE WORDS OF THE HIME VILLAGE HEADMAN...
"IF YOU ARE TO BE THE KING...
"...YOU AND A CHOSEN WOMAN WILL CREATE A NEW WORLD TOGETHER."
MAYBE THAT WOMAN IS MIKUSA...
KOTOHA!
HOW CAN YOU SAY THAT?!

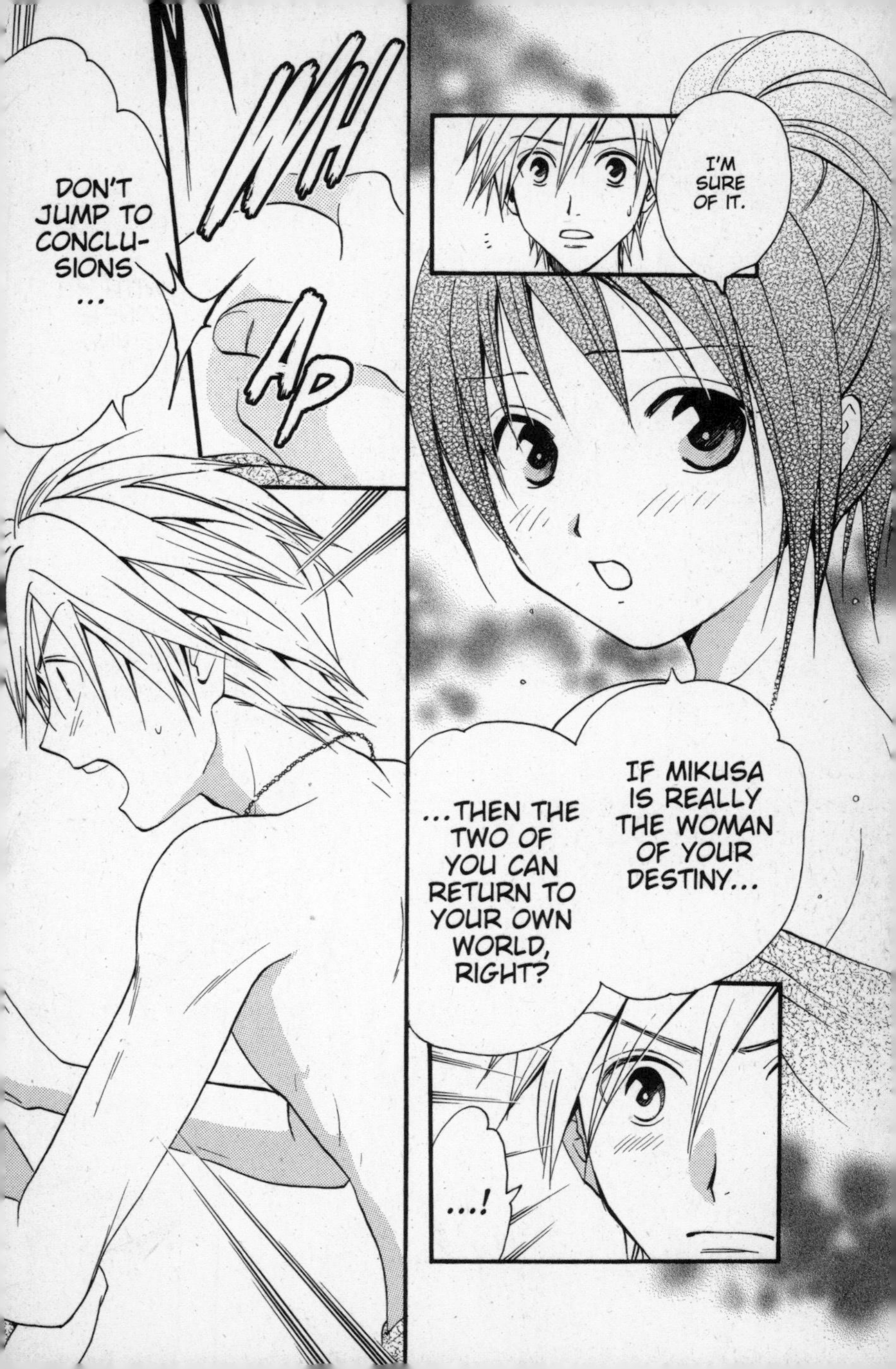
I'M SURE OF IT.
IF MIKUSA IS REALLY THE WOMAN OF YOUR DESTINY...
...THEN THE TWO OF YOU CAN RETURN TO YOUR OWN WORLD, RIGHT?
...!
WAH
DON'T JUMP TO CONCLUSIONS...
AP

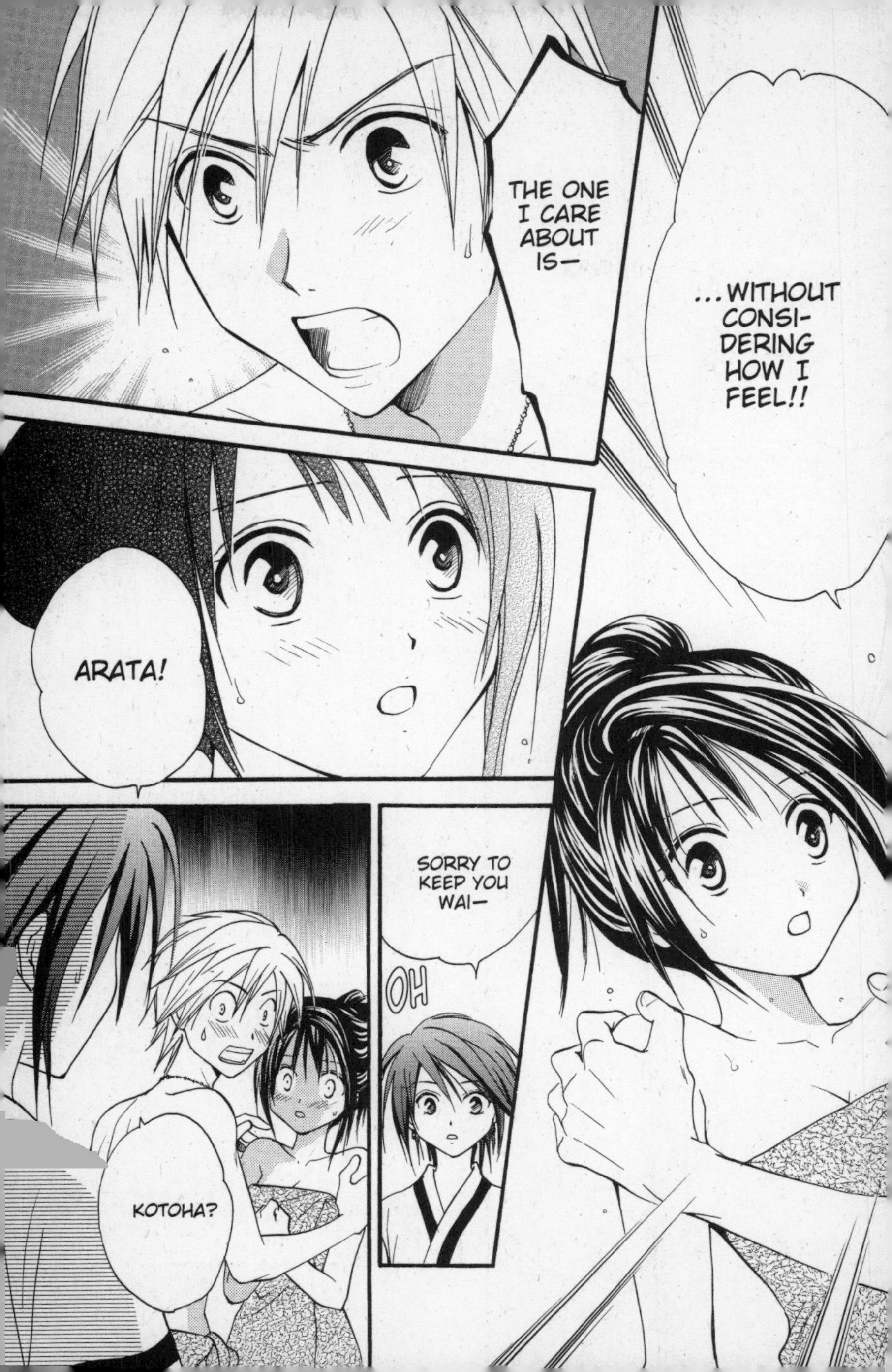
...WITHOUT CONSI-DERING HOW I FEEL!!
THE ONE I CARE ABOUT IS—
ARATA!
SORRY TO KEEP YOU WAI—
OH
KOTOHA?

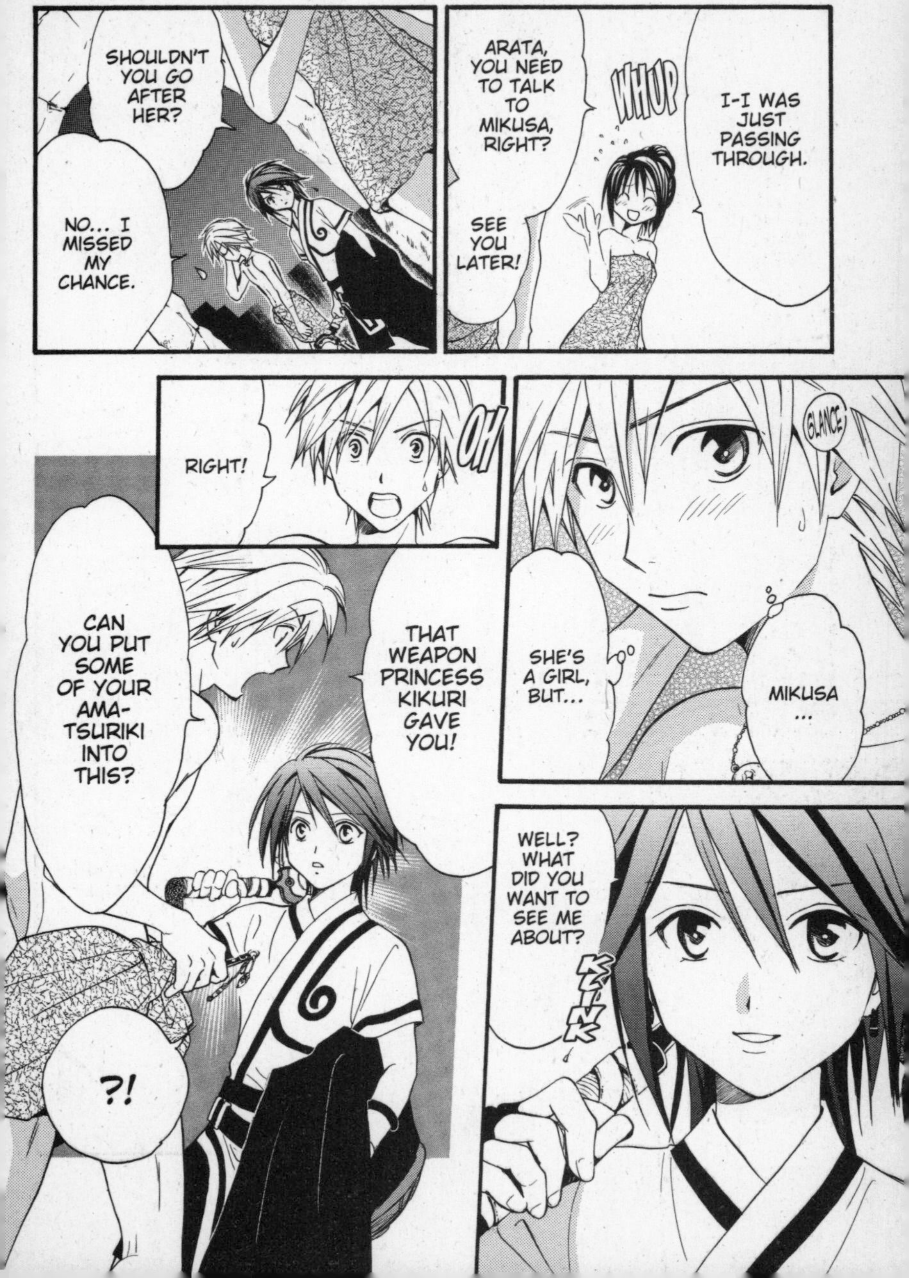
I-I WAS JUST PASSING THROUGH.
WHUP
ARATA, YOU NEED TO TALK TO MIKUSA, RIGHT?
SEE YOU LATER!
SHOULDN'T YOU GO AFTER HER?
NO... I MISSED MY CHANCE.
GLANCE
MIKUSA ...
SHE'S A GIRL, BUT...
OH
RIGHT!
WELL? WHAT DID YOU WANT TO SEE ME ABOUT?
KLINK
THAT WEAPON PRINCESS KIKURI GAVE YOU!
CAN YOU PUT SOME OF YOUR AMA-TSURIKI INTO THIS?
?!

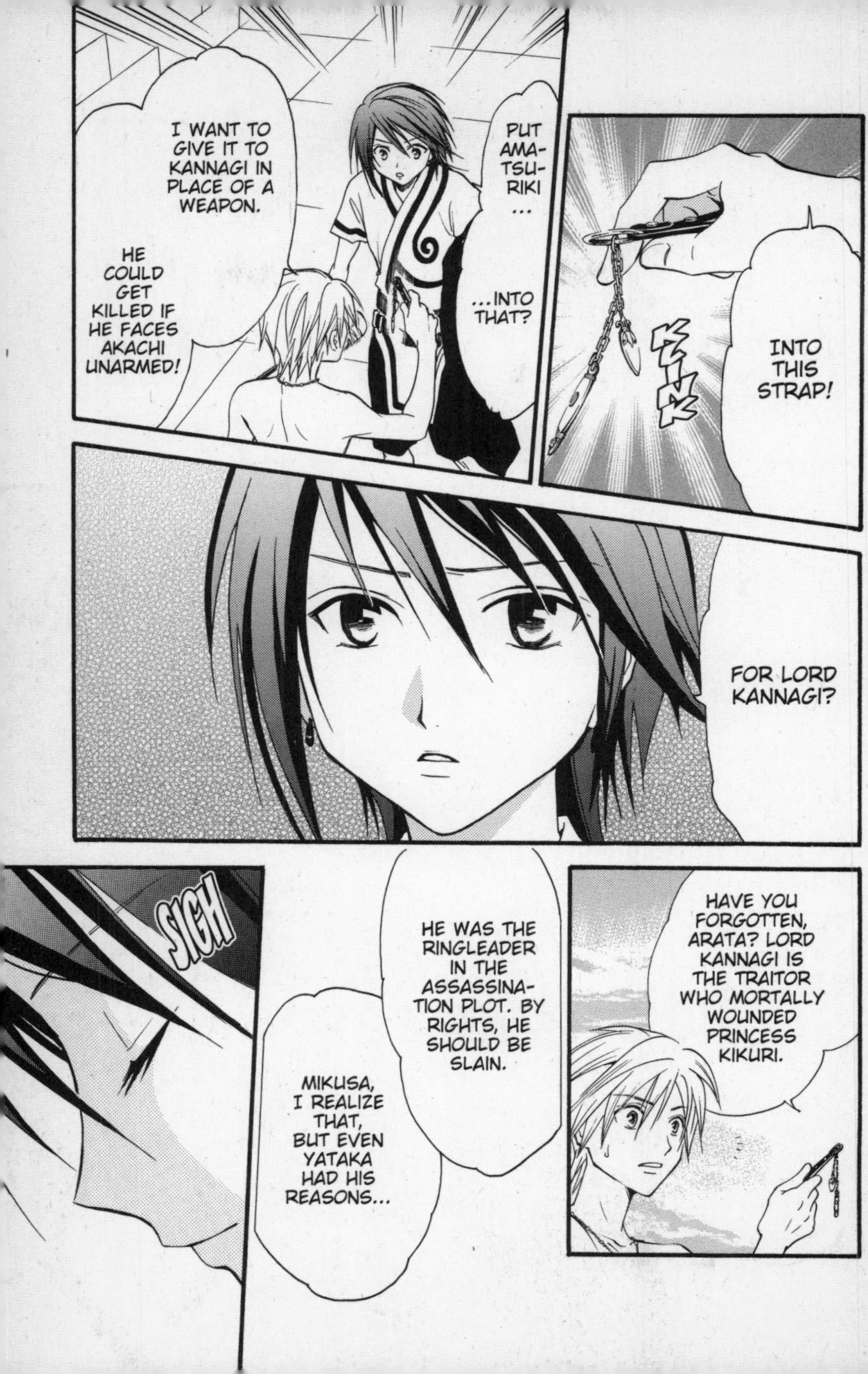
INTO THIS STRAP!
KLINK
PUT AMATSURIKI...
...INTO THAT?
I WANT TO GIVE IT TO KANNAGI IN PLACE OF A WEAPON.
HE COULD GET KILLED IF HE FACES AKACHI UNARMED!
FOR LORD KANNAGI?
HAVE YOU FORGOTTEN, ARATA? LORD KANNAGI IS THE TRAITOR WHO MORTALLY WOUNDED PRINCESS KIKURI.
HE WAS THE RINGLEADER IN THE ASSASSINATION PLOT. BY RIGHTS, HE SHOULD BE SLAIN.
MIKUSA, I REALIZE THAT, BUT EVEN YATAKA HAD HIS REASONS...
SIGH

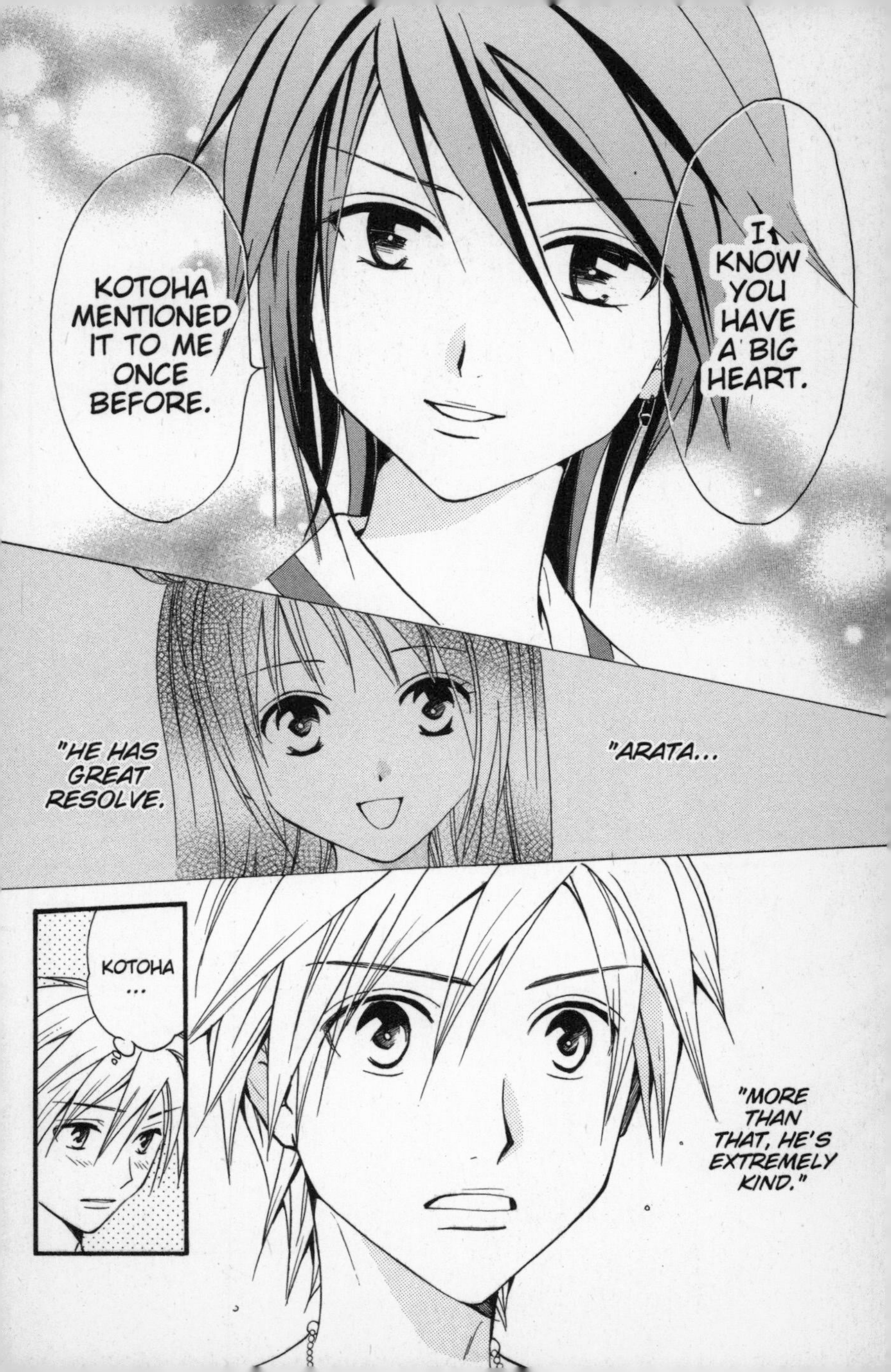
I KNOW YOU HAVE A BIG HEART.
KOTOHA MENTIONED IT TO ME ONCE BEFORE.
"ARATA...
"HE HAS GREAT RESOLVE.
"MORE THAN THAT, HE'S EXTREMELY KIND."
KOTOHA ...

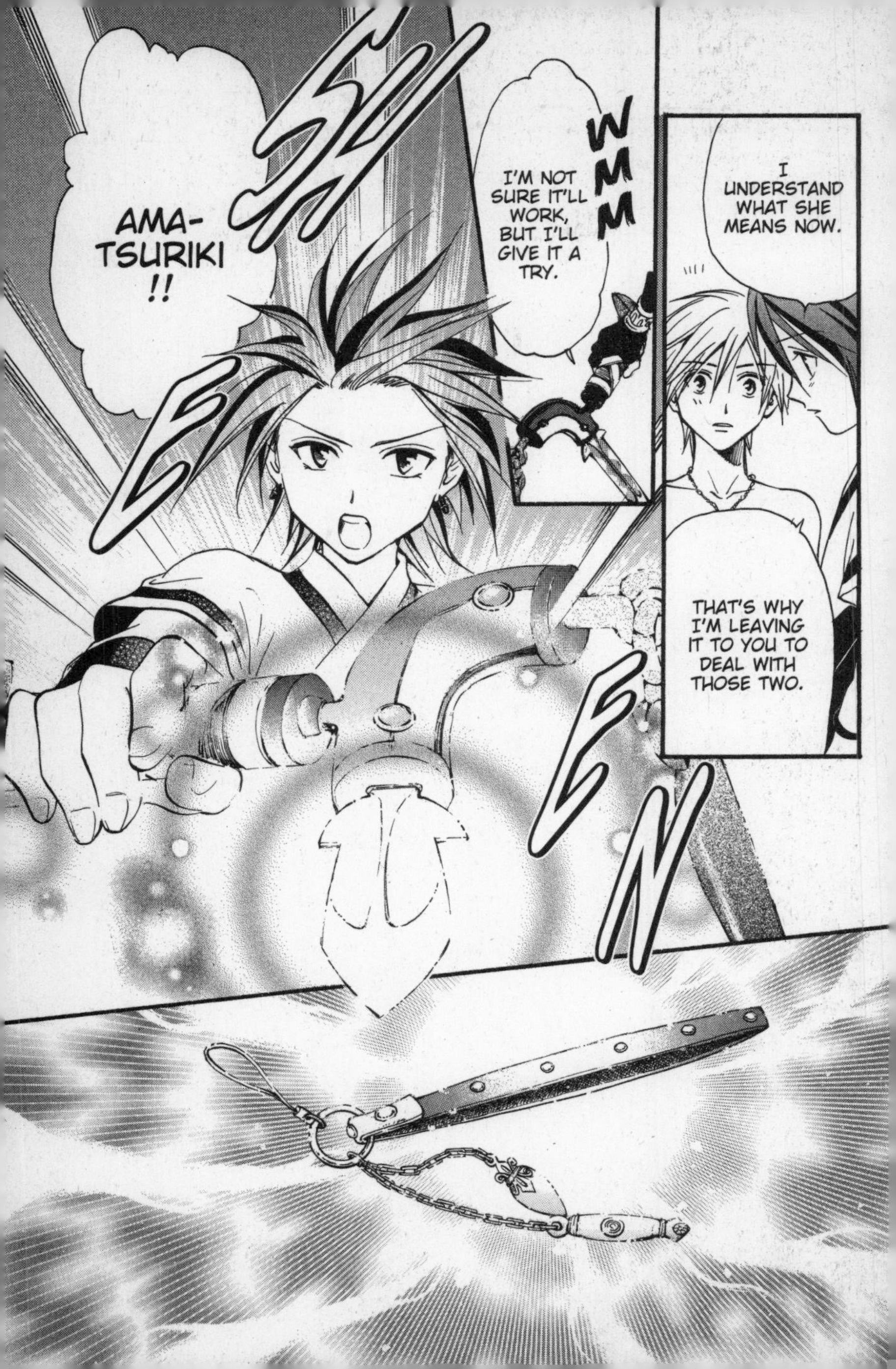
I UNDERSTAND WHAT SHE MEANS NOW.
THAT'S WHY I'M LEAVING IT TO YOU TO DEAL WITH THOSE TWO.
WMM
I'M NOT SURE IT'LL WORK, BUT I'LL GIVE IT A TRY.
AMA-TSURIKI!!

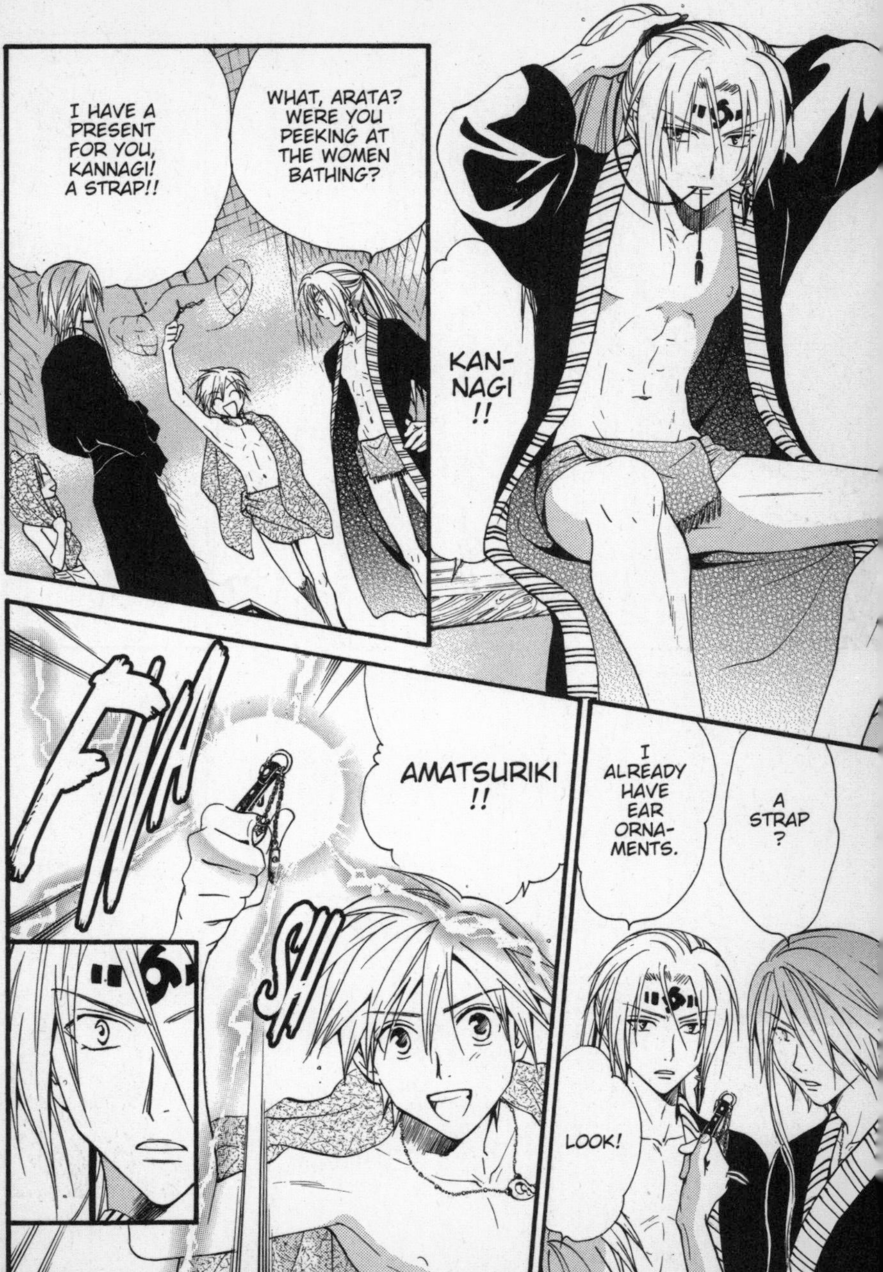
KAN-NAGI!!
WHAT, ARATA? WERE YOU PEEKING AT THE WOMEN BATHING?
I HAVE A PRESENT FOR YOU, KANNAGI! A STRAP!!
A STRAP?
I ALREADY HAVE EAR ORNA-MENTS.
LOOK!
AMATSURIKI!!

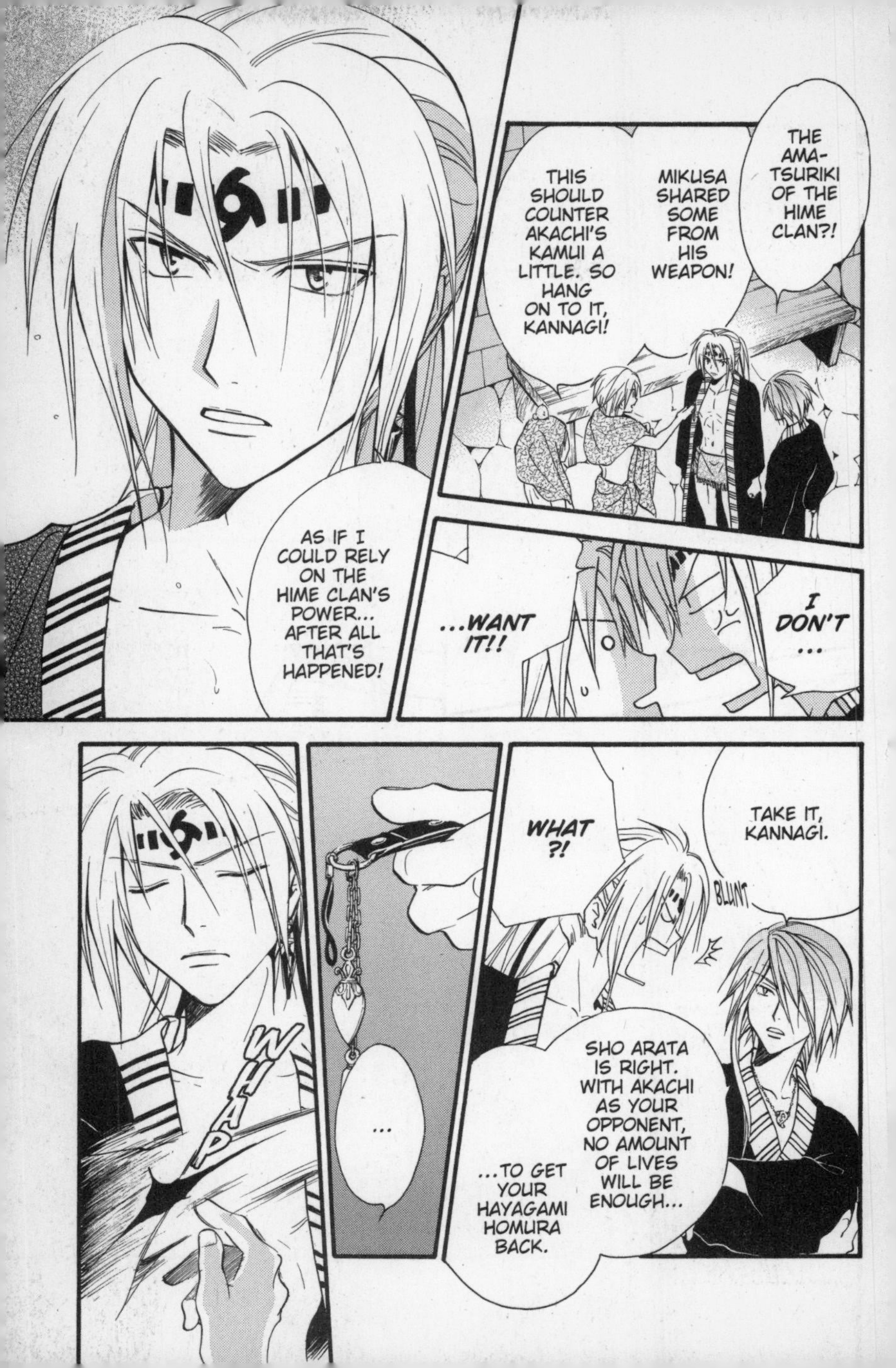
THE AMA-TSURIKI OF THE HIME CLAN?!
MIKUSA SHARED SOME FROM HIS WEAPON!
THIS SHOULD COUNTER AKACHI'S KAMUI A LITTLE. SO HANG ON TO IT, KANNAGI!
I DON'T ...
...WANT IT!!
AS IF I COULD RELY ON THE HIME CLAN'S POWER... AFTER ALL THAT'S HAPPENED!
TAKE IT, KANNAGI.
BLUNT
WHAT ?!
SHO ARATA IS RIGHT. WITH AKACHI AS YOUR OPPONENT, NO AMOUNT OF LIVES WILL BE ENOUGH...
...TO GET YOUR HAYAGAMI HOMURA BACK.
...
WHAP

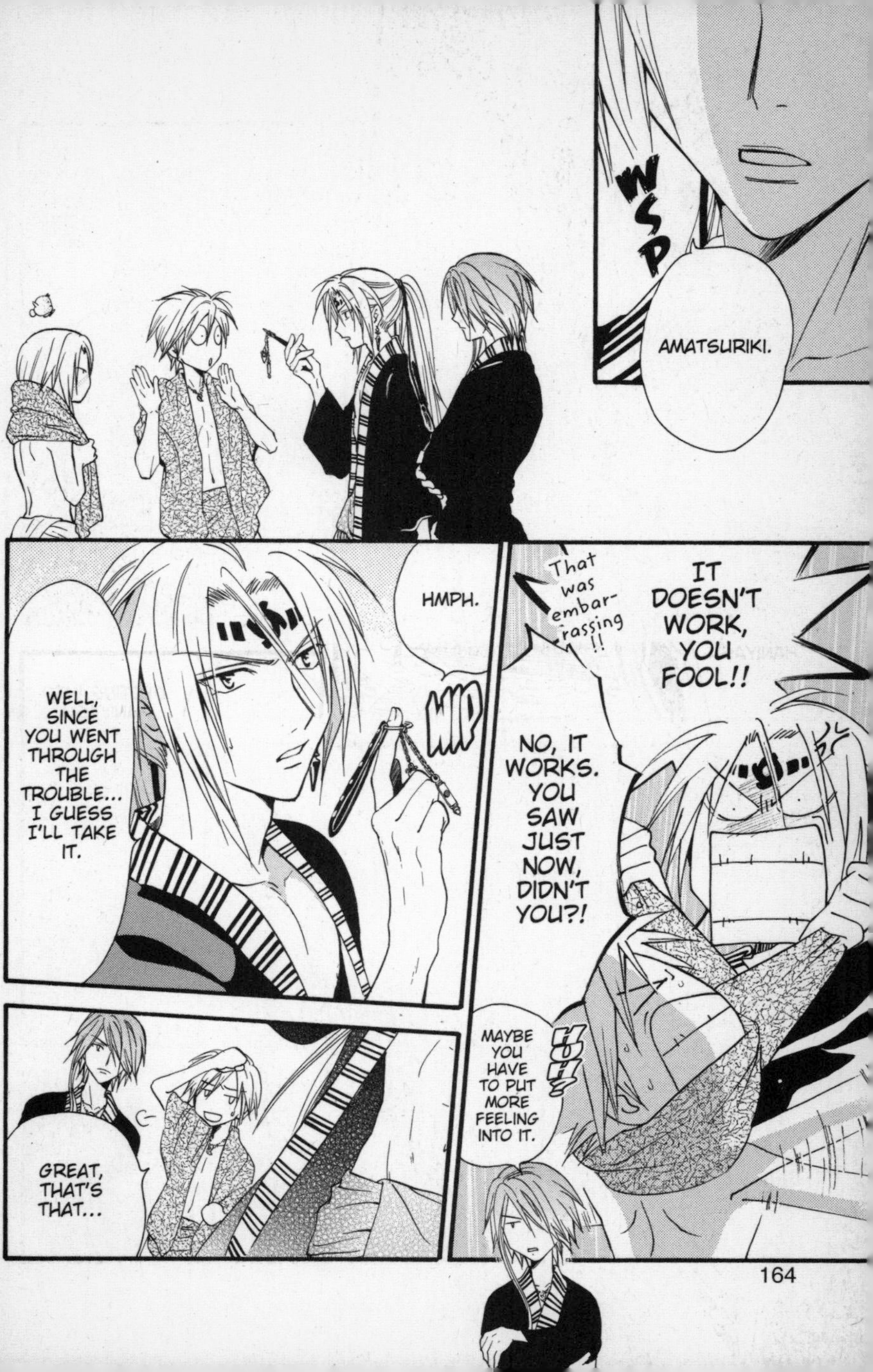
WSP
AMATSURIKI.
IT DOESN'T WORK, YOU FOOL!!
That was embarrassing!!
NO, IT WORKS. YOU SAW JUST NOW, DIDN'T YOU?!
MAYBE YOU HAVE TO PUT MORE FEELING INTO IT.
HMPH.
WHIP
WELL, SINCE YOU WENT THROUGH THE TROUBLE... I GUESS I'LL TAKE IT.
GREAT, THAT'S THAT...

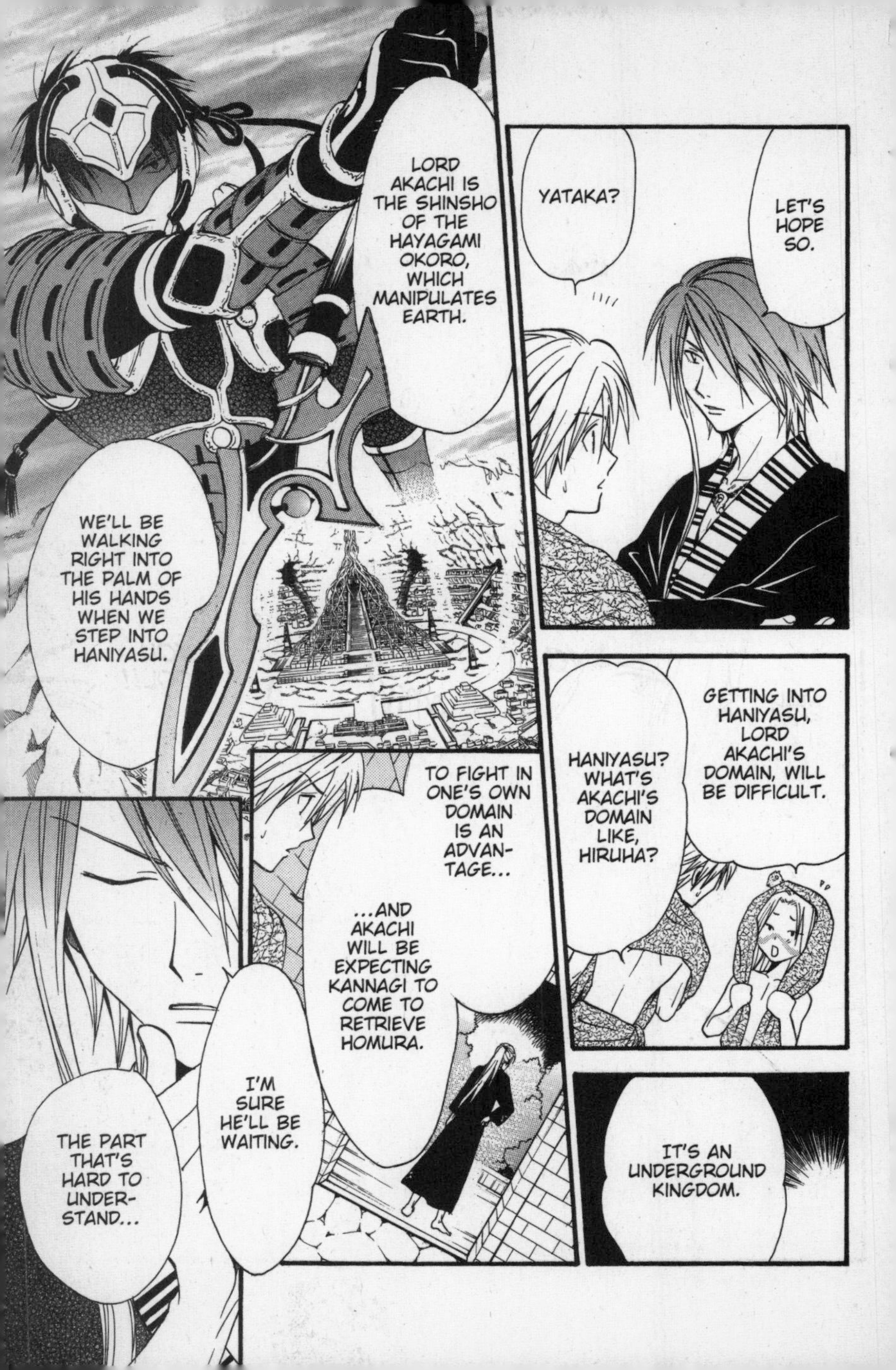
LET'S HOPE SO.
YATAKA?
GETTING INTO HANIYASU, LORD AKACHI'S DOMAIN, WILL BE DIFFICULT.
HANIYASU? WHAT'S AKACHI'S DOMAIN LIKE, HIRUHA?
IT'S AN UNDERGROUND KINGDOM.
LORD AKACHI IS THE SHINSHO OF THE HAYAGAMI OKORO, WHICH MANIPULATES EARTH.
WE'LL BE WALKING RIGHT INTO THE PALM OF HIS HANDS WHEN WE STEP INTO HANIYASU.
TO FIGHT IN ONE'S OWN DOMAIN IS AN ADVANTAGE...
...AND AKACHI WILL BE EXPECTING KANNAGI TO COME TO RETRIEVE HOMURA.
I'M SURE HE'LL BE WAITING.
THE PART THAT'S HARD TO UNDERSTAND...

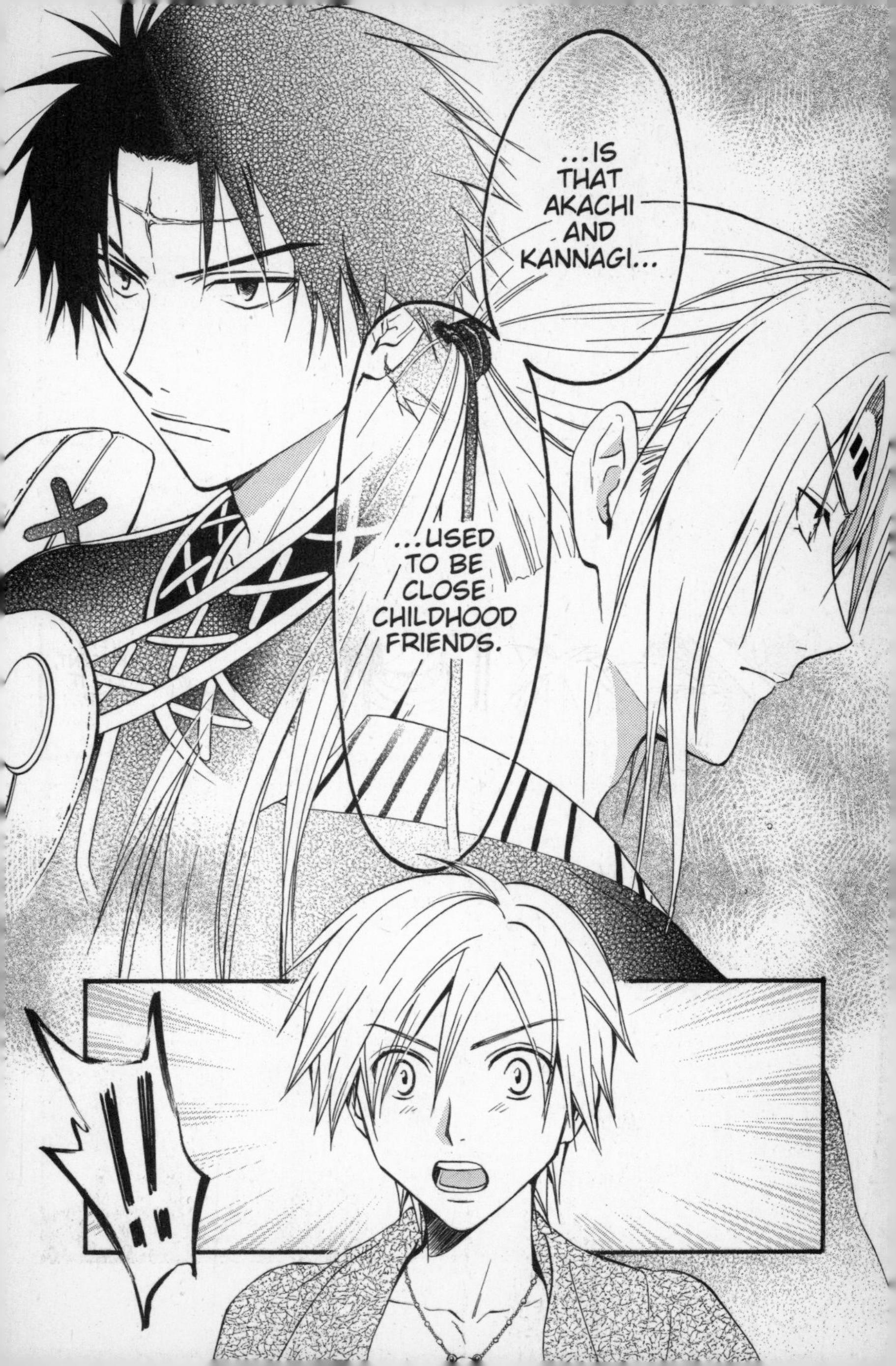
...IS THAT AKACHI AND KANNAGI...
...USED TO BE CLOSE CHILDHOOD FRIENDS.
!!

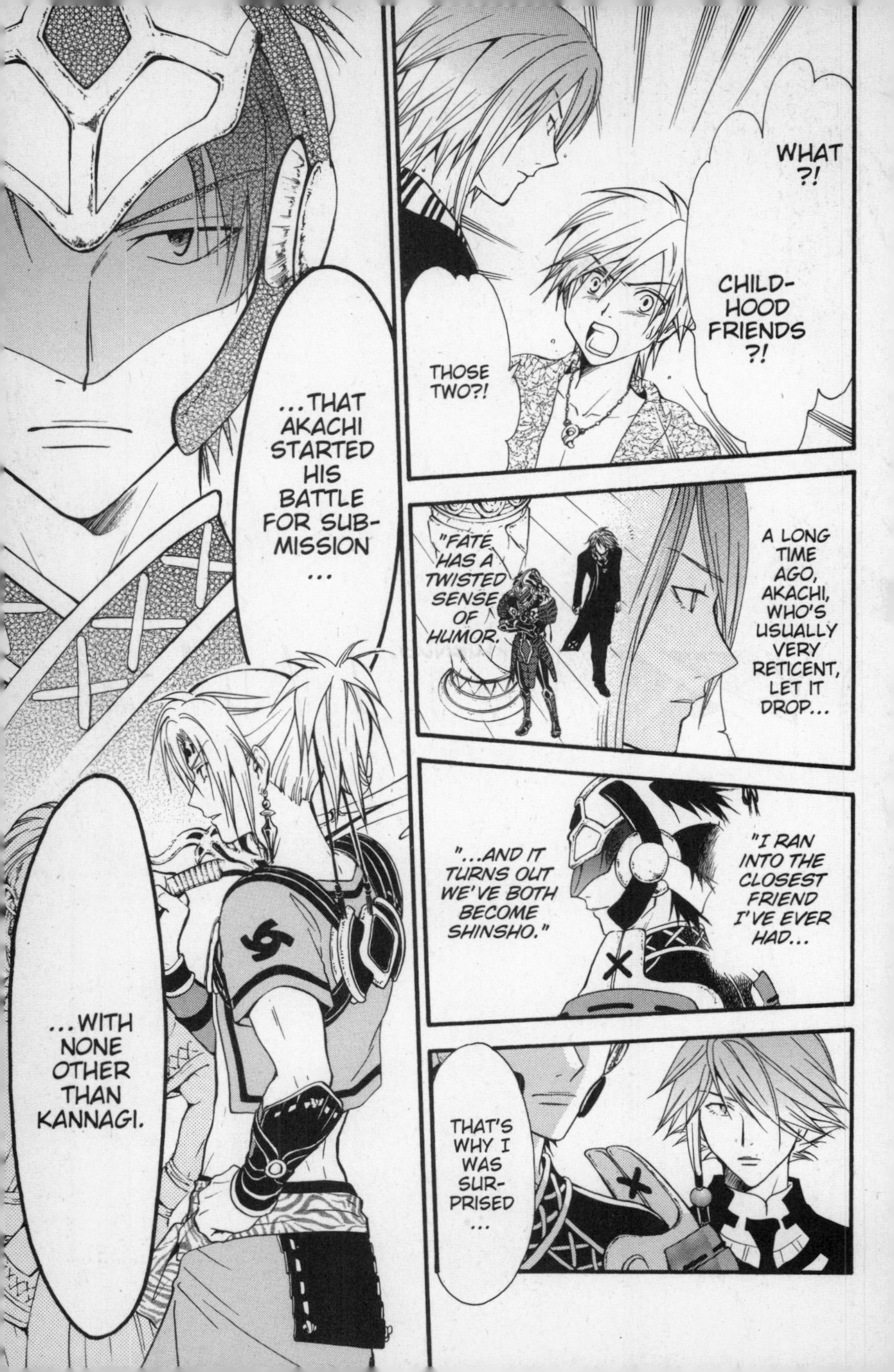
WHAT?!
CHILDHOOD FRIENDS?!
THOSE TWO?!
A LONG TIME AGO, AKACHI, WHO'S USUALLY VERY RETICENT, LET IT DROP...
"FATE HAS A TWISTED SENSE OF HUMOR.
"I RAN INTO THE CLOSEST FRIEND I'VE EVER HAD...
"...AND IT TURNS OUT WE'VE BOTH BECOME SHINSHO."
THAT'S WHY I WAS SURPRISED...
...THAT AKACHI STARTED HIS BATTLE FOR SUBMISSION...
...WITH NONE OTHER THAN KANNAGI.

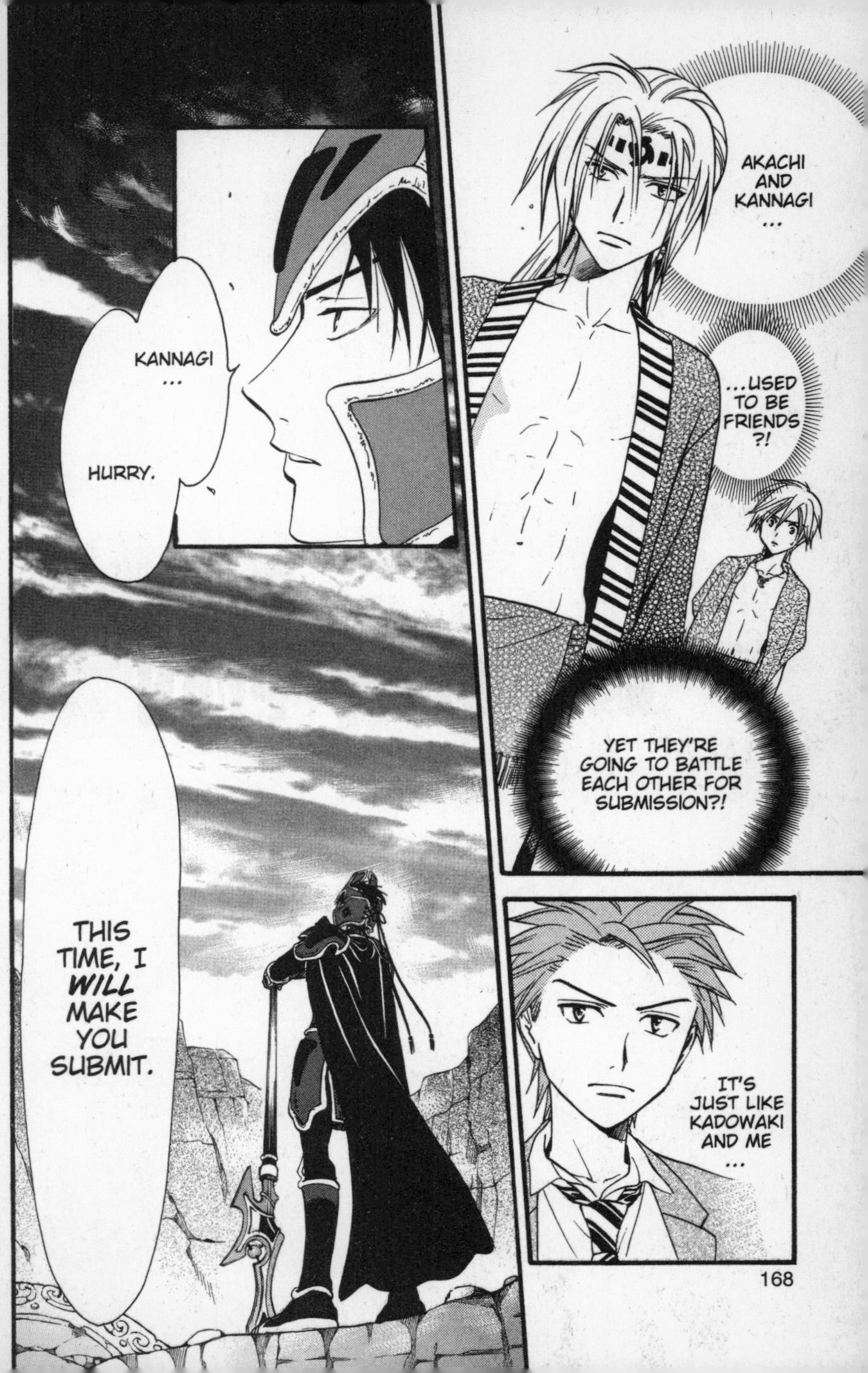
AKACHI AND KANNAGI ...
...USED TO BE FRIENDS ?!
YET THEY'RE GOING TO BATTLE EACH OTHER FOR SUBMISSION?!
IT'S JUST LIKE KADOWAKI AND ME ...
KANNAGI ...
HURRY.
THIS TIME, I ***WILL*** MAKE YOU SUBMIT.

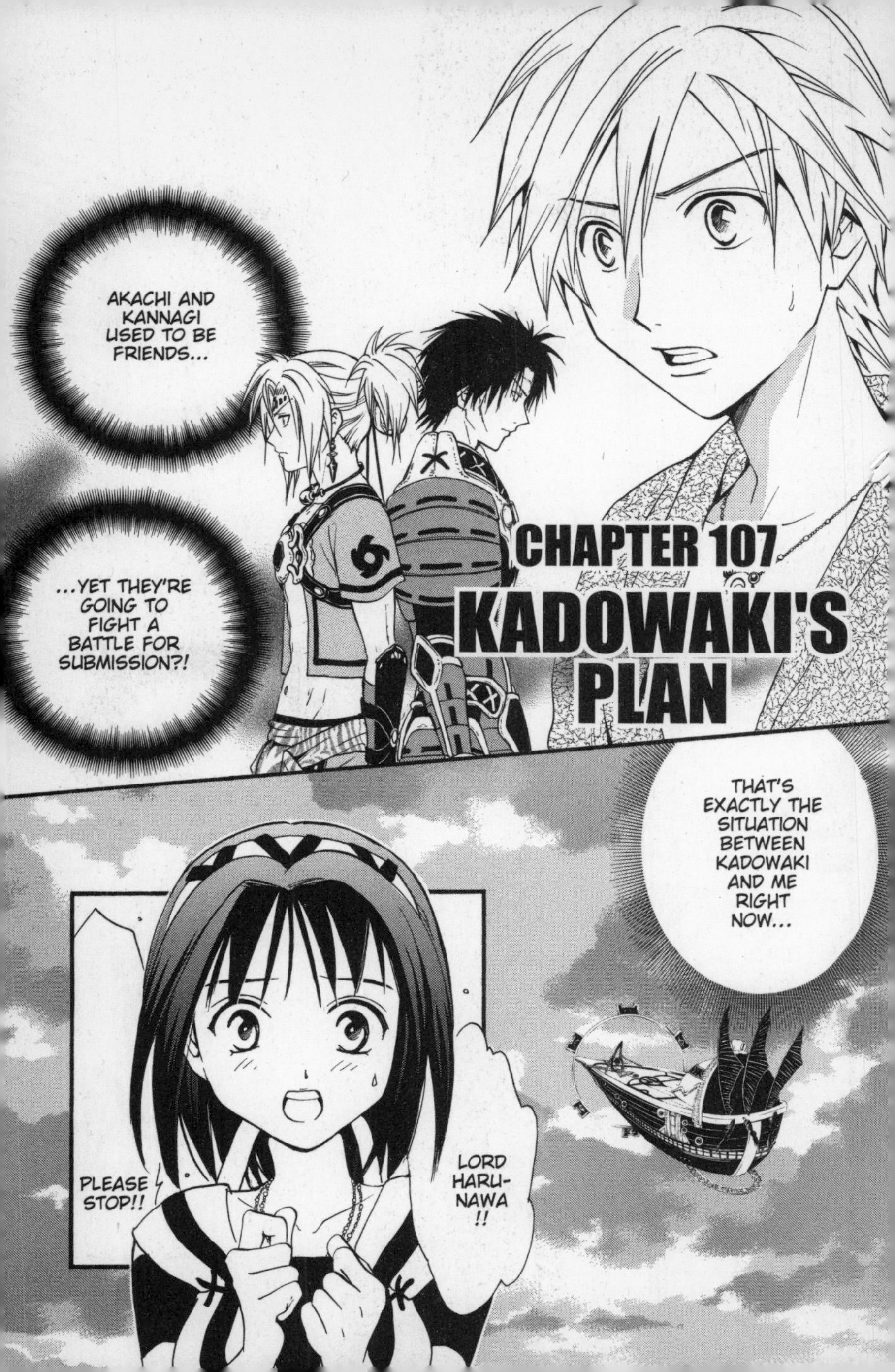
CHAPTER 107
KADOWAKI'S PLAN
AKACHI AND KANNAGI USED TO BE FRIENDS...
...YET THEY'RE GOING TO FIGHT A BATTLE FOR SUBMISSION?!
THAT'S EXACTLY THE SITUATION BETWEEN KADOWAKI AND ME RIGHT NOW...
LORD HARU-NAWA!!
PLEASE STOP!!

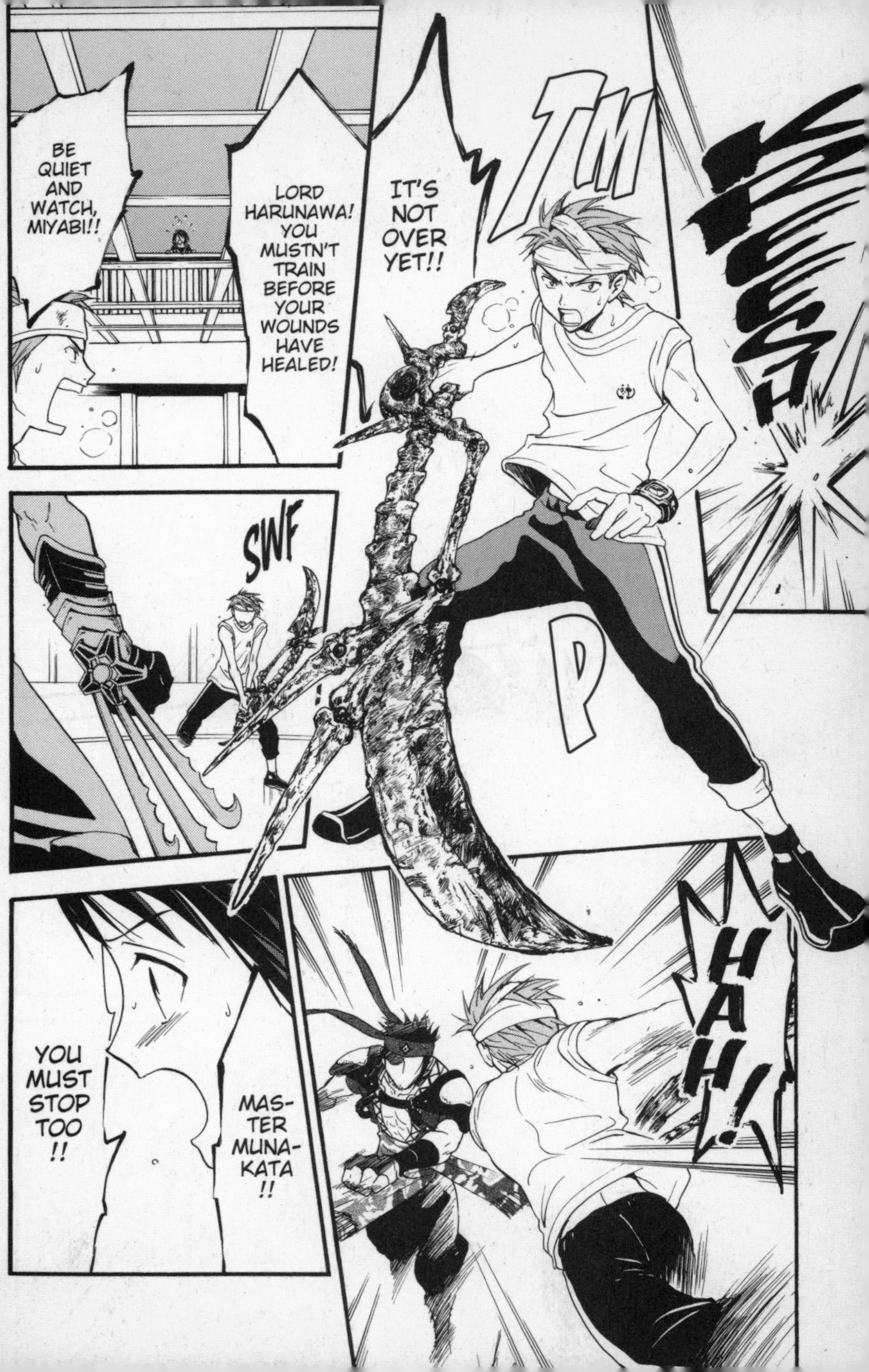

IT'S NOT OVER YET!!
TM
P
LORD HARUNAWA! YOU MUSTN'T TRAIN BEFORE YOUR WOUNDS HAVE HEALED!
BE QUIET AND WATCH, MIYABI!!
SWF
HAH!
MAS-TER MUNA-KATA!!
YOU MUST STOP TOO!!

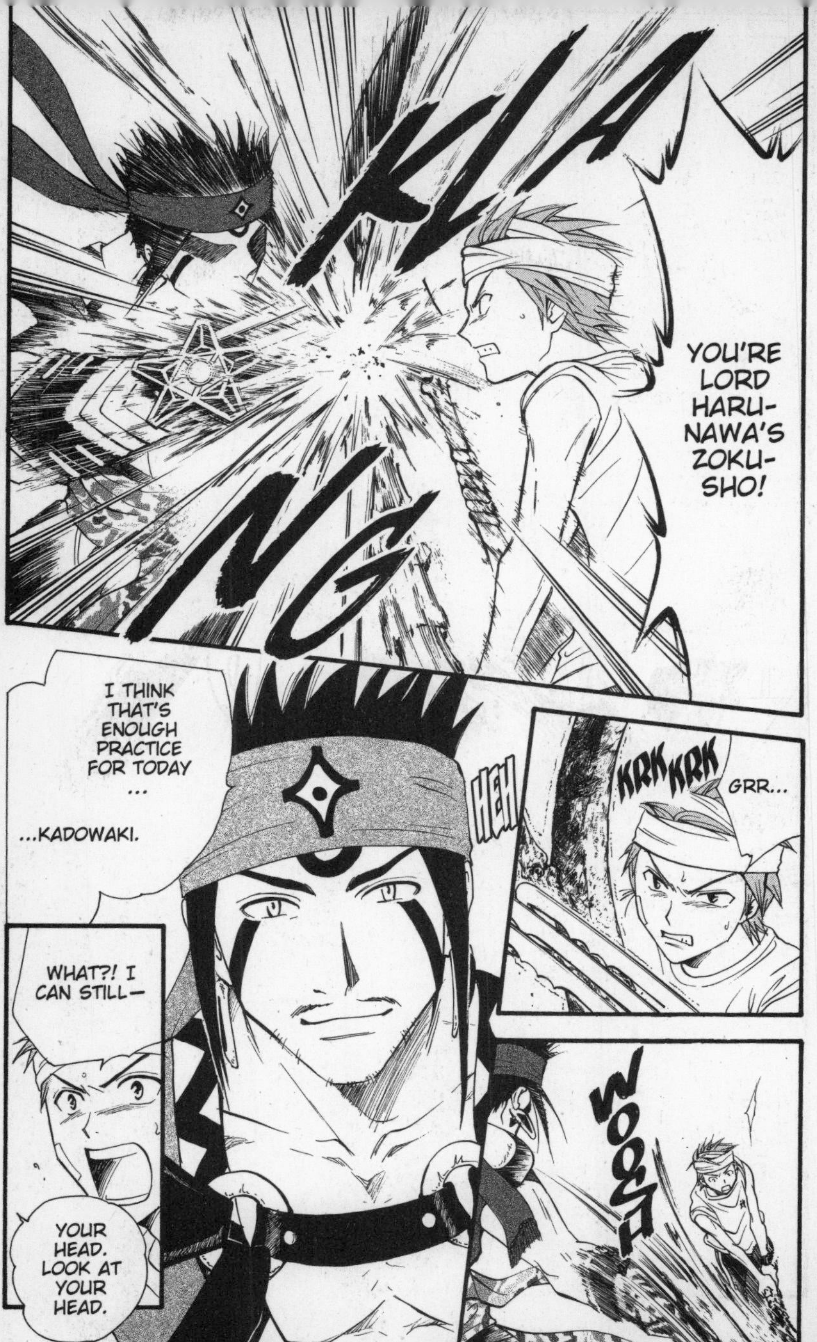
KHANG
YOU'RE LORD HARU-NAWA'S ZOKU-SHO!
KRK KRK
GRR...
HEH
I THINK THAT'S ENOUGH PRACTICE FOR TODAY ...
...KADOWAKI.
WOOSH
WHAT?! I CAN STILL—
YOUR HEAD. LOOK AT YOUR HEAD.

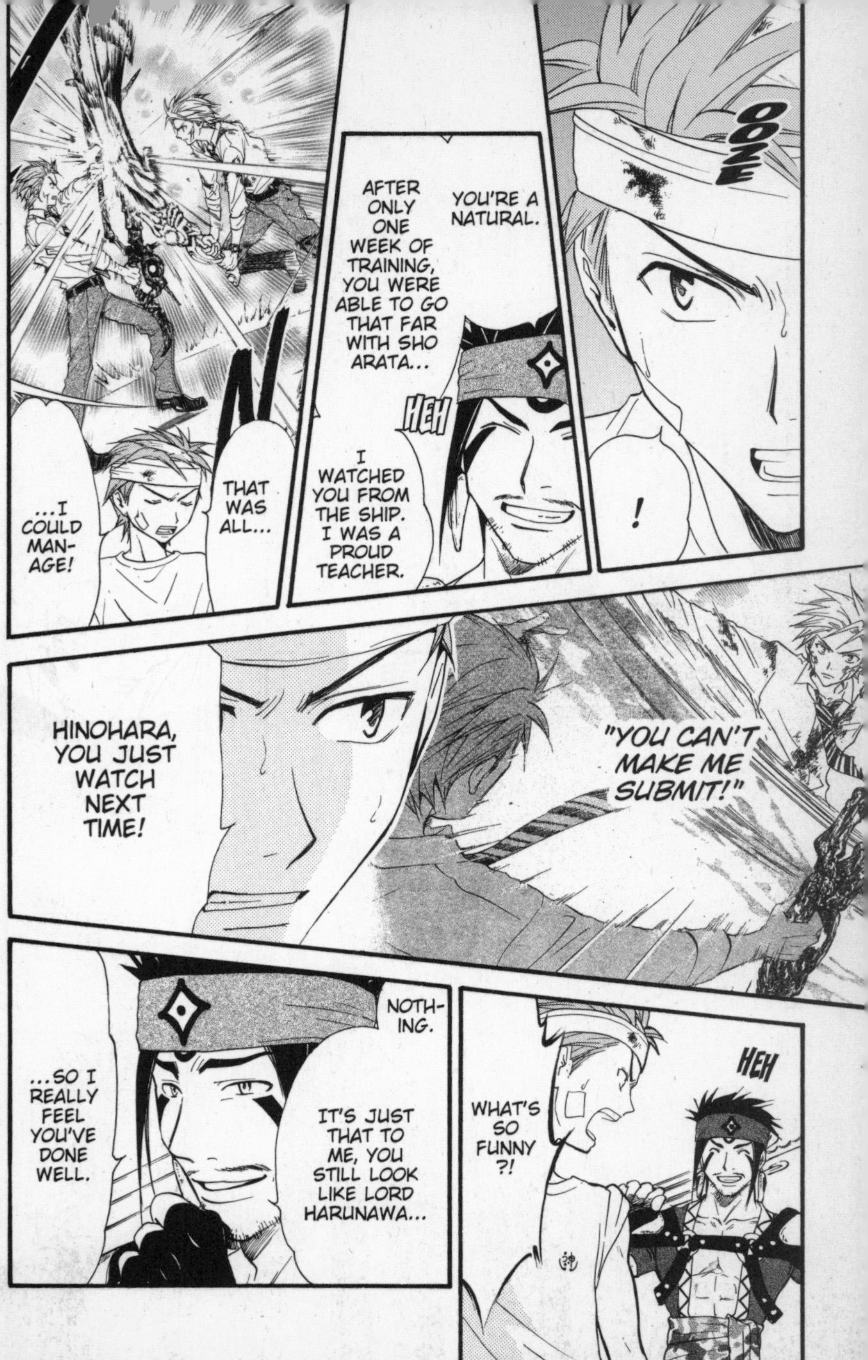
OOZE
!
YOU'RE A NATURAL.
AFTER ONLY ONE WEEK OF TRAINING, YOU WERE ABLE TO GO THAT FAR WITH SHO ARATA...
HEH
I WATCHED YOU FROM THE SHIP. I WAS A PROUD TEACHER.
THAT WAS ALL...
...I COULD MANAGE!
"YOU CAN'T MAKE ME SUBMIT!"
HINOHARA, YOU JUST WATCH NEXT TIME!
HEH
WHAT'S SO FUNNY?!
NOTHING.
IT'S JUST THAT TO ME, YOU STILL LOOK LIKE LORD HARUNAWA...
...SO I REALLY FEEL YOU'VE DONE WELL.

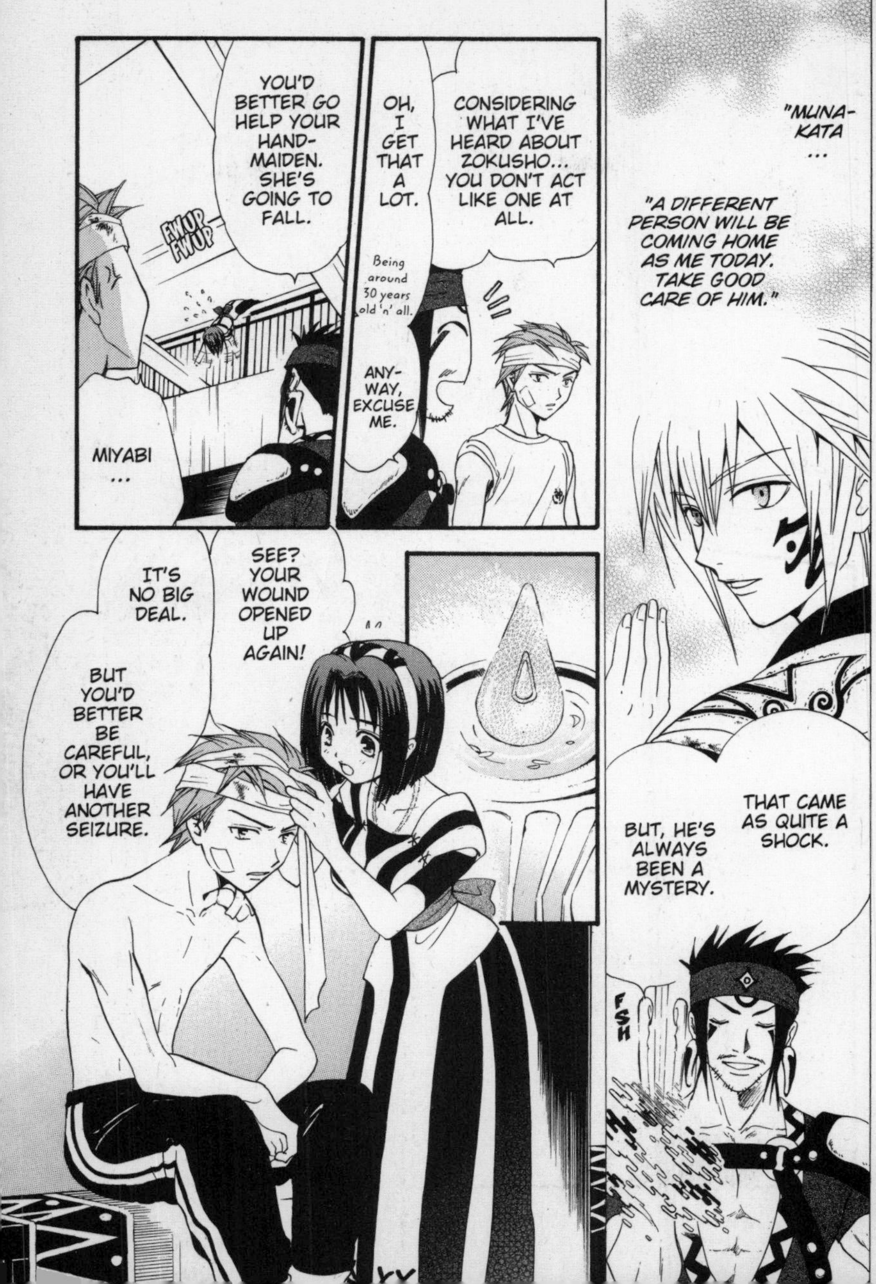
"MUNA-KATA ...
"A DIFFERENT PERSON WILL BE COMING HOME AS ME TODAY. TAKE GOOD CARE OF HIM."
THAT CAME AS QUITE A SHOCK.
BUT, HE'S ALWAYS BEEN A MYSTERY.
FSH
CONSIDERING WHAT I'VE HEARD ABOUT ZOKUSHO... YOU DON'T ACT LIKE ONE AT ALL.
OH, I GET THAT A LOT.
Being around 30 years old 'n' all.
ANY-WAY, EXCUSE ME.
YOU'D BETTER GO HELP YOUR HAND-MAIDEN. SHE'S GOING TO FALL.
FWUP FWUP
MIYABI ...
SEE? YOUR WOUND OPENED UP AGAIN!
IT'S NO BIG DEAL.
BUT YOU'D BETTER BE CAREFUL, OR YOU'LL HAVE ANOTHER SEIZURE.

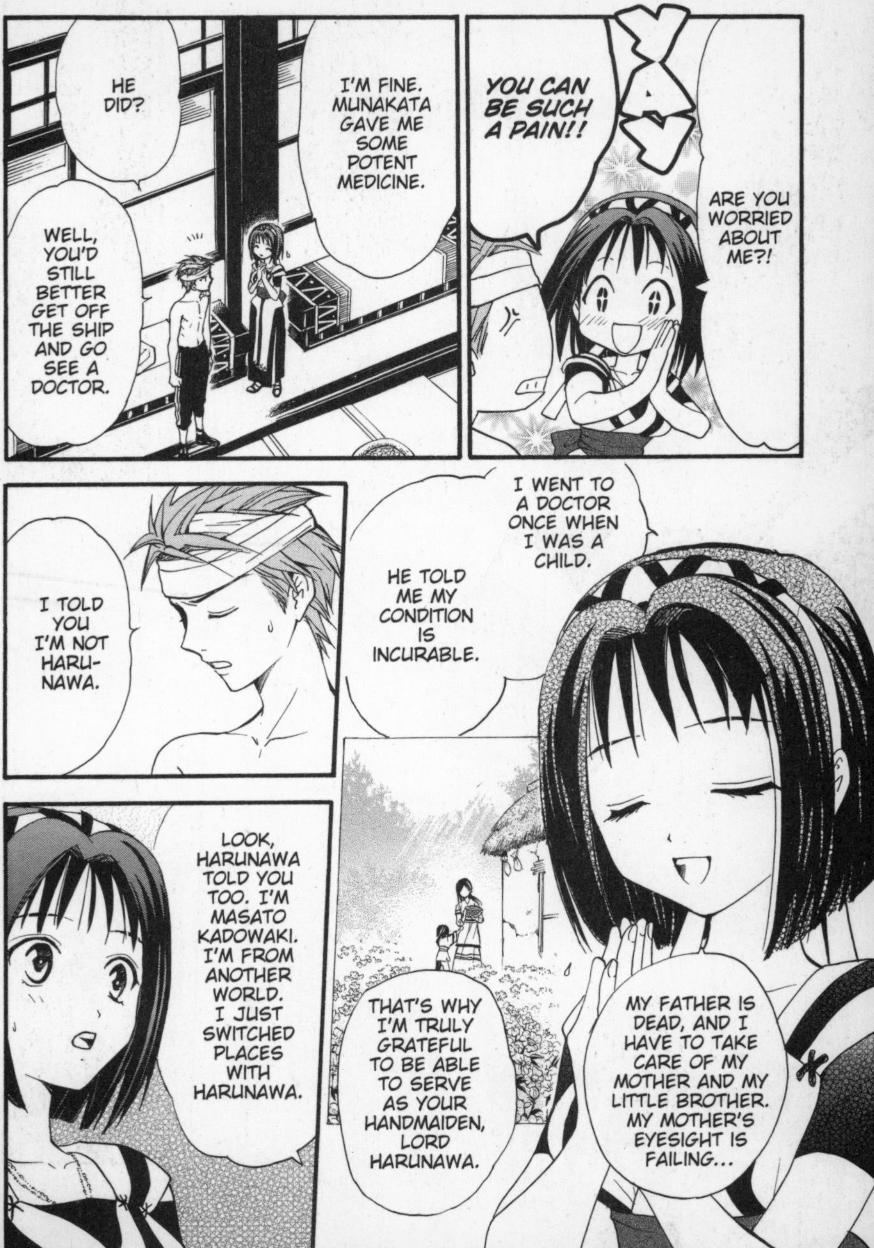
YOU CAN BE SUCH A PAIN!!
ARE YOU WORRIED ABOUT ME?!
I'M FINE. MUNAKATA GAVE ME SOME POTENT MEDICINE.
HE DID?
WELL, YOU'D STILL BETTER GET OFF THE SHIP AND GO SEE A DOCTOR.
I WENT TO A DOCTOR ONCE WHEN I WAS A CHILD.
HE TOLD ME MY CONDITION IS INCURABLE.
MY FATHER IS DEAD, AND I HAVE TO TAKE CARE OF MY MOTHER AND MY LITTLE BROTHER. MY MOTHER'S EYESIGHT IS FAILING...
THAT'S WHY I'M TRULY GRATEFUL TO BE ABLE TO SERVE AS YOUR HANDMAIDEN, LORD HARUNAWA.
I TOLD YOU I'M NOT HARU-NAWA.
LOOK, HARUNAWA TOLD YOU TOO. I'M MASATO KADOWAKI. I'M FROM ANOTHER WORLD. I JUST SWITCHED PLACES WITH HARUNAWA.

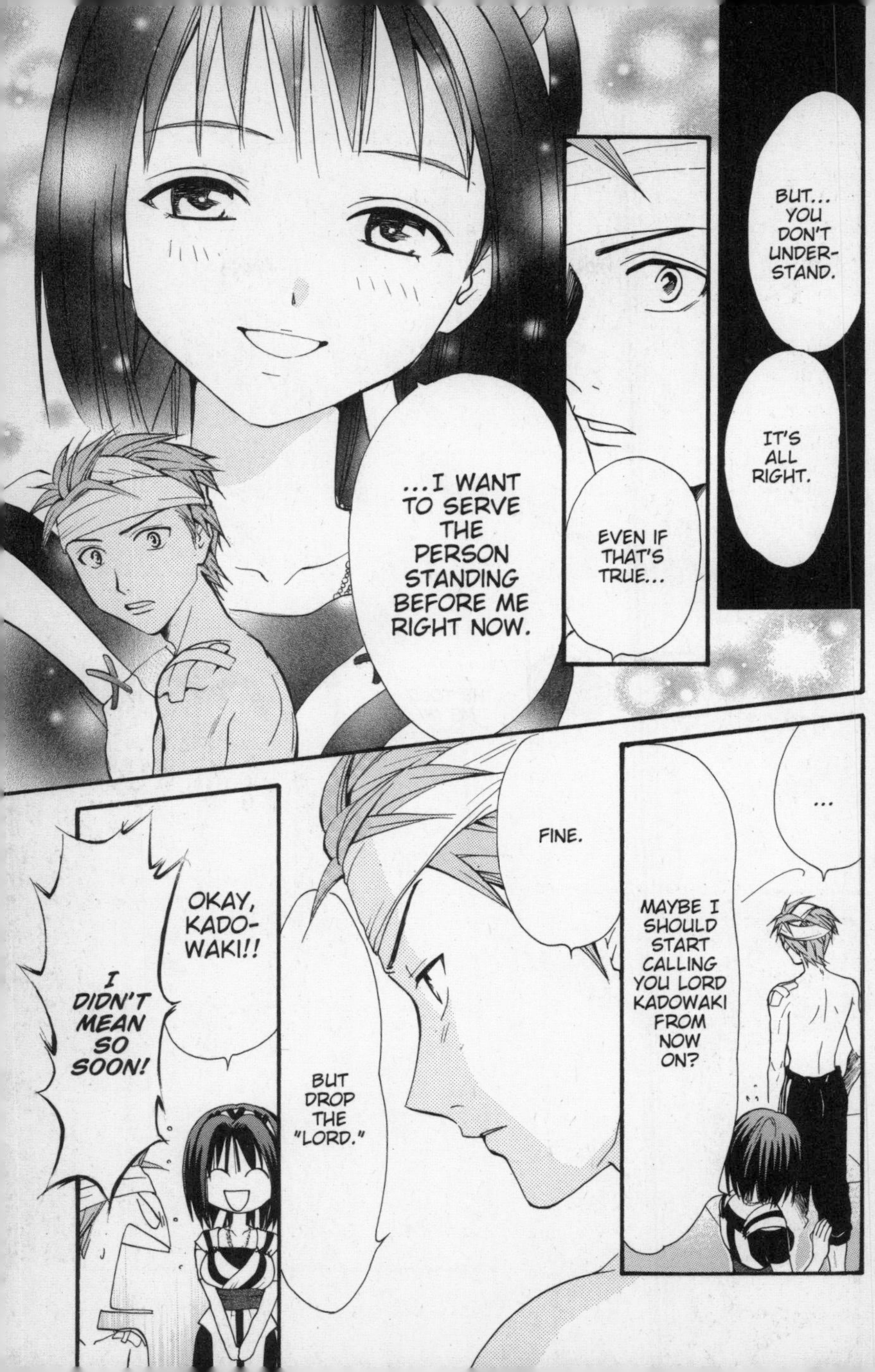
BUT... YOU DON'T UNDER-STAND.
IT'S ALL RIGHT.
EVEN IF THAT'S TRUE...
...I WANT TO SERVE THE PERSON STANDING BEFORE ME RIGHT NOW.
...
MAYBE I SHOULD START CALLING YOU LORD KADOWAKI FROM NOW ON?
FINE.
BUT DROP THE "LORD."
OKAY, KADO-WAKI!!
I DIDN'T MEAN SO SOON!

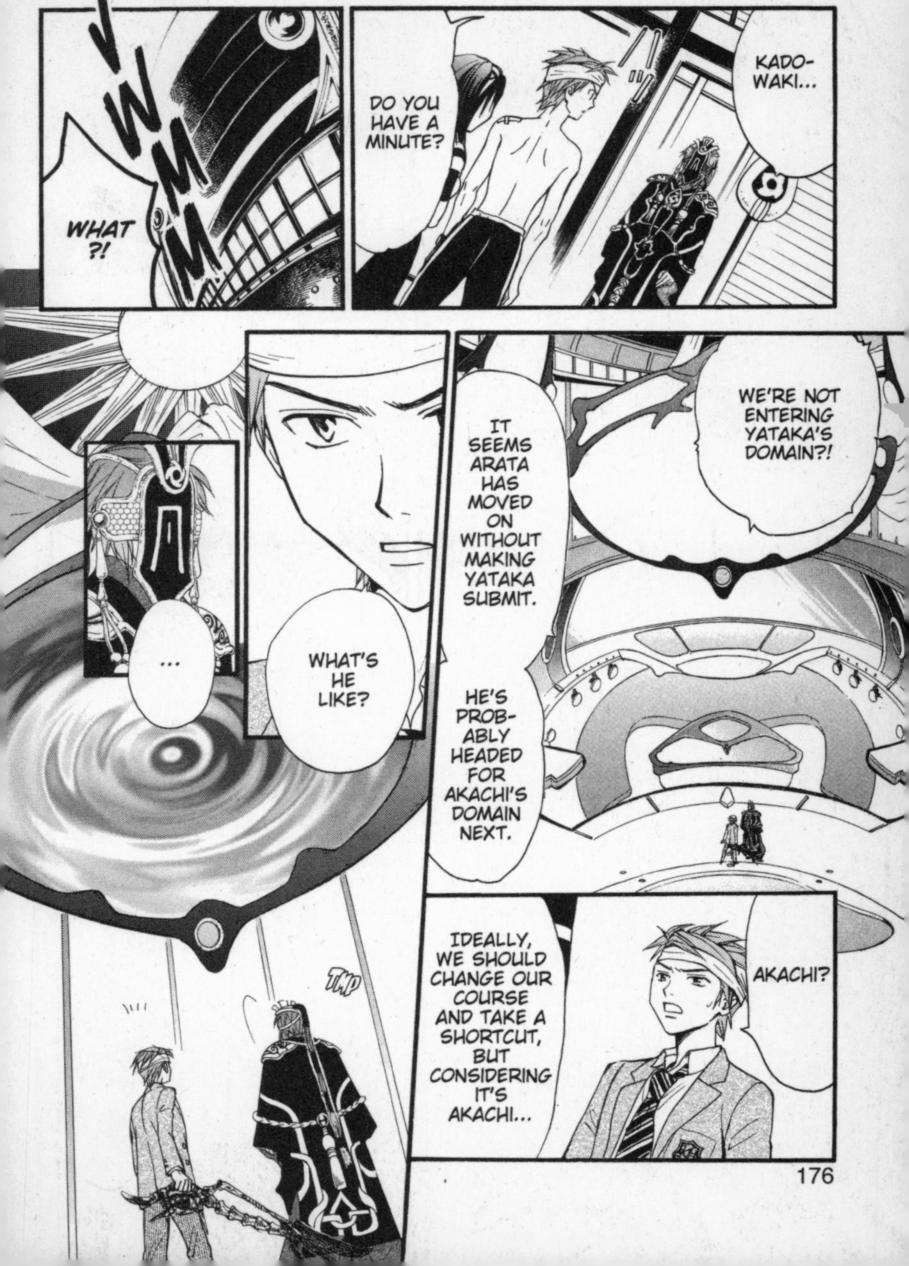
KADO-WAKI...
DO YOU HAVE A MINUTE?
WMM
WHAT?!
WE'RE NOT ENTERING YATAKA'S DOMAIN?!
IT SEEMS ARATA HAS MOVED ON WITHOUT MAKING YATAKA SUBMIT.
HE'S PROB-ABLY HEADED FOR AKACHI'S DOMAIN NEXT.
WHAT'S HE LIKE?
...
AKACHI?
IDEALLY, WE SHOULD CHANGE OUR COURSE AND TAKE A SHORTCUT, BUT CONSIDERING IT'S AKACHI...
TMP

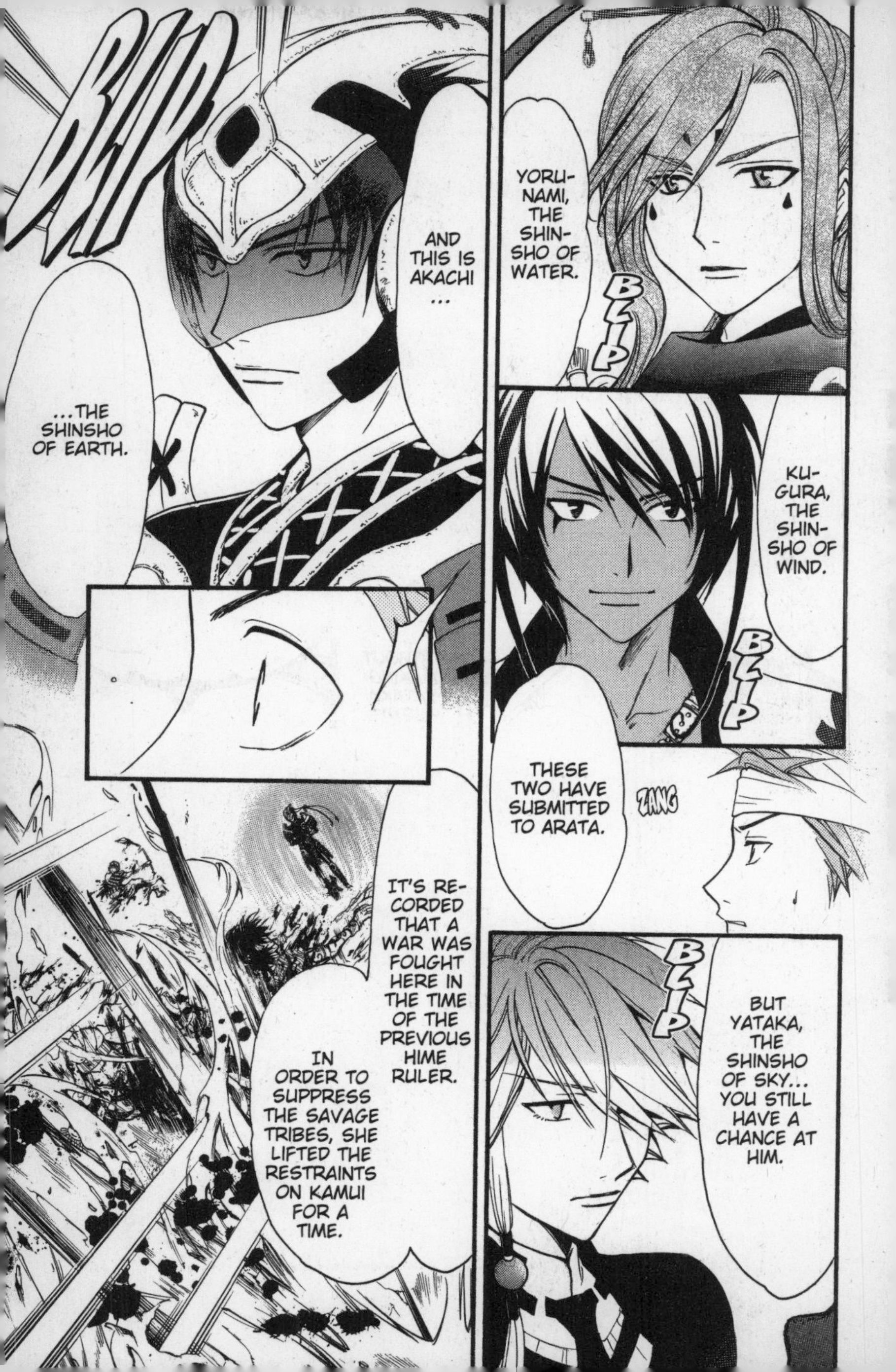
YORU-NAMI, THE SHIN-SHO OF WATER.
BLIP
BAP
AND THIS IS AKACHI ...
...THE SHINSHO OF EARTH.
KU-GURA, THE SHIN-SHO OF WIND.
BLIP
THESE TWO HAVE SUBMITTED TO ARATA.
ZANG
BLIP
BUT YATAKA, THE SHINSHO OF SKY... YOU STILL HAVE A CHANCE AT HIM.
IT'S RE-CORDED THAT A WAR WAS FOUGHT HERE IN THE TIME OF THE PREVIOUS HIME RULER.
IN ORDER TO SUPPRESS THE SAVAGE TRIBES, SHE LIFTED THE RESTRAINTS ON KAMUI FOR A TIME.

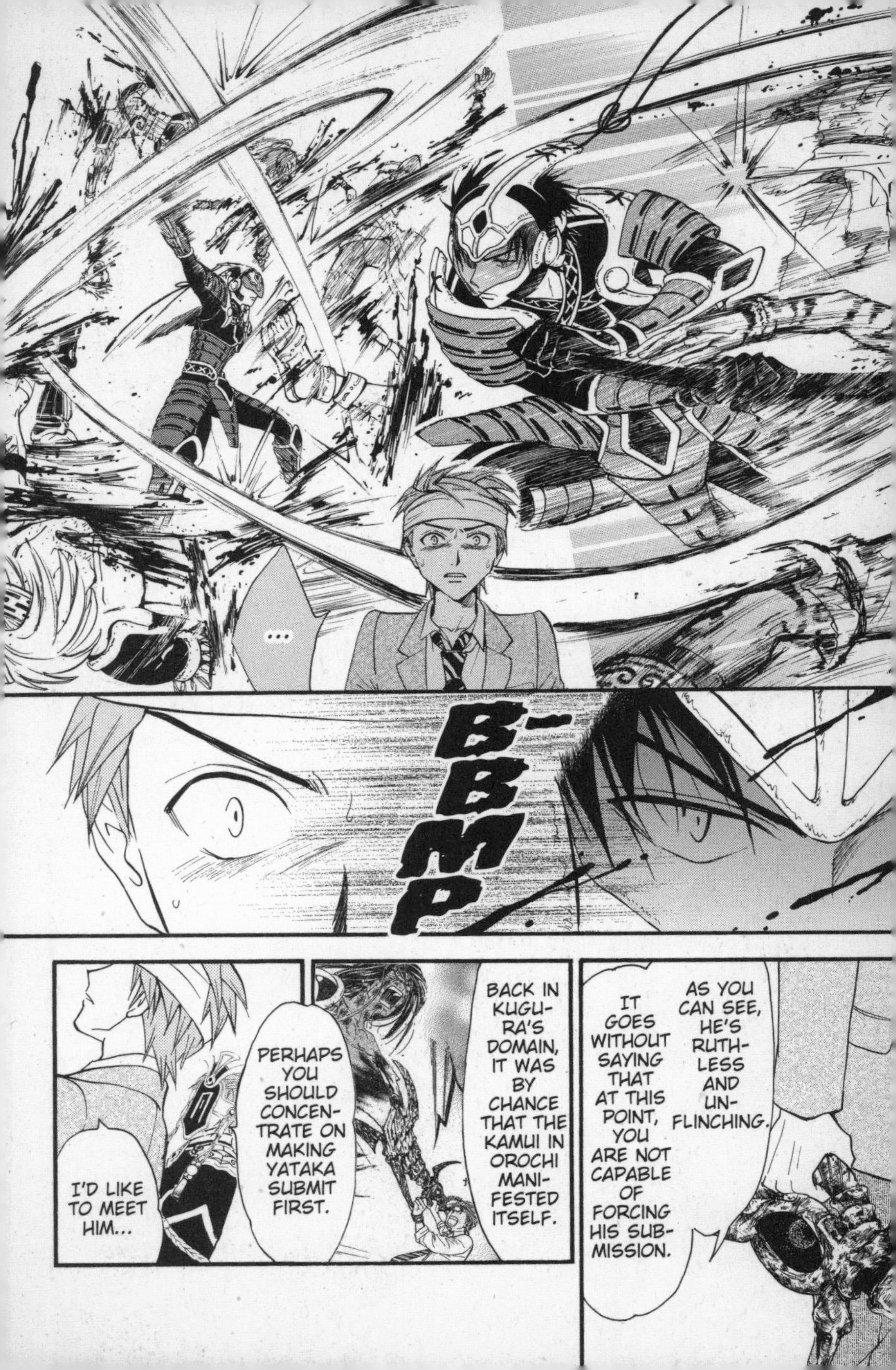
...
B-BBMP
AS YOU CAN SEE, HE'S RUTHLESS AND UNFLINCHING.
IT GOES WITHOUT SAYING THAT AT THIS POINT, YOU ARE NOT CAPABLE OF FORCING HIS SUBMISSION.
BACK IN KUGURA'S DOMAIN, IT WAS BY CHANCE THAT THE KAMUI IN OROCHI MANIFESTED ITSELF.
PERHAPS YOU SHOULD CONCENTRATE ON MAKING YATAKA SUBMIT FIRST.
I'D LIKE TO MEET HIM...

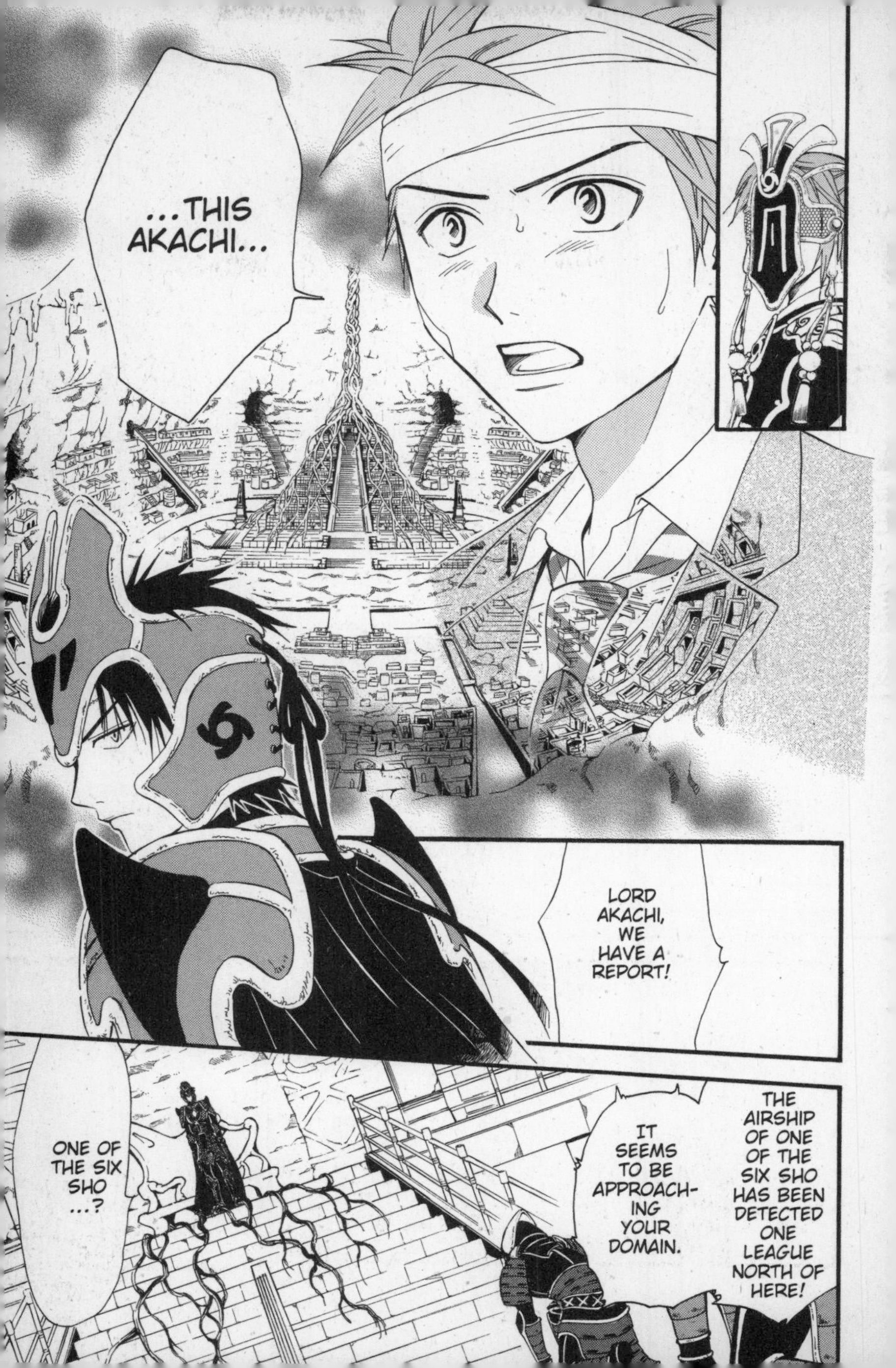
...THIS AKACHI...
LORD AKACHI, WE HAVE A REPORT!
THE AIRSHIP OF ONE OF THE SIX SHO HAS BEEN DETECTED ONE LEAGUE NORTH OF HERE!
IT SEEMS TO BE APPROACHING YOUR DOMAIN.
ONE OF THE SIX SHO ...?

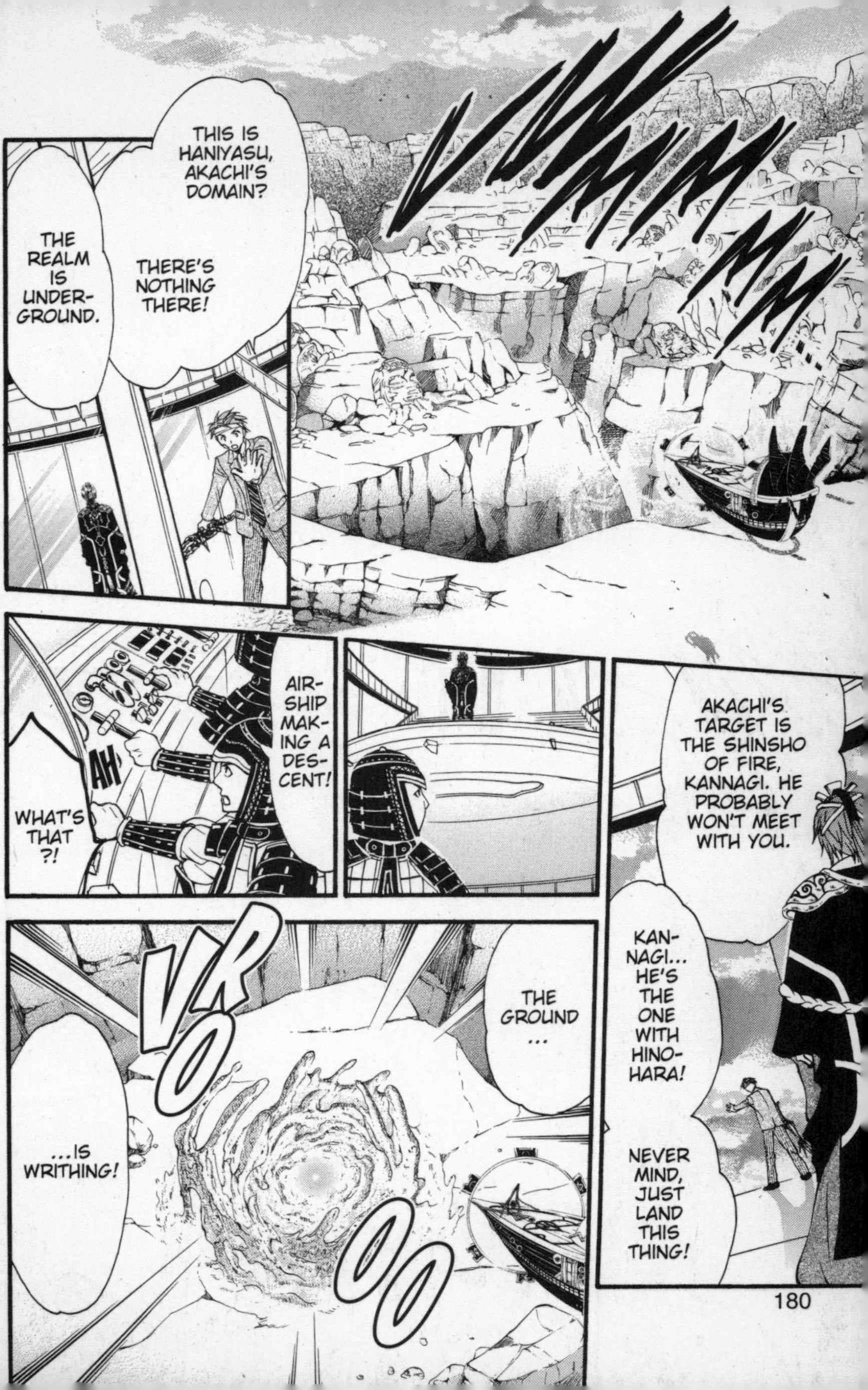
VUMMMMM
THIS IS HANIYASU, AKACHI'S DOMAIN?
THERE'S NOTHING THERE!
THE REALM IS UNDERGROUND.
AKACHI'S TARGET IS THE SHINSHO OF FIRE, KANNAGI. HE PROBABLY WON'T MEET WITH YOU.
KANNAGI... HE'S THE ONE WITH HINOHARA!
NEVER MIND, JUST LAND THIS THING!
AIRSHIP MAKING A DESCENT!
AH
WHAT'S THAT?!
VROOOO
THE GROUND...
...IS WRITHING!

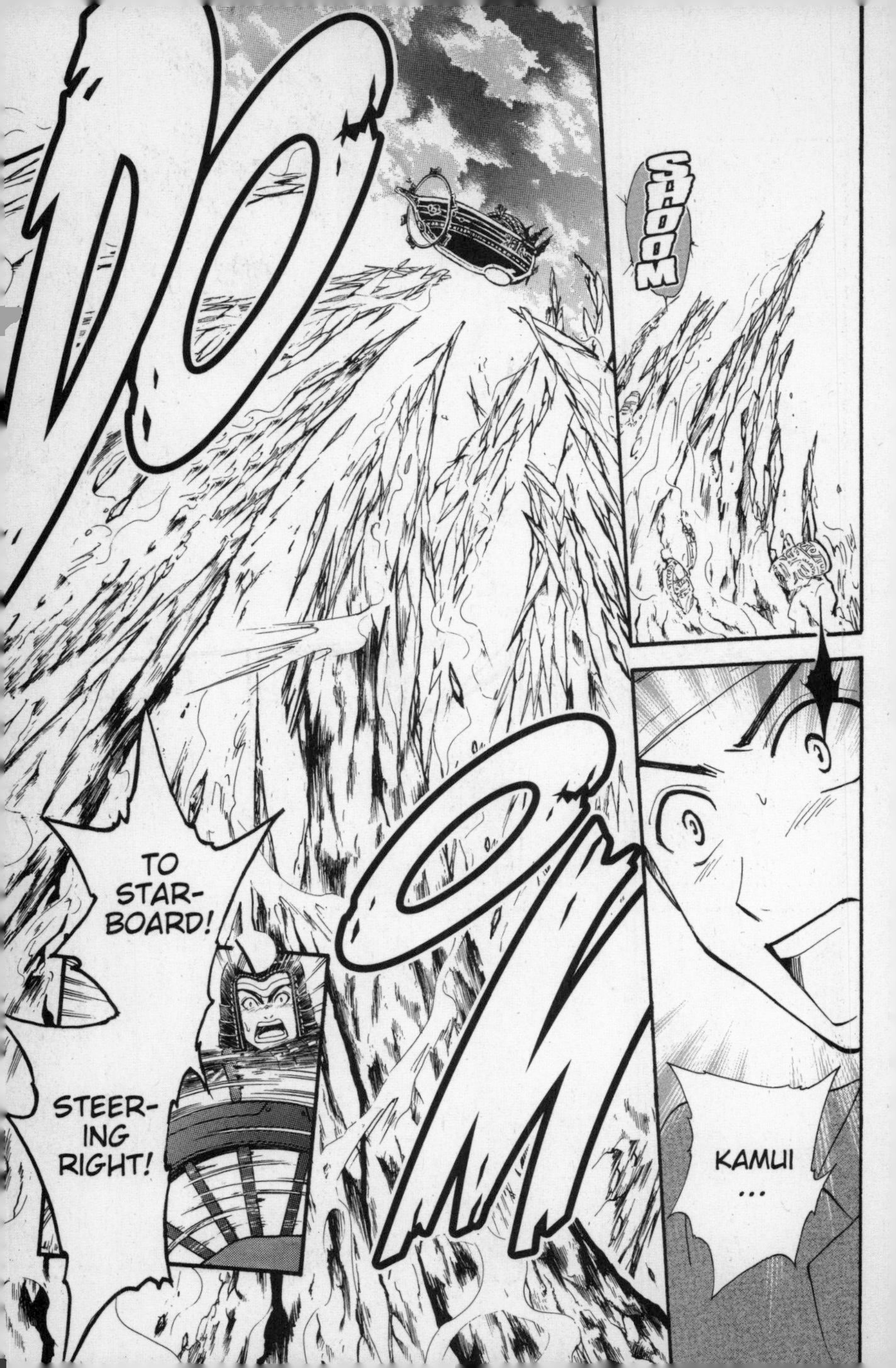

SHOOM
KAMUI ...
DOOM
TO STAR-BOARD!
STEER-ING RIGHT!

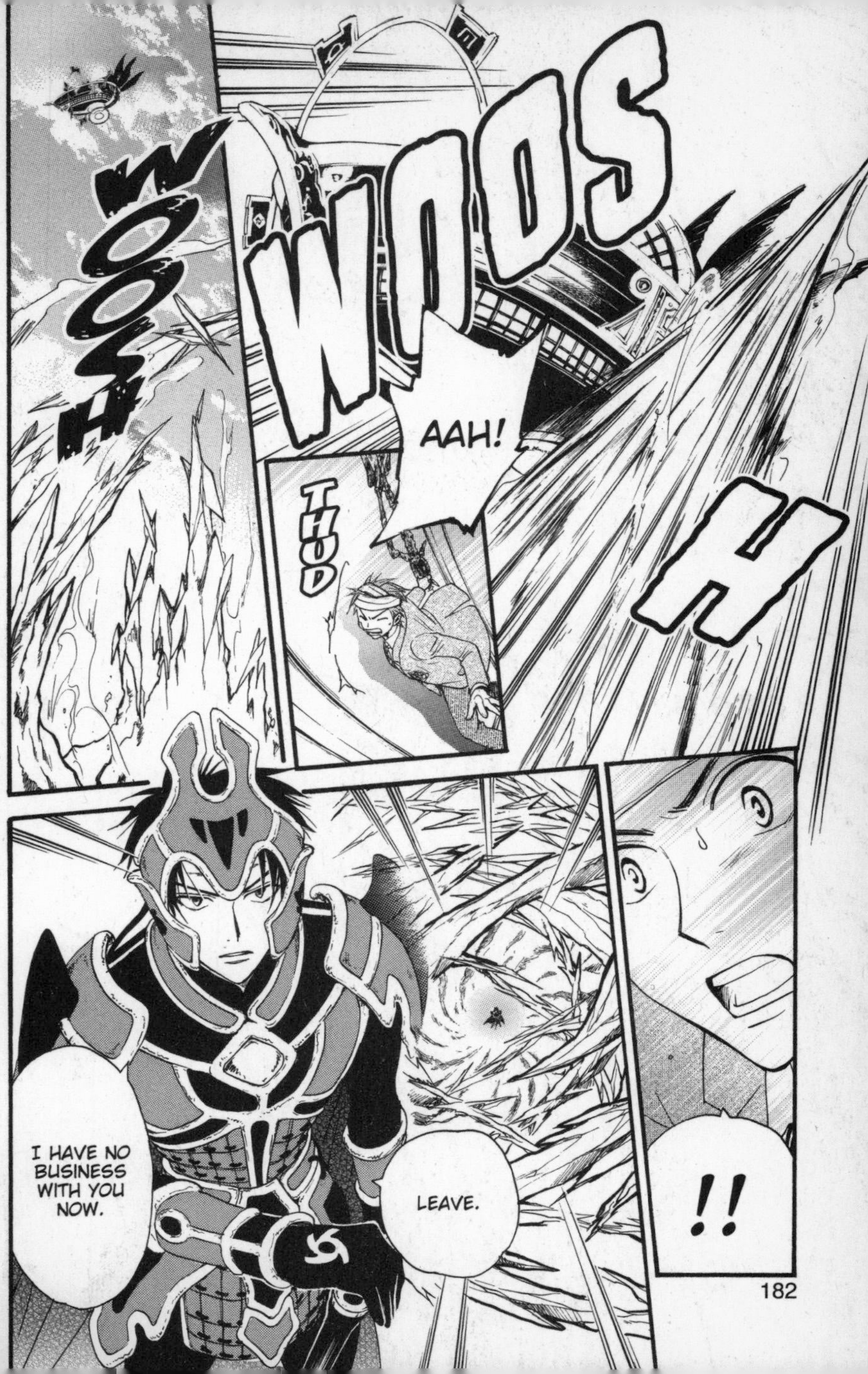
WOOS
H
WHOOSH
AAH!
THUD
!!
LEAVE.
I HAVE NO BUSINESS WITH YOU NOW.

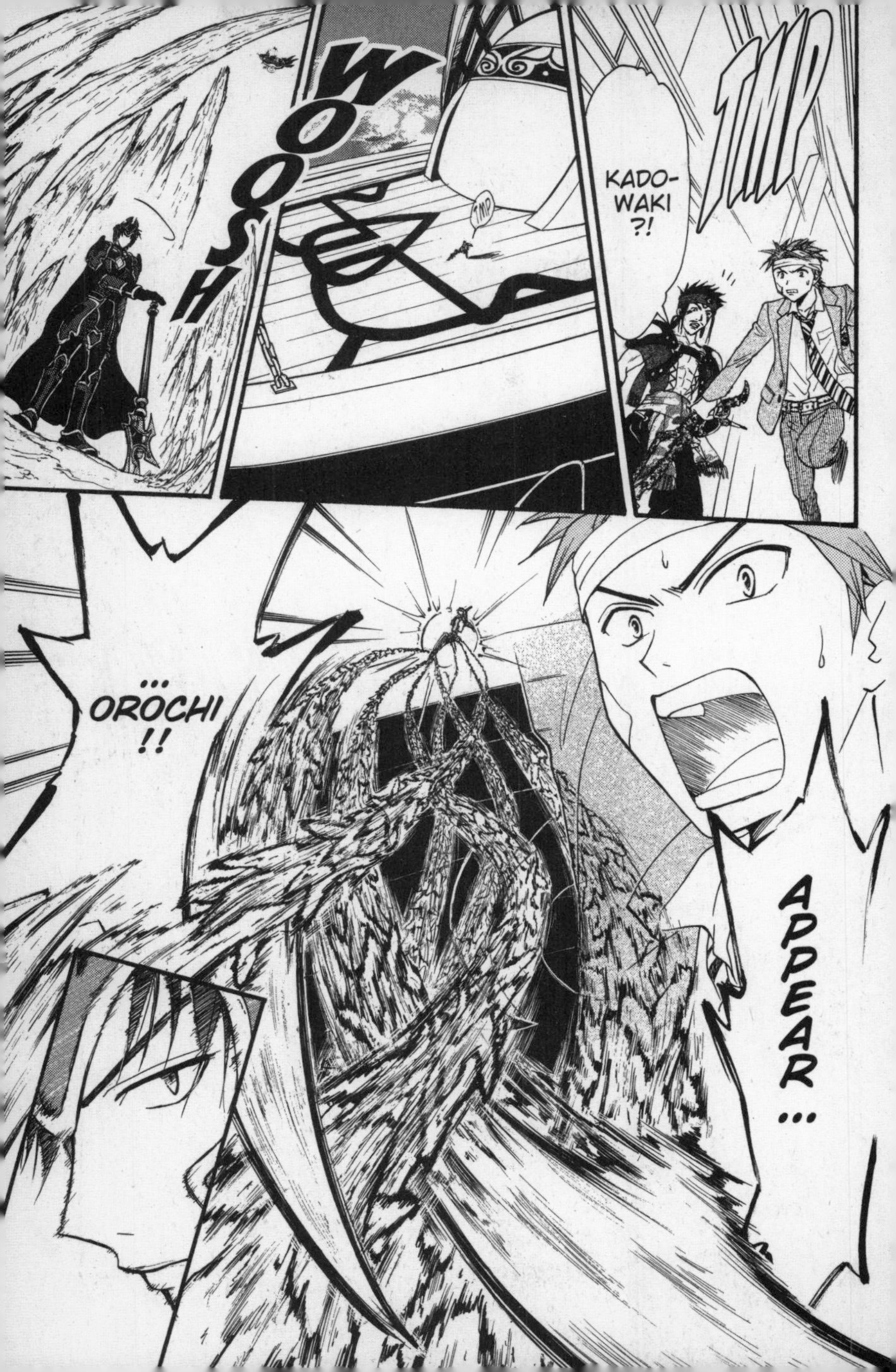
TMP
KADO-
WAKI
?!
WOOOSH
TMP
APPEAR
...
...
ORÖCHI
!!

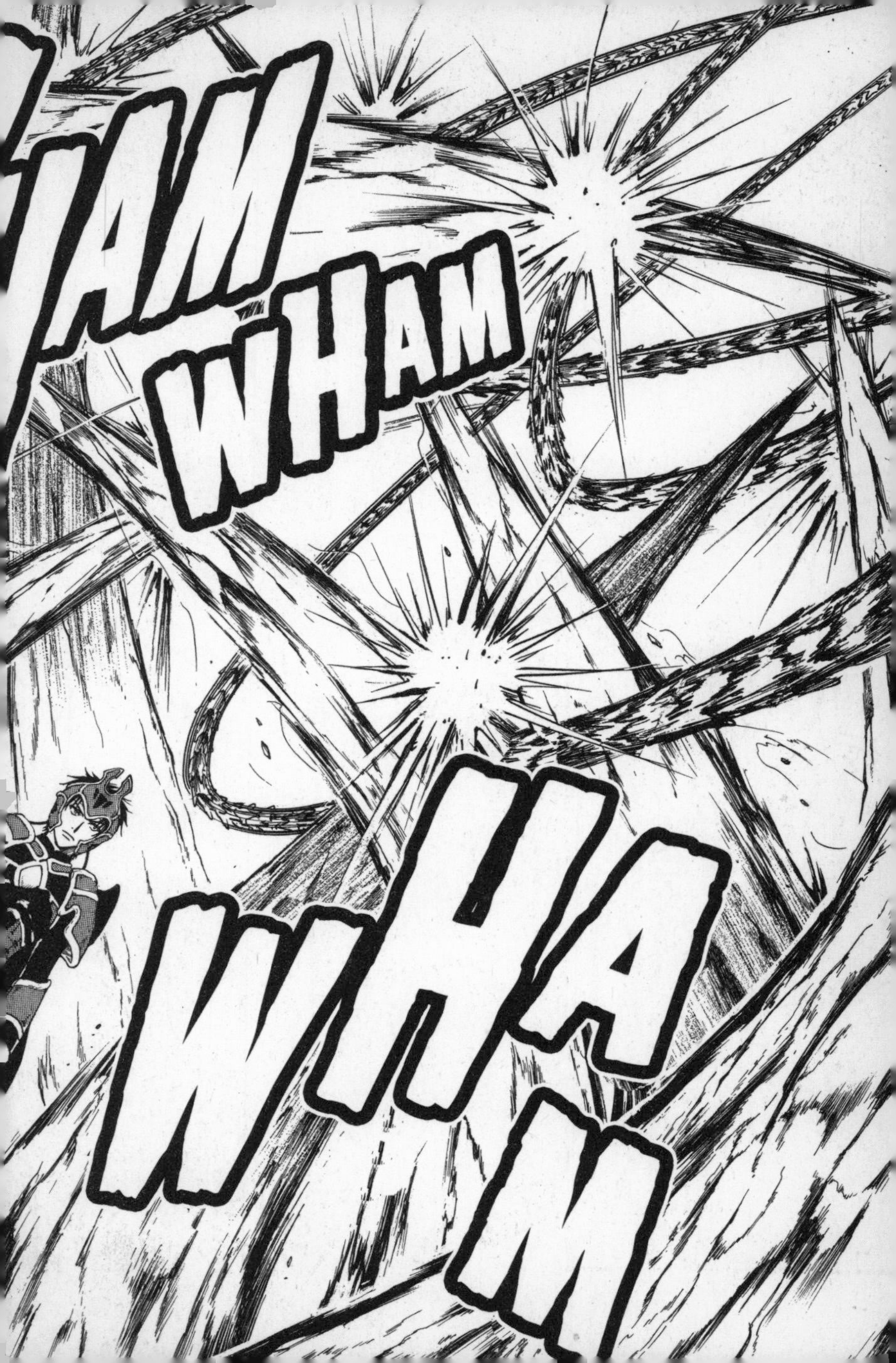
WHAM
AM
WHAM

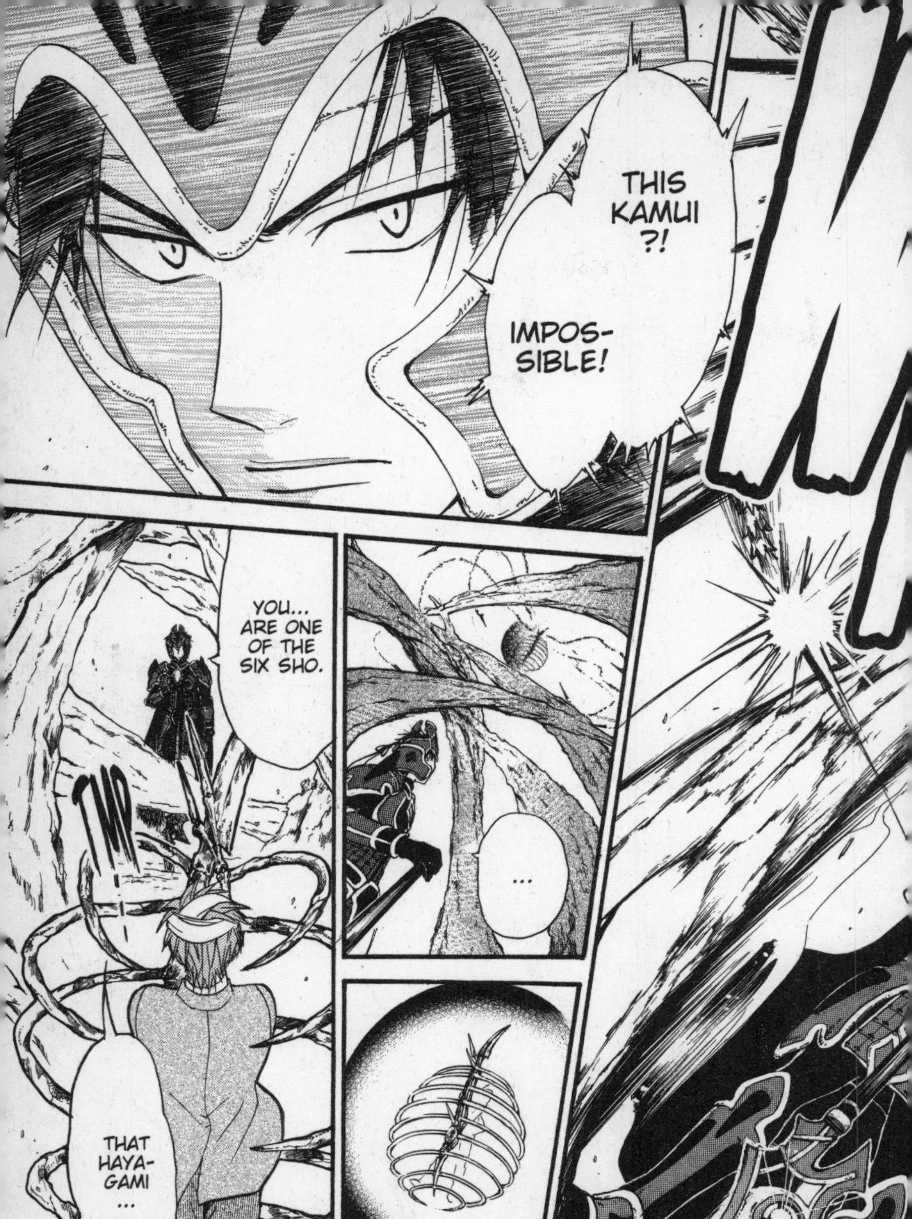
THIS KAMUI ?!
IMPOS-SIBLE!
...
YOU... ARE ONE OF THE SIX SHO.
THAT HAYA-GAMI ...

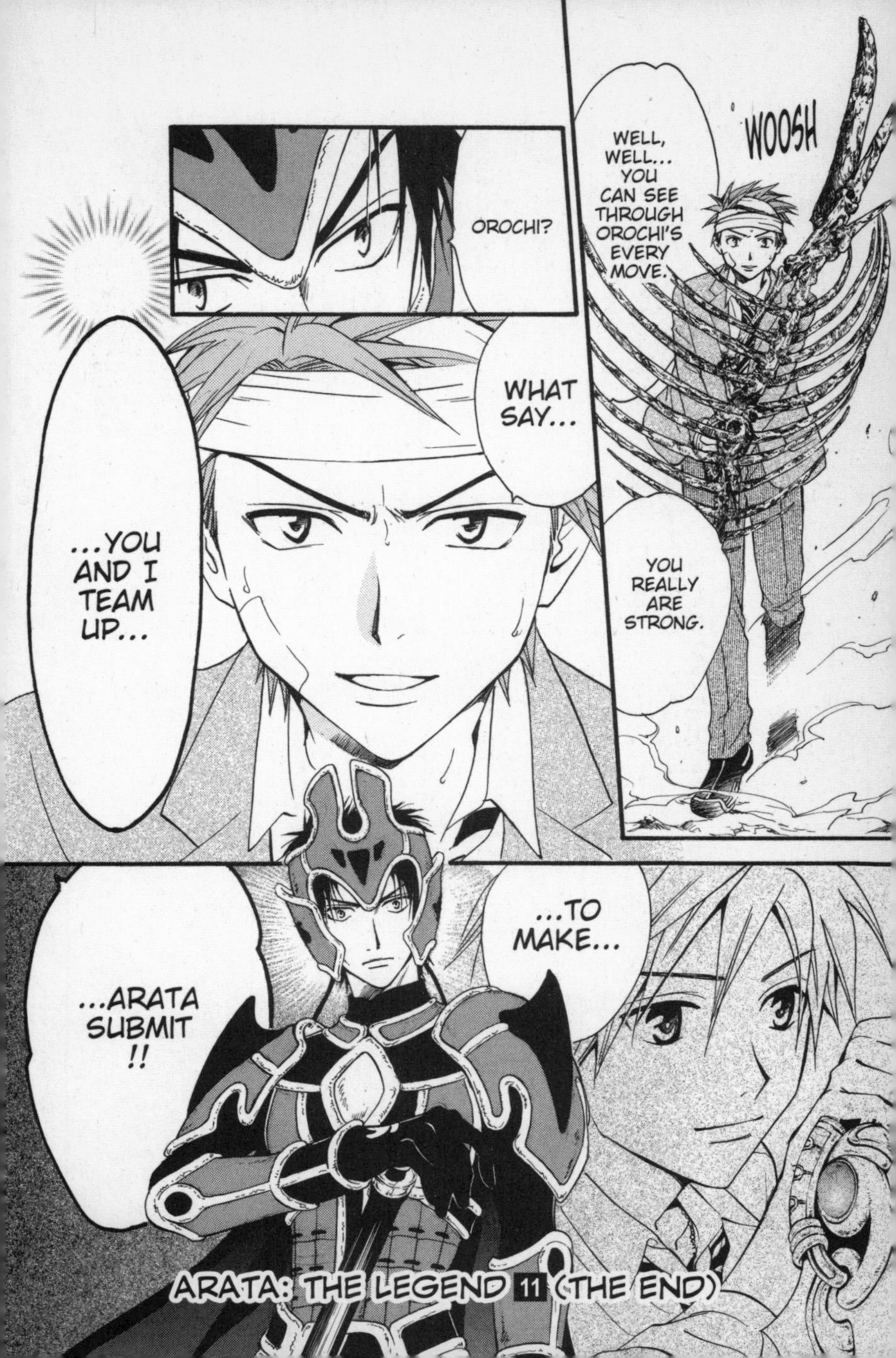
WOOSH
WELL, WELL... YOU CAN SEE THROUGH OROCHI'S EVERY MOVE.
YOU REALLY ARE STRONG.
OROCHI?
WHAT SAY...
...YOU AND I TEAM UP...
...TO MAKE...
...ARATA SUBMIT !!
ARATA: THE LEGEND 11 (THE END)

OHIKA AND
KANNAGI IN
HAPPIER DAYS

OHIKA BECAME A ZOKUSHO AT AGE 19. SINCE HE HAS SERVED SO LONG, THEY SEEM TO BE THE SAME AGE. (HA HA) BUT AFTER HE MET HIS WIFE, OHIKA DECIDED TO AGE AND GROW OLD WITH HIS LOVE.

IN OTHER WORDS, TIME STANDS STILL FOR KANNAGI AND ALL SHINSHO, BUT ZOKUSHO HAVE A BIT OF FREEDOM. THEY CAN CHOOSE TO SERVE THEIR MASTERS ETERNALLY OR GROW OLD AS HUMANS. UNLESS, OF COURSE, THEIR SHINSHO DISAPPROVES. BUT THAT ALMOST NEVER HAPPENS. SHINSHO, FOR WHOM A HUMAN EXISTENCE IS OUT OF REACH, ARE HAPPY WHEN THEIR ZOKUSHO CHOOSE MORTALITY. I'M SURE THERE IS SOME SADNESS. THEY ARE HUMAN, AFTER ALL. (I WORK FROM THE IDEA THAT, WITHOUT EXCEPTION, SHO ARE HUMAN BEINGS.)

AFTER MARRYING, OHIKA BEGAN TO AGE AND WAS EVENTUALLY BLESSED WITH A CHILD. HE'D EXPECTED TO CONTINUE WORKING AS A SHO AFTER BECOMING A FATHER AS WELL AS LIVING AS A MORTAL UNTIL HIS DEATH, BUT... (YOU CAN READ ABOUT IT IN VOLUME 3).
IN CONTRAST, ETO IN VOLUME 8 CHOOSES TO SERVE KUGURA ETERNALLY. A MONTH BEFORE THE RELEASE OF THIS VOLUME, OKIMA DECIDED THAT HE WOULD SOMEDAY LEAVE HIS MASTER AND CHOSE DEATH (AFTER 52 YEARS OF SERVICE!).

NOW IN THE CASE OF DEATH, AS WITH FUTAI IN VOLUME 8, IF A SUCCESSOR IS NOT FOUND, AT THE MOMENT THE SHO DIES, HIS HAYAGAMI DISAPPEARS AND LIES IN WAIT AT AN APPROPRIATE LOCATION FOR A SUITABLE SHO. IN GENERAL, SHO INSTINCTIVELY KNOW WHO TO NAME AS THEIR SUCCESSORS, AND THE HAYAGAMI WOULD NOT REJECT THEIR CHOICE.

IF SOMEONE BECOMES A SHO AND DECIDES HE DOESN'T REALLY LIKE IT (HA!) AND TRIES TO DISCARD HIS HAYAGAMI, HE'LL FIND THAT HE CAN'T GET RID OF IT SO EASILY. (HEE) IT'S JUST LIKE A HUMAN RELATIONSHIP. "YOU'RE THE ONE WHO PICKED ME UP!" THE HAYAGAMI WILL USUALLY DO THE APPROACHING AND START THE CONVERSATION. (IN ARATA'S CASE, TSUKUYO FORCED ITSELF ON HIM AS IN, "OH, HE'S THE ONE!")

THE SAME GOES FOR ALL OF THEM. IF YOU'RE APPROACHED AND ACCEPT IT, FOR EXAMPLE, BY GRABBING IT, AND THE HAYAGAMI TAKES A LIKING TO YOU, IT'S OVER. JUST BE PREPARED FOR THAT. (HA HA...)

YOU'LL NEED THE TENACITY TO STAY PARTNERED FOR SEVERAL YEARS UNTIL YOU FIND SOMEONE ABOUT WHOM YOU CAN SAY, "HE'S BETTER SUITED TO YOU," AND YOU CAN FINALLY MAKE THE BREAK. ← WHAT'S THAT SUPPOSED TO MEAN?

REJECTING A HAYAGAMI AND IGNORING IT INSIDE YOUR BODY, LIKE KANNAGI OR ARATA IN VOLUME 6, CAN RESULT IN THE HAYAGAMI BEING INADVERTENTLY STOLEN, SO BEWARE. (HEE)

HOWEVER, AS LONG AS THE HAYAGAMI HAS NOT BEEN MADE TO SUBMIT, NOT EVEN TEKO WOULD OBEY, SO THERE IS NO CHANCE OF EVILDOING.
JEEZ, THIS WASN'T ABOUT ZOKUSHO. IT'S MORE LIKE AN OPERATOR'S MANUAL FOR HAYAGAMI! (HA HA)

BY THE WAY, IT IS THEORETICALLY POSSIBLE FOR A SHINSHO TO FIND A SUCCES-SOR AND RELINQUISH HIS POSITION. HOWEVER, HAVING REACHED THE HEIGHTS OF POWER AND INFLUENCE, WOULD A MAN BE WILLING TO GIVE IT UP? THAT IS THE QUESTION. AFTER ALL, HE WOULD'VE SACRIFICED A LOT TO GET TO WHERE HE WAS. LOOK AT KUGURA, WHO WAS SERVED SO LOYALLY BY ETO, THE ZOKUSHO CONSIDERED BY HIS HAPPUJIN COMRADES AS A MAN OF TRUE CHARACTER. KUGURA HAD TO BE PRETTY GREAT. A SUPERIOR WHO APPRECIATES A GOOD SUB-ORDINATE'S DEDICATED SERVICE IS PRECIOUS, ISN'T IT?

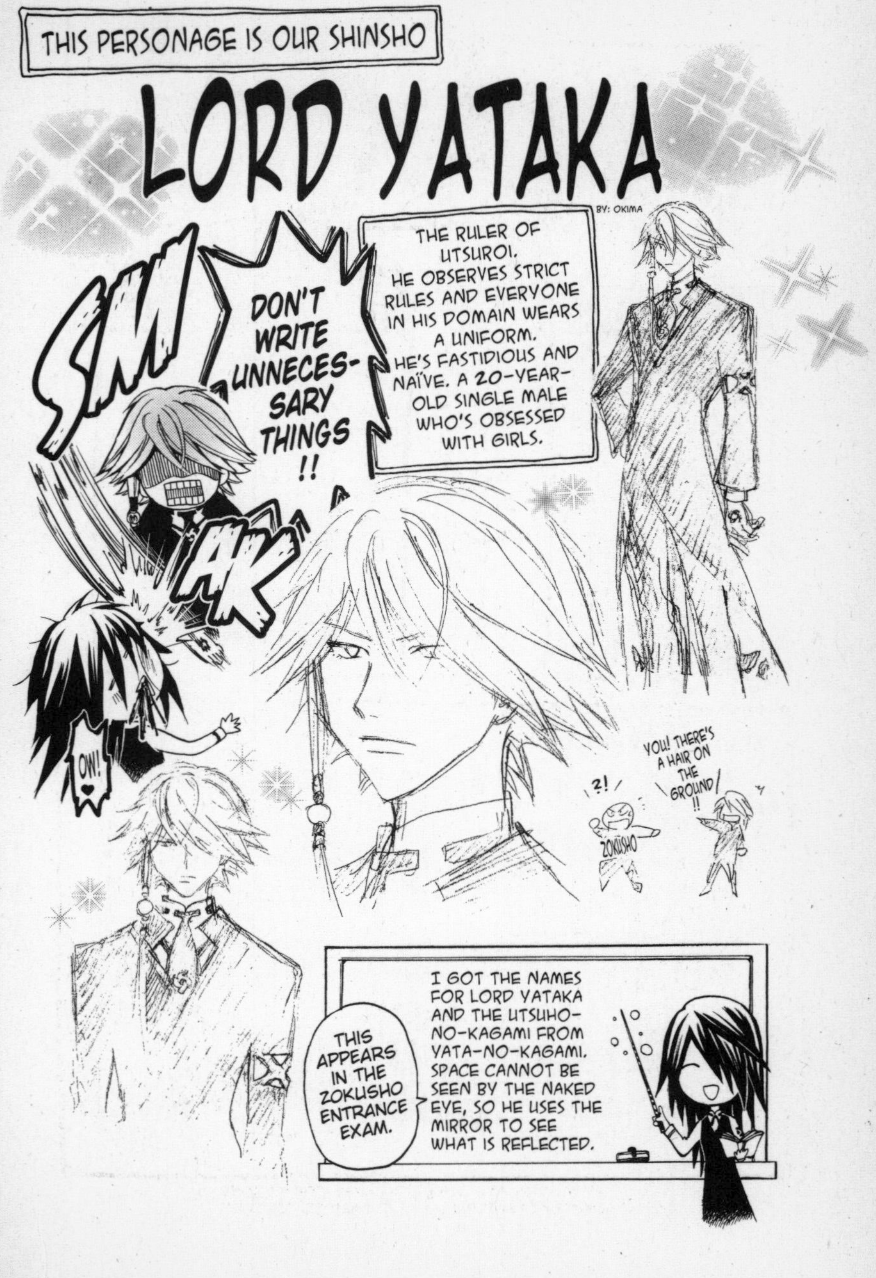

THIS PERSONAGE IS OUR SHINSHO
LORD YATAKA
BY: OKIMA
THE RULER OF UTSUROI. HE OBSERVES STRICT RULES AND EVERYONE IN HIS DOMAIN WEARS A UNIFORM. HE'S FASTIDIOUS AND NAÏVE. A 20-YEAR-OLD SINGLE MALE WHO'S OBSESSED WITH GIRLS.
DON'T WRITE UNNECES-SARY THINGS !!
SMAK
OW!
YOU! THERE'S A HAIR ON THE GROUND!!
?!
ZOKUSHO
I GOT THE NAMES FOR LORD YATAKA AND THE UTSUHO-NO-KAGAMI FROM YATA-NO-KAGAMI. SPACE CANNOT BE SEEN BY THE NAKED EYE, SO HE USES THE MIRROR TO SEE WHAT IS REFLECTED.
THIS APPEARS IN THE ZOKUSHO ENTRANCE EXAM.

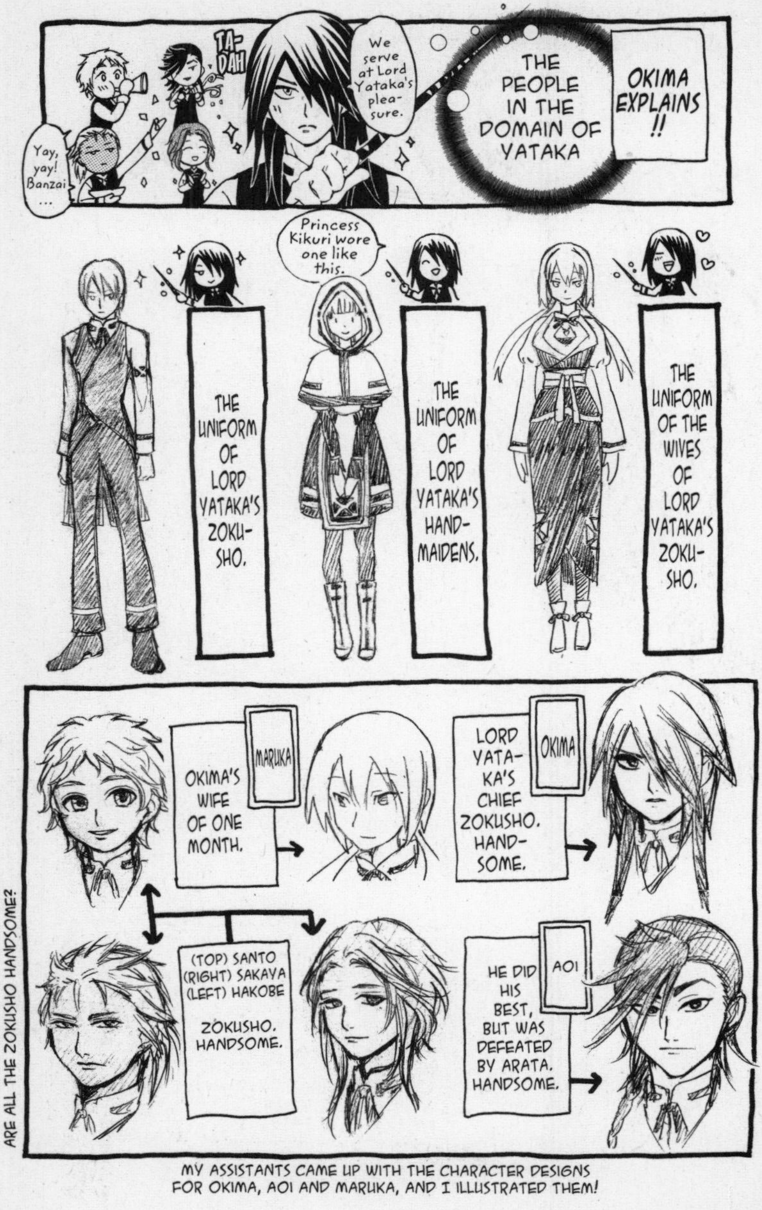
OKIMA EXPLAINS !!
THE PEOPLE IN THE DOMAIN OF YATAKA
We serve at Lord Yataka's plea-sure.
TA-DAH
Yay, yay! Banzai...
THE UNIFORM OF THE WIVES OF LORD YATAKA'S ZOKU-SHO.
Princess Kikuri wore one like this.
THE UNIFORM OF LORD YATAKA'S HAND-MAIDENS.
THE UNIFORM OF LORD YATAKA'S ZOKU-SHO.
OKIMA
LORD YATA-KA'S CHIEF ZOKUSHO. HAND-SOME.
MARUKA
OKIMA'S WIFE OF ONE MONTH.
AOI
HE DID HIS BEST, BUT WAS DEFEATED BY ARATA. HANDSOME.
(TOP) SANTO (RIGHT) SAKAYA (LEFT) HAKOBE
ZOKUSHO. HANDSOME.
ARE ALL THE ZOKUSHO HANDSOME?

MY ASSISTANTS CAME UP WITH THE CHARACTER DESIGNS FOR OKIMA, AOI AND MARUKA, AND I ILLUSTRATED THEM!

It's been a few months since the earthquake disaster*, and while I pray for the quick recovery of the areas affected, I can't help but worry about the rash of global natural disasters lately.

Currently in our series, the Sho are able to manipulate earth, water, fire, wind and sky. All this has taken on a larger significance now, and I think, "If this were a manga, we could use their powers to stop these disasters."

When nature goes on a rampage, we humans can do little to defend ourselves. ...Be strong, Arata. (?)

–YUU WATASE

*The author wrote this comment during the summer of 2011.

AUTHOR BIO

Born March 5 in Osaka, Yuu Watase debuted in the *Shôjo Comic* manga anthology in 1989. She won the 43rd Shogakukan Manga Award with *Ceres: Celestial Legend*. One of her most famous works is *Fushigi Yûgi*, a series that has inspired the prequel *Fushigi Yûgi: Genbu Kaiden*. In 2008, *Arata: The Legend* started serialization in *Shonen Sunday*.

Arata THE LEGEND

ARATA: THE LEGEND
Volume 11
Shonen Sunday Edition

Story and Art by YUU WATASE

Original Japanese edition "ARATAKANGATARI"
published by SHOGAKUKAN Inc.

English Adaptation: Lance Caselman
Translation: JN Productions
Touch-up Art & Lettering: Rina Mapa
Design: Ronnie Casson
Editor: Amy Yu

Printed in Canada

Published by VIZ Media, LLC
P.O. Box 77010
San Francisco, CA 94107

10 9 8 7 6 5 4 3 2 1
First printing, September 2012

RATED T FOR TEEN

PARENTAL ADVISORY
ARATA: THE LEGEND is rated T for Teen and is recommended for ages 13 and up. This volume contains fantasy violence.
ratings.viz.com

viz media
www.viz.com

MANGA STARTS ON SUNDAY SHONEN SUNDAY
WWW.SHONENSUNDAY.COM

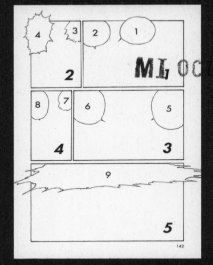

← Follow the action this way.

THIS IS THE LAST PAGE

Arata: The Legend has been printed in the
original Japanese format in order to preserve
the orientation of the original artwork.

Please turn it around and begin reading from
right to left. Unlike English, Japanese is read right
to left, so Japanese comics are read in reverse order from the way English comics are typically
read. Have fun with it!